I0681877

Prophet

Loss

Kennedy Weible

East West 792 *Publishers*

East West 792 *Publishers*

Brooklyn, NY

Published by East West 792 *Publishers* 2016

Copyright © Kennedy Weible 2016

The author asserts the moral right to be

identified as the author of this work.

ISBN: 978-0-692-76126-7

ISBN: 0692761268

Library of Congress Control Number: **2016914341**

East West 792, Brooklyn, NY

Cover design by Kris LoCascio

This is a work of fiction. Names, characters, businesses, places, events, and incidents are either the products of the author's imagination or used in a fictitious manner. Any resemblance to actual persons, living or dead, or actual events is purely coincidental.

All rights reserved. No part of this publication may be reproduced, stored in a retrieval system, or transmitted, in any form or by any means, electronic, mechanical, photocopying, recording, or otherwise, without the prior permission of the publishers. A version of this story first appeared in the magazine *Fogged Clarity*, in the June 2010 issue under the title, *Zoar*.

For my mother, with love.

Prologue

New Zoar Tabernacle of the Living Faithful

In the early days of the compound, before rape was followed by champagne and before she helped murder a man, Celia crouched over a baby bird. Its feathers were nothing like feathers as she knew them, but a gray down resembling fur that parted in the breeze, revealing a thin line of nude, raw flesh, like a scar. "Repent," she demanded. The bird peeped unrepentantly.

Her friend Rebekah, squatting beside her, thrust a splay-fingered hand over the bird and cried out, "Cast your sin to the…"—she turned her head into her shoulder, pondering whither the bird's sin would best be cast—"…the wolves," she decided. "And taste the bread and jam that is Christ's salvation." The bird shat small and white in the dirt.

"It poops in protest," Celia declared. The girls laughed. The bird peeped. Overhead its mother's screams poured through the branches of the tree. Celia and Rebekah had been out back of the farmhouse Celia shared with her parents, singing a song about hell, when they discovered the fallen starling. Celia had invented the song, sung to the tune of "My Boyfriend's Back," a song she and her mother had listened to in their old lives:

My Savior's back and you're gonna be in trouble

Hey la, hey la, you'll roast in hell

He hates your sin; He'll condemn you on the double

Hey la, hey la, prepare for hell

Celia had taught the song to Rebekah, and they were developing a dance routine for it. Since their imaginations were already on the subject, they condemned the bird for the purposes of make-believe.

"He has been cast out as a sinner," Rebekah said. "He has fallen from above and landed in the dirt."

"It's up to us to bring him salvation," Celia announced. She rolled the little bird onto its back. With the tips of her fingers, she gently spread its stumpy, undeveloped wings.

"Open yourself to Jesus Christ the Lord and Savior's healing power, and he will forgive you," Celia said.

"He suffered and died on a cross for your sins," Rebekah said. "Don't you even care about that?"

The mother bird swooped close above them, and Celia said, "*Not now,*" as though she were talking to her own mother. The bird went back to its hysterical shrieking in the tree.

"Let's turn our backs on this creature," Rebekah said finally, after the baby bird continued to refuse Christ's mercy.

"Yes, for it is dark with sin and unworthy of our sight," Celia agreed. The girls stood and marched off righteously. They became involved in another game and forgot the baby bird hopping nervously in the dust.

The next day it was still there. Celia stopped when she saw it. It still peeped—but quietly now. Its cries went unanswered. The tree was silent. The mother bird was gone. Celia moved the baby bird closer to the tree trunk and brought out a bowl of water. She didn't want to bring the bird inside in case its parent came back.

"Maybe someone touched it," Celia's mother said that night. "If a human touched it, the mother won't have anything more to do with it."

Celia looked out the window through her own thinly reflected face. The tree was a dark arm and fist against the starlight. The baby bird was somewhere beneath it. It was just a game, but they had been right: the bird was so full of sin its own mother could no longer stand to have it in her sight.

The next morning the baby bird was gone. There were scratches in the dust where it had sat. A few inches away, like a signature, was the single perfectly formed pawprint of a fox.

Chapter 1

We're brave, right? That's us—Stalwart in times of trouble—The shirtless prince and warrior princess of the American South—Like it to rain every Saturday so I never have to leave—Barrett Higgins—Behind the Food Lion—Numbers don't lie, unfortunately—There are no vacuums—A new *something*

Celia's family came to know Barrett Higgins when Celia's father lost his Sunday shift delivering newspapers. Six days a week her father rose at 3:00 a.m. He drank a cup of coffee and smoked cigarettes at their kitchen table. Sometimes Celia's mother got up with him and scrambled eggs with cheese before going back to bed, but he didn't always let her do this. The bad hours and early mornings were his sacrifice, and he enjoyed having a sacrifice to make. The job was love's receipt, and he wanted to show he had bought and paid. Sometimes when he emerged from the bathroom those early mornings to find his wife in the kitchen, half-asleep, squinting into the light of the refrigerator, he would grip her gently by the back of her neck and say, "Get yer butt back to sleep, baby. No reason for you to be up this early." He'd steer her back down the hall, stroking her neck with his thumb, steadying her groggy walk, her smooth legs unsure white stalks sprouting beneath the long T-shirt she slept in.

"I wanna make you some breakfast. You'll be hungry," she would mutter. He was too skinny, she told him. Too much coffee and too many cigarettes, and he couldn't be trusted to feed himself during the day when he was out in the truck.

"I'll be fine. Here, you hold my spot for me till I get home." He'd lead her around to his side of the bed on these mornings and pull the covers back over her.

By four o'clock every morning, he was at the warehouse loading a white box truck with bundles of the local paper. He'd deliver his route, then return for the day's shoppers and pennysavers. He would return home at two in the afternoon, shower, and sleep. When he rose again in the early evening, their day as a family would begin. He would emerge from the hallway, calling out, "I'm up."

Each day he made the same lap of the kitchen, kissing Celia and his wife. Then it was a string of questions and chatter as he caught up on what he'd missed: "How was everyone's day?…What'd you do in school?…Did you get the oil changed?…Dale didn't rip us off, did he?…You won't believe what this son of a bitch said to me…Remember old Patch from the Blue Wave? I saw her walking down Highway Nine…Of course in her robe, when you ever see her in anything else?…What about you, Cee-bear, still the smartest girl in school?…Well, that's what I heard…Everyone, that's who, all over town, everyone tells me…Nah, I just got up, no beer yet, how 'bout that tea…Cee, honey, your colored pencils are going all over. What are you coloring?…Science papers?…Oh, I see, you color the plant's cell parts. What's that?…The ribosome? That's not a real thing, is it?…What about that?…The *what*? Say it again…Ha! You're messing with me. One more time…The mogli—sorry, the Golgi apparatus. Golgi apparatus. And what the heck does the googly apparatus do?…Distributes chemical products out of the cell? Just like your daddy. You'll remember that on the test now, won't you? The googly…Right, the Golgi apparatus has the same job as your dad. He takes newspapers out of the warehouse and distributes them all over, and the goggly distributes whatever it distributes, cell farts or whatever, to all over…Oh, all right, I'll leave her alone…Mama wants you to finish up. Here, I'll set the table…Ha, did I tell you what Dwayne said to Billy—can't believe a grown man lets hisself be called Billy, but there you are…" This would carry on through the meal until the dishes were in the sink and the leftovers in Tupperware and Celia's mother sent him out of the kitchen.

Celia would help with the dishes, then quietly make her way to the den and crawl into her father's lap. Television was forbidden until she finished her homework, a law legislated by her mother and upheld with the full support of her father. When he was tired, though, with Celia in his lap, he would sometimes click on the set and negotiate with the rulemaking cabinet, saying, "Just this once won't kill her. Let me relax with my baby girl for a bit."

Her mother invariably was leaning against the kitchen doorway at this point, having realized a scheme was afoot. She'd stand with one hand on her hip (*tip me over and pour me out!* Celia would sing in her head) and give her husband his line: "Ask her if she's finished her homework."

"You finish your homework?"

"Yes."

"Celia Ann Waters, that is a bald-faced—"

"There's just that one work sheet left, and Mr. Chandler doesn't even check them! It only takes, like, two seconds anyway."

"He wouldn't assign it if he didn't check it."

"How would *you* know? I'm the one who's in his class."

"Don't sass me, or I'll—"

"All right, all right, look. She'll do the work sheet before bed, OK? You'll do it right before you brush your teeth, won't you, honey?"

Celia would sigh an exasperated, "Yessss."

"OK?" her father would ask her mother again.

"Fine. But I don't want to hear any complaining and whining about it."

"OK," the put-upon Celia would snap with an eye-roll.

Her mother then would retreat into the kitchen and Celia into her father's side, inhaling the scent of his shirt and Vantage Lights. Her mother was her friend and ally in everything except television. Everything would be perfect, Celia thought, if her mother would get on board and accept that television was currency in school. What shows you could talk about opened doors to a social life. Braiding her hair in the mornings, singing along with the radio in the car, making cookies together as a surprise for her father when he got off a double shift—these things were fun, but they got you nowhere at the sixth-grade lunch table.

Four weeks before losing the Sunday shift, Celia's father wrenched his back tossing bundles of pennysavers. He felt a spasm in his lower back as he swung the papers toward the day-lit opening at the back of the truck, behind the Food Lion. His left hand failed him in the moment and didn't release the pennysavers. Their weight and momentum pulled him off his feet, and he splayed out on his stomach. He lay in the grit on the truck's floor, trying to comprehend how he got there. Perversely, he was concerned about whether he could finish his route. How much time was he losing lying there? He limped through the rest of his shift, slowly carting the papers out the tail end of the truck, and checked back in an hour later than usual.

That night Celia's mother helped him into a hot bath. Celia waited outside the bathroom, ready to hand in his cigarettes and ashtray when her mother called for them. "Goddamnit, baby," she heard him say to her mother, "it feels like someone put out a pack of matches in my back meat."

"We're gonna soak that pain out of you."

"I hate this. I feel old."

"You're not old enough to be old. You're strong. You stay in there and soak. I'll bring your dinner up. Celia, hand me the—" Celia's hand shot through the cracked door with the ashtray, the cigarettes, and the good lighter. "Thanks, sweetie."

"You helping take care of your old man?" her father called through the door.

"You're not old," she said, echoing her mother's reassurance. "You're the Golgi apparatus."

Celia knew what old looked like: darkened hands, shapeless mouth, fingers that were always cold and looked like twigs dipped in wax—her grandmother, years back, before she died. Her father did not resemble old. He threw the football back to the Johnson twins across the street when it bounced, pathless and erratic, out of their yard. They were long bombs that Scott and Derek would sprint beneath, slapping and pushing each other, competing for the catch. He had picked up the snapping turtle they found under the car with his bare hands, holding it at the back of its shell while it craned its neck and chomped the air, inches shy of his fingers. Celia and her mother had screamed, and Celia had watched in terrified delight as he marched it a hundred yards into the woods behind their house, putting wild nature back in its bottle.

Celia dogged her mother's heels as she trayed a plate of ham, green beans, potatoes, tomato slices in a bowl with oil and vinegar and salt and pepper, and two leftover chicken legs from the night before. Celia carried a glass of tea and a can of light beer down the hall, following her mother and the tray back to the bathroom. Her father draped a towel over his parts, and their procession filed in. He lay back in the tub, arms out to the sides, his feet atop each other and his knees bent to fit the tub's length. Celia's mother pulled the stopper and ran fresh hot water. She stubbed out his cigarette. Celia pulled the tab on his beer. "How is it?" her mother asked her father.

"Feeling better in here. We'll see when I stand up."

"You're not standing up yet. Stay put." She pulled her shower cap out of the cabinet and stuck it on his head. "There, now you look properly ridiculous." He laughed and winced. He reached for the cap.

"No, leave it," Celia said. She was scared of losing the only levity they'd had since he came home.

"You want me to eat like this?"

"It's funny."

The shower cap stayed, the cellophane crinkles cutting the light into diamond patterns around his head.

"You're dripping into the potatoes." Her mother took a hand towel and dried his forearms while he forked up ham and beans.

"Woman, you'll lose a finger getting between my food and my mouth."

"You'll have to burp it back up. I need it to haul your ass out of here."

Celia laughed so hard she collapsed onto her side on the thick bathroom rug they had gotten for next to nothing because it was a hideous yellow.

Before moving to the neat brick house with the bay window by the kitchen table, they had lived in the Blue Wave Mobile Home Community, a treeless rectangle of land out by the county line. It was unclear whether it had been named Blue Wave as a wish and a prayer for a life that was easy and tropical or as a poetic reference to the depression that washed over its inhabitants. They moved to their *real* house when Celia was eight. She didn't have bad memories of the Blue Wave. She remembered lots of dogs, a few friends, and an excessive amount of gravel. A single remaining grandmother had still been alive then and stayed with Celia during the day while her parents were at work and after school, once she got old enough for kindergarten.

An older couple her parents called Patch and Dangle lived in the trailer across from them. Their names derived from the couple's habit of wearing nothing under their bathrobes and sitting splay-legged on their small porch, giving anyone who passed by an eyeful. Dogs were plentiful at the Blue Wave, rarely confined and never leashed. Dangle hated dogs and kept a flyswatter to hand for defense should any of them bother him and his wife, though few ever did. Being untethered made the dogs calm; mostly they just padded around looking for other dogs to pad around with. Sometimes a group would bark together a few trailer-rows over, and Dangle would rise and step to the porch's edge, flyswatter up and poised for action.

"Is it dogs?" Patch would ask through the barking.

"Think so," Dangle would answer over a howl. But the dogs would go off and eat trash somewhere, and he'd be left with nothing to do but resume his dangling, unmolested and unthreatened. When any dog came by, Dangle was on his feet in an instant, leaning over the porch rail, swinging the flyswatter like a ship's flag in the dog's general direction. Usually, the dog would bound over and jump for the swatter, twisting in excited circles, thrilled with the game. Patch would shriek and upset the flowerpot where they dropped their spent cigarette butts, yelling, "Get it! Get it." Dangle would keep up the assault until the dog got bored and wandered away. After, they'd tell any passerby who'd listen what happened, threatening the unknown owners of all the dogs with a phone call to the dogcatcher, who didn't exist.

An especially dense and lovable beast named Bobo famously managed to catch the flyswatter one day, briefly ending Dangle's impotent reign of terror. In the tug-of-war that followed his capture of the swatter, Bobo nearly pulled Dangle over the porch rail, leaving the old man teetering from his waist with his legs in the air. Patch, stalwart in times of trouble, clung resolutely to one of her husband's feet, screaming her face off for someone to get a gun and save them. Dangle was forced to release the swatter or risk plummeting four feet onto his head, and Bobo raced away for about three seconds before he stopped and turned politely to await pursuit. Patch and Dangle had retreated inside though, lest Bobo return and use their weapon against them. Bobo sat down and chewed the swatter for a while before falling asleep in the road. He stayed there until Loomis, from three trailers down, pulled up in his truck and blew the horn till Bobo woke and ambled to the edge of the street, where he shat, ate it, and wandered home.

"Sounds like a major success for Bobo," Celia's father said when he got home from work and Celia filled him in. She had watched it all from the window. It was the most exciting thing that had ever happened to her.

"He ate the flyswatter," Celia reported happily. "It's not food, but he ate it. I saw, I saw the stick, and there was no—"

"It's called a handle, sweetie," her mother said. "Things you grip like that are called handles."

"—and there was no more of the, the top, and..." In her excitement, Celia skipped back to the window without finishing her thought, hoping it would happen all over again.

Celia's mother dropped her voice to the volume that suggested Celia shouldn't hear more than it actually prevented her from doing so. "Old Dangle's lucky Bobo didn't get something else, or we'd have to start calling them both Patch."

Her father laughed the way he only did at things his wife said.

"What does that mean?" Celia asked, running back over, wanting to get it, wanting in.

"Nothing, honey. Go wash for supper," her mother said.

Her parents' distaste for the Blue Wave became apparent only in their excitement to leave. For a few months they had been having conversations full of phrases Celia didn't have a place for in her head.

"They're asking two hundred with fifty down for that place in The Heights. I drove past it on my route today."

"The only thing high is *them*, if they think we can pay that."

"Three bedrooms, two and a half bathrooms."

Half a bathroom, Celia thought. How was that possible? What a mess half a toilet and sink must make.

"We can't half afford it, so it doesn't matter. It's too much house anyway. Who wants to clean all that?"

Too much house. There must be extra walls and ceilings, each room with four or five doors.

"I really liked that other place."

"You liked the pool table."

"I can't help it. I'm a man of refined tastes."

"Liking pool tables ain't refined."

"Neither is saying *ain't*. Little ears pick up that habit—"

"You're right, I know. She'll end up talking like your mother."

"Or hers."

"Ooh, someone is funny tonight. The pool table wouldn't come with the place anyway, funny guy. I liked that one, too, but it was too much, and there wasn't any storage."

Storage must be stores. Did houses sometimes have stores attached to them?

"We don't have anything to store, and I bet Cee would like a pool table," her father said, scooping her up as she slid out of her chair, overcome with the sudden urge to see if she could fit a sock over the head of her stuffed bear. "You want a pool table, little monkey?" He swung her around, his strong back and arms making her light as a doll. A swimming pool the size of a table sounded far less scary than the monstrous public pool she lived in anxiety over all summer. So she said, "Yes." Whatever her parents were talking about, they were both bouncy and excited. Her father tossed her up and down lightly, as though he were nervously playing with a football.

"Put the little monkey back in her seat, please, and set the table. This is almost ready. Celia, where are you going? I just said we're about to eat."

"I need a sock."

"Maybe they'll come down on their price."

"The agent said they were firm."

"Well, maybe they ain't."

"See, you do it, too. Talk like that when we negotiate with them, and they'll know we're a couple of hicks from Blue Wave."

"If they come down twenty K, we'll be a couple of hicks from Garden Estates."

Another night Celia was outside her parents' bedroom door. She had awakened in her small bed in the dark and wanted to crawl into their bed and sleep between them. Their bed was massive, which was more fun than her own; plus sleeping together was the least scary way to pass the night. Her parents, however, for reasons that eluded her, failed to appreciate these two points. She paused to listen outside their door. Her best chance of getting in was for them to be asleep. Then they were too drowsy to take her back to her own bed and argue with her. If they were awake, it was useless.

"What's the point if we never see you? It's too tight and too much. The numbers don't lie, unfortunately," she heard her mother say through the door. It was a saying they used to describe decisions that were not actually decisions, but imperatives: ten-hour workdays, not going out to dinner, cutting your own hair. The numbers referred to were the rent and car payments, the electric bill, groceries, school supplies, the possibility of braces.

"You'll still see me. This is what we've always wanted. We want to raise our daughter in a house, not this trailer. A Sunday shift just opened up, and Dwayne said it's mine if I want it. And they're willing to come down enough on the price that we can just make it if I take it."

"It's six days a week. We'll only get you on Saturdays."

"Then we'll make them the best Saturdays ever. This is *our house*. I know you feel it. You love that place."

"What about you? You're not going to get a pool table, and you're going to be at work so much..."

"Baby," he said, chuckling a little, "I know I'm not getting a pool table. I don't care. I want to give my family a house."

"But it's just—"

"You'll have that big kitchen," he interrupted.

"Yeah."

"With all the windows, so it's nice and bright."

"Yeah."

"And a washer and dryer in the place."

"Yeah."

"And there's a yard and a nice neighborhood and a decent-sized room for the monkey."

"We could paint her room yellow."

"We can paint every room any color we want. All the colors, they're all ours. We can make every wall different if we feel like it."

"I'm scared, though. What if it's too much for us?"

"We just have to be brave. It'll all be fine. We're brave, aren't we? That's us."

"Yeah."

Celia heard other noises start then. She didn't know what they were doing, but she knew they weren't asleep and she had no chance of getting into the big bed. She tottered back to her own room.

The big move: from the Blue Wave to a new neighborhood half an hour away. Two low brick walls framed the entrance road to the new house; one read Garden, the other Estates. There were few actual gardens, and none of the plots could properly be described as estates, but the lawns were well-kept, and kids rode their bikes in the street with impunity. These were modest houses inhabited by modest people. Owing to her age, Celia was incapable of thinking of her parents in terms of their being happy or unhappy—their presence was all-encompassing, too great to be reduced to the simple emotions discovered and resolved during story time at school. It would have been like wondering if God was happy. But the emotions of the gods trickle down and form the shallow pools from which their creations drink. Celia was happy during this time. They all were.

Celia's father's father was a nonentity. Her father never knew him, though he'd heard he had been around briefly when he was a baby. His mother never indicated she felt any particular way about this missing figure. She was a trim chain-smoker who automatically distrusted everyone and everything. She held jobs at grocery stores and gas stations and worked long hours. She once remarked, "I ain't ever worked no place didn't sell milk, condoms, and cigarettes." Celia's father modeled himself on his own father in reverse, using the blank spots left by that mysterious man's absence. His road through fatherhood was pocked with holes, not to avoid, but to painstakingly fill in, one by one. Since his own father had been around for precisely nothing, every act was a blank canvas on which to paint a scene—sometimes in sad, touching colors: "My own dad was never there to throw me a birthday party. I just want it to be special," Celia's father told his wife when he wanted to overspend on Celia's eighth birthday party by renting a pony. Other times he painted the scenes with broad strokes of stupefying banality: "I'd of been thrilled if my dad had been around to hog the bathroom," he once said, after Celia and her mother fussed at him for locking himself in there with a newspaper and a cup of coffee for forty minutes.

Celia's mother's parents had died within six months of each other, the year after their only daughter got married. Her father succumbed to a heart attack. He held on for just over a week before his heart surrendered entirely. They mourned and cried, but between his angina and the mild manner that was the hallmark of his personality, they had all been prepared, even expectant. Her mother's aneurism sometime in the night as she slept, however, was a razor's painless path over her stomach, opening her up before she had time to comprehend the act. Celia's mother's mother had been a fierce creature who babied and nursed a husband who was perpetually unemployed or on disability, and who coached her daughter in a style of hard work, vigilance, and aggressive homemaking meant to tame one small piece of the world and make it safe.

Celia's own parents had met when her father was still working as a laborer with a landscaping crew and her mother was working the front desk at a Days Inn that employed their services. Celia loved the story of their early courtship. The retelling still possessed the qualities of flirtation, resistance, and pursuit that had been present in the actual moment. "I didn't like the look of him one bit," her mother would say. "I wanted nothing to do with him."

"That ain't—isn't—true," her father would break in. "She'd take an extra-long time getting in her car in the parking lot 'cause she was waiting for me to come over and talk to her. Finally, one day, I said to myself, 'Hell, son, what's keeping you? A girl like that's only gonna pretend to lose her keys in her purse so many times waiting for you to make a move.' So one day she came out and I threw down the edger I was using and went over and asked her out."

Celia's mother would ignore this and say, "He never wore a shirt, like he thought he was hot stuff. And he was always so sweaty. Then one day he runs his skinny little ass across the parking lot and asks me 'if I wanted to get a beer sometime.'" Here, her mother dropped her voice to something close to a mongoloid's.

"I don't sound like that."

"I laughed right in his face, got in my car, and drove out of the lot."

"That's true. She said no," her father would say. Then he'd wink at Celia. "But I asked her again the next day, and she said yes. And she ain't ever said no to me again."

That was also true. Celia loved the story, but she was tormented by it, because she hadn't been there. She wanted to own that time the way they did, to have known them then—this shirtless prince and warrior princess of the American South. Her mother had fallen in love with her father's peculiar sense of neediness—to work and take care and push himself for the sake of someone else. Her father had fallen in love with her mother's ability to absorb his efforts and put them with her own in order to mold a life for them and give it shape. "It didn't hurt that she was a real bombshell," Celia's father once told Celia, when she asked why he'd run across that hot parking lot to talk to her mother all those years ago. Celia's mother rolled her eyes and went to refill her tea. "And still is," he called after her.

Celia's remaining grandmother passed away a few months after they moved. To everyone's great surprise, she had a life-insurance policy that went to her only son. This was a woman had who referred to anyone who didn't make their own curtains as "highfalutin" and thought any man who wore a suit to work was a "crooked son of a bitch."

"I'd love to find the crazy bastard who convinced my mama to buy a life-insurance policy," Celia's father said when he got the letter informing him he was the beneficiary.

"Find him and what?" her mother said. "Kiss him?"

"I guess." He laughed, then grew quiet again. "No, I'd ask him if she said why she bought it."

"She bought it for her son."

"Isn't like her."

"Look at me. Whatever else your mother was, and Lord knows I had words with the woman over the years, she was a mother first. And there's nothing decent that's not in a mother's nature when it comes to her children. She loved you and Cee, and she wanted to leave you something."

"She loved you, too, in her way."

"Let's not go telling stories now."

Ten thousand dollars. At last, with his mother, love had a receipt. Celia's father ignored this opportunity to get a pool table and passed the still-warm example of motherly devotion to Celia by providing her more time with her own. The whole insurance check went to the mortgage, and with the wiggle room this created, Celia's mother cut back her work hours to part time.

This was the *new* most exciting thing that had ever happened to Celia. She had loved her grandmother because she had been told she loved her. It was a word she had thrown out there since she'd been taught to say it. But what was there to love, really? The old woman was nice enough, but she didn't do anything or stir any response in Celia. Mostly she sat on the couch watching TV shows that were so boring even Celia didn't care about them. Sometimes she handed Celia food. Celia adored her parents, on the other hand. She loved them the way they loved each other, especially her mother, who was exciting and full of movement and songs. Now when Celia came home from school, the house was full of sounds that weren't the shopping channel, full of smells that weren't stale ashtrays. Together they painted the bedrooms bright shades of yellow, the kitchen a deep red. There was always music. Her mother had shoeboxes full of tapes, most of them compilations dubbed off the radio over the years. She played them constantly, at high volume. Where her father's modus operandi had been their house, her mother's was their home. She reigned from the kitchen with her tapes, a bowl of strawberries, and her coffee pot. Bird feeders stationed outside the windows attracted avian throngs that drove the neighborhood cats to distraction.

One Saturday, her father's only day off, Celia woke to rain. She lurched into the kitchen as usual and sat down on the floor by the table, over the floor vent that oozed steady warmth. A lone cardinal perched on one of the feeders, braving the drizzle.

"Such a dreary day out," her mother said offhandedly, scraping eggs she hadn't finished onto her husband's plate, where they were promptly relocated to his mouth.

"Good," he said, through the last forkful. "Then I don't have to feel bad about not leaving this house all day." He carried their plates to the sink, then retook his seat, lighting a cigarette. "I'd like it to rain every Saturday, so I never

17

have to leave again."

Celia silently agreed, then dozed off against the wall.

Celia's father got up stiffly the day after he wrenched his back and went to work. Each night her mother put him in the tub to soak. She rubbed Tiger Balm into his lower back before bed. When he lost the Sunday shift a few weeks later, no one said it was because he had slowed down. "They cut half the trucks going out," her mother said. "It's nothing to do with you personally. You work damn hard, and they know it. People just read less newspapers."

"Goddamn Internet," her father said. "Mushy liberals don't want to get their hands dirty with anything, even reading their biased newspapers." He fumed in his armchair. Celia didn't know what a mushy liberal was yet, but she agreed with their preference to keep their hands newsprint free. Her own travails with the comics page left her hands grimy and, consequently, her face and clothes dotted with fingerprints, like a piece of evidence in her own manhandling.

Trying to clamor onto her father's lap in those days elicited a hiss. "Ah, goddamnit, Celia, no. My back can't take it. Just let Daddy rest." The TV wasn't clicked on. Nothing was on.

"Other people lost shifts, too," her mother said.

"And I'm one of them because of my goddamn back," her father replied. He was not a man who went happily to doctors, but the debilitating pain and the important loss of a day's pay each week tore through his prejudice. A cheerful young back specialist prescribed OxyContin and told him to stay off his feet for a while.

"Yoga can help back pain as well," the young doctor said. "You might want to think about attending classes a few times a week."

"What do they teach these assholes in med school?" her father wondered aloud on the ride home.

The painkillers got him moving the rest of the week and got Celia back in his lap and in front of the TV when he came home. Sunday mornings, though, he couldn't sleep. The early-morning hours were etched into his bones, and though the back pain and the Oxy scrambled to wear down the scrimshawed pattern of his working life—in other words, his life—they were finding his habits too deeply cut to cover quickly. Since he was up anyway and it couldn't hurt to have a higher power on his side, he started attending sunrise services at a storefront church called Living Faith in a half-empty strip mall called Green Pines Plaza. "Are there other color pines?" Celia's mother asked.

"Maybe out west," her father mused. "You know the kind of silly shit that goes on in California."

Living Faith was where he met Barrett Higgins.

Her father had been home an hour already from his first Living Faith service when Celia came barefoot into the kitchen, half-lynched from her sleep-twisted nightgown. "There's the sleepy bear," her father said. "C'mere." Celia drifted over, and he pulled her nightgown straight and pushed her hair back from her face. "There, now you almost look like a real girl."

"You want some juice, sweetie?" her mother said, the refrigerator door already open. Celia nodded. She took a chair next to her father. She didn't speak upon waking. She liked the exterior stimulus of her parents' conversation or the TV to jog her memory of the waking world first. She stared drowsily at the light brown wood of the table. Her father picked up a monologue he'd been on before she came in.

"I thought I was the first one there, but after I'd been sitting a minute, I saw this fella up front I hadn't noticed when I came in. The minister said he hisself'd only been there five minutes before I showed up, so this guy musta been waiting when he opened the door."

"You met the minister?"

"He introduced himself. He was setting up chairs when I got there. Place doesn't gather more'n fifteen, twenty people."

"Well, how many of y'all you expect to be up at sunrise? The later services probably get more."

"There's just the one service. Don't know how the place stays in business. Must rent it out for bingo on the weeknights."

"You enjoyed it, though?"

"It was kinda singy and dancy."

"It was *what*?"

"You know. Hands in the air, clapping, people closing their eyes, and their heads tilted back like they're in a shampoo commercial."

"Oh, of course, singy and dancy," her mother said, rolling her eyes.

"'Cept that guy up front. The one who got there before me. He kept it pretty solemn. Didn't seem real thrilled with the carrying on going on around him." He chuckled. "The minister was pretty good though, I guess. Gave a decent sermon." He went on, summarizing the moral lesson presented to him that morning.

The solemn man in the front corner of the church, the one seated and reading his Bible before all the folding chairs had even been slung open and placed, was Barrett Higgins. Celia's father didn't speak to him on that day.

Didn't even see his face. He saw the narrow shoulders so straight across you could use them as a level to hang a picture. He saw the back of Barrett's head, the unkempt hair swirling madly like the cosmos, expanding away from his head, the point of creation for the new world they would soon be born to.

"Are you gonna go back?" Celia's mother asked her father.

"Shit, I hope not. I need my Sunday shift back if a spot opens up. I hope I can't ever make it back."

But he would.

Celia's father met Barrett Higgins in the flesh the following Sunday. He was feeling back up to his usual speed, thanks to the painkillers. This sense of returning to his normal strength carried over from his workweek and sparked his competitiveness. He drove to the Living Faith church earlier than he had the week before, thinking he would arrive before the serious man who sat up front, but found he had been beaten again. The serious man was sitting on the walkway between the Living Faith Church and the Wok and Roll Chinese Restaurant, reading his Bible.

"Looks like we both beat Reverend Steve here this morning," her father said, still wanting to best somebody at something. The man looked up, startled, "Like I'd walked over and stepped on his balls," her father would recall later that morning. Months later, the story of that first meeting took a more reverent tone. Her father would say that the man looked up, "Like I'd interrupted a personal conversation with our Lord, and I think that's exactly what happened. It was the closest I'll ever come to the voice of God." That would also change, but for now the startled man blinked a few times at Celia's father and came out of his reverie.

"Good morning, peace of Christ be with you," he said. He stuck his hand up and out toward Celia's father, who gripped it and helped haul the man to his feet. "Barrett Higgins," said Barrett Higgins. He gave Celia's father's hand, which he was still holding, a firm shake.

"His hair was sticking up like he got a shock and he's got this one kinda lazy eye," her father recounted at the breakfast table, while a zombie Celia stared, a bit lazy-eyed herself at that time of morning, at a pancake that had appeared before her on a blue glass plate. "But he was put together normal otherwise. Just must not own a comb. I was thinking: I wish I just sat in my truck 'cause now I gotta talk to this weirdo."

In the future this, too, would be recounted differently: "When he stood up, I just felt this pull toward him. He had that quality about him. You just knew he was something special. You could feel the presence of Christ around him. You all probably know exactly what I'm talking about from when you met him yourselves. A piece of me knew right then I'd follow that man. That he was worth following."

In this first telling, though, in the kitchen of their small brick home with the wide flat lawn staked here and there with pillars of tall pine, the two men chatted idly under the morning's pink-rinsed sky until Reverend Steve came and unlocked the glass doors, one of which still carried a sticker with credit-card logos, left over from whatever business had been there before the church moved in. Barrett and Celia's father stood in the back while the reverend set up the folding chairs, then sat together up front. Together they didn't sway or throw their heads back in ecstasy as though they were in a shampoo commercial. Together they didn't sing. Celia's father sat and listened quietly, and Barrett kept his eyes closed in concentration except when he followed along with the scripture readings in his Bible. A curious thing Celia's father noted but did not ask about as they shook hands after the service and parted ways was that, as Barrett followed the readings in his Bible, he occasionally clucked his tongue and shook his head in annoyance—annoyance over what, precisely, her father couldn't tell.

They sat together again the next week, and after the service, Celia's father bought Barrett Higgins a cup of coffee at the gas station across the highway from the strip mall.

"He's staying in a house someone gave him 'bout half a mile away," her father was telling her mother when Celia came into the kitchen that morning.

"Someone gave him a house?" her mother repeated with doubt.

"Yep, gave it to him."

"Why would someone give him a house?"

"She was just really affected by his ministry."

"His ministry?"

"He's a minister."

"Does he have his own church somewhere?"

"No, he ain't—isn't—a minister like that. He's more, you know, freestyle."

Celia's mother looked up from her chopping block. "You're gonna have to explain that one."

"He, like, ministers to people as they need it. He doesn't have a set church, so he isn't constrained by dogmatic squabbles or internal politics."

"That's how he described it?"

"Yeah. He ministers on a more personal level."

"Do people pay him? How does he make money?"

"Says he doesn't need money."

"Guess not, if you're buying his coffee."

"It's not like that. This woman who gave him the house, she had problems in her life, strife. Barrett counseled her, prayed with her, helped her through her time of darkness." Celia's mother stopped slicing tomatoes and focused on these words and phrases that did not belong to her husband. "She was pretty well-off and happened to have a second house, like an investment house she was fixing up to sell. He helped her, and she wanted to help him, so she's letting him stay there. That's how he gets by. He helps people, and they help him. You know, like, God provides. He doesn't worry about bills or taxes or money shit. He takes care of people, and through them, God takes care of him. He just trusts in the Lord, and things work out fine."

Celia's mother hesitated before she replied. Celia saw her squint slightly at her husband, the way she would size up an appliance she had never seen before and the function of which was unclear. "I suppose it's good his faith provides for him," she offered.

Her father lost the tightness he had briefly displayed. He brightened, taking in his wife's turn of phrase. "Yeah, that's it exactly. His faith provides for him."

Her mother turned the conversation elsewhere, and her father followed. Celia waited for the mush in her brain to solidify and noted idly that there was a new word she didn't have a place for in her head. She wondered what *strife* was.

Celia's world went askew the day she came home from school and saw her father lying on the living-room floor. His truck hadn't been in the driveway. He was never awake when she came home from school. His presence in the living room at this time on a school day, his supine position between the coffee table and the TV as though he were auditioning to be a third piece of furniture, meant tragedy. Her mother came out of the hallway, where she must have been in the bathroom. She was carrying a damp washcloth and did not see Celia. Her father, flattened on the floor, had not seen her come in. Her mother knelt over her father and wiped his face. Celia realized that her father was doing the impossible. He was crying. "I'm so sorry," he whispered. His hands were clenched in fists on his forehead. Her mother shushed him and continued to clean his face, clearing away the tears that shouldn't be. "I'm so sorry," he said again.

"Sh, stop it now. It's not your fault. There's nothing you could have done. We're going to be fine. We're going to be brave," her mother said.

"I tried so hard for us. It's not fair," said her father, who did not, as a rule, believe in fairness. Nothing was fair. Fair didn't factor into things. But now: "It's not fair. I worked so goddamn hard. I'm sorry, baby. I tried so goddamn hard."

"I know you did. I know. It's going to be all right."

"I worked so goddamn hard!" he shouted, and her mother leaned over him and hugged him, and he fell into true sobs.

"It's OK. It's OK."

Celia pulled the door back open noisily, then slammed it. Her mother turned and looked over her shoulder. "Honey, go to your room. I'll be in there in a minute." Celia stared back at her. "Go," Celia's mother said more firmly, not wanting her to see.

Celia wished she hadn't.

Had the OxyContin made him sloppy? Reckless without realizing it? He didn't think so. But he did know they made him numb. He hadn't felt any pain, so he couldn't pinpoint exactly what caused his immobility—hefting open the back door of the paper truck maybe, or slinging the half-dozen bundles of newspapers toward the opening it left. Whatever it was, he'd suddenly found himself frozen; then his legs had gone out, and he collapsed onto his face. That's how he got the black eye. He was parked behind a Roses out off the highway. No one came by while he lay there.

He was scared but not panicked, because nothing felt real. He couldn't move. He had a sideways view out the back of the truck, as in some dream. Birds hopped circles in a puddle outside by a stack of plastic soda crates and wooden loading pallets. Then the pain slowly made itself a presence. It began in his lower back and poured slowly through his legs and shoulders like lava, boiling and viscous, being introduced into his bloodstream from some valve in his spine. Through the pain he gained some movement. Pain was, at least, a feeling. He found he could move his arm a little. He managed to flop over onto his side and get his phone out of his pocket.

When Celia's mother got there, her husband was still on his side. If this was her husband's love, this spectacle of twisted limbs showing the damaged proof of his efforts, his receipt, then her love was an account that stored interest from his payments, squirreling love away in increments until it was strong enough to hold something massive. Now it held him. He had inched across the floor of the truck toward the opening, but the bundles of newspapers he'd tossed there might as well have been the bars of a cage. She pulled them to the ground and helped drag him to the edge, four feet above the ground. She spread her legs, braced herself, and took his weight. When his feet hit the ground, there was a flood of profanity. In the back of her car, he lay twisted, hissing with each bump until they arrived home, where Celia found him, strewn across the floor like a shattered globe.

The first time he'd wrenched his back, the doctor prescribed OxyContin and taking it easy. Because he had a mortgage and a family, the second part of that prescription hadn't been an option. Subsequent weeks of back-damaging work, amplified by the push to go faster and win back his Sunday shift, tore and chewed the delicate muscles, wires, and cords that ran through and around his spine, his center. The painkillers kept him from feeling the damage he was doing to himself.

"Diagnosed as a broken goddamn CD player," he said, leaving the doctor's office with a prescription for higher milligram OxyContin. "Skipped discs."

"Slipped, baby," Celia's mother said. "Slipped discs."

"It doesn't matter, does it? What they're called. My back's fucked."

Three slipped discs, torn muscle tissue, nerve damage. Disability.

"Going on disability doesn't make you disabled," her mother told him.

"How the hell else am I gonna interpret the word *disability*?" he snapped. He was in an irritable mood that was rapidly becoming his de facto personality. He swallowed another pill and left the kitchen for his chair. Celia didn't attempt to crawl into his lap. She didn't even attempt to occupy the same room anymore. "You're too big for that," he'd said when she'd last tried to sit with him. "You're almost twelve, for Christ's sake. Go finish your homework."

Her mother made the kitchen a sanctuary, putting bowls of carrots with ranch dressing on the counter for them to snack on. She kept the radio on the windowsill going constantly with tapes, played low now—the *Dirty Dancing* soundtracks and other oldies. The smell of chained Vantage Lights wafted in from the other room. Ever-smoldering cigarettes and painkillers gave the den its own atmosphere: overcast. The room and the man in it both were hazy. Celia's mother went back to working full time.

"I spent six days a week in that truck so you wouldn't have to be full time," her father slurred. It wasn't an argument—someone had to work—but it was a lament for the loss of all they'd had.

"Numbers don't lie, unfortunately. There's no point discussing it," she said, both because there wasn't, and because communication with him in his mentally neutered state hardly qualified as discussion. "Besides, I'll be damned if we're going back to the Blue Wave."

When Celia's mother dropped from full to part time, the dentist for whom she was the office manager had assured her he would take her back on her old schedule whenever she wanted. He kept his word and not only took her back, but gave her a raise. This hurt her father worse than his back did. Celia's father was a man who complained about work only when he didn't have any. Watching his wife slip effortlessly back into a full-time position with a raise after he'd lost his Sunday shift and gone on disability unraveled his faith in the world and obliterated his sense of self.

He was not a ticking time bomb. He was not prone to rage. He wasn't even sarcastic. He was nothing except self-pitying and morose. He drank on top of his meds. It made him loopy and incoherent. Celia's mother stopped keeping beer in the house.

"Where'sss my beer?" her father said. He pushed a few items around in the refrigerator and knocked over the canister of parmesan cheese without righting it. It rolled from the shelf onto the floor. Her mother returned it to its place, shutting the refrigerator door.

"Why don't you go sit back down, and I'll bring you some iced tea," she said

"No—what? Where'sss my beer."

"There's no beer. Now do you want some iced tea or not?"

"Jesst get my beer." He teetered on his feet and spoke as though he were searching for unfamiliar words buried in his memory.

"You're not getting beer," she said, trying to lower her voice some because Celia was in the room doing homework at the kitchen table. "You piss all over yourself when you drink."

"I don't—"

His wife grabbed his arm and squeezed it, trying to rouse a moment of clarity and understanding through pain and force. "Yes, you do. Go sit back down."

"Jesst go get my fucking beer," he whined, trying to pull his arm away. "Jesst, look, look, I'm fine, jesst get me some fucking beer, OK? OK?"

"Go sit back down," Celia's mother said through gritted teeth.

"I'm in pain." It was a true whine now. "You don't know how it feels, and then you won't get the beer, and jess, jess…" He closed his eyes and steadied himself against the counter. "Jesst get fucksing beer!" he shouted. "Fuck you, jesst get it."

Her mother turned back to the sink and the potato she had been peeling when he reeled into the room. The top was shiny and slick already, like a bald head, but she resumed whacking at it with the peeler anyway. Celia sat frozen over her paper, not wanting to look up at either of them, reading the same math problem over and over. Her father leaned against the counter with his eyes closed and his mouth open. They stayed like this for several long minutes, locked into their positions, the top of the potato being whittled away, the math problem going unsolved, the counter holding up an unstable man. Celia thought her father had fallen asleep on his feet until he said her name.

"Celia." His eyes were still closed. "Celia, be—be good girl and go get Daddy some—"

"No!" her mother shouted, and she threw the potato at him. It bounced off his head, and he stumbled away from the counter. "Don't you dare ask your daughter to get you beer! What the fuck is wrong with you?" She struck out at him, smacking him on his head and shoulders and arms. "That's your daughter, you miserable piece of shit." He put his hands over his head.

"Stop, fuck," he said. He fell, and she kicked him once, then stood over him.

"How could you ask your daughter to get you beer?" she screamed.

"Get, fuck, away from me!" he roared back. Celia fled the room, hearing behind her as she went, "I wasssn't gonna let her drink any."

Ultimately, Celia's father got his beer. Her mother went and got it for him after he tried to leave the house and get it himself. She couldn't let the neighbors see him, lurching down the street, a grown man in a grimy shirt and basketball shorts, no shoes, clutching a handful of change he'd taken from the jar in their room. It was something that would happen at the Blue Wave— omeone desperate for a drink to make them feel less desperate.

Celia's mother saw him through the kitchen window, past the sparrows and finches hopping from feeder to bath. She caught him at the end of the driveway. "I'll get it. I'll get the beer. No, just stop talking and go back to the house this instant, and I'll get it. Shut up. Shut. Up. Go now, and I'll get it for you." When she came back, she threw each of two six-packs at him from the doorway. The cans blew out of their rings on impact with his shoulder. He recovered one and opened it without a word.

"I started to get a twelve-pack," she said, coming into Celia's room. "But it was too heavy for me to throw."

An hour later, he was passed out on the couch, soaked in his own urine. Celia went to bed with her mother in her parents' room. They locked the door. It was unnecessary, but they felt, somehow, that it made a point, if only to themselves.

Celia had never been overly talkative anyway. Now she shut up almost entirely. After school she walked from the bus to their house and let herself in through the back kitchen door to avoid the front room and her sedated father, bathed in blue light from the TV, a room she had begun referring to in her head as the Crypt. She had not known change on this scale could take place. She changed grades each year, but the school building itself was the same, along with all the people in it, just in different chairs. She had changed residences, but her family had remained consistent: their sounds, the cars, bedsheets. Then her father became a different man, literally taking pills that changed him, his shape, the way he spoke, acted, treated her. He dragged her mother along with him, making her desperate and angry, his change necessitating hers. How could Celia trust these people? Or anything else for that matter.

"Honey, you've been so quiet this whole semester," her English teacher, Mrs. Rivlin, said one day as she was packing her bag, the last one to leave class. "Is everything OK?"

What was there to talk about when you didn't understand anything? All she'd ever thought she understood had proven unreliable. Celia nodded at Mrs. Rivlin. "I'm fine," she said. From then on, she packed up quickly and tried to be the first one out the door, lest Rivlin or another teacher accost her with more passing concerns she couldn't address.

Her mother didn't press her to talk and tried to make things seem normal, which only proved how much they were not. Since when did they *try*? Celia sat in the kitchen when she came home from school and did homework. When her mother finally came home, Celia unclenched slightly, for though she didn't understand how this had happened and now knew that her mother was also capable of becoming a different person, she at least felt safe around her. Music, snacks, random observations about what was in the fridge and what was needed—these were the only things that remained unchanged. Celia did all her homework, then invented more homework. She read ahead in all her textbooks. She copied her math problems neatly onto another sheet of paper after completing them. As long as she was doing homework, she was doing what she was supposed to do, and there would be nothing to discuss. She was being good and would be left out of whatever this was going on around her.

After so much time in her textbooks, Celia thought in statements: the Treaty of Versailles ended World War I; X equals 15.67. But there are no vacuums, she thought, musing on all the scientific theories that existed in so-called vacuums, empty of all matter and influence. Nothing could be empty of matter or things that mattered. She knew that now. Celia had believed that they—"they" as a family, the house, the Saturdays off and the Sunday shift that brought in overtime pay, the yard, even the Blue Wave with Patch and Dangle croaking and squawking next door, all the collected elements that made up the existence she thought of as "they"—existed in a vacuum. That was wrong, though. All those elements were sewn together, connected at the seams like an overmended shirt, vulnerable through every loose stitch. There was no end to the things that could get through to them.

As if to prove her point, she came home one day, let herself in the back door to avoid the Crypt, and found her father drying dishes over the sink. He had showered. His hair was combed back and still damp. He had shaved, put on clean clothes. The smell of something besides his cigarettes and unwashed body drifted through the house.

"Hey, Cee-monkey," he said, too casually. "I put a casserole in the oven. Figured I'd give your mom a night off from the kitchen. She deserves…" His voice faltered a second, catching on some realization. "She deserves a break, I think," he managed. He resumed his act of normalcy. "You wanna watch a little TV together till she gets home?"

Celia ran to her room and shut the door, more frightened than ever.

He told them the whole story that evening, but not before her mother had her own run-in with the unexpected and horrifically normal man in the kitchen. Her father's voice must have been low and contrite; Celia only heard her mother's side through her bedroom door.

"What the hell is going on? Where's Celia?"

…

"What do you mean, *you don't know why*? Because she doesn't know what's going on. I'm sure you scared her half to death. What are you doing?"

…

"No, your family isn't afraid of you. Just your daughter is afraid. Your wife is fucking pissed at you."

…

"So just like that, it's all OK? Huh? That's what you think?"

…

"Who?"

…

"The weird church guy?"

…

"I'll call that loser whatever the fuck I want. Don't you tell me—"

…

"You're damn right you're sorry. One sorry piece of—"

…

"How did he know where you live?"

...

"No, no, just stop right there. Just stop. If this is going to be some kind of apology or explanation, I'm gonna get Celia. You owe her both, too."

Her mother collected her from her room, and they sat together at the kitchen table, her father opposite them. Celia wanted the roof to cave in and destroy them all. It was so formal and planned, so unnatural that they should be sitting here like this about to have a talk. Her mother sat with her arms crossed, defiant. Her father leaned forward in his chair, cigarettes and the good ashtray in front of him. He shifted now and then, wincing at the pain returning to his back as sobriety overtook him.

"Well? Go on," her mother said irritably.

What had happened was this: Celia's father had not risen that morning, as was his recent custom. He didn't rise anymore. He fluttered to a loose consciousness after Celia and her mother left the house. He'd eaten a couple pieces of bread from the loaf on the counter, dropped some slices of ham into his mouth, then washed it down with a squirt of mustard straight from the plastic bottle.

Her mother shook her head. "Can't even assemble a boring sandwich."

"I know," her father said. "It's undignified. Everything about me was undignified, and I felt, just, worthless. Useless."

He'd found a few beers left in the fridge and took them back to the Crypt with him, where he began the daily routine of befouling himself and the couch. "I got a steam cleaner from the grocery store today and cleaned that, by the way," he said. "It's still a little damp."

That's when the miracle had happened. As Celia's father sat withering on the sofa, there was a knock at the door. He ignored it, as usual, but the knock persisted. It grew louder and more forceful.

"It wouldn't stop, this hammering. Just pounding away at the door." When he finally answered it, Barrett Higgins stood on the other side.

It took Celia a minute to place the name. When she finally did, she spoke her first words directed at her father in over two weeks.

"The church man with the weird hair?" she said. Her parents gave her a look that showed her silence had not gone unnoticed. Her father seemed relieved to hear her address him, and Celia was struck by the sensation of her words having power for the first time in her life.

"That's exactly who it was, baby," her father said.

"How did he know where we lived?" Celia's mother said.

Her father shook his head. "Just let me finish, first."

Barrett Higgins stood on the front step and took in her father's appearance. "Lo, brother, but you have fallen on ill times," he said. With the sun behind him, his hair cast a shadow through the room like that of a tree.

"Oh, fuck off," her father had replied.

But Barrett Higgins did not fuck off. He pushed his way into the house, an action that would have been unthinkable, dangerous even, if her father had been his old self.

"You are weak, my friend," Barrett said. "Is this a man? Someone who can't defend his own home. What if I had come for your possessions? Or your family?" Her father lunged at Barrett who easily sidestepped him. Celia's father pitched face-first onto the floor. "I could come and take all you have, brother. Only the righteous can rely on the protection of the Lord, and there is no righteousness in you." Her father attempted to stand, but Barrett shoved him down again and kicked him over onto his back. He stood over Celia's father, who lay sprawled, foggy, and, to hear him tell it, genuinely frightened.

"The way he was talking about how he could take my family, and I…I just," he said, lighting a third cigarette as he recalled the moment. "I was only sort of just realizing who this guy was. It was like he was parting the curtain, and I was kinda able to see again."

So Barrett stood over her father. Celia was reminded of the time she'd come home and found her mother kneeling over him while he sobbed. All recent major events seemed to be prefaced by his being knocked down in his own living room. Barrett Higgins's hair rose from his scalp like furious wisps of smoke. He carried something in his hand. Through the haze, her father had believed it to be a weapon, had believed Barrett had come to kill him, bludgeon him to death with whatever it was he carried, then run off with the TV maybe.

"And I realized I didn't care," her father said. "I was relieved. I wanted him to kill me and just let it all be over." Celia's mother put a hand over her eyes as he spoke. "I thought he was gonna kill me, and I wanted him to hurry up and get on with it already."

Barrett bent low, and Celia's father hoped whatever he was going to use wouldn't cause too much of a mess. He'd given his family enough trouble without them having to spend a week scrubbing bloodstains from the carpet. Barrett had reached out and placed one hand on her father's head; he pressed the object he carried to his chest. It was his Bible.

Barrett whispered to her father: "I know you are a good man. A good father and husband. You're an honorable worker, a man who has tried to do everything right and still ended up in this state, but it's OK. I can fix you. Put your faith in God the Father. He will see your good life, and he will be proud of you. The father of all will be there to help you. Trust him. Trust me. We will help carry you through this."

Then he began to pray.

"Merciful Lord," Barrett called out. "This is a good man. He has done his best to provide for and care for his family. But circumstance and the evil of the world have had their way with him and left him broken, unemployed, and suffering from addiction and self-pity. He has done all a man can do, Lord, but alone he is not enough. He needs you, Lord. He wants you. I know this, for I have seen him in your house, seeking you. He is open to you, Lord, but he is confused and uncomprehending of your ways and your mercy. With your help, oh Lord, he will rise again, for you are the father of us all, and you will care for him and guide him as a father does. Come into him, Lord. Enter this man's heart that he may see that, through you, all things are possible and your grace will guide him in all matters for the rest of his life. Come into him, Lord. Come into him!"

"And I felt it," her father said. "When he called on God the Father to enter me, it happened. I felt his presence, I—it's hard to explain, but I really felt…this peace. That's it. It was a peace. And I heard him, God, inside me, saying it would all be OK if I just put my trust in him. And I did." Celia and her mother sat in silence on their side of the table. Her mother's eyes were pink and raw, but there were no visible tears. They smelled something. "Oh, my casserole," her father said. He got awkwardly to his feet with noticeable pain, slid the dish off the rack, and placed it on the stovetop, then sat back down. "Anyway, I—Barrett stayed, and we talked for a while. When he left, I flushed all my pills down the toilet and took a shower. I want to apologize to both of you. I'm…I'm just sorry. I've not been the man or father you deserve. Christ has opened my eyes now, and with him as my witness, I promise the two of you I'll—"

"That's enough," her mother said. It was abrupt and harsh. She leaned forward, placing a hand over one of her husband's and said it again more gently. "That's enough. Let's just…let's just have some dinner, OK? That's just—it's enough for right now, OK?" She stood and went to the stove, touching her husband's shoulder for a brief moment as she passed him. She sniffed and pulled on the oven mitts and moved the casserole dish over to the table. "Cee, can you set the table, please?" she said.

Outside, the sun dropped below the pines and threaded its light between the branches and trunks, like a child peeking at a movie through his fingers. Celia's father got up and dropped the blinds to cut the glare so the sun cast their arms, plates, and glasses in the day's last light. Their heads, in the shadow above, kept quiet as they ate. Halfway through the meal, Celia realized she was exhausted. She asked to be excused. Her face must have shown her tiredness, because her mother just nodded.

Celia closed the door to her room, then changed her mind. She opened it again, quietly, and sat on the floor leaning against the doorframe. She listened for her parents' conversation, but they were quiet. The occasional tink of a fork on a plate and clonk as a glass was replaced on the table after a swallow were all that signaled life was going on in the kitchen. Otherwise, there was nothing.

It had been a long time—months—since there was nothing. It felt like stalling, but Celia wasn't sure she was ready for a new *something* to come along yet. The last something had ruined each and every day and made the living room smell like pee. Celia closed her bedroom door and switched off the light. Plastic glow-in-the-dark stars swirled across the ceiling. Celia lay across her neatly made bed with her clothes on and stared at the stars.

She did not feel better about the Crypt turning back into the living room. She didn't feel better about her father walking and talking again like a normal man. She felt trapped and suffocated by her parents and their lives, which, she noticed for the first time, had nothing to do with her. Celia hadn't known that before. Now she couldn't *un*know it. Her life took place at school or out in the neighborhood with Sloane. The crap that went on in this house was someone else's problem because she wasn't invited to help solve it. The disintegration of all decent behavior (pissing on the couch! throwing beers and potatoes!)—these two people had moved beyond her, or she had moved beyond them. Her heart hurt, literally felt sore in her chest, at the thought of the Blue Wave, and painting the rooms of the new house, and listening to tapes in the kitchen.

She lay under her fake plastic stars and experienced her first pangs of nostalgia.

Chapter 2

Shot in a war or run down by a bus—In the Lord's hands thanks to cheap Vantage Lights—Barrett Higgins at church—A health immunity to the effect her words have on others—It'd be nice to be Baptist—Celia the Chosen One—Darlington Speedway—A magical place to be alone—The schism—At least it ain't the Blue Wave

The next Sunday Celia was in the backseat of her mother's car, wearing the dress that was usually reserved for school-picture day. Her father drove. Celia had never been to church before. Her parents had told her about God when she was younger. She had received cursory explanations of heaven and hell and been assured she was bound for the former rather than the latter. She knew God had a son, Jesus, but that Jesus's mother was married to some other guy, Joseph. Celia knew of several people at the Blue Wave in similar situations.

Her friend Sloane's family went to church every Sunday. "It's really boring, but you're not allowed to say so," Sloane told her.

The night Celia's father cleaned up the living room, made the casserole, and apologized to her and her mother, things went sour—not sour the way they had been, but another *something* came along. Nothing really exists in a vacuum, Celia observed, not even nothing. She fell asleep in her clothes that night with the small reading lamp burning beside her bed. She awoke to sounds of retching. Her father was vomiting in the bathroom. Withdrawal had set in. All his painkillers were down the toilet already, leading the way for the half-digested casserole that now followed. The next day he was back on the couch, that portal he'd traveled through to turn into the beast he was and through which he now returned to himself. The living room remained steeped in fluids and smells, albeit new ones. Celia continued referring to it as the Crypt. Her mother brought Valium home from the dentist's office, but her father refused any of "the devil's chemicals."

"You look like the devil's already inside you, the way you're shaking," her mother said.

"I'm freezing," her father said while sweating through his shirt and the two blankets wrapped around him. "You can't go outside. The lake turned to fire, and I couldn't get to you in time. I couldn't get to you and the baby. I was stuck on the shore."

"He's delirious," Celia's mother reassured her. "It's OK." She wasn't worried. Her mother doted on her husband when she came home from work, returning to something like her former self. Her father was working on it, she guessed. His withdrawal symptoms were a relief to Celia's mother. She hummed along with her tapes in the kitchen, pausing occasionally when a splashing sound carried in from the Crypt. "Sounds like he threw up again," she'd say, giving Celia a bright smile.

"Hooray," Celia replied.

"Men are weak when it comes to illness," her mother said. "They can't handle it. They prefer getting shot in war or run down by a bus or something."

"Or tearing up their back?" Celia asked.

"Exactly. He was angry and energetic about that. Now he's overcome."

Celia's father made it through the worst of the withdrawal in three or four days. The living room aired out, but Celia permanently declared it the Crypt. Her present had died in there and made way for the future in which they now lived. The Saturday night after the casserole and apology, her mother stuck her head into Celia's bedroom. Celia was cutting pictures of pretty women out of one of the magazines her mother brought home from the dentist's waiting room. She glued the pictures into collages. "You should get to sleep early tonight," her mother said. "We're going to church in the morning."

Celia sleepwalked through the morning. She dressed with one eye open and shuffled out to the car. She came fully into the day sometime after they pulled out of Garden Estates. They drove along the thin highways of Brock, South Carolina. The road split fields and forests like pages in an open book as they traveled the spine. Tobacco and cotton grew on the flat, square stretches. Celia looked for the dilapidated barns and smokehouses she loved, stranded in the middle of fields, left standing for unknown reasons, calling out the passage of time. Her favorite was a lone chimney and hearth left in an unplanted field, its house torn down or worn away. Its resolute existence made her think of structures blown in by hungry wolves or carried off by a typhoon.

They pulled into the strip mall. The grocery store that served as the strip's anchor store had closed. A Dollar Store, a discount cigarette outlet, a Dress Barn, a Payless Shoes, and a Prudential Insurance office soldiered on resolutely with the church and Chinese place. Celia's father parked the car, and they all sat a moment.

"How do you feel?" her mother asked her father. She put a hand to his forehead.

"Kinda bad, but all right. Queasy." He shifted to hunch awkwardly over the steering wheel, relieving the pressure and pain on his bad disks.

"Have you heard from this guy, Barrett, since he was at the house?"

"No, has Geraldine mentioned him?"

Geraldine worked at the dentist's office with Celia's mother. She and her husband also attended Living Faith Church. Celia's mother generally was not one to reveal too much about her personal life to others, but she had known Geraldine on and off for years, and in the course of her days at the office, while her husband moldered in the house they were struggling to make payments on, she found she needed to talk to someone. Anyone. Geraldine became that anyone. Geraldine enjoyed people telling her their woes. She believed it meant they thought she was handling her own life particularly well.

Geraldine and her husband, Beaufort, recently had met an enigmatic man at their new church. The man was devout and incredibly intense in his beliefs. He had a stormy head of hair on him and something wrong with one of his eyes. His name was Barrett Higgins. The fact that this interesting and deeply religious man had befriended her—and even was friendly with boring old Beaufort—confirmed for Geraldine that Beaufort and she were the kind of commonsense people who carried the proper values. Geraldine told this man at her church about her coworker's husband, Celia's father. Geraldine said he was suffering from demoralization and addiction and said she was praying for him and his family, and would Barrett keep them in his prayers, too? Barrett said of course and asked the man's name. After that he consulted the phone book. That was how he came to find Celia's father at home that day. That was how her father became well, so to speak. And that was how they found themselves here, in the parking lot, stalling before going to meet the man, and his deity, who had authored all this.

They got out of the car and made their way to the church. The glass door bore a cross made from blue painter's tape. It was nothing like the churches Celia knew from TV, or even from just driving around with her parents. Living Faith's proximity to the discount cigarette outlet explained how her father had discovered the place though. They were in the Lord's hands now, thanks to his need for cheap Vantage Lights by the carton.

Barrett was waiting for them when they stepped through the door. He shook hands with Celia's father. "Welcome back," he said. His tone was thick with knowing weight, implying more than just a return to Living Faith Church. It hinted at a return to the living in general.

"Thank you," her father said. He held Barrett's hand a long moment, and Barrett nodded in understanding. "This is my wife," her father said, breaking his grip and gesturing toward Celia's mother.

"I'm pleased to meet you," Barrett said.

"You, too," her mother said. "I'd like to thank you as well. Everything's been much—" She stopped, and her face hardened as she composed herself.

"Well, it's not me who deserves the credit," Barrett said, covering her emotional moment. He gestured upward. "But I'm glad to see you both and hear that—"

"Hello, hello," a voice broke in. A man was striding across the room toward them, his hand already out while he was still a few paces away. "Hello," he said a third time, reaching past Barrett to Celia's father. "Pleasure to have you back again," he said, shaking Celia's father's hand. "I'm Reverend Ste—"

"Reverend Steve," Celia's father said. "I remember." The reverend wore the traditional black pants and black shirt. He had a thick mop of sandy blond hair and rimless glasses that were nearly invisible until the lenses caught the light. He was thick in the waist and thin in the shoulders. He smiled too intently, as though he were waiting for the answer to a question no one had heard him ask. "Nice to see you again, Reverend. This is my wife."

"Reverend Steve, pleased to meet you," the reverend said. "I was just setting up the last of the chairs. I see Barrett is acting as our greeter." He gave Barrett a terse smile. Barrett tersely returned it. The reverend stepped past him to Celia's mother. "This is your first service with us, isn't it?"

Barrett turned from the conversation to face Celia, who stood watching. "You must be Celia," he said, offering his hand. Her father had reported accurately on Barrett's hair. It appeared to be its own entity, curly in some places, spiked in others, and all of it growing with the survivalist abandon of jungle vegetation. His left eye pulled away from his face as if it wanted to go be with his ear. What her father had failed to notice, or perhaps to appreciate, was how handsome Barrett was despite these things—or maybe because of them. His face was made up of clean lines and a strong jaw, with good dark eyebrows. The untamed hair and eye were like things casually neglected on a face of abundance, like a mansion whose wealthy owners didn't worry about the creeping ivy and drafty antique windows because they could always afford brick repair and heat.

"Hi," Celia said, trying to focus on the good eye. She shook the outstretched hand.

"I'm Barrett Higgins." Barrett pulled a chair from the back row where they stood and turned it around. He sat, leveling his height with Celia's. "I'm a friend of your dad's." Celia nodded. "How old are you, Celia?"

"Thirteen."

"That's a good age. I remember being thirteen." Adults always talked like this. All thirteen meant to Celia was algebra and no driver's license.

"It's all right," Celia said.

"Do you know who I am?"

"You helped my dad," Celia said.

"I showed him the path, but he walked it. Your father helped himself. Not everyone can do that. He's a special man." They both looked over at her father. Reverend Steve must have asked about Celia, because they overheard her father say, "She turned thirteen a month ago. She's a good kid, smart as a motherf—smart as her mother." He put his arm around his wife. "The women got all the brains in the family. They just keep me around 'cause I'm good-looking." He winked at his wife.

Barrett turned back to Celia. "I imagine you're a very special girl, too."

"We have to do our service early, before the rest of the stores open," they heard Reverend Steve say. "Otherwise the customers from the Wok and Roll stand outside and stare."

"Maybe you could hang some curtains," Celia's mother said.

Reverend Steve either smiled or winced. "Of course, I'm getting to that one of these—"

"Yes, one of these days," Barrett said, standing and turning his attention back to the adults. "If only there were a place to buy curtains today. But alas—"

"Yes, thank you, Barrett. Your position on this matter has been duly noted," Reverend Steve said. He smiled at Celia's parents. "It was a pleasure to meet you. Welcome to our Christian family. If you'll excuse me, we're going to start shortly." He stepped away, then stopped. Barrett had left his chair turned the wrong way. Reverend Steve sighed and righted it, then continued to the podium at the other end of the room.

"The good reverend has a theological opposition to everything I say," Barrett said to Celia and her parents. "Especially in regard to those curtains. And he believes mightily in the order of his chairs."

Reverend Steve took his seat behind the podium, facing the congregation. To his left, a middle-aged woman with a guitar took up a corner. A small table with a CD player, a triangle, and a tambourine stood beside her. The reverend arranged his chairs on either side of the room, leaving space for a center aisle. The place wasn't a third full.

"I'd consider it an honor if you sat with me," Barrett said to Celia's parents. He gestured to the front as though he were inviting them into his home.

"Absolutely," Celia's father said.

They made their way to the front. Geraldine and Beaufort came in the back as they took their seats. Geraldine waved to them energetically. She pressed her hands together in the shape of prayer and held them to her lips as she looked at their family.

"Aw, crap," Celia heard her mother sigh quietly, realizing the connection that now bound her more tightly to this woman. Geraldine hustled down the aisle, Beaufort trailing, and sat behind them.

"Praise the Lord," Geraldine whispered to Celia's mother, squeezing her shoulder.

"Yeah," her mother replied.

The woman with the guitar suddenly brandished the tambourine and shook them all to attention. There was silence. She closed her eyes, guitar pick poised above the instrument. They all waited. The woman threw her hand against the strings, bursting into the chords and verse simultaneously. "He walks with me/Through the valley/Brings peace to me/Indubitably." Celia's mother stifled a laugh. No one else seemed to notice. Barrett Higgins rolled his eyes. There were no hymnals, but the song must have been a Living Faith anthem, because the rest of the congregation sang along. Behind them Geraldine's voice rang out in a deranged aria above the rest of the singers: "If I'm lost at sea/He'll rescue me/The Lord He be/Yes, He, He, Heeeeeee."

When the second verse kicked in, people jumped to their feet. Hands were raised like antennae for better reception of the Lord's grace. Celia's mother leaned over to whisper to her husband, "Right, singy and dancy." Her father nodded and shrugged. Reverend Steve smiled in his chair, eyes closed, swaying back and forth. Barrett Higgins glared wrath at him. Celia guessed everyone's eyes were closed to keep from being embarrassed by the sight of themselves.

The song lasted seven minutes. The woman leading them concluded with a violent ringing of her triangle.

Reverend Steve took the podium. He smiled out over his congregation. "We're going to read from Matthew this morning," he said. "A lot of you are probably already familiar with this reading." Celia wondered what constituted "a lot" in a crowd less than twenty strong. "'When Jesus saw the crowds, he went up the mountain, and after he had sat down, his disciples came to him. He began to teach them, saying: Blessed are the poor in spirit, for theirs is the kingdom of heaven. Blessed are they who mourn for they will be comforted. Blessed are the meek, for they will inherit the land. Blessed are they who hunger and thirst for righteousness, for they will be satisfied. Blessed are the merciful, for they will be shown mercy. Blessed are the clean of heart, for they will see God. Blessed are the peacemakers, for they will be called children of God. Blessed are they who are persecuted for the sake of righteousness, for theirs is the kingdom of heaven. Blessed are you when they insult you and persecute you and utter every kind of evil falsely against you because of me. Rejoice and be glad for your reward will be great in heaven. Thus they persecuted the prophets who were before you.'"

Reverend Steve looked up from the open Bible and gazed out at them. "What's Jesus telling us in this passage?" Celia panicked. She hadn't known church would have questions like school. What if she was called on? But the reverend answered his own question. "He's telling us not to worry. He's telling us it will all be OK and we need not struggle so. He wants to love us as we are. The peacemakers, the clean of heart, the poor in spirit, the meek, the insulted, the mourners, the hungry and thirsty! It covers everyone! We're all included in this list. God loves us, and the kingdom of heaven awaits us." Celia hoped that meant they could wrap this up and go home, but despite the admitted simplicity of the passage and its meaning, the reverend managed to drone on for forty more minutes. Celia found it impossible to be attentive. She drifted in and out, catching snatches of the sermon.

"We're all God's children, and our mistakes are immediately forgiven if we just ask, the same way you would forgive a child for making a mistake." Celia thought about Marcus Havenfelt in her class. He got in trouble almost every day. He was indifferent to punishment and his frequent trips to the principal's office, not terrified the way Celia would have been. Marcus was cute though. "When all the pressures of the world seem like too much, take comfort. That's what he's saying. Those challenges are your salvation." If she and Sloane tied their bike tires together, could they make a tandem bike like they saw in that movie? Wait, that wouldn't work. The rope would catch against the bike frame. How *do* you make a tandem bike? Glue? "Paradise is right there, it's ours for the taking. God wants to give it to us. All we have to do is open our hearts to him and accept him as the supreme ruler of our lives and thoughts. Give all ourselves to him, and let him take control. That's all. It's that easy." She wished she had boobs. Sloane was getting hers, but she didn't like it. They embarrassed her. How unfair. Cheese eggs: that's what she wanted for breakfast. Was her mom taking requests this morning? Celia could help her. She liked grating cheese, the solid hunk ripping to strings as the cheese dragged against the grater.

At last Reverend Steve drew to a close, though the service continued. There was another song, then a prayer everyone—except Celia's family, who didn't know it—said together, and some closing remarks from the reverend.

After a final song, the service concluded with a last riot from the tambourine and a wild thrashing of the triangle. The congregation stood and made their way to the door. The service had lasted more than an hour. Geraldine had somehow contained herself throughout and now happily burst, standing and reaching over the chairs to hug Celia's mother, who barely had time to turn around.

"Oh, honey, praise the Lord," Geraldine said. "I'm so happy for you."

"Hey, Gerry. Thanks," Celia's mother said, extracting herself from Geraldine's grip. Geraldine's hair was an armory that protected her head, Celia thought. It was sprayed stiff and rarely deigned to move. None of its soldiers ever broke rank into flyaways or unruly strands. Her prominent bangs descended in an even and orderly fashion from her strictly held hairline. She wore large earrings and had more teeth than anyone Celia had ever met.

"It's amazing, isn't it? I had no idea Barrett knew you all. I was just asking him to pray for some people like I always do, and I mentioned…" Geraldine's eyes grew wide, and she nodded her head to say *you know what*.

"The painkillers," Celia's mother said in a sharp tone.

"Right," Geraldine whispered, then returned to her normal loud voice. "And as soon as I mentioned your two names, Barrett said, 'I know this man. He is a child of God.'" Geraldine gawked at Celia's mother. "Can you believe it? I mean, I don't know how people say they don't believe in miracles. When you think what the odds are of this happening, it's impossible not to see it was clearly God at work." Geraldine shook her head in wonderment.

"Yes, clearly," Celia's mother said, trying the words out to make sure they were the right response. Celia felt as if they were in a play.

A few feet away, her father and Beaufort were listening attentively to Barrett to keep from having to make awkward conversation with each other. "His heart's in the right place, but I think his sermons often miss the point of the scripture they're supposed to enlighten," Celia heard Barrett saying in a low voice.

"Music's nice and lively," Beaufort observed.

"That's one way of putting it," Barrett said with a dry roll of his eyes.

"Beaufort and I would love to take everyone out for breakfast," Geraldine was saying. She stared at her husband. "Right?"

Beaufort looked up from studying his loafers and said what he always said when his wife was 100 percent wrong about what he would or wouldn't love to do: "Of course."

"That'd be great," Celia's father said.

"Honey, we need to get home. You're still not feeling well enough to be out too long," her mother said. Celia's father looked at her and said what he always said when he was 100 percent sure that he shouldn't, no matter what, contradict her: "You're probably right."

"You poor thing, I forgot about how you must be feeling," Geraldine said.

"He'll be all right. He just needs some rest," Celia's mother said. Her father nodded.

"Barrett, you'll still come, won't you?" Geraldine said. There was a measure of pleading in her voice.

"Of course," Barrett said, echoing Beaufort. It was impossible to tell if he was mocking him or if Geraldine simply aroused defeat and acquiescence in the men she spoke to.

"It's such a treat having him discuss the scripture with us. I learn more than I do during the actual sermon," Geraldine said. Reverend Steve came up behind her just in time to hear this, but Geraldine possessed a healthy immunity to the effect her words had on others and was able to press on despite his arrival. "I can't wait to hear your thoughts on what we heard this morning," she said. "Hello, Reverend. Sorry we came in late. I couldn't get Beaufort out of the bathroom."

"Probably in there trying to hang himself," Celia heard her mother mutter into her purse while pretending to look for the car keys she knew her husband had in his pocket.

"Quite all right," Reverend Steve said. "I just wanted to thank everyone for coming."

"You gave a fine sermon this morning, Reverend," Beaufort said with a nod of his bearded head. "I found it powerfully inspiring."

"Thank you, Montford," Reverend Steve said.

Beaufort didn't bother to correct him. He took his keys from his belt loop and said, "I'll be in the car."

"I hope we see you again next Sunday," Reverend Steve said to Celia's parents.

"Absolutely," Celia's father said at the exact same time her mother said, "We'll see." There was silence while everyone waited for whatever was going to gloss over their discrepancy of opinion.

"Celia, it was sure nice to have you here this morning," Barrett said.

"Thank you," Celia said quietly.

"We should be going," Celia's mother said. She ushered them toward the door.

"Breakfast next Sunday, promise me," they heard Geraldine saying behind them. They crossed the lot to the car. As they pulled away, Celia saw Geraldine and Barrett walking toward a car where Beaufort sat behind the wheel. A man stepped out of the Wok and Roll and opened a sandwich board advertising a Peking duck special. Through the glass front of the church, she saw Reverend Steve by himself, quietly folding the chairs one by one.

Celia's parents sat in silence on the way home. There was a conversation they wanted to have, but weren't having. Celia felt excluded. They weren't having it because she was there. She knew what the conversation not taking place was. Her mom didn't like going to that weird church. Her dad did. Her mom disliked the instant familiarity everyone pushed on them. Celia didn't blame her. The whole ordeal had been too early and boring.

Her father spoke at last as they pulled through the entrance to Garden Estates. "Did you enjoy the service, Cee-bear?"

She had not. What was there to enjoy? But that miserable storefront church obviously meant something to him. She didn't want to hurt his feelings by saying how much she hated it. Nor did she want to take his side against her mother, whose feelings she shared. Why should she be the one who had to talk about the awful morning, anyway?

She gave the staple answer of her age group. "I don't know." Her mother fixed her father with a grimace. He stopped looking at Celia in the rearview and put his eyes on the road. The rest of the neighborhood was just confronting the day. Dads in gym shorts and T-shirts sauntered to the ends of their driveways for the newspaper. Here and there people watered flowers before the sun got too high. They pulled into their carport. Celia got out before her father had even put the car in park. She ran to her bike, the one that was too small for her really but that she had learned on and trusted.

"Celia, not in your dress," her mother called after her as she cruised to the end of the driveway and onto the blacktop of the street.

"Just once around the block," Celia hollered back. "Promise." She pumped the pedals, the wind blowing her hair back. She closed her eyes and worked her legs in frantic circles, feeling the rush of possibility that came from not knowing if she'd hit something. She kept them closed longer than she usually did when she played this game. Then a little longer still.

She came back around the block and leaned her bike neatly in the corner of the carport. She entered the house through the Crypt and heard her parents in the kitchen. They hadn't heard her come home. It was the conversation that had been missing in the car.

"...and he's rude to that poor minister," she heard her mother say.

"He's just at odds with him over—"

"The hell is that? 'Just at odds with him.' That's what I'm talking about. All of a sudden you talk like this. You sound ridiculous. You're putting on religion the way other people put on airs."

"Fine. They got some tension between them. Part of it has to do with the curtains—"

"That's another thing. Why would we go to a church where the minister is such an idiot? Why aren't there curtains?" There was a quick, repeating, banging sound Celia recognized as her mother's good knife whacking against the cutting board as it annihilated some vegetable. Her mother liked to chop and tear when she was agitated. Celia suspected they would be eating an aggression salad with dinner that night.

"Christ said that—" He was cut off by what sounded like the cutting board being lifted and slammed back down. There followed a long pause.

"I need you to stop talking like that and talk like an adult if you want me to keep having this conversation," her mother said in a low, controlled voice. "Jesus Christ, it's so—"

"Please don't blaspheme. I know this is coming at you quick, and you don't have to feel like I feel, but it's—"

"No, you're right," her mother interrupted. "It's a bad habit, anyway." It was quiet for a bit. The chopping sound took on a more regular rhythm, and the force of the blade dropped from intent-to-wound to average food prep. "Why couldn't we become Baptist?" her mother said.

"I know the past half a year hasn't been easy," her father said. "Most of that's on me."

"You couldn't help what happened to your back."

"No, I couldn't help what happened with my back. Or shit, maybe I could've, who knows. It wasn't intentional at any rate. But the rest of it, you know, I wasn't at my best. And I think to myself, how could I have got so bad? I was so," he thought for a moment, "soft. So weak."

The knife halved some poor vegetable with a loud thwack. "You are not weak, and you ain't ever been. You're the strongest—"

"Would you let me finish? C'mon." The chopping resumed. "I got everything, you know? A beautiful family, a beautiful home, everyone's healthy, but a hardship came along, and I stumbled and fell." The chopping got louder, but Celia's mother didn't comment on the drift of her husband's rhetoric. "And it was because I didn't have God in my life. And when I found him, I didn't feel weak anymore. And I knew this was something we needed in our lives that we'd been neglecting. He's real. It's all real. It's God who saved me and brought us out of a bad time. I know you see that."

The chopping stopped and there was another pause, then her mother said, "I do. I feel that's true." Celia heard her father get up and open the refrigerator door. "I still think it'd be nice to be Baptist," her mother said. "They build such nice facilities."

"The Baptists are crazy," her father said, indifferently. "Maybe we could ask people to chip in a couple bucks and just buy the curtains ourselves."

Celia went to her room and shut the door with something less than a sense of gloom. Her parents weren't fighting about church; that was positive. On the other hand, now they had to go to church. They'd never gone to church before, and they didn't talk much about God. There had always been the tacit understanding that they, as a family, believed in God's existence, but it was a rainy-day-fund kind of belief. It didn't cost anything to say it, and it made people less suspicious of you.

What needled her anxiety most was the suddenness. Being churched-up came with a lot of intangible accessories. She knew church-going kids at school. They talked about politicians they hated, and they had to leave during certain parts of science class. Here they were, jumping right in. Her father at least had a rock-bottom from which to rebound into this. How were she and her mother supposed to be sincere?

That night at dinner, for the first time ever on a nonholiday, Celia's father said grace. "Let us bow our heads," he began, a formality Celia thought was a bit much for a dinner of aggression salad and mac and cheese. "Dear Heavenly Father, it is through you that this meal is before us. We ask you to bless this bounty, and we eat it only through your glory. In your most blessed name, amen." He raised his head and looked at his wife and daughter, both of whom stared back, baffled, unsure if it was safe to begin eating yet. He gave his wife a look that seemed to want a response.

"Amen?" she ventured. He smiled and looked to Celia.

"Amen," she mumbled.

Her father picked up his fork, and Celia and her mother did the same. They sat silently and ate in God's glory.

Reverend Steve bought and hung curtains after the parishioners all ponied up a couple dollars. A service was added at nine in the morning. There, for Celia, the improvements in Living Faith Church stopped. They began attending the later service, but not without her mother cajoling her father.

"The sunrise service is too early for Celia," her mother said.

"God gives her everything, from her life to the air she breathes. She can sacrifice one measly early hour to him a week. That's not asking too much," her father said. He looked over at Celia, who was watching TV on the couch. They were all sitting in the Crypt on a Saturday night. Celia was nonplussed; Sloane couldn't spend the night because they had to go to church in the morning. "Is it?" her father asked her.

"Honey, don't—" her mother started.

"It's fine. She's a big girl. God gives you the whole week, Cee. Do you think it's too much for you to give him an hour and a half?"

Celia had known this God character for only a few months now, but she already knew she didn't like him. He mainly was thrown in her face as someone she took for granted and let down simply by being his creation. She also knew she didn't have a choice of when she went to church, so there was no point dissenting. She said, "No."

"Well, then it's not too much for *you* to give him *three* hours," her mother said to her father in a sweet voice.

"What?"

"Celia and I will give him *our* hour and a half at nine. I'm at work all week, and Cee is in school. We don't need to get up so early on a Sunday. You're still looking for a job, so it certainly won't hurt for you to go to service twice. You'll go to the sunrise service, then go again with us at nine, as a family. You don't mind giving him twice as much time, do you? After everything he's given you?"

Her father sat with his mouth open for a moment, realizing what had just happened. "No," he said when he recovered his tongue. "I don't mind."

"Good. That settles that." Her mother took the spot next to Celia on the couch. Celia appreciated her mother's intervention, but it was like someone promising to make a slap in the face hurt no more than it had to—it was trying to make something lousy sound like a favor. Celia found it best to keep quiet. If she said she didn't want to go to church, she was guaranteed not only to have to go to church, but to have a long conversation about why she should want to go and how ungrateful she was for not wanting to.

Celia's mother had "come around," as Celia's father put it. Living Faith grew on her. Her worries about her family, her quick temper, her husband's inability to find a new job—she sent her emotions about all these things express to God and found peace in sharing her tribulations with a being as large as thought itself. It was God, after all, who had returned her husband to her, God who saved her family from going over the edge. She carried some resentment, of course, for the deity who stepped in to save her husband when she alone hadn't been enough. Even her resentment, though, found a place in her new faith, thanks to Barrett. They were all out for doughnuts after service one Sunday morning: Celia and her parents; Geraldine and Beaufort; recent acquaintances Harmon and Stacy Landross; and another couple whom Celia's parents had met at the new nine o'clock service, the Eubankses. The Eubankses were the same age as Celia's parents and had a daughter named Rebecca.

"The good reverend means well," Barrett was saying. "It's just..." he paused, making a face while he decided how to put this delicately.

"Oh boy. Here it comes," Geraldine said, looking around at the others to let them know they were in for a treat.

Celia saw Barrett catch her mother's eye. He made a barely perceptible face at Geraldine's buffoonery. Her mother smiled and sipped her coffee. "The reverend has a little too much of a feel-good take on faith for me. You sing a few songs, God loves you, and that's it. Now, I'm not saying that your faith shouldn't be a joyful thing." The others around their table sat quietly, listening. "It's fine to take joy in your faith. But we're talking about our eternal souls here, heaven and hell, damnation or salvation, leading a superior life through Christ's grace or souring our existence with Satan's false promises and deceit. This is, to put it mildly, rather important. It is the *most* important. Would you want to see one of your children end up in hell? Or your spouse? Or yourself? Of course not. So I think the reverend, who I respect and, like I said before, who means well, he really does—I think he takes it all a little too lightly with the guitar in the choir and his insistence that God loves you no matter what and everything will be OK. He wants his religion to be something that makes you feel good all the time. That's not worshiping the Savior. That's worshiping yourself. I mean, take all these homosexuals out there now." The group stiffened. They hadn't been prepared for someone to go and toss homosexuality at them over a doughnut and coffee. "There's churches and preachers out there who say that's OK. Men loving men. They say God created them that way, so it must be all right. Well, he didn't create anyone that way, first of all, and that's a fact. You can look right in the Bible where God says man may not lay with man, and there's your proof of fact. Now, I'm not saying the reverend has ever said that's OK, but he's also never outright said it's not. People want everything to be OK, and the simple truth is a lot of things aren't. Especially homosexuals. That's truly disgusting in God's eyes."

"Most everyone else's, too," Harmon Landross chimed in. He got a good laugh from around the table.

"Amen, Harmon," Barrett said. "Maybe you even know a homo and he seems nice enough, but I'm sorry to say, he's going straight to the worst part of hell. No one likes to hear that about a nice enough person, but it's a fact. You have to accept it. It's OK for your faith to be a challenge." Barrett looked at Celia's mother. "For it to be something you have to work at. The world is tough, isn't it?"

Nods from around the table. "You're damn right it is," Celia's father sighed.

"You know it firsthand," Barrett said to him. He shot a look at the others. Their eyes locked on him. "You all know it firsthand. Your faith has to be strong, to stand up to the world." Barrett held his hands up in a boxer's pose. "Think of a horse. In the past, they were animals people relied on for transportation, for getting work done, for everything. You needed a good horse, a strong horse, one that could handle a tough time. But horses aren't a thing that sits stagnant till you're ready to use it. They have to be handled, trained, fed. Sometimes they get a little wild. Sometimes they get spooked, and you'd have to get control of that horse again, by force. Your faith is like that. Get in a fight with it, it's OK. It's gotta be tough." He looked back to Celia's mother. "It won't always be easy. You might not even like your faith sometimes, but like that horse, you know you need it, and that everything would be a thousand times harder without it."

In the car later, Celia's mother said, "We should have Barrett over for supper one night."

"We absolutely should. That's a good idea." Her father was quiet for a moment. "You think we should invite—"

"Yes, hell, Geraldine'll have a conniption fit if she thinks they were left out. We can have the Eubanks over as well. I like them." She turned in her seat and looked at Celia. "You like Rebecca, too, don't you?"

Not really, Celia thought. Rebecca was three years younger than her. She copied everything Celia did. When Rebecca's mom, a twiggy little brunette barely larger than her daughter, asked what kind of doughnut she wanted, Rebecca invariably looked at Celia. "What kind are you getting?"

"Coconut," Celia said, a flavor she hated.

"Coconut," Rebecca repeated to her mom. When it was her turn to order, Celia pretended to have changed her mind and got a double chocolate.

With her mom asking if she liked Rebecca, though, Celia gave the standard reply she used for everything these days: "I don't know."

"What do you mean, 'you don't know'?" her father said. He didn't care for Celia's attitude lately, as he'd told her repeatedly. "What's wrong with her? She's a perfectly nice little girl."

"I guess."

There was a dangerous silence from up front, and Celia saw her father's eyes dart to the rearview to take her in. "Are you testing me?" Celia didn't say anything. "I asked you a question, young lady. Answer me."

"No."

"When I ask you something—" he began, raising his voice.

"No, I'm not testing you. Not no, I won't answer you," Celia said, making sure her voice held a tinge of exasperation.

"You're on thin waters, young lady. I'm sick of this attitude of yours. It's rotten."

"Ice," Celia heard her mother say softly.

"What?" her father said. "What about it?"

"It's thin *ice*," Celia said, sliding out right onto some. "Not thin *waters*. That's not the expression."

That dangerous silence from up front, again. "Why don't you just sit back there and not talk? That'd be nice," her father said.

That's what I was doing! Celia shouted in her head. You two spoke to me. You keep asking me what I think and how I feel, but it's only a trick to prove that my thoughts and feelings are wrong. It's none of your business how I feel, because it doesn't matter. All that matters to you is how *you* feel.

Celia leaned her head against the window. "Fuuuuuuuuck," she said in her head. "Fuuuuuuuck. Fuuuuuuucking baaaaaaaalls. Fuckballs." This was her mantra. She cursed elaborately in her head, and her parents couldn't stop her from doing it. She could think whatever she wanted. Right then she thought her parents sucked.

The guest list for dinner grew. Over the next two weeks, more couples were added from Barrett and her parents' "group." In the end there were eleven people: Celia's parents; Barrett, of course; Geraldine and Beaufort; Rebecca's parents; Stacy and Harmon Landross; and another couple, the Altmans. The dinner party was lively. The bon vivant that alcohol usually provided for such occasions was replaced by unanimous dissatisfaction with everything except one another's company and opinions. Disgust with the state of the government and declining American values replaced beer. Instead of glasses of merlot, the group passed around arrogant sympathy for Reverend Steve's efforts.

Celia's parents ordered a pizza for her and Rebecca and let them sit in their bedroom and watch the small TV on their dresser rather than have to eat dinner with the adults. Rebecca was thrilled; Celia felt rejected. She slumped against the foot of her parents' bed, slowly chewing a slice of Domino's. Rebecca peppered her with questions that she answered with grunts or shrugs.

"Can I see your room?" Rebecca asked.

"No," Celia said.

"How come?"

"I don't feel like it."

The door to the bedroom was open, and snatches of conversation drifted in from the Crypt, where the grown-ups were sitting after dinner and before coffee and dessert.

"…bunch of Ivy Leaguers who think because they got an expensive education they have the right to tell us how to live. They don't listen to people like us, the people actually out working and living in America. They rob us blind and expect us not to notice. They're trying to destroy American values."

"Oh, don't even get me started on values. It's terrible what's going on. No one cares about family or morals anymore."

"Public schools. There you go right there. Public schools. You can't pray in school anymore. You can listen to that rap crap music on your headphones, but you can't pray."

"And of course they teach them all about sex."

"Oh, yeah. You wouldn't want to take sex out of the schools, but praying, that's got to go. Wouldn't want the kids to learn to respect and fear the Lord and grow up to be decent folks. Much better for them to think they can have all the sex they want as long as they use a condom. Sheesh."

"I'll tell you what I'm sick of is all the gays on TV. They just rub it in your face."

"What's worse is them rubbing it in each other's faces."

"That's disgusting. Don't even joke."

"Ain't a joke. It's worse."

"I, for one, am tired of feeling like I'm under attack from the world. The government, the media. I feel like my faith is constantly under attack." Celia recognized her father's voice—her father who'd had his faith for about six months. The silence after his statement was confirmation from the others that this summed up their feelings as well.

"Amen," a voice said. It was Barrett's. "Amen, Brother Waters. You just hit the nail on the head. You feel like your faith is under attack. Well, you should, because it is. They want to steal your faith. They want to knock it down and replace it with TV, malls, designer clothes, movie stars. They want you and your children to focus on these things instead of on yourselves and your relationship with Christ. And I'll tell you something else. They want the world to think that gays and fags are normal and OK, because that creates another market for them to sell things to. They want your children to think it's OK to be a fag so they can sell them on the lifestyle, while the children of America sell their souls as sodomites. They want to take your faith and religion away because it scares them. Christ empowered the meek and the poor and made them righteous and strong. That's what they want to stop. They don't want a strong class of the poor and the downtrodden to challenge them, so they hide behind all these things, all this media and nonsense, and they try to steal your love of Christ."

Celia, who had been waiting for a lull, decided one wasn't coming and stood up. "I'm getting more soda," she said to Rebecca, caving in and being just a little bit nice. "You want some more?" Because Celia wanted more, Rebecca wanted more. Celia carried their glasses down the hall. Barrett was still talking, the rest of the room doing everything short of taking notes.

"And you say you're tired of feeling under attack? You should be. You have every right to be. This country was founded on God's love, and you are all free men and women under its constitution. You should never have to fear for your faith. There is a time—" He stopped. Celia was standing where the hall emptied into the living room. She was afraid to cross the room and interrupt the scene of solemn adoration she had come upon. Something about it held her in place. Now, to her utter terror, Barrett had locked his eyes on her and stopped speaking. All the heads in the room swiveled to see what had ended the sermon. Celia's breath quickened, and her heart beat oddly in her throat like it might choke her. It was same sensation that always made her want to faint or cry when she had to read in front of the class. "Celia," Barrett said. "There is a time of great upheaval and distress coming."

"OK."

"Do you believe you can face it?" He nodded his head slightly in the affirmative as he said this. All eyes were on Celia.

"Yes." The word was exhaled. "I believe I can face it," she said, awkwardly restating the question.

Barrett turned to Celia's father and mother. "You have a very special child, for there are adults, even among those here, who could not truthfully answer as she has." Every adult in the room looked down guiltily at his or her feet. No one exempted themselves except Barrett. When their eyes found Celia again, there was a different look in them. They wanted something from her. Not the way people usually did. Not the way teachers wanted answers, or her fellow students wanted something funny and embarrassing. They looked at her the way everyone looked at popular kids at school. They wanted acknowledgment, benediction, approval. "Thank you, Celia," Barrett said. The rest of them nodded their thanks, too, for pointing out their failures, she guessed.

As Celia went back down the hall the way she had come, she was filled with something unfamiliar. The glasses she clutched to her chest were still empty. Rebecca looked from the TV to Celia the second she came through the door. Again, Celia saw the look of need and want. She felt light and loose in its glow.

"Is there no more Coke?" Rebecca asked.

Celia knelt down in front of her. She reached out and took a strand of Rebecca's hair and smoothed it back behind her ear. "Would you like me to French braid your hair?" she asked.

Rebecca's face broke open at the eyes and mouth in rapture.

The night after the dinner party—"Well, that was a success," Celia's mother said. "God blessed that event," her father said. Her mother suggested instead it might be all the cooking and planning she had done. "Well, who do you think gave you the gift of cooking so well?" her father countered, needing to be right, taking from them the only small things they ever had—Celia's father said grace before their own private meal. He placed one hand on Celia's head.

She looked up at his arm bridging the distance between them, like a hairy trunk growing from her forehead.

"Heavenly Father," he began. "Bless this meal and this family through this child, through her unattainable innocence. And help her keep that divine understanding she now carries throughout her life. Through this child I ask that you help me find work, so that my hands may be useful for my family. In your Heavenly name we pray."

"Our child," Celia's mother interjected, at the point where she was supposed to say Amen. "Bless us and keep us through *our* child."

"Amen," her father said.

"Amen."

He still hadn't found a job. Three mornings in a row he lined up behind the 7–Eleven as a day laborer. "Hola, hola," he said to the mostly Hispanic group of men the first day he showed up, pronouncing the H. He was hired out the third day and made $150 hauling lumber from a truck up to a work site for a large house by the river, its frame a blond-wood skeleton the wind blew through while it waited for the men to finish fleshing it out. When he got home, he could barely walk, and his wife sent him back to the bathtub. He soaked miserably and didn't go back the next day to wait with the others.

"It's no good to ruin your back totally," his wife said. "We'll have to find you some other kind of work. Your disability is still coming in."

"Disability won't last forever."

"Your *actual* disability will if you don't quit this kind of work. It won't be an injury anymore. You'll be for real disabled." She read the wound this comment inflicted; it hung all over his face. She added, "Pray about it. I know you are already, but keep your head up. Or down, I mean, in prayer." She swirled her hand in the bathwater and pushed his hair back from his forehead. "It'll work out. We're brave, remember? No one is braver than us."

He spent part of his next disability check on twenty quarts of oil and a book on minor engine maintenance. He spent a week in the driveway with his truck up on jacks, lying on a creeper he built with a board and the roller skates Celia had outgrown, teaching himself how to change a car's oil. He applied for work at every Jiffy Lube and gas station in a forty-mile radius.

Was it owing to the enthusiasm at the dinner party—whether that success rested with God or Celia's mother—that led to Barrett forming the weekly Bible-study group? Maybe it was the post-service breakfasts or, and Celia thought this was most likely, he just knew it would irritate Reverend Steve. At any rate, Geraldine wanted to host the first one.

"What a blessed and fabulous idea," she squealed when Barrett mentioned it after service one Sunday. "You're doing the first one at my house. I insist. You wouldn't say no, would you, Barrett?"

"I would not, Geraldine. It's kind of you and Beaufort to open your home," Barrett said, smiling. Geraldine looked back over her shoulder to where Beaufort was standing, as if she had no idea who he was talking about.

"We're happy to rotate hosting duty," Harmon Landross said.

"An' I bet the chil'ren would love to see the chickies and piggies," his wife Stacy said. She looked at Celia and Rebecca. Celia had previously been thinking how much she hoped the Bible study was a grown-ups-only event, but the lure of pigs changed her mind. Of all her parents' new friends, Stacy Landross was the only one she really liked. Her husband, Harmon, was a thick pillar who resembled the shape of the cigars he constantly chewed, unlit, in the corner of his mouth like a thought he was keeping to himself. He always nodded to Celia and Rebecca, and there his acknowledgment of them ended. Stacy talked to them as she did everyone else, with a glint in her eye that said she'd take any excuse to smile. She was country in a way that even Celia's countrified parents called out, widening their eyes at the irony of their labeling her such and using the word as its own adjective: "Stacy is *country* country."

Celia liked Stacy who was *country* country, and she liked the idea of meeting chickens and pigs—specifically chicks and piglets. She imagined thin, hard, tanned Stacy catching a piglet and handing it to her, saying, "G'on now, this'uns yours to keep. He's special, won't never get no bigger'n this."

"We'd like that very much," Celia said to Stacy's comment about her and Rebecca visiting her farm's menagerie. She turned to Rebecca. "Wouldn't we?"

"Very much," Rebecca repeated.

"They're like sisters, these two," Kent Altman said. Geeky and drab, he and his wife, May, looked more like brother and sister. Kent was an out-of-work contractor. Out of work was the only way you could imagine him as a contractor, Celia once heard her mother say.

"Sisters in Christ," Celia said.

"Bless their hearts."

"From the mouths of babes."

"The children shall lead, says so right in the Bible."

Celia treated her new exterior life, the one lived around her parents and their new friends, as a play in which she was the star. She played the lead role as a character who would eventually be revealed to be the Chosen One, who would vanquish something or someone evil and go on to lead some group of people to something or somewhere better than whatever had existed before. She was getting rave reviews, despite the thinness of her plot.

"That's kind of you, Geraldine, Harmon," Barrett said. "But I thought I might hold the meetings at my place. Save everyone the trouble of planning where to go each week."

Everyone stared at him. No one thought of Barrett's having a "place." They thought it was incumbent on them to take him in, provide him shelter. He belonged to nowhere particular and drifted among them; that's how they defined his presence in their lives. Now he had a location, a point on a map.

Geraldine said, "Well, Barrett, we should hold the first one at your place, then, for sure. It's the maiden voyage, after all." On the drive home, Celia's mother would observe, "She didn't want her house to be the waiting room. She knew everyone was dying to see where he lived, and she'd be second fiddle."

"Geraldine, you will help me plan it, won't you?" Barrett said, placing a hand on her forearm.

"Of course, of course," she said, placing her hand over his, which he then took back.

"Could you get everyone's e-mail or phone numbers for me? I'll get in touch with you about directions." He handed her a small slip of paper. "This is what I'd like everyone to read for the first meeting." He turned to face the rest of them. "You'll probably recognize it. You've all heard it at least once before. If you'll excuse me now, I'd like to walk a bit and reflect on all this: our upcoming discussion, this fine group of men and women, our place in God's plan..." He trailed off and smiled. "I'll see you all Wednesday."

He nodded good-bye, and left. They were the only parishioners remaining in the storefront church. A somber and momentous feeling came over them. Geraldine looked at the piece of paper Barrett had handed her. "It's the scripture we heard at service today," she said.

Around them, Reverend Steve snapped his chairs flat and carried them to a corner, scowling in their direction. Outside, Barrett walked along, heading back, presumably, to wherever it was they were all going soon.

It was only three days till Bible study met, but Celia's father showed an impatience "like waiting for the second coming," as her mother put it. During the day, while his wife was at work and his daughter was at school, he tinkered with his truck in the driveway, pulling out spark plugs and putting them back in, removing air filters and replacing them. He disassembled and reassembled his engine, seeking to maintain the shape and structure it already had, while gaining insight into why it had it. Evenings he did the same with the Bible passage Barrett had asked them to read. He sat at the kitchen table with a couple sheets of loose-leaf Celia had given him and a pen, making notes.

His wife came and leaned over his back, her arms over his shoulders and crossed against his chest. "Baby, it's not going to be a test. Don't push it so hard," she said in a low voice near his ear. "We'll all discuss what it means."

"I just want to know what I'm talking about for a change," he said.

"You want me and you to talk about it some beforehand?"

"No," he snapped irritably. Then, calmer, he said, "I want to have my own thoughts on it, not just what you've explained to me." She kissed him on the head and left him to his work. Celia observed that her father was lousy at studying. This observation became a revelation. He was a terrible student. With a truck engine, he could see what to do and do it. But this required extrapolation, theorizing, and abstract thought. He slumped at the table with his forehead in his palm and his hair tangled in his fingers, making incomprehensible notes in his bad handwriting. He came back to Celia's room Tuesday night and asked for more paper. The next morning she found the first sheets balled up in the kitchen trash can when she was dumping a used coffee filter for her mother. She put one of the sheets in her pocket and opened it on the bus. There were a handful of ideas enumerated:

Luke 13:22

1. Why can't the people who asked questions get into kingdom? What does a narrow door to kingdom have to do with not being strong enough? Narrow door is easier to break down.

2. "He will say to you I do not know where you are from." Importance of hometown? Doesn't God know everything?

3. First will be last last will be first. God can mess with time.

4. Avoids answering the question—Will only a few be saved? Maybe a trick question.

The notes had a violent scribble over them—the kind done in a sudden fury. The pen had scratched through the paper in some places. She folded the wrinkled page neatly and put it in her backpack. She pictured her father slaughtering his thoughts with the pen in a fast angry gesture, then wadding the paper into a ball and hurling it across the room. She saw him, in her mind's eye, sitting dejected with his head in his hands the way he did, the other pages already balled up and scattered around the trash can. She saw him sigh, stand, and gather the paper wads and place them neatly in the trash can. By the time he got to her room to ask for more paper, he was calm again, patiently waiting while she tore some sheets from a notebook and saying, "Thanks."

Celia felt pity and contempt. It was hard not to feel bad for her father as he sat there desperately trying to understand something that meant so much to him. Simultaneously, she hated his ignorance. How could he care so much about something he couldn't understand? And worse, how could he not get it? Scripture was vague to the point of absurdity precisely so you could impose upon it any meaning you wanted. Reverend Steve preached what the scripture meant, and some people believed him. Barrett said he was wrong and it meant something else, and some people believed him. It wasn't complicated. Yet her father somehow interpreted "some are last who shall be first and some are first who shall be last" like a plot point in a time-travel movie. She had figured out a lot when Barrett put her on the spot at the dinner party. It should have been obvious to everyone present that she only answered the way she did out of nervousness and obliviousness, yet it became a moment because everyone chose to see it the way they preferred—or the way Barrett preferred they see it. Celia wanted to feel bad for her father, but really, how hard was it to understand something where you could literally make up any answer you wanted? Her own one-girl show had been going on for weeks based on the ease with which this material could be ad-libbed.

Just the past week, May Altman had been chatting idly with Celia and Rebecca at the doughnut shop after service, asking the kinds of questions about school and homework that adults mistakenly think children find interesting, when she jokingly said, "Celia, what about you? You behave at school?"

"Christ is good in all things," Celia replied. "All he asks is that we try and be the same, so I try." She delivered the last line with a little shrug, as she'd seen people on TV do: Whadayagonnado?

May about fell over in shock. "That's the truth, isn't it? You have a good heart, Celia." She looked over at Rebecca, who was just happy to be there. "You, too, little miss."

May went back to the adults' table, and Celia and Rebecca went back to their double chocolate doughnuts. Celia pretended not to be watching, but from the corner of her eye, she saw May repeat their conversation to the others in a whisper. Heads shook in amazement, and someone said something about learning from the simple faith of children.

Throughout the school day, Celia periodically pulled out her father's mangled page of idiotic notes. She looked around her history class at the notebooks of the other boys. Trey Dantzel's paper bore similarly stressed-looking letters running crooked across the page. What was with him? The paper had lines on it to keep their words straight. Was Trey what her father would have been like at her age? As she pondered this, Trey looked up and caught her staring at him. Celia's heart shot into her throat, and she threw her eyes down to the textbook open on her desk and didn't look back up. Even when the bell rang, she left the classroom watching the floor.

Celia brought her lunch to school but waited in the cafeteria line with Sloane to keep her company. As they crossed the mayhem of the lunchroom, Celia saw Trey watching her from his usual rowdy table. She immediately believed she would trip and fall. For the remaining five seconds it took for them to find seats, she was so overwhelmed by the possibility that she nearly threw herself to the floor just to get it over with. A spectacular tumble, she thought, where my lunch bag flies through the air and sprays crackers and egg salad around the room like a food bomb. The fall must not have happened, though, because she found herself sitting across from Sloane at their usual spot and Sloane saying, "Are you OK? You look, like, all flushed and crap."

When she got home from school, her father was in the driveway under the hood of his truck, his regular haunt the last several weeks. Dale, a sort-of-but-not-really friend of the family, owned a small repair shop where they took their cars, despite their steadfast belief that he would rip off his own mother. Dale and her father had once been on a landscaping crew together. He had given Celia's father work at his shop. He paid him cash off the books, ten dollars an hour, for three days of work each week, but her father went in on his days off, too, hanging around with the other mechanics, learning how to replace carburetors and spark plugs and reassemble mufflers. He spent the rest of his time practicing on his own truck, which, to his credit, continued to run.

Celia's father popped his head out from under the hood as she came up the drive. "Hey, Cee, you have a lot of homework tonight?"

Celia shrugged.

"Well, get it done, whatever it is, so we'll all be ready to go when your mama gets home."

Celia went into the kitchen and opened the lid of the trash can. There was a new trash bag, still empty. There was no sign of any more discarded notes. His study station of Bible, paper, and pens was missing from the kitchen table where it had been the last few days.

Celia did her homework and reviewed her notes from the day. She'd had straight As since the first days of the Crypt and enjoyed maintaining them. Perfect grades were a haven; they were logical. Effort in, results out. Studying provided a legitimate excuse to isolate herself without being accused of being shy, and the high marks she got in exchange looked like a path. A path elsewhere. The idea of *getting out of here* had recently lodged in her mind. Every A was a stepping stone across that river. She imagined going to college, living in a dorm. She had seen cities and jobs on TV—different jobs than the ones the adults around her had: office jobs, with air conditioning. Marketing, whatever that was. Jobs where you got a cubicle all to yourself, or maybe even an office. If you felt like it, you could go out after work, or you could go home and be alone with your pet. A dog would be lonely all day. Celia figured maybe a cat. Maybe Trey, a voice in her head suggested. Maybe shut up, Celia suggested back.

By the time Celia's mother got home, her father had showered and was pacing around the house. Celia went and sat with her mom in the kitchen. Her father appeared in the doorway for the second time and said, "You 'bout ready to go?"

"I just got home," her mother said. She looked at the time on the microwave. "We'll leave at six. We'll be there by six thirty." Her husband nodded and went back to pacing around the house. "I haven't seen him this wound up since he went to Darlington," her mother said. "Remember that?"

A man at his old job, Billy (a name her father didn't approve of for a grown man but used anyway), had gotten free tickets to a race at the Darlington Speedway and invited Celia's father. It was on a Saturday, his one day off. Her father listened to NASCAR on the radio and watched on TV, but he'd never been in person before. Celia was younger then; they had just moved from the Blue Wave to their house. Her father spent the night packing and repacking a cooler full of sandwiches, cold fried chicken, and pasta salad his wife had made and chain smoking Vantages. Celia was watching videos in the living room. Every time he passed through the room, he picked her up and tossed her in the air a few times. "You gonna watch the race tomorrow?" he kept asking. "You gotta look for your daddy on TV." After a few hours of this, both Celia and her father were balls of manic energy.

"I'm gonna put both of you down for the night if y'all don't relax," her mother had said. "You, put that food back in the fridge until the morning so it stays cold. What kinda fool packs a cooler the night before? And you, little miss, might end up in the fridge, too, to cool your heels."

Her mother put the race on the next day with the sound off. "I'm dumb enough from the races I've already heard," she said, "I don't need to hear another one." Celia checked the TV throughout the day but never saw her father. He came home that night drunk and sunburned. He fell asleep in his chair almost immediately, and Celia sat on his lap and watched TV. Her mother smeared aloe on his sleeping face around the white patches from his sunglasses. She rubbed more onto his arms and neck. He slept through two more applications before she made him get up and go to bed.

"You could barely get him out of that chair," Celia said.

"You sat on his lap like he was a parade float. He never moved. He brought that cooler home empty, too. I must have put a whole fried chicken and six sandwiches in there. How he and Billy ate all that I'll never know. All he talked about for weeks after was that race."

"He couldn't get over the guy with the number shaved into his chest hair."

"Earnhardt's number. Three, I think. The guy had shaved it into his dog's fur, too."

"And the noise, how loud it was."

"It must have been thunderous if he could hear it over his own mouth."

They laughed. Celia's father reappeared in the doorway, cracking his knuckles and pulling down half the length of a Vantage in one drag. Celia and her mother stared at him.

"What?" he said. "What are you two grinning at?"

"Nothing," her mother said. "Why don't you go change into that other shirt I hung up?"

He looked down. "What's wrong with this shirt?"

"Nothing at all. I just like you better in the other one."

He nodded and vanished down the hall. Celia's mother winked. "It'll give him something to do." She sat down at the table across from Celia. "You don't have to come tonight if you don't want. I'll tell your daddy you're staying home. Say I want you to study."

Celia laid her head on the table and stretched one arm out toward her mother, who took her hand and lightly massaged it. "No, it's OK," she said. "I'll come. Rebecca'll have to go. She'll be by herself if I stay here."

"You sure?" her mother said. "Rebecca'll be OK one night."

"I'm sure. It's fine."

Celia was enjoying her role in the play she was performing. It was liberating to be a version of herself, an imagined Celia, for a little while. She liked Church Celia, as she called her. She was more like Sloane: more confident, more talkative. And because Church Celia wasn't real, everything she said and did felt consequence free. She simply stepped out of her role later and resumed her life, knowing she could go back whenever she felt like it. She didn't mind Rebecca anymore either. She was kind of funny, and Celia enjoyed the adoration.

She kept her head down while her mother massaged her palm, so she missed the frown, the look of concern and worry, that rode her mother's face until her father came back in the new shirt and it was time for them to go.

They drove to Barrett's in Celia's father's truck, the three of them sitting up front together, because he wanted to make sure it ran properly with the new spark plugs he'd installed. "It's gonna be one crappy evening for all of us if it doesn't," her mother said, climbing into the cab.

"I'm confident," her father said. He turned the key, the engine fired, and they backed out of the drive.

Barrett had always come to them, one man going to a group. Now the whole group sought out a single man, led by Geraldine's directions printed from an e-mail and signed with a smiley face. Celia's father turned the truck off the highway and down a side road.

"It says to drive about ten miles on this, then it turns into a dirt road and we go another mile on that," Celia's mother read from the sheet of paper. She looked around at the passing woods and fields. "Doesn't seem like there's too much back here."

The paved road ran out as promised and turned to dirt. "He walks all this way to church every Sunday?" Celia's mother said. "Someone should start picking him up. This is ridiculous."

The dirt road stretched off into fields of unplanted farmland. There was a low brick house in the distance, at the edge of the cleared land, where the woods began. From the front it was wide, two and a half times the width of their own house at least. As they pulled around to park next to Beaufort's car, they saw the house had three wings: one extending back from each corner and a third from the middle. From the air the house would have looked like one of the blocky Es from an eye-exam chart.

"He lives here by himself?" Celia's mother said.

"Far as I know."

"And some woman just gave him this whole spread? Does she live out here, too?"

"I think it's just him. He said something about the woman living over in Georgia now. She moved after her husband passed or something. Left this for Barrett. He's like a caretaker, I guess."

They exited the truck and stood admiring the house. There was no one around. There was one other vehicle besides theirs and Beaufort's.

"I guess we just go knock on the—" Geraldine's head popped out the door before Celia's father could finish. She called down to them from the front porch.

"Hey, y'all." She waved her arm over her head, though they were no more than fifteen feet away and there was no one else outside. "C'mon in." They mounted the steps and went through the door behind Geraldine, who gave each of them a hug once they were inside. "Barrett asked if I would mind waiting out here to show people in, and of course I didn't mind. I was happy to do it." She dropped her voice into a faux-whisper. "Can you believe this place?" She switched back to her usual pitch. "I don't know where I thought he lived, but it wasn't here."

They were standing in a room with couches, end tables, and a few nice chairs. It looked like the waiting area at the funeral home where they'd had Celia's grandmother's funeral. "We're gathering back this way," Geraldine went on. "Follow me." She led them out of the front room and down a hallway. The walls were bare and looked dangerously white to Celia. A handful of closed doors were the only things that broke the clean white monotony of the hallway as they walked. Finally, they found themselves in a sizable room with a circle of chairs. Beaufort and a couple with an infant occupied three of them. The rest were empty.

"I have to get back out front," Geraldine said. "To lead the rest back here. I'll see y'all in a bit." She scooted out of the room, which promptly surrendered to an awkward silence. Celia's father was the one to break it. "Where's Barrett?" he asked no one in particular, tossing the question out into the center of the ring.

"Haven't seen him yet," said the father of the infant.

"He was here when Gerry and me got here," Beaufort said. "Said he needed to prepare a bit and asked Gerry if she'd mind playing usher."

"I bet she didn't mind," Celia's mother said.

Beaufort came as close as Celia had ever seen him come to a smile. "Nope. She didn't mind," he said.

"Look who's here," Geraldine sang out as she reappeared in the doorway, as though Beaufort's near-smile had summoned her to come extinguish it. Kent and May Altman came in behind her and went around greeting everyone, same as Celia and her parents had done. Celia had a very mild urge to pee and a powerful case of curiosity. She had never been in a house this big. She waited until Geraldine left again so she wouldn't be offered an escort. Then she turned to her mother and said, "I'm going to use the ladies."

"Well, wait till Geraldine comes back, so she can show you where."

"I can manage."

"I don't know if it's a good idea to go wandering—"

Celia dropped and tightened her voice. "I don't really want to make a huge deal out of it in front of everyone. I just want to use the bathroom." She stared at her mother, annoyed. Her mother nodded and looked apologetic, a look Celia ignored. She left the room as Kent, behind her, said, "This is like my old theater classes in high school with the circle of chairs."

Celia left quickly and quietly; she didn't want company. The room they were in was in a wing, one of the three that extended off the back of the house. Celia reversed the way Geraldine had brought them in till she came to the long hall that connected all three wings at the front of the house. Through a doorway, in the front, Celia heard Geraldine's long, drawn-out, "Heeeeeeeyyyyyyy," as she greeted another arrival. Celia sped along the hall and turned left into the middle wing before Geraldine could pop in with the new guests.

The middle wing of the house was another long hall with blank walls spotted with doors along the left side. Celia carefully opened one. It looked like a guest room. She opened another. Same. All down the wing there were empty guest rooms. She ran back to the connecting hallway, conscious of not being away too long. She was exhilarated. Her blood ran a little quicker, and she breathed a little harder. She had never been bad before, not that she was being terribly bad now. If someone discovered her, she could just say she got turned around.

When she checked the final hall to make sure it was Geraldine-free, she knew right away it was Barrett's. It was all Barrett's, of course, or that mysterious lady's who lent it to him or gave it to him or whatever, but this wing was the only place that looked lived-in. The carpet in the hall was worn, and the walls were still blank but bore the scuff marks Celia had sensed were imminent in the other wings, discolorations and smudges where someone passed too close. The doors to the rooms were open.

Celia crept to the first one, where the blue glow of a television flickered through the doorway. She peeked inside. It was another bedroom. There were some men's clothes on the floor and a master bathroom. A TV on top of a dresser was showing the news with the sound off. The next room was an office. A third room had big windows and a sliding glass door that looked out into the space between that wing and the middle wing. The open area had been bricked over into a patio with a small fountain in the middle, some lounge chairs, and what appeared to be a hot tub. Celia looked back at the bland hallway, then again at the patio. The house was impressively large, but it was impersonal, vaguely clinical even. It stood in contrast to this oasis. The wing opposite the one she was in didn't have any windows along that side, so the patio was hidden from view except from this room. She stepped inside. A high wooden fence at the end spanned the two wings with a giant fir guarding it from the outside, blocking the view from anyone who walked around the back of the house.

"Celia," a voice said to her left, and she spun around with a jerk. Barrett was sitting in an armchair in a corner of the room. His one good eye met hers. The rogue eye studied the fountain outside. "You found my sanctuary," he said. Her mouth opened and closed, but nothing came out sound-wise. Barrett stood and approached her. He was dressed neatly as usual. He wore a blue Oxford button-down, neatly pressed, over rough and worn-in jeans with his beaten leather boots—half college professor, half field hand. Celia could smell a mix of soap and his laundry detergent when he came close.

Barrett put a hand on her shoulder and led her over to the sliding glass doors. They stopped at the glass and stared out. The sunlight was slowly whirling down the drain of the horizon, and their reflections in the glass grew more substantial and solid as it faded. "Do you have somewhere you go?" Barrett asked her. "When you need to be alone for a while?"

"My room?" she said, aware of the heavy presence of his hand still on her shoulder.

"Are you asking me?" He looked down at her.

"My parents come into my room whenever they want. I don't have anywhere."

"You should find a place. It's nice to have one. This is mine. This room and out there. You can't see it from anywhere else in the house. No eyes but those of God." He looked down at her again. "And yours, I guess." He went quiet. They stood in front of themselves in the glass. Barrett leaned forward and breathed slowly onto the window, blotting out his face. "Before there was anything, God had an idea of the world." He breathed again, expanding the foggy patch. "His idea included all of us: the planet, every living thing on it, every dying thing on it, all the fish under its oceans. He had an idea, and he breathed life into it." Barrett exhaled once more, and with his free hand, wrote Celia's name in the fog. "Just like that." The fog of Barrett's breath faded slowly around the letters. "He made us in his image. And he gave us the same power. To breathe life into an idea. To imagine something, then make it real."

Celia raced over his words in her mind. No one talked to her like this. Lights shone through the water of the fountain and the hot tub in a soft wet glow. Celia exhaled on the glass herself, and because he had chosen her name, she took her finger and wrote his in her own breath. He smiled. "That's right," he said, though about what she couldn't guess. But she held the moment as long as she could, memorizing everything. "Your parents think you're in the bathroom?" Barrett guessed. She nodded. "You better go on back. I'm almost ready. I'll be right behind you." The hand left her shoulder

Celia turned and walked toward the door, watching Barrett over her shoulder on her way out. He remained at the sliding glass door, his back to her, staring out into his private Eden. The boring hallway hit her like a spell-breaker when she reentered it. She jogged back until she found the room with the circle of chairs, almost all of them filled now and the flat, incomprehensible sound of a dozen mixed conversations roiling in the center. Rebecca had arrived with her parents and was looking around anxiously for Celia. Celia waved to her. Celia's mother wore the same anxious look.

"Is everything OK?" her mother asked as Celia retook her chair.

"I got turned around coming back."

"It just seemed like you were gone awhile."

"Believe it or not, Mom, I can use the bathroom all by myself," Celia said. Her mother turned away from her and crossed her legs and arms. Celia did the same.

She wondered if Barrett would mention their meeting to her parents. She had wanted the thrill of spying, but she had been caught. Instead she would settle for the thrill of a secret meeting. Breathing life into an idea. That's what she had done. She had gone sneaking around wanting something exciting, only for herself, and she made it happen. Assuming Barrett didn't spoil it, of course.

The chatter around the room died out in a receding line when Barrett appeared in the doorway, like a string being pulled out the back of the room. He paused, watching them all, just long enough for the silence to register, then said, "Hello, faithful. I'm glad everyone could make it." He cast his eyes around the room. "Geraldine," he said, finding her across the circle between Beaufort and Celia's mother. "Thank you for helping lead everyone in. Celia," he said. For a moment she believed he was going to say something in front of everyone, but he only lingered on her name, catching her eye, before adding, "And Rebecca. So good to see the youth came as well. It's great to have you participate."

Barrett took the remaining empty chair, near the door, and the circle was complete. He opened his Bible, the gilt edges of the paper flashing.

"Let's begin with a prayer," Barrett said. "Celia, would you like to lead us?"

Celia absolutely would not. In fact, few things sounded less appealing. Celia the Chosen One, however, could not say no to such a request. So Celia the Chosen One nodded her assent and said, "Let us bow our heads." The room obeyed, and Celia felt something stir in her at their obedience. She closed her own eyes, which helped, and pictured herself in the movie version of her life, Christ's child prodigy leading her amazed followers in prayer. "Heavenly Father," she began, then launched into the first religious concept she had on hand. "You had a beautiful dream of the world, so you breathed life into your wonderful idea called Man." She sprinkled in some rewording of prayers she had heard the grown-ups say. "But we don't always deserve your love. We can be bad and not—" Good? No, that sounded idiotic. "—worthy of the goodness you have given us." OK, *good* still slipped in, but that was better. "But we are gathered here tonight, blessed Father, to better understand you. To do better in our relationship with you." The relationship with God, that was one of Barrett's mantras. "With your help, Lord, we'll take these words, these ideas, you have provided for us and breathe life into them in our own way, so that we become closer to you." Celia looked up, pleased with this poetic touch at the end, to find everyone else still head-bent and shut-eyed. Except Barrett. He was leaning forward, elbows on his knees, clocking her with his one good eye while the other appeared to be admiring Kent's shoes. He nodded to her. "Amen!" she blurted.

The rest of the room opened their eyes and sat up straight. "That was really beautiful," Rebecca's mother said. There were murmurs of agreement around the room.

Celia's father turned to her. "That was good," he said. "What made you think of that? Breathin' life into the words, I mean."

"The prayer just came through me," Celia said, thinking of her father struggling with his own understanding of scripture and God. How nervous he'd been about this night. "It just flowed right through me," she added. Her father looked down at his Bible and frowned.

"Celia, that was truly inspiring," Barrett said. "And true." He held up his Bible. "We are indeed going to breathe life into these words, because they have a life. They come from the source of all life, but until we put something of ourselves into them, we can't fully know them." Barrett thumbed his pages open and began to read. "Jesus passed through towns and villages, teaching as he went and making his way to Jerusalem. Someone asked him, 'Lord, will only a few people be saved?' He answered them, 'Strive to enter through the narrow gate, for many, I tell you, will attempt to enter but not be strong enough. After the master of the house has arisen and locked the door, then you will stand outside knocking and saying, "Lord, open the door for us." He will say to you in reply, "I do not know where you are from." And you will say, "We ate and drank in your company and you taught in our streets." Then he will say to you, "I do not know where you are from. Depart from me, all you evildoers." And there will be wailing and gnashing of teeth when you see Abraham, Isaac, and Jacob and all the prophets in the kingdom of God and you yourselves cast out. And people will come from the east and the west and from the north and the south and will recline at table in the kingdom of God. For behold, some are last who will be first, and some are first who will be last.'"

Celia had tuned in at last Sunday's service long enough to hear Reverend Steve read the passage and had read it over since then in her father's Bible, left open on the kitchen table in a puddle of his frustration. What stuck with her the most about the story was how irritating it was to ask Jesus a simple question. Will only a few be saved? Yes or no, Jesus?

Barrett asked if anyone had any questions or wanted to tell the group their impression of the reading. As in school, Celia noticed all the sane people avoided going first and that, reliably, there was one lunatic who relished the opportunity to put herself out there and break the ice.

"Well, I have to say," Geraldine began, "that I had some trouble understanding this. It seems a little, well, I hate to say it, but it seems a little mean. I know that's awful and I'm just not smart enough to understand it, but—" There were murmurs around the circle. Others who'd felt the same frustration nodded.

"It's not awful, Geraldine," Barrett said. "Not awful at all. And you're plenty smart, but sometimes the word of the Lord is challenging. He's talking about things that exist on a plane far, far above our normal lives. Not getting it right away is OK. That's why we're all here. I want you to hold that thought about Jesus's words sounding unkind, because we're going to come back to that and discuss it. Let's hear from a few others first, though." A hand went up, a bald man Celia didn't know, new to the group. "Gardner," Barrett said. "Go ahead, what'd you think?"

One by one, around the circle, Barrett let them each confess their ignorance of the meaning of Christ's words. He offered light encouragements. "This is why we seek guidance." "There's no shame in being confused. God's ways are deep." "The important thing is that you know you don't understand, and you're open to receiving insight." Then Celia's father raised his hand. "'Bout time we heard from you," Barrett said jovially. "You've been awfully quiet. That's not like you."

Celia's father smiled at the friendly recognition, but it was merely a motion, not an emotion. His face promptly fell back to consternation. "I really twisted myself up over this passage," he said. "I walked away from it a bunch of times. Gave up even trying to get it. Figured it was beyond me." He fell silent for a moment. Celia stared at his quiet mouth—her father, Mr. Popularity, Mr. Talk-to-anyone, suddenly struggling to find words. "But then…then it was like it came to me all at a sudden. That it was too hard—that's what it is. Or what it means, I mean. The words of Jesus are hard. Understanding them is hard. Living them is harder. That's the narrow door we strive to get through. I work damn hard. My whole family does. It ain't just—it isn't just me. They work hard and try hard, too. I'm sure everyone in this room does. And it's a narrow way and it's tough, boy. Like wedging yourself under a car and trying to fix it. It's tight and it isn't pleasant, but you gotta keep working, striving, to get through that tight space. Even just to understand that the way is hard is pretty dang hard. I think Jesus is telling this fella he's talking to that doing what's right, and doing it his way, it's a lot harder than this fella thinks. A lot harder than a lotta people probably think. And his number's gonna come up and this fella and them others are gonna realize that they didn't try hard enough. God's gonna look out his window at 'em all lined up like they're waiting for a paycheck and say, 'Son, I don't even know you. You haven't been at work, or I would have seen you. You thought it was easy and you had it all figured out, so you just rode on cruise control the whole time. I gave you the chance and now it's over. Sorry.' 'Cause if you don't at least know how hard it is, then you haven't even begun to know anything."

Celia's father kept his eyes on the floor as he spoke. Celia saw the doubt sewn all through his features. Barrett had closed his Bible and sat watching her father. Or her. They were sitting next to each other, and the rogue eye left some doubt. After a moment, when it was clear her father was through, Barrett looked around the room at the faces watching him, waiting for his pronouncement.

"Amen," Barrett said. "I say to you, brother, Amen. For that is precisely what Christ is saying" He stood and took a few steps toward the center of the circle. The rest of them leaned in, needing to be closer to his words. "This man in the passage, he meets Christ and asks him what a lot of people would probably ask him: Will only a few people be able to get into heaven, or a lot? He wants the answer to be a lot. He wants to know that only the really bad people are left to burn in hell and that the majority of people get into heaven. Because that includes him. He's one of the OK people. He's not great, not truly good, but he isn't really bad. What he's really asking Christ is: Can I get into heaven without having to work real hard and disrupt my life overly?" Barrett turned in a slow circle, letting each one of them see the baffled grin on his face. It was contagious. They all smiled back. Some were shaking their heads. "Gardner, you're shaking your head. Why?" Barrett said to the bald man Celia didn't know.

"'Cause the answer to that man's question is no," Gardner said.

"The answer is what?" Barrett said. He put a hand to his ear as though he were hard of hearing and continued to spin, prompting all of them.

"No!" More people joined in this time. Almost the whole group.

"Of course it's no!" Barrett exclaimed. "What would be so special and important about heaven, about eternal salvation, living forever in bliss and harmony and basking in God's unending love, if it were easy? No, of course not, you have to do the work. And it isn't easy work. Following God's path is hard. It's another full-time job. But the reward is so sweet. Now, I don't want to speak too poorly about the good reverend." There were a few giggles, knowing that was full well what he intended to do. "But the reverend would have you believe that just showing up to service once a week and feeling good about yourself while you sing some songs is all it takes. But if that was all it took, almost everybody would get into heaven, and Christ tells us right here." He held up his Bible and thumped it with his fist. "Right here in the Bible. The Bible that you all have a copy of. The Bible that's free to take from any motel room. The Bible we can all read. He tells us right here that that is not the case. That only a few will be strong enough to enter. That only a few will get through that narrow gate. As our wise friend over here described it," he gestured at Celia's father, "like working under a car. The path is narrow. It is specific. And we must walk it correctly." His voice became more serious. "The people in this room are on that path, and they are trying to walk it correctly. I know that because you're all sitting here tonight, on a weekday. You could be home, tired from a long day's work. Watching TV, watching commercials that want you to buy this soap, upgrade your TV, get a better computer. Distracting you with things. Objects. Gadgets. Crap you don't need. Lulling you away from your freedom to believe and to worship by making you a consumer, by making you a follower of some TV show instead of a follower of Christ. The closer you are to him, to the Lord Almighty, the less you'll want their things. Their products. So they don't want that. They don't want that, because then what would they sell you? The government doesn't want that, because when they sell you things, you pay taxes. Not only do they take your money for taxes—because let's be honest, you don't pay taxes, they take taxes—but then they use it for people who don't work. People on welfare who don't feel like working. Mexicans who sneak into our country, steal jobs from Americans, take advantage of all this country offers, then send that money back to Mexico without so much as paying a dime to Uncle Sam. They're criminals. And if they weren't already criminals, then they are the minute they break the law by sneaking across the border. Because it's illegal! On top of it all, you have to listen to politicians try to convince you this is all OK. Try to convince you to let them make laws that say this is all OK. For you to pay for others who are too lazy, to give your country away to criminal outsiders, for them to destroy the sanctity of family. This is a great country, but there is an element out there that wants to ruin it, tax you to death, take you away from Christ, and distract you with a bunch of TV shows about queers and people who have unwed sex. That's why it's a battle. That's why it's a fight. All this stuff of the world, all these distractions, they crowd the edges. They fill up the sides. And that makes the path narrow. Following this"—he shook his Bible gently over his head, slowly turning in the center of their circle—"is a narrow path, but it is the righteous path. And all of you I see before me. You. Are. Righteous."

Barrett's last words faded into silence. He went back to his chair slowly, like a boxer who'd just left the favorite-to-win KO'd on the mat in front of a stunned crowd. He sat with his head down and his eyes closed, spent. When he looked up again, he said, "The Lord has spoken through me tonight. I could not have said things so well if not for his divine guidance. Let us all join hands and offer a final prayer."

In the truck on the way home, Celia's mother said, "Looks like I got two of Bible study's superstars on my hands." She smiled over at Celia and rubbed her husband's shoulder as he drove them back out along the shaky dirt road. Celia returned her mother's smile, but when she turned away, Celia let her face fall back into the scowl she had been wearing. The scowl was directed at her father. He had outperformed her in front of the group. A day ago he'd thought "some are last who will be first, and some are first who will be last" had something to do with time travel. Tonight he pulled off some country-boy-faced-with-the-eternal mumblings about wedging himself under a car. Bah. She wanted to kick him in the shin or bite his ear.

Celia let her eyes close. She visualized the glassy sunroom Barrett had all to himself, closed off from the world, the fountain outside burbling thick streams of water and the hot tub blowing bubble sunbursts as the water roiled on top, lit from underneath by yellow lights. She visualized standing next to Barrett, breathing on the glass. It was the first magical thing that had ever happened to her.

Bible study carried on in two ways: joyously for the members of Barrett's tribe, and miserably for Reverend Steve. The reverend began noticing that more and more often as he approached his congregants, chatting in small groups before or after a service, their conversation dried up. He received pitying smiles. Trite pleasantries. Barrett's head shaking and eye-rolling during the reverend's sermons had not gone unnoticed. The jerk sat in the front row after all, though sometimes he sat back a few rows with one of his toadies. Now when the reverend looked out at his flock during his sermon, he saw the same condescending looks on a dozen faces, some of them smirking at one another.

Eventually, Reverend Steve mentioned it in a sermon. He tried to make it casual, but it came out as awkwardly as someone angling for an invitation to a party.

"If any of you out there ever want to discuss the readings that we hear each week, you can always reach out to me. As your minister, that is precisely what I'm here for, to help guide you in your faith. We know from the Bible that Jesus lectured and taught his disciples and followers, and that's the tradition we ministers carry on. So come to me, if you ever feel the need to explore the teachings of Christ in more detail."

"Oh, my God bless America," Geraldine said after the service. "That was so sad."

"I think he just wants to be involved," May Altman offered weakly, trying to be nice.

"No, he don't," Gardner Creech, said. He was the bald man Celia had noticed at the first Bible-study meeting. He allegedly had a wife, but she didn't come to service or Bible study with him, and no one had ever seen her. "I've been coming here for over a year, and that's the first time he's ever offered to discuss anything with anybody. He ain't nothing but jealous and competitive." Gardner's contempt for Reverend Steve always seemed to run a little truer than the rest of theirs, who didn't hold him in contempt as much as they simply couldn't help noticing he wasn't Barrett.

The exact details of what happened next were more legend than known fact. Barrett left Living Faith Church; that was a fact. He started holding his own services on Sunday mornings. That was also a fact, and one they all knew because they left the church with him and attended services out at his house. The exact how and why, though, were as mysterious and difficult to translate as anything in the Bible.

Stacy Harmon claimed to have been there when Reverend Steve asked Barrett if he could come into his office and speak with him. "They went back and talked, I guess. I ain't asked what for or 'bout. Weren't none'a my business 'n' I ain't figuring to make it any," she said. Best they could all decipher that meant Stacy didn't know jack.

Rebecca's parents claimed it was the other way around. "Barrett had been waiting to have a word with the reverend for a long time. After he started Bible study, the reverend realized he's the smartest guy in the church when it comes to understanding Christ," Rebecca's dad said. "I think the reverend realized that and kicked him out because he was jealous, plain and simple."

"Barrett gave the reverend two options: get your act together, or I'm leaving your church. Simple as that. He told the reverend, 'You owe us a better church and a better service, and if you don't start delivering, I'm outta here.' So he quit." That was Gardner's opinion, phrased to sound like definitive knowledge.

In any case, Barrett left, and they all left with him. Barrett's only comment on what had happened was "It was time." Sundays at ten in the morning they drove to Barrett's house, where each week, someone brought doughnuts and coffee. It wasn't like the service at Living Faith. There was no singing, no clear mark of the beginning or end. Barrett simply entered the room, and they all got quiet and took their seats. He read from the Bible, and they all followed along until he was finished; then he would speak. Sometimes there was no reading at all, and Barrett just began in his own words. Only they weren't his, he told them at the end of each service. The Lord had been speaking through him. The Lord who looked down on them—these people gathered of their own free will in this blessed free country—and was pleased. So pleased that the Lord sent his words through Barrett, his servant, for them, because they were righteous and deserving of them.—perhaps the only people in the whole rotten, liberal, faggy, secular (but free, and blessedly free at that) country who were deserving of them.

Celia's parents easily turned their backs on Living Faith. "This feels way more right than Living Faith did," her father said, clearly forgetting how right Living Faith had felt after the depths of his painkiller addiction. "This is what a church is supposed to feel like, like a family."

No, Celia thought, that's what a *family* is supposed to feel like. He had it backward. The church felt like his family, and he treated his family as though they were always in church. He roamed the house as though he were a missionary in a godless foreign country. Television was banned outright, severing any remaining affection Celia held for her father and his faith, except for the news, and then only the right news. "None of that liberal-media garbage about how great it is to be homosexual," he declared. Lingerie catalogs that showed up in the mail were thrown in the garbage with enthusiastic disgust. "Why do we get this filth?" he demanded of Celia and her mother as though there were some devious reason other than someone needing a bra.

"Because we have an address and I have tits," her mother answered in a cold and measured voice that suggested he better bottle up his nonsense.

"Well..." He paused his tirade and thought. Slowly, Celia observed. He thinks so slowly. She could not help hating him. She was tired of his problems. His problems with himself and his problems with everything that wasn't Barrett Higgins and his new church family. "We should get ourselves taken off the mailing list," he said more mildly. "It's just smut. I don't want it in the house."

"Fine, take us off the mailing list. I have to be at work," her mother said, knowing full well he had no idea how to do something like that.

Her father's back was functional again, thanks to a series of shots called transforaminal injections around his slipped disk. He still hadn't found a job, though, something Celia could tell was beginning to irk her mother, because for the first time he wasn't trying. During the week, while her mother made appointments for wisdom-teeth extractions and Celia navigated the science fair, her father drove out to Barrett's to talk God with him or help him around the grounds, fixing up an old tractor Barrett had found in the barn on the north end of the property, mending fences and loose porch steps.

"He paying you for that work?" Celia's mother asked, already knowing the answer.

"There's a different kind of reward for my work. Not money."

Her mother sighed. "Nothing in this world is free, it seems, not even the grace of God."

"Now that's—"

"You can't keep going out there every day," Celia's mother said. She didn't raise her voice. There was no steel edge in it. "The numbers don't lie."

"Unfortunately."

"Right. Unfortunately."

Celia was in the Crypt drowning herself in homework. School was her refuge. A place to go that wasn't her house, and homework was something to do that wasn't talking to her parents. And one day she would get a scholarship, even if it was only to the University of South Carolina a few hours away in Columbia, or maybe Coastal Carolina in Myrtle Beach, where they'd vacationed once when they were a different family with different lives. She could go to the beach whenever she wanted. School promised another life one day. She wondered if that's what church was like for her parents, with its promise of heaven and angels and peace after a lifetime of trying to pay the bills.

"You have to find a job," Celia's mother was saying in the other room. "I don't care if it's bagging groceries or flipping burgers, but I need you working again. I've prayed about it, and something has to change. Something *will* change."

Celia's father didn't say anything. Celia knew he was frowning, nodding, the *antithesis* of the laughing jovial giant he used to be. The word was at the top of the list of new vocabulary words they had gotten that day. Her father was his own *antithesis*. *Becalming* was next on the list, but she didn't know that one yet.

Something did change. Dr. Pearson, the dentist for whom her mother and Geraldine worked, went bankrupt. He had bought three houses, intending to fix them up and flip them. He took outrageous loans from the bank to do this, confident he would have the houses sold again in no time. In no time turned into *at no time*, and the houses stood where they always stood, empty and unsold. He was underwater on all three, plus his own home. He let all his employees' benefits lapse, and finally, he let his employees themselves lapse. Pearson filed Chapter 11, moved his family into an apartment and his practice into a smaller space in a strip mall, and Celia's mother and Geraldine joined her father in the nether regions of unemployment a few weeks before Celia's fourteenth birthday.

The payments on their mortgage were unpayable, as were all their other bills. When Celia's father lost his job, it had been devastating, but they rallied. When he had been that ghost of himself, blurry from OxyContin and cheap Coors, it had been hard, but they persevered. This time, when her mother didn't merely lose her job but saw it annihilated, they were defiant. They felt lied to and let down. It had all been a sham, everything they had believed to be true about hard work, strong values, and the promises of their country, things that, because they were born poor and managed to rise slightly higher, they had put all their faith in—because they had to be true. There had to be some hope, otherwise why not just settle for welfare and avoid the hassle?

They lost their faith. Not in God, but in everything else. When their faith went, they tossed their ideals and pride out along with it. Everything must go. America was still there, but it wasn't there for them, and it turned out it never had been. God was all there was and the only one there to help.

Barrett Higgins had an empty farmhouse on his property. He wanted to know if they'd like to live there—rent free, of course. He could use the company and a couple good pairs of hands around the place. He wanted to get the farm up and running again, a small output to start. With no rent and no utilities, their combined unemployment and disability checks would provide more than enough for them. Celia could be homeschooled. Public schools were a breeding ground of sin, anyway, as well as outright breeding grounds.

They accepted Barrett's offer, and Celia's parents defaulted on their mortgage. They left her mother's car and her father's truck to be repossessed by the bank. It was all she could do, her mother said as they left the house where they could paint all the rooms any color they wanted, not to throw a match in the place and let it burn. It was a symbol of their unattained wants, all their pointless striving, all their fruitless efforts: working so hard to live in a house you would never fully own.

There was one other option, but the last scrap of nobility left in this prince and princess of the American South wouldn't accept it. Celia's mother said it on their first night in the farmhouse, throwing her concerns for proper language on the imaginary fire at their old house: "At least it ain't the Blue Wave."

Chapter 3

The farm—French is Satan's bedroom language—God loves an early riser—When we used to be happy—The first neighbor—Like an idiot robbed a flea market—Surprise!

Celia's family moved out to the farm—more specifically, to the old farmhouse, the one someone else had abandoned to build something better. It had been left on the property as a remembrance of the past. Before they moved into it, it was being used for storage. Barrett swept and cleaned it for their arrival, but there was always the lingering smell of old camping equipment about the place. It had a front porch and a screen door. There was the main room and two small bedrooms off to each side like shoulders. The primitive bathroom stapled onto the back of the place represented the last technological upgrade the cabin had received. Celia stood in the center room and looked up into the open ceiling, the two halves drawing to a point above her.

Celia's father was filled with righteous rage. He behaved as though this move were something he'd been threatening if the world didn't shape up, and now he was left with no choice but to go through with it. It was modern America's loss that he would no longer participate in her corrupt game. Celia's mother unpacked boxes with quiet contempt. She hated the Blue Wave because it was beneath them. She hated Garden Estates because it was above them. And now she hated the farm because it was all they could manage. Celia lay on the cot in her room and cried, mashing her face into the pillow so her parents couldn't hear. She had never felt so helpless. She wanted to go home, to any home. The Blue Wave, Garden Estates, it didn't matter. She realized her parents had no control over their lives. It was a deeper truth than any she had ever hit upon, and she had barely been able to speak for the rest of the day, she was so shocked by its simple veracity. Now she cried it all out. The only thing they had control over was her. She was in the hands of fools.

It was them and Barrett on the property. In the mornings, her father rose early, before first light. He dove back into his old schedule as though it were a pool he had missed since his boyhood summers. Stacy and Harmon gave them some chickens, and Celia's father built a coop. He got the old tractor running, hitched the plow and tilled a quarter acre for corn.

If Celia had to credit her father with something, it was getting them through those first weeks. He threw himself at their new life with his old energy and mania. His enthusiasm and the delusion that he was turning his back on a status quo he no longer believed in let them pretend their situation was a new project they were embarking on. If he wasn't exactly his old self—if self-righteousness had replaced his goofy self-importance—he was as close to it as he had been since losing his job.

Celia helped her mother unpack and together they started, then abandoned, Celia's homeschooling. The decision to pull her from school and take her education into their own hands was part of the con they were running on themselves, meant to lend credence to the idea they were pulling out of the secular world.

"No more brainwashing," her father said.

"How was I being brainwashed?" Celia asked. "I took algebra. What's so liberal about math?"

"See, you don't notice it. They make you think it's all normal."

"That all what is normal? You've never been to my school, not even for a PTA meeting. I don't understand how you could dislike something about it." Celia often had no idea what her father was talking about anymore.

"Well, there's the fact that they're telling you evolution is real when even the world's top scientists will tell you it's just a theory." Celia resisted the urge to ask him who these top scientists he was referring to were. What would he say if she asked him to name one top scientist?

"No teacher in my school has ever said to us that evolution is real. I don't think we've ever had an evolution lesson."

"It's all implied with the stuff they do teach. Cell transformation and biology, it's all implied that it's in the service of evolution. They don't teach you the falseness of evolution, do they?"

"I don't—what?"

"They don't tell you that it's not true. It's the liberal agenda to get rid of religion, little by little. And Spanish."

"It's the liberal agenda to get rid of Spanish?"

"No, Spanish is another liberal trick. Do you even know why you take Spanish?"

"Because you said French was Satan's bedroom language."

"It's because of all these illegals coming into our country. Not only are they sneaking in here, but they want you to talk like them." Celia was pretty sure her school didn't have enough funding to implement an agenda. They had to have a bake sale to buy textbooks. "What's wrong with English? That's what I'd like to know," her father said.

"But I take English."

It was no use. She was pulled from school so her mother could homeschool her. The fact that neither of her parents had any educational training didn't dissuade them. Nor did the fact that they didn't have any books. They didn't have the Internet nor a computer to access it if they did. For lack of anything else to read, Celia started the Bible.

"Best education in the world, right there," her father said the first night he came in and saw her.

They saw a lot of Barrett Higgins. While Celia's father was up before the sun feeding chickens—Celia had strong suspicions the chickens were still asleep when he got to them—Barrett slept in. He showed up at their cabin after her father left and before Celia finally dragged herself out of bed. Celia heard him first, through her bedroom door, his deep voice muffled. When she emerged into the center room, Barrett was always standing at the kitchen counter, close to her mother's shoulder as she got breakfast ready.

"Morning, Miss Celia," Barrett would say as she shuffled across the wooden floor. The boards made tiny squeaks and creaks as she went, like she was trampling puppies. The cabin was always with them when they were in it. Every movement garnered a reaction, from the floor to the door hinges. It was like living in the belly of some animal.

Barrett moved to the table. Celia took a chair next to him and put her head down. She gazed up at him through heavy eyelids and met the lazy eye looking back down at her while the other followed her mom. Did he see that way? she wondered. The two of them simultaneously? Or was it just an illusion, the dual directions, and did the vision in the errant eye track with the other one? By the time a plate appeared in front of her, Celia was ready to speak and issued a long-delayed response to Barrett.

"Good morning."

The first time this happened, Barrett laughed in a guffawing outburst. "I've never seen someone rouse so slowly," he said.

"Yeah, our little flower opens to the sun at a leisurely pace," her mother said.

They ate their breakfast with a side of idle chitchat until Celia's father came in from his morning chores.

"Morning, everyone," he said. "Celia, what time'd you appear this morning?"

"Leave her alone," her mother said.

"That late, huh?"

"It's only nine thirty now," her mother piped up again.

"She can—"

"I'm working on it, Father. The Lord didn't bless with me with your easy ability to conquer the morning, so I'm working on changing on my own. A little bit more every day," Celia said.

"Well," her father said, always thrown off by her turns of sincerity. "That's good to hear. God loves an early riser." He looked over to Barrett, forever searching for confirmation when he declared what God did or didn't love. "Not sure I like you calling me 'father.'"

"Must be all this farm air," Celia said.

"Celia, that's mighty admirable, you taking on a personal-growth project like that," Barrett offered.

"Yes, I think it actually means something if you work at it, instead of only doing it because it's in your nature," she said. She kept her eyes on her breakfast plate for a moment before looking up and smiling at her father. "Well, if I can be excused, I have some studying to do."

She left the table and went to her room, where she usually went back to sleep for another hour. As she drifted off, she could hear the conversation through the door.

"It's amazing she's so responsible about her education."

"She's a blessing. A really good kid." That was her mother. "Isn't she, honey?"

"Yeah, she is. It's tough to keep on the straight path at her age, though. Teenagers. All you can do is try to set an example, pray for 'em."

"Cee has never been anywhere near a crooked path, unlike some of us," her mother said, in the tone they all recognized as the warning shot, a tone she was using a lot more these days.

"What do you say we head out?" Barrett said to Celia's father. "Get our day started for the second time?" This was their little joke. Celia's father had already been up tending to various things, and Barrett had allegedly been up for hours preparing sermons, answering mail, and praying. Or something. Whatever you could imagine falling under the heading of "work" for someone like him. He never specified, and they never asked. Barrett and Celia's father climbed into the old truck Barrett had bought and her father kept running and toured the property. They talked farming. They talked God.

"You know Barrett thinks we can make a run of it farming. Says there's real money in food from small independent farms," Celia's father said one evening. Another night he told them, "Barrett was telling me about farm subsidies today. Did you know the government just gives farmers money? It's to keep prices stable. Forty thou per person or eighty thou for a couple. You imagine us making eighty grand a year?" And another time: "Farming is a pretty sure thing. It's not like people are ever going to stop needing food."

"Crap. How'd I end up married to a farmer?" Celia's mom said. They were all three sitting on the front porch of the cabin when this last exchange took place. Celia's father looked down at his hands, bobbing just the smallest bit in the old rocker he was sitting in, as though any more swing would be an indulgence. His face pulled in toward his nose as it always did when he was hurt, his eyebrows dipping down like a lowered limbo bar and his lips drawing up like a cresting wave.

"Why would you say that?" he asked in a flat voice.

"Honey, I was teasing," her mom replied from the other rocker, where she was leafing through a five-year-old *Marie Claire* she'd found in one of their moving boxes.

"You were and you weren't. You were saying what you meant but pretending it was all in fun so you could get away with it."

"Hey. That's not—"

"I'm the head of this family and its spiritual leader. I deserve respect. The Bible says a wife shall respect and demure to her husband. That doesn't happen around here, and I'm getting damn sick of it." He stood up and stormed into the house, letting the screen door, on its old rusty hinges, swing shut with an agonizing scream and slam. He was gone before anyone could point out that he meant *defer* and not *demure*.

Celia looked over at her mother, who stared at the closed door between her and her husband before sighing and leaning back in her chair. She closed the magazine on her lap and looked out across the flat land with its dirt trails and bordering forests. "Remember when I used to be funny?" she said after a while.

"Remember when we used to be happy?" Celia said.

Her mother crossed the porch and put her arms around her. "We're still happy, sweetie. Somewhere in there. It's still there. We've just had a rough couple of years." She put a kiss on the top of Celia's head and gave her a squeeze. "We've made it through worse. Remember the Blue Wave?" Celia thought of Bobo and Dangle and Patch and all of them snug in their wonderful little trailer. A child's memory, she knew, far from the considerations, both economic and social, of grown-ups. "I'm gonna go talk with your dad. It'll be OK."

Celia's mother let her go and went inside, holding the screen door as it closed and keeping it to a grumpy whine. Celia took her father's rocker and thought how nice the evening air was now that they were both out of it.

The next morning, Barrett was in the kitchen as usual. Celia, in her drowsy state, listened to their conversation from her door. She could only make out pieces, but heard in Barrett's tone the formal counsel of a preacher rather than the genial houseguest.

"...must be a support to him now. God has great plans for us out here…your immortal soul, his, and your daughter's."

"…strong enough for this…so confused."

"…beautiful…the fire that keeps this all going…"

Then a laugh from her mother.

"I'll speak with him as well."

Celia opened the door and came out into the room. Her mother and Barrett were standing close by the sink. They turned when she emerged.

"Hey there, Cee-bear," her mother said in the nursery-rhyme voice she had used when Celia was younger.

"Morning, Celia," Barrett said. "The flower looks a little more open this morning than usual. And lovely as always." He smiled at her. She nodded a hello, more than she usually mustered, and tried for a smile in return that ended up looking like a spastic twitch. She had slept in her clothes to appear more awake than she really was. They went through their usual routine, everyone in their places, Celia struggling to wake up into her starring role. On cue her father returned from her morning chores and entered stage left.

"Morning, everyone," he said. Casual, normal. He took his place at the table, and his wife slid a plate in front of him. He looked over at Celia. Her moment was coming. "You're dressed," he said.

"With the Lord's help and your encouragement, yes. I'm slowly getting the hang of mornings," Celia said. She tried for a quick smile in his direction and then shoveled a groggy and uncoordinated mouthful of eggs into her face. She waited. She had conceived of this development for her character the night before, alone on the porch.

Her father nodded thoughtfully and smiled to himself. He reached out and combed back a piece of her hair, and his smile grew more confident. "Good girl. I knew you could do it." He bent to his own plate. He had done it. Through faith and solid parenting, his unschooled daughter, who lived in a creaking farmhouse they didn't own, was up and wearing clothes slightly earlier than usual. This was the right path after all. Any lingering tension in the room dissipated, and they ate peacefully until Barrett and Celia's father left and Celia returned to her room and fell back asleep.

When Celia woke later, she read for a while, until the rhythm of the Bible's prose threatened to pull her back to the land of sleep. She came out of her room and found her mother asleep on the old couch, as usual, the box fan they kept in the den blowing air and white noise over her. Her mother slept more and more of the day away as the weeks went by. Celia let her be and went out to wander the farm. As when she'd gone exploring in Barrett's mansion, she crept, not wanting to be seen, for reasons that welled up from somewhere deep within her and turned her isolation into a game she was playing. She trotted down the dirt paths until she spotted Barrett and her father, sometimes seeing the dust gyres from the rattly gray truck off in the distance or the two of them on Barrett's porch. Once she discovered where they were, she avoided them and was alone with the world.

Because she was getting almost no stimulation or education, Celia thought mainly in images. There was nothing to learn except Bible stories, nothing new to think about, no conversations worth going over in her head. With the exception of a few repetitive lines at breakfast each morning, she didn't even have the role of Celia, The Chosen One, to play. Her mother on the couch. Her mother and Barrett at the sink. Her father rising in the predawn gray and lighting his first cigarette of the day. The old truck with its blooming tail of dust, plump like an angry cat's. The way the untilled fields looked from inside the shade of the woods where she liked to walk: the sun's bright wash made the green of the weeds and grass appear white sometimes vanish altogether, a trick of the light and her eyes. She saw all these things, and without words they made sense, formed their own language. She wondered how long she could go without speaking. She saw their life on the farm as images from the Book of Genesis—nothing, then Barrett created a farmhouse. It was then, after they'd been living on the farm for a month, that they got their first neighbor.

Celia and her mother heard the news from Celia's father, who was put out by it and trying not to show it. He smoked on the front porch with a little crease of worry in the skin between his eyebrows, like the bunched fabric of pants that were too big in the crotch.

"Gardner's coming," he said.

"To what?" her mother asked.

"To here."

"Like for dinner?" She got a little wrinkle in her forehead, too.

"To the farm. To live. Like us. Barrett just told me."

"Well...when is he coming?"

"There." Celia's father pointed back toward the dirt road that led to and away from the farm. There was a dust-fog rising above the tree line where a vehicle approached.

"What, now? He's moving here now? How long have you know about this?"

Celia's father leaned on the porch rail stared at the ground. "Barrett told me about ten minutes ago. Gardner and him've been planning it for a few weeks."

"And he didn't even mention it to you? You see him almost every day."

The "almost" was a sore point. There were days when Celia opened the door to her room in the morning and discovered her mother alone at the kitchen table. It was impossible to miss her mother's obvious hurt. When her father came in the door those days, his face fell. There was never any warning when these days were coming, nor any explanation when Barrett once again graced them with his presence. Once they didn't see him for three days.

"Nope," her father said in response to his wife's question about Gardner. "I guess he didn't think he needed to discuss it with me." He lit a second cigarette off the first, and the two of them watched the approaching cloud.

Gardner Creech came in his pickup, the bed loaded with tools and supplies, towing a pop-up camper behind him. There was no sign of a wife. He parked a hundred yards away from Celia's family, popped up his camper, and announced he would begin building a home for himself the next day.

"Will your wife be joining you when it's done?" Celia's mother asked. She added, "We can't wait to finally meet her."

Gardner stiffened, but all he said was, "No, she ain't coming."

"Come by the cabin tonight," Celia's father said, only being polite. "Have a good supper with us. Welcome you to the farm."

His wife seconded his invitation. "Yes, come have a good meal on your first night."

"Appreciate it," Gardner said in a tone that sounded much like he didn't. "But I'd like to just get my site set up this evening before I lose the light. Maybe another night." He turned back to the bed of his truck. It was filled near to the top with loose tools and appliances, small wooden end tables, duffel bags swollen to capacity, a loose pillow with no case, and other miscellaneous items.

"Can I give you a hand with anything?" Celia's father said.

"No. I'm fine," Gardner said without looking up.

They left Gardner with his truck full of crap and went back to the cabin. "You believe he's got his tools just sliding around loose like that?" Celia's father said when they were out of earshot. "No tool bag? If a man can't take proper care of his tools, he sure as heck don't know how to use them."

"The back of that truck looks like an idiot robbed a flea market in the dark," Celia's mother said, and though it wasn't one of her best lines, her husband laughed aloud once more, the way he only did for her.

Barrett didn't surface the day Gardner moved in, and he didn't show up the next morning either. Late in the afternoon on Gardner's second day, though, there was a knock at the door that startled Celia as she climbed back in her window from a secret afternoon excursion and woke her mother on the couch. It was Gardner. "Barrett's having a welcome dinner for me up at the house tonight. Wants y'all to come, too." He didn't add anything to indicate that he also wanted them to come.

"Oh, that's so nice," Celia's mother said slowly. Celia knew she was thinking how they had not been invited up to the house for any reason aside other than the regular Sunday service and Bible study, never mind a dinner welcoming them—not that Barrett hadn't been generous enough just letting them live there for free and giving her husband work with the farming and all. But still. "Should I bring anything?" she added.

Gardner shrugged. "He didn't say anything about it. I guess you could if you wanted." He nodded good-bye and turned to go.

"Mr. Creech," Celia called after him. He stopped and turned. "I think it's a real blessing to have you out here with us. We're making a family in Christ."

Gardner Creech gave the closest thing to a smile they'd seen on his face since meeting him at Living Faith. "Thank you. It's nice to be out here. See y'all at dinner."

Her mother closed the door and looked at her. "That was nice of you."

"His wife left him."

"How do you know that?"

"Isn't it obvious?" Celia said. She had never cared for Gardner Creech, his bald head, or his habit of folding his arms across his chest when someone spoke to him, waiting for them to finish blathering what he clearly thought of as their astonishing stupidity, with his eyebrows raised in amazement. She was bored, though. If she had to live out here, she at least wanted something to do, someone for whom to perform her role of Celia the Chosen One. Celia didn't know much, but she knew when you found a man carting around a pillow with no case (one he no doubt intended to sleep on that way), whatever woman had been in his life was gone. Whether Gardner was here because she threw him out, or she threw him out because he wanted them to move here was anyone's guess, but somewhere out there was a woman who no longer had a pop-up camper cluttering up her yard or a Gardner Creech cluttering up her bed.

"It'd of been nice of Barrett to give us a little warning," Celia's mother said, pulling the ponytail holder out of her hair and combing her hair out with her fingers.

Yes, Celia thought, remembering the scene the evening her father came home with his injured back. She imagined them all in the bathroom again, the plate of food in her father's hand, the shower cap on his head, ashtray on the tub's edge, and a bright red light flashing throughout the house while a siren's wail swarmed the rooms. Warnings, she thought, would be nice, though if they went off as often as we actually needed them we'd just grow used to their constant sound.

It took Celia's mother a long time to get ready for dinner. She sat at the little cracked mirror in the bathroom applying makeup, then wiping it off and starting over, like she was erasing and rewriting a sentence she couldn't get right. "It's weird he didn't say anything to you about it," she called to her husband, who sat chain-smoking in the other room.

"It ain't weird. Guys just don't make plans like that. You just say, 'Hey, you want to come to dinner?' and the other guy goes, 'Yeah, sure, see you in an hour.' And that's it. It's women who have to plan everything days in advance." He got up and paced the room for a minute, then sat back down and lit another cigarette. "I mean, he just isn't thinking he needs to come give me a personal invitation, or that I'd expect one. We aren't like that, him and me."

Celia sat in her room, blocking both of them out, and ran lines in her head. She imagined someone saying something about praying, about their doubts that God heard them, Gardner preferably. She'd never spoken to him much and wanted to work against a new character. "God's voice is all around us," she'd say. Geez, no, how cliché. "The events of our lives are where we find God's voice. The ups and downs. How we react to them is where we find our own voice." Better. A little long, but she could work on it.

They walked to Barrett's house. The sun dropped below the tree line, creating a false sunset, bits of light visible through the odd gap here and there like something caught in a net. They stopped at the front door and stood together. No one made a move until Celia's mother said, "Well, knock or something," and her father gave a nervous laugh and said, "Hell, you'd think we'd never been invited to someone's house for dinner before." He rapped on the door as they all stood realizing that they hadn't. Before any of them could comment, though, the door swung wide, and there was Geraldine on the other side yelling, "Surprise!"

Geraldine hopped out the door and gave Celia's mother a hug she neither expected nor wanted. "Isn't it exciting?" Geraldine said.

"What? Dinner?" Celia's mother asked.

Geraldine let go and clapped her hands over her mouth. "Oh, I can't believe I did that—"

"Yes, you can, you know damn well—" Celia's father didn't clap his hands over his wife's mouth, but he reached over and placed his hands firmly on her shoulders, which for them amounted to much the same gesture.

"Can't believe you let what slip, Gerry? All you said was isn't something exciting. What's exciting?"

"Come on in, come on in," Geraldine said, turning and stepping inside. "I'll let Barrett tell you. It's his news and his dinner."

"I thought it was Gardner's dinner," Celia's mother said.

"Yeah, he's here, too," Geraldine said with indifference. "Through here," she said. Celia and her parents were ushered into a hallway, passively herded along it like cows in a chute. At the end of the hall, they came out into the dining room with a long eight-person table of dark, shining wood, place settings, and candles. Gardner was in one corner of the room, holding a glass of tea, and Beaufort was in another. Celia didn't know which corner not to go to first. Her father, ever the statesman, cut right and hit Beaufort first with a firm handshake, then swung around the room to Gardner before finishing up with his family back in front of the door.

"Can I get you anything to drink?" Geraldine asked.

"Iced tea'd be great," Celia's father said. Celia nodded that she'd like the same. Geraldine looked at Celia's mother.

"I'll come help you."

"That's not—"

"Geraldine, show me the kitchen," her mother said in a voice that was half threat. Geraldine nodded and smiled and led the way past her husband.

"How's it going, Beaufort?" Celia's mother said as she passed.

"Same as with you, pretty soon," Beaufort said. Celia's mother made an uncomprehending face, but Geraldine was already pushing through the kitchen door, and she had to follow.

Celia was going to excuse herself to the bathroom again, but before she could, she felt a pair of hands slip over her shoulders, the fingers extending over her collarbones. Above her head Barrett's voice said, "Welcome, all." He had come in so quietly he caught the other men by surprise. They all tripped over themselves and one another coming around the table to shake his hand.

"Got that fence about fixed," Celia's father said to him.

Barrett took one hand off of Celia's shoulder and put it on her father's. "Excellent work, my friend," he said, smiling. "We couldn't do this without you." Barrett turned to Gardner. "And you, brother?" Celia's father stiffened slightly at this. "How's your move coming along?"

"Pretty well set up in the pop-up," Gardner said. "Aim to start building myself a cabin soon as I can."

"That's great to hear." Barrett turned back to Celia's father. "Gardner will be riding out with you during the days now. It'll be good to have an extra pair of hands."

"Oh...great," Celia's father said. "Be a little tight with three of us in the cab, but—"

"I won't be coming along much anymore," Barrett said lightly. "So there'll be plenty of space."

"You know much about farming?" Celia's father said to Gardner with apparent skepticism and not-so-apparent hypocrisy. He himself knew next to nothing. "It's tough work."

"Never farmed so much as a garden."

"Despite the name, huh?" Beaufort said. They all turned toward his voice, suddenly remembering he was there.

"Beaufort, it's a joy to have you here," Barrett said.

"No, I'm more hunter than gatherer," Gardner went on. "Got my guns in the pop-up. Figure I'll get out in the woods and bring us back some game from time to time. You hunt at all? Or just farm?"

"No, I—"

"Oh, Barrett, you're ready!" Geraldine's voice cut in behind them. She put the iced teas down on the table. "Everybody sit, sit. I'll start bringing out the food." She was gone back into the kitchen before her voice had totally faded from the room. Celia's mother shook her head.

"Hello, Barrett," she said, as she came around the table. She stuck the glass of iced tea she was carrying into her husband's hand. She exchanged a light cheek-kiss greeting with the host. "Where've you been hiding?" she asked.

"Locked away in my study," Barrett said.

"You should come up for air every now and then, and a cup of coffee. God's voice'll find you better out in the world. It's all around us out here."

"Aguh," Celia said. Everyone looked at her, and she turned red.

"What was that, honey?" her mother said.

It was the sound of a word dying in her mouth as she heard her mother speaking her lines nearly verbatim. Celia had started to yell out, "Hey! No! Mine!" but the words imploded into a mongoloid grunt.

"Nothing," Celia said, and cleared her throat. "Just a tickle in my—" she patted her throat and reached out for her father's iced tea. Her mother, that bitch, was stealing her leading role.

"I hunt a bit," Beaufort said to Gardner.

"Everyone sit, sit down." Geraldine's voice bit through them again as she came back in carrying a casserole dish.

"Gerry, let me help you," Celia's mother said, sighing.

"No, you sit right down with everyone else. You just relax."

"Screw it, fine," Celia heard her mother say under her breath. Louder she said, "Thanks, Gerry, that's sweet of you. Here, Barrett, come sit. I'm going to take the place next to you. We've missed you at breakfast. I need to catch up." She pointed Barrett to the head of the table and took the seat next to his. Celia's father jerked to attention, but it was useless. Gardner took the seat on the other side of Barrett, and he was reduced to taking the seat next to his wife.

"You and me can get out in the woods and bring back some protein then," Gardner was saying to Beaufort. Celia's father snapped his head over to see the two of them conferring across the table from him. "We'll get you set up with a gun, too." Gardner said to Celia's father. He thought for a moment. "A varmint gun or something. Then you can keep the gophers out of your crops."

Geraldine swept in and out of the kitchen door, dropping off bowls and dishes that crowded together like ships in a bay. At last she took her seat next to her husband. Celia took the seat opposite Barrett at the foot of the table.

"That's not a seat for a child," her father said, finally finding someone on whom he could exert some control. "Move over here." He pulled out the one empty seat next to him.

"Actually, I like looking down the table and seeing young Celia there," Barrett said. "Always having to hang around with us grown-ups, she never complains about it. She's very mature."

"Thank you," Celia said for the compliment. "When we're all together, it's usually in Christ's service. I guess that one purpose levels the field some when it comes to age."

"Well said," Barrett replied.

Geraldine beamed at her, and Gardner gave her a little half salute with his glass of iced tea. Celia fixed her father with an expressionless stare, one she hoped said, "Don't mess with me."

"Let's take hands and offer a blessing," Barrett said. Celia reached across the empty space between them and took her father's hand. Geraldine gripped her with soft, cold fingers on the left. "Powerful Savior," Barrett began. "We humbly ask that you bless this food we are about to eat, that it may make us strong in body while you make us strong in spirit. Lord, we are united here, on the verge of something mighty, but we know we can only pull it off with your grace. We welcome Gardner onto this land and into this family. And we thank you for the Waters family, who were the first. They led the way so that others might follow. Without their first step, we would not be here today with the second and third." Celia looked up now and saw her parents had opened their eyes as well and were exchanging puzzled looks. The rest of their fellow diners still had their heads bowed in prayer, eyes mashed shut. "Lord, we will set an example for the rest of the world. We will be a testament to the way you want all mankind to live. We are so pleased you have brought Geraldine and Beaufort to live here with us, for they are two strong pillars of faith. With your blessings, more will follow, and we will create a strong community true to you and all you want for us. In your name we pray, amen."

They all opened their eyes. Celia's parents were looking from face to face around the table, realizing what everyone else already knew. Geraldine's reaction when she came to the door made sense now, but just in case they hadn't remembered, she yelled out again, unable to contain herself.

"Surprise!"

Chapter 4

Three months later

Rebecca and Rebekah—Farm animals don't got names—Proselytizing gravy—Sticky with sap—The Second Coming, not too bad of a burden—Spreading the good news

It was a drizzling summer morning. Celia walked in the damp grass along the edge of the trail to avoid the mud. Everyone did this once the path got muddy, so the sides wore down as well and the path got wider and muddier, spreading the mess they were all trying to avoid. When the sun was out, it baked everything into dust.

Geraldine had lost her job along with Celia's mother. Beaufort hadn't worked in years. He simply didn't care for it. He spent his days on the Internet, running a business that was supposed to design websites and develop software. He had no clients, a fact he blamed on Microsoft having a monopoly.

"You believe that?" Celia's father said. "A man letting his wife work full time while he sits at home playing on a computer?"

Geraldine and Beaufort had managed to sell their house and most of their belongings. They bought an RV, drove it to the farm, and parked it near Celia's family's cabin. The Landrosses, Stacy and Harmon, came next, sleeping in a tent until Harmon could "whack up a domicile" as he put it. He built them a three-room structure with an ease and swiftness that totally discouraged Gardner from his disastrous attempt to build himself a cabin and left him settling for the pop-up indefinitely. Harmon and Stacy had been living on a farm and were happy for the company, the help, and the lack of rent involved in this new community. Harmon took over the farm's agricultural activity, and Celia's father was again out of a job. He had to settle for being even with Gardner as one of Harmon's assistants, though he still ranked above Beaufort, who didn't care for manual labor any more than he did the other kind and promptly fell out the back of Harmon's pickup his second day on the farm, claimed a twisted ankle, and went back to his RV.

Rebecca's family, the Eubankses, came next. In honor of their joining the community, they changed the spelling of their daughter's name to Rebekah after Isaac's wife, from the Bible. Celia was immensely pleased to see her number-one fan, however her name was spelled. She was glad to see all of them as they arrived over the weeks. Kent and May Altman set up an enormous tent at first. To everyone's surprise, Kent actually knew his trade and, like Harmon, he had a shelter erected quickly. Everyone helped with everything. The men roamed the property in their pickups, moving from chore to chore: framing a new room for Harmon and Stacy; checking the rows of crops; insulating windows for Kent and May; and, most energetically, building a large, covered amphitheater with a stage at one end for services. Beaufort's ankle healed, but he sprained his wrist when he tripped over a pig, so he returned to his RV.

Celia approached the old barn where Trevor, the donkey, lived and pushed through the large doors, freshly painted red by the enthusiastic citizens, complete with white paint for the frame. Inside, the air was dense with outdoor odors trapped inside between the walls and roof. The concentrated smells of dust, idle tools and equipment, and Trevor with his mouthful of hay all slipped around Celia as she came in and closed the door behind her. Trevor didn't make much fuss, just farted and shook his head. Celia liked to believe this was meant as a greeting.

Celia had unofficially adopted the donkey as her personal pet. She'd been the one to name him Trevor. Every time Celia went to visit him, he was munching hay. It was his only hobby. Celia remarked on this to her father. "He's of a singular focus and cannot experience God's love the same as we can, so his pleasures in life are small," he had said, in his newly adopted way of ruining conversations.

Trevor had come along with Stacy and Harmon from their place. Celia had fallen in love with him on first sight when, stamping and snorting, he'd refused to come out of the trailer he'd ridden in to the farm.

"What's his name?" she had asked.

Harmon had looked down at her as if wondering when she'd learned to talk. "Farm animals don't got names. They got jobs," he finally said.

"His name's donkey," Stacy said, bending slightly and putting her wild smile closer to Celia's face. "He's a donkey, so he gets called donkey." Celia wasn't buying that. She decided on Trevor.

Celia and her family had arrived at the farm in early spring. It was now late summer. The heat was still mesmerizing but had stopped escalating and would taper off soon into the pleasant snap of fall. Celia stroked Trevor's long soft ears and fed him the carrots she brought. It was Barrett who'd sold her on the idea of a place of her own, a secret place, and this was it. Solitude in a large building filled with hiding places, nooks and crannies, the hayloft, shadows, and thick still air. And Trevor. A pet. He was like a large, docile dog who never wanted to run or go anywhere, so you always knew where to find him. Barrett's hot-tub grotto was fancier, but this worked just as well for her.

After Gardner, Geraldine, and Beaufort arrived, Barrett became a rare commodity. Once the Landrosses and Altmans showed up, he only made appearances at Wednesday and Sunday Service Gatherings, as they were calling them now. Celia's father slipped into a funk over this, feeling abandoned, until one day Barrett summoned him out of the fields to come up to the big house and "talk awhile." Celia's father came back from this talk with an air of gravitas that would have sunk him if he'd gone for a swim.

"We discussed what comes next. Where the path leads once a man, a family, is walking it. When he starts talking, you listen, boy. Let me tell you." Celia's father sat at the picnic table Gardner had set up outside his pop-up with several of the other residents of the farm gathered around him, listening. "You can just see in his eyes that his thoughts are on another level. That he's seeing things we can't even imagine."

"What's he see?" said a man everyone except Celia's father called Biscuit. Her father, ever disparaging of nicknames for grown men, called him by his real name, Ashley. Ashley's wife, Nancy-Lynn, sat beside him, equally engrossed in any message from Barrett.

"Deep and dark things, Ashley," Celia's father said. Celia herself listened quietly next to her mother, standing just outside the circle that had formed around the table. She wasn't playing her role at the moment. She knew when she was upstaged. Right now, the spotlight belonged to her father.

Her mother stood at her side, examining her nails. "I feel like they never look completely clean out here," she said.

"It's hard to try and tell you all exactly what we discussed. We sit down and it's like an energy, a presence overtakes us." Celia's father held up his hand as though holding back an accusation that hadn't been spoken. "And that's all coming from him. From Barrett. I'm just there trying to open my heart up to the power he's channeling, trying to hear and help in whatever way I can for whatever reason he calls on me to be there. But I can tell you one thing he said to me, he said, 'Brother Waters, we are the center of something important. Why us—why me to lead, why you all to follow—I can't say. When this all first began back at Living Faith, I was just following the push I felt God stirring in my heart. And now we've come this far, and I feel this thing growing. We'll be asked to go further. We are very much in God's favor. As long as we do whatever he asks, we'll remain that way. We just have to listen and be open.' Now that right there about put me over on my you-know-what. It's a mighty thing to realize that your faith, when you truly live it like we're all doing, has such power. Everybody's faith can do that, if they let it. And we've all let it."

"Amen."

"Yes, sir, amen."

A dozen voices around him gathered in affirmation. Her father was happier now, the happiest he'd been since they moved, less riddled with stress and failure—as long as you didn't mind every banal exchange of pleasantries being smothered with a proselytizing gravy. Telling him, "Good morning," fetched you a response ranging anywhere from, "Thanks be to God," to "No morning will be good enough until my Savior returns."

Celia's mother was invited up to the house quite a bit, too. She came back in a different mood than Celia's father. Though the visits were for "spiritual guidance," her mother returned with little to discuss in the way of the spirit.

One day, Celia was sprawled on the musty couch in the center room when her mother returned from a visit to Barrett's. It had been days since Celia had seen her mother other than at the breakfast table. During the day, Celia wandered the farm while her mother slept or visited with Barrett. Celia wandered the farm at night as well. She would slip out her small window after the tense and self-righteous voices coming from her parent's room had died away. She walked the black fields and woods, a darker universe than the one above, with its salting of starlight and the waxing-waning glow of the moon. She visited the dwellings of the tenants and believers. Gardener would be in his pop-up, door open, cleaning his hunting rifles. Geraldine and Beaufort played rummy at their kitchen table. Barrett was usually in his hot tub. She discovered she could climb into the fir tree that hid the fence and peer down through the branches. The first time, she saw Barrett lying in the hot tub, his head tilted back against the edge, visible only from the neck up. The roiling bubbles from the jets hid everything lower until they abruptly cut off. The water cleared, and Celia saw he was naked. She had seen naked men before on the Internet at Sloane's house, but this was her first in body and blood. The dark area of his manhood was less awful-looking than what she and Sloane had witnessed online. It was like a flower that had been glued to his crotch by its unappealing, hairy bloom, and the thick, fleshy stem swayed pointlessly in the warm water. When she came out of the tree, she was always sticky with sap.

When her mother returned from Barrett's and found Celia on the couch, she said, "Oh. Hey," clearly surprised. Celia had been staring at the ceiling in boredom, unable to read any more of the Bible for the day. Her mother looked around the dismal space and sighed. Despite her efforts, the farmhouse refused to feel like anything other than an old, borrowed farmhouse. The photos of their family, the throw pillows from their old house, the careful organization of her kitchen command center—none of these things overcame the fact of the three small rooms with the floor, walls, and ceiling all meeting at uneven angles.

Celia's mother pushed back the front curtain an inch and peered out. "Here she comes," she said. Through the small crack Celia could see Geraldine power walking along the path from her and Beaufort's RV. "She watches me," her mother said. "It's creepy. She waits to see when I leave Barrett's and come back." Celia noticed her mother's hands. Her fingernails were free of the grime that so plagued her, as though they had been boiled clean.

"What do you think she'll want this time?" Celia said, not changing her position of one leg and arm hanging off the couch. She turned to stare into the rafters, taking note of the small cobwebs and little toes of dust that clung to the beams.

Celia's mother thought about it. "Sugar," she said finally.

"I'll say salt."

"You're on."

Celia's mother pulled the door open the second before Geraldine could knock. Geraldine was startled and speechless. "I was just getting ready to knock," she said when her tongue got back to work.

"Heard you come up onto the porch. This old place, a body can't move an inch that it doesn't give you away," Celia's mother said. "C'mon in."

"Hello, dear Celia," Geraldine said.

Celia raised one hand in Geraldine's direction but didn't move to get up. "Howdy," she said.

"Would you like a cup of coffee?" Celia's mother asked.

"You'd be such a peach, thanks. You know, I was just getting ready to come over and ask to borrow a quarter cup of salt"—Celia raised a fist in triumph over the back of the couch, and her mother pretended not to notice—"when I saw you coming down from Barrett's. I hope everything's OK. It's so rare that anyone sees him outside of the gatherings."

"You know Barrett and I meet occasionally for spiritual counseling," Celia's mother said, casually.

"That is so wonderful," Geraldine said. "You're doing that regularly now, it seems like." She wasn't smiling. "With so many of us, he could hardly have time to spend with everyone like that. You're really blessed that he picked you."

"I think it's because he and Brother Waters meet and chat now and then. My meetings with Barrett are a sort of collateral damage from that." She did a light imitation of Barrett's voice when she said "Brother Waters," trying to lighten the mood.

"He values your husband's counsel. That's very special. And you can tell your husband knows how special it is," Geraldine said. "He's happy to serve Barrett and God."

"Yeah," Celia's mother said, becoming serious. "He's become very happy to serve."

The Service Gatherings became more intense. Bible study had been absorbed into them, and instead of a discussion, they all read the same passage and listened as Barrett expounded on it. All the meetings had moved to the outdoor pavilion for the sake of space and comfort. They rigged thick plastic sheets to the roof of the pavilion to be rolled down and fastened tight so they could run heaters in the winter.

Celia closed her eyes and pressed her ear to Trevor's side, listening to the unseen world churning within him, keeping him alive. The donkey's blank stare told that he knew nothing of all that and held no control over what went on inside him. Celia thought of her own heart, stomach, and guts all cranking inside the border of her flesh. She could no more will her heart to stop than she could will a tumor to go away if she had one. Her hair color, the rate at which her fingernails grew, her skin tone, the size of her nose and feet, the angle of her teeth—she had no control over these things, or anything really. If someone yawned, she yawned. Her thoughts were the only place she exercised any autonomy, and even that was subjective. Her brain ambled along doing whatever it wanted in the background, even while she concentrated on a bird or a color. An organism barely aware of itself: that's what she was. She thought things about her life but decided nothing about it. She merely observed her own existence while freckles blossomed like flowers along her arm and her hair lost the sun and turned a shade darker in the fall along with the leaves.

Celia opened her eyes and saw Barrett sitting in the corner on a bale of hay. He must have been there since she came in. His hair had grown wilder in the months since they'd come to the farm. His skin was markedly lighter than the rest of theirs. When he took the stage to lead their worship, he was a pale specter speaking to a sun-dark tribe.

"Hello, young Celia," he said when he saw her notice him.

"Hi." Celia took her ear off the donkey and stood straight.

"Come here," Barrett gestured to a bale of hay next to his own. Celia crossed the distance between them and sat. "I see you found a private place," he said. "Somewhere to be alone."

Celia thought she had, but now here was Barrett perched on a lump of hay, spying on her from a corner. She was flattered, though, that he remembered their conversation. That he remembered her. With all the people clamoring for his attention, her father not the least of them, she felt a slight thrill at being granted a space in his memories. "I come here to see Trevor," she said.

"Trevor?"

"The donkey." She pointed at the beast, who lifted his tail and shat as if in reply.

"Ah, well, he's a very special animal," Barrett said. "You're very special, too, you know." Celia was pleased to be told so without her having to shit on the floor as well. "Do you remember when I asked you if you were prepared to handle times of great upheaval and distress?"

"Yeah."

"Do you remember what you said?"

"I said yeah."

"That's right. Those times are coming."

Celia was unimpressed. Those times were always coming, according to everyone around her. It was the perverse promise they made themselves to make the present seem tolerable. A hurt back, a lost job, a foreclosed house—these things were nothing compared to the impending doom of upheaval and distress that was forever on its way. Still, she nodded politely. She tried to slip into her Celia the Chosen One persona, but it was hard with just Barrett. The role needed a specific audience, one that was playing along themselves. Barrett, she sensed, wasn't playing.

"Celia, may I burden you with something that's been weighing on me?" he asked.

"I guess so."

He leaned in close to her face. "I have returned," he nearly whispered. "Christ your Savior has come back, and I am him." He was so close she could smell the soap on his face. His hair brushed against her forehead, and the bulk of his adult body, though not actually touching her, was close enough to imagine its weight pressed against her. He leaned away, his good eye meeting hers.

"Well, that doesn't seem like too bad of a burden," was all Celia could think to say when she found her voice. He sat back farther and cocked an eyebrow at her. She cleared her throat and went on more forcefully. "I mean, you love Jesus, so you should be thrilled. And everyone else already loves you, and they love Jesus, too, so they're going to be all happy about it. Plus hasn't everyone been waiting for the second coming for, like, *ever*? So really, when you think about it, it's probably good news." She patted him on the back. It was the first time she had ever touched him, and her hand found its way there before she was aware of what it was doing. The barely aware organism, she reflected, feeling the contours of his bone and muscle in the space between his shoulders.

Barrett's face struggled for a moment, the deep worry and thoughtfulness breaking into unrecognizable expressions that it fought before giving in and turning into a smile. "Thank you, Celia, for putting that into perspective," he said. "It *is* good news. I guess I referred to it as a burden to convey that it was *big* news." His face found its way back to its previous expression of otherworldly concern. "It's quite a lot to accept."

"You'll be great," Celia said, still patting him on the back. She knew she'd been doing it too long, but she couldn't stop. He solved this for her by reaching over his shoulder and taking her hand in his.

"Thank you for listening, Celia," he said. Somewhere outside, a small voice called Celia's name, echoing his own pronouncement.

"That's Rebekah," Celia said. "I'm supposed to meet her over by these trees."

Barrett nodded. "You better go see your friend. I'll try to remember that this is your special place and not disturb you in it again."

"It's OK," Celia said. Rebekah's voice called out. "I guess I gotta go."

Barrett nodded and released her hand. Celia jogged to the barn door. She looked back to wave before she passed through into the screaming sunlight that pressed through cracks and openings in the barn as though the outside was overpopulated with such light. Barrett had his back to her, petting Trevor. The scene reminded Celia of a painting or a drawing, something staged. She kept her wave to herself and dipped out into the sun.

Celia and Rebekah pretended they were ponies. It was a game, like many of theirs, for which Celia was really too old. With no other children around, though, she and Rebekah both operated below their respective ages. Who was there to care?

"We'll be ponies who are sisters," Rebekah said.

"And princesses," Celia added.

"But we're really smart."

"And we have to take care of our father. Because our mom is dead."

"He needs our help because he's not good at running the kingdom anymore."

"So we have to step up and take care of everything."

"Because he's hopeless."

The cantered and galloped around for a while, getting into various adventures and handling all the things for which their put-upon grieving father was no longer suited.

"Barrett told me that Christ has come back, that he's the second coming," Celia said during their game.

Rebekah stopped midgallop and stared at her. "He did? When?"

Celia reined herself in a little and trotted in place alongside Rebekah. "Earlier. This morning."

"Did you tell your parents?"

"No. I started playing ponies."

"My dad says that the second coming is what we're all waiting for. He says it's gotta be coming soon because the world has gone so bad."

"My dad says that, too. Because of gay marriage and terrorism, which he thinks are basically the same thing."

"I think you need to tell your parents," Rebekah said.

They sat around the table in Celia's parent's cabin. Celia and Rebekah sat next to each other with the grown-ups eyeing them as though the conversation were about sneaking out to a party or bringing home an F. There had been an odd moment, an unclear reaction from her parents, when Celia came into the cabin and announced that Barrett had revealed himself to her. They had disbelieved her; she was sure of that much. They looked at her as though she'd told them animals in the forest had spoken to her. Then she explained about the second coming of Christ, and their mouths fell open, their ears too, it seemed, and they wanted her to repeat exactly—"Exactly, Celia, tell Daddy exactly what he said. Word for word."—what Barrett had said to her. She recounted the conversation, and her and Rebekah's parents sat back in their chairs considering this news.

"In the Bible, Jesus rode into town on a donkey on Palm Sunday," Rebekah's father, Mr. Eubanks, said. "The people knew him then to be their Savior. Do you think there's a connection there? With Barrett revealing himself in the presence of the donkey?"

"Trevor," Celia corrected.

"I think we'd be fools not to see the connection there," Celia's father said. Celia's mother sat staring down at the table. "What do you think?" her husband asked her.

She looked up blankly for a moment, stepping away from the parade of her own thoughts. "I was thinking how I guess I'd kind of expected this in some back part of my brain, but how I'd never really let myself believe it, like I knew it but doubted my own belief. That's probably a sin. Or anyway a lesson to be taken away. Or something. It's amazing."

"If it's a sin, I think it's one we all share," Celia said. They all looked at her a touch surprised, having forgotten she was there after she'd relayed her news. She wasn't going to let them forget her, though. She knew why Barrett had chosen to reveal himself to her now, why he had invaded her private place. He believed she really was special. He wanted to show everyone just *how* special by giving her this miraculous news, by making her his Gabriel, sent to announce his arrival. "God knows it's not easy for the human heart to accept things such as this, even when they can see it for themselves. That's why he uses a messenger." Me, she didn't say. That's why he used me, not you.

Mr. and Mrs. Eubanks nodded gravely. "She's right," Mrs. Eubanks said. "I feel the same way you do," she said turning to Celia's mother. "I guess that's why we're being told like this. It's like saving us from ourselves."

"Celia, honey, why don't you and Rebekah go outside and let us think a little bit?" Celia's mother said. Celia looked up at her, and the hurt must have shown on her face, because her mother said, "I think we all just need a little time to digest this, honey."

"The grown-ups need to talk. Go on outside," her father added, just to horn in on giving an order.

Celia didn't say anything else. She left the table and went out the door. Rebekah followed. Outside, Celia stood in the dusk with her hands on her hips and fumed. How dare they kick her out while they discuss something she brought to their attention? She pictured her father with a group of Barrett's followers around him, telling them about the Second Coming. Telling them her news. Then her anger abated. A new vision swam before her, and she smiled. She turned to Rebekah. "Is Beaufort still nursing his sprained wrist?" she asked.

"His wrist got better, but he thinks he broke his tailbone sitting in the back of the work truck when Gardner drove over a log. Aunt Geraldine is making him sit on a pillow."

"Aunt Geraldine?"

Rebekah shrugged. "That's what she told me to call her."

"Why don't we go visit Aunt Geraldine, now?" Celia said. "And bring her some good news."

Geraldine ran out of the RV when Celia told her about Barrett being Jesus returned to Earth to lead them in his glory. She left Beaufort sitting on a stack of pillows waiting for the sandwich she had abandoned on the counter. Celia and Rebekah went out after her and pulled the door closed behind them. She was pretty sure Beaufort would find the strength to get that sandwich himself once they left.

"Should we go spread the good news some more?" Rebekah asked. They watched the retreating form of Geraldine as she went near-hysterical down the path to Celia's family's cabin. Farther along the path, past her home, Celia saw Gardner Creech out in front of his pop-up with Harmon, who was helping him lay the foundation for a proper home. They were cleaning up their work site in the failing light. Celia took Rebekah's hand and together they galloped down the path to take care of the things that needed taking care of.

Chapter 5

A blessing and a fall—Take a wife, so sayeth the Lord—No you there for me anymore—
Burning the whole place down with you in it—A pile of unloved dresses—The man
without a cigarette for more than one day—The kind of thing you really oughtn't have to
tell people—The grotto—Job had everything taken away, you still have a bowl of pasta—
Getting left on the losers' side feeding chickens—Two were there was once one

"The Lord, your God, has spoken to me," The Prophet said, and his
followers believed him and so made it true. "You all please him very much
indeed." The Prophet stood, eyes closed, in the center of the dais his followers
had built for him. "He has brought you all here to this beautiful place. Created
for you this community of like-minded and blessed individuals. You have built
him this temple," The Prophet said, eyes still closed, as he gestured around him.
"It is not made of marble or decorated in gold ornaments. It is simple wood, cut
and shaped by simple, honest Christians, and that makes this temple pure. That
makes this temple more beautiful than any cathedral built in God's name but
designed to bring glory to the builder. This temple is God's temple!" Amens and
hallelujahs issued forth from the congregants. "This land is God's land! This
people is God's people! He is pleased with you!" More affirmations from the
seated, louder now. "You are my people!" His followers already knew. "I am
pleased with you! The Lord, your God, has come back through me." He needn't
have announced it. His messenger had already visited each of them, a dusty-
footed child with a bright smile who was rumored to be spiritual beyond her
years. "He has spoken to me. He has had me prophesy my own return. He has
commanded me to shepherd you through the end-times. He will reveal the
secrets of the Book of Revelations to me and he will lead you through my
voice!"

There was a great uproar from the congregation. Nancy-Lynn fell from
her chair and began speaking in tongues on the wood floor, kicking in spasms
against her husband's legs. A few others dropped after her and began chanting in
unidentifiable languages. The Prophet left his post at the front and moved into
the crowd, laying his hands on his followers, some of whom dropped into
rapturous oblivion at his touch. Geraldine rushed to the front to receive The
Prophet's blessing. He placed his hands on her head, and she toppled backward
into the arms of Gardner Creech, who had sidled up next to Barrett and was

snatching bodies as they went down and laying them off to the side like caught fish. Beaufort gathered up his pillow and the crutch he hobbled around on and made for the back, lest he end up healed. Celia's father copied Gardner and took a spot on the other side of Barrett helping to catch the blessed, who now surged forth en masse to be touched by the Savior.

Celia sat up in the cross beams of the amphitheater in the back corner and watched. Mr. Eubanks lifted Rebekah up before the prophet, and she was blessed and went limp in his grip like a handful of spaghetti. He handed her off to Gardner, then took his own blessing and fell. Celia's father caught him and laid him in his row.

Celia saw a single figure emerge from the back of the pavilion out into the night. It was her mother. She turned and watched the proceedings, much as Celia herself was doing from her perch. She was wearing jeans and one of her husband's old shirts, the tail twisted into two lengths and tied in a knot at her stomach, like a younger version of herself. Her hair was pulled back, her face clean of makeup. She wore an old pair of sneakers. Celia thought of what her mother used to look like. The colorful high heels, the skirts, the dark thread of makeup that ringed her eyes and the red burst that colored her lips. Here she looked stripped and reduced, her layers mined and never replenished. She was a strip of land that had been deforested, had its rivers diverted and drained, and its topsoil collected and bagged so that nothing remained except a loose, sandy stretch of dirt and the thin, still air that separated it from the heavens. Celia watched her mother watching Barrett and her husband dispatching the faithful, giving them the brief mercy of rapture. Her mother stood that way for a while, then turned and began slowly walking in the direction of the big house.

Gardner came first and announced The Prophet was coming to the three-room farmhouse to pay them a visit. They were humbled and honored that he should bless their dwelling with his presence. Celia's father might have chafed a bit that Gardner was sent to announce something that was once a common occurrence, but it would have been blasphemy to chafe at something ordered by the Risen Christ. So in the end he didn't chafe; he thanked Gardner and began straightening up around the cabin. It was less tidy than anywhere they'd ever lived. Celia's mother went into the bedroom and closed the door. Gardner left, and a short while later, Celia saw him escorting Barrett down the path from the big house. Geraldine was already out of her RV and hustling toward them before Gardner turned her back with a shake of his head. Geraldine watched as they mounted the front steps and entered the cabin, then she hustled off toward Kent and May Altman's house instead.

The Prophet came in and surveyed the place as though he had never seen it before. He sat at the kitchen table, and the three of them sat with him. Gardner stood sentry by the door. It had been a few weeks since the announcement of Christ's return in the form of Barrett, who now went by The Prophet.

The Prophet appeared regularly for the Service Gatherings, but he disappeared immediately afterward and was never seen in between. His weight gain became more noticeable because of this. His appearance was scrutinized, and each time he emerged from the big house, he resembled it more. Not huge, just bigger. Everything about him, his house, faith, stomach, dwarfed the counterpoints in the rest of them. He hadn't bought new shirts, and he filled his old ones out completely now.

"Thank you for having me in your home," The Prophet said.

"It's our privilege," Celia's father said. "The place is a little messy, if we'd of known you were—"

"Celia, how wonderful to see you," Barrett said, cutting him off.

"Hey, Barrett," Celia said.

"You address him as The Proph—" her father started to growl, but again Barrett spoke over him.

"It's fine. Do not grow in anger toward this child. The youth are our most important allies in the times to come. Their clarity and honesty is pure. Plus Celia was there at my birth, in a way. Or should I say my rebirth. She's my own personal Gabriel." The Prophet reached over and took Celia's hand. He gave it a gentle squeeze. He turned his attention back to Celia's father and became serious. "The Savior has returned. You know this, Brother Waters. You were an early disciple, and your dedication to your Heavenly Father and to your faith has been unfailing. You have put tremendous trust in God, first with your injury and addiction. He brought you through it, and now you are clean and sober, fit and strong. You put your faith in him again when you lost your house, bringing your family out here. You were a pioneer. And now look around you. You have a community, friends, food, and work. Your faith has been strong, and you have been blessed. "

Celia's father nodded, pleased with this praise and easily understood summary of his achievements in belief. "I have been truly blessed."

"My father has been speaking to me, Brother Waters," The Prophet said. "He has a plan for us. You know he has a plan, don't you? You have seen it unfold personally. Things that seemed hard at the time, defeating things, challenges. When they occurred, you couldn't see how these things could be God's work. But your faith grew stronger, did it not?"

"It did."

"You were provided with a home and place to worship."

"I was."

"Your soul and the souls of your family members are saved now, are they not?"

"They are."

"Saved from the torments of hell eternal, from the claws of demons ravaging their flesh and yours. You have saved your family, regained your strength and your soul."

"I have. Oh, yes, I have."

The Prophet reached across the table and placed a hand on Celia's father's forearm. He gave it a manly shake. "Indeed you have, Brother. Now the Lord speaks to me and tells me that the Second Coming needs a companion." Celia saw her father's face begin to break into a smile. "A partner," The Prophet said. Her father nodded and appeared to be on the verge of shouting *yes*. "A wife." Her father's face went limp. He took a deep breath and forced a gentle cough to cover his disappointment. "God has commanded me to take a wife," The Prophet continued. "This command is deeply important—so important I am not permitted to choose for myself. God has chosen for me, and I must honor my father's wishes." He paused. "As must you."

Celia's father was preparing to announce how he was always willing to honor God's wishes when he saw The Prophet's eyes flicker toward his wife. He looked to his wife as well. She hadn't spoken since they had sat down at the table. She didn't speak now. They all stared at her, The Prophet, her husband, and her daughter. She stared back, silent.

"You mean—"

"God wants me to take a wife, Brother Waters. He wants me to take your wife as mine. God asks sacrifices of us all. He tested Abraham by asking him to kill his only son. And Abraham was willing to do what God asked. You must decide if you are willing."

"I don't—It's not that—Ain't it, I mean, isn't it her choice?"

"A wife will go where her husband commands. The Lord has commanded she be the wifely companion of The Prophet and Savior," The Prophet said, referring to himself in double third person.

"I don't understand," Celia's father said.

"It is not for us to understand, only to obey. God has chosen your wife to be the mate of his son's second coming. She is to play a part in our salvation."

Her father looked back and forth between The Prophet and his wife enough times for it to be comical. "I think she and I should pray over this," Celia's father suggested.

"The Almighty has already decided this issue. If you refuse, I'm sorry, but you must be cast out." There was a pause. "So sayeth the Lord," The Prophet added.

This command from the Lord was both awful and flattering, though her father wasn't supposed to think it was either. Not awful, because what God decreed could not be so. Not flattering, because that implied The Prophet coveted Celia's mother, which was a sin, something the Second Coming of Christ was incapable of. There was a long silence.

"If—if it be his will," Celia's father said quietly. "His plan has led me to the path of righteousness. I'll continue to follow it."

There was a loud scrape as Celia's mother pushed her chair back from the table. The Prophet's new wife stood up, her face still impassive and unreadable, and made her only contribution to the conversation thus far.

"I'll pack."

The Prophet thought God wouldn't mind if Celia's parents took a little time to say their good-byes. "I shall return to the house while you ready yourself," he said to his new bride. "Gardner will help you with your stuff." He turned to his henchman/apostle. "Wait outside if you would, Gardner. So they can take a little time to give thanks."

No thanks were given, and their byes weren't good. Celia sat at the table, immobile, and watched as her mother stalked around the cabin, shoving things into a bag. She filled a duffel with clothes and opened the front door. "Heads up, Gardner," she said, and tossed it over the porch railing at him. She shut the door and got a second bag, which she began to fill, starting with her coffee mug. Then she moved into the bathroom.

This was how it went. Her father loved God and The Prophet. He had come this far. He had turned his life over to this love for the two of them. If he refused this request, then what was he saying? That he didn't believe as strongly as he claimed to believe? That he had moved out here to this farm at the behest of a charlatan? His faith was not dissimilar to the car engines he had taught himself to fix. Everything had to be uniformly tight. Loosen one bolt and you get a rattle. A rattle turns into a shake. A shake loosens something else that begins to rattle. If her father denied the sanctity of this request, then he was saying he didn't believe it came from God's authority. And if this didn't, what else that Barrett had told him, told any of them, was untrue? If he didn't believe this was a real request from God—and you can't just go around turning God down, can you?—then maybe gays and environmentalists weren't evil either.

Maybe God wasn't watching and weighing their every action. Maybe he didn't have to go to church. If her father loosened this bolt of his faith, what else might begin rattling? No, he had come too far. Everything had to be uniformly tight. He loved God and The Prophet, and now he was a man living on the other side of admitting he loved them more than having his wife.

What about his wife? If you had been watching through the window, you might think her reaction was basically no reaction. But her husband knew better. His wife had a reaction to everything. Sympathetic, volcanic, passionate, enraged: all reactions he had come to know, that he was able to read. The first time he had seen her in that parking lot, her legs scissoring back and forth on the way to her car, he knew he wanted a reaction out of her. He asked her out and she laughed right in his face, and that had been enough. He was back the next day to get another reaction out of her, and that had been his happiness ever since, to make her notice him; even after years of marriage, her attention was all he ever sought. Until Barrett came along. Now he stood stunned, amazed by the choice he had made. Celia watched as he lit cigarettes and set them in ashtrays, where he forgot them, then lit new ones.

Celia sat at the table, watching. Why wouldn't her father do something? Or her mother? Either. Why didn't one of them call a halt to this? Her incapable father stood, gawking, with cigarettes burning down all around him. Her mother kept packing, her face placid and expressionless. Celia felt as though her father had been driving them all down a winding road along a cliff face. A road with no guardrail. Now, suddenly, the steering wheel had torn loose in his hands, and at the same moment, a swarm of bees slipped through the window.

At last her mother collected the final item and zipped the second bag. She turned and stared down her husband. Waiting for anything. A final chance.

"I'm—I'm sorry he has to take you—"

"He isn't taking me," Celia's mother said, calm and flat. "I'm leaving you. I stood by you. I knew you as a strong man and husband, but you, you just couldn't see or feel it yourself until you found God. I'm the one who believed. I believed in you and knew you were good, and God came along and got all the credit. And now you're just—you're just—you're gone. There's no you there for me anymore." She crouched down in front of Celia, still rooted in her chair. She spoke just above a whisper. "I'm sorry, baby. I'm so sorry. But you'll see. It's going to be OK. I'm going to take care of things, and you'll come and stay with me up at the big house. Right now you'll stay here with your dad until I can—" Here she paused, her mouth trying to form the words for a plan that didn't exist. "Until I can figure things out." She put her arms around Celia and squeezed. "I love you so much, baby. I'm going to make it better for us. You'll see."

Celia's mother stood and wiped her eyes. She picked up her bag and headed for the door.

"It's what the Lord wants," Celia's father offered feebly as she passed him.

Her mother stopped at the door. "The Lord has no wants, darlin'. Only men have those. That's what assholes like you don't understand." The door shut, the porch groaned, and she was gone.

Celia did not get up and go to the front window, but she could picture her mother and Gardner walking up that path, Gardner carrying her bags, the house like an E from an eye-exam chart waiting at the top. The big house sat only slightly higher than the rest of the property, but in her mind's eye, Celia pictured them trudging dramatically upward, climbing away from her and her father.

So this was love, Celia thought. Love was a house with rooms painted in whatever colors you wanted. Then one day all your favorite reds, and oranges, and yellows came to embody the fire they represented, burning the whole place down with you in it.

"You saw it when you were out there," The Prophet said, marching left and right on his dais. "You saw it with your own eyes. Sodom and Gomorrah right in your own towns, right on your own streets, before your very eyes. Faggots. Baby-killing abortionists. Illegals. Minorities who don't work and contribute only violence to our nation. Pornographers. Pot smokers and drug fiends. You've seen these sinners presented to you as victims. As a persecuted class. They want to pass laws that protect their baby murdering. Their drugs, their right to sneak into this nation illegally, which makes them criminals, outright international criminals, their right to produce smut, their right to marry and sanction their filthy sodomy. You've seen with your own eyes the direction society is taking."

Celia's mother sat to the side of the dais, facing the congregants. She was set apart from the rest of them physically, but she was also apart from them in appearance. Her dress was simple but new and well-made, while the rest of their clothes were grim and worked-in. She had showered somewhere proper. Somewhere with water pressure, unlike the farmhouse she used to inhabit, and definitely somewhere better than the tin trough Gardner, Harlan, and Stacy used or the communal showers Kent had rigged up for the rest of them. In the summer the cool water they bathed in was fine, welcome even, but in the winter a fire had to be built and maintained to get any hot water, so the residents designated two days a week for showering with a rotating crew manning the fire.

Celia waved to her mother. Her mother stared back into the crowd, blank.

"Yes, you've seen it for yourselves," The Prophet went on. "Society standing on the verge of collapse. And rest assured, brethren, society will crumble. It will topple under the weight of all this disgusting sin and criminality. And those who look back and mourn for it will not merely be turned to pillars of salt. No. Not this time. They can look forward to simmering in the scalding pain of hell, tortured and mutilated servants of Satan, for all eternity."

Celia and her father sat in the front, but on the far side of the dais from her mother. Her father kept his eyes closed and his hands raised slightly, palms up, as though receiving this message from God as a beggar. His devotion, since his wife's departure, had tripled. He threw himself into prayer and work. Everyone else on the farm couldn't believe how totally blessed Celia's father had gotten. "It's an incredible honor," Rebekah's father had said, later the night Celia's mother had left. "To have God, and God's returned son, recognize your family in such a way..." He trailed off, unable to even articulate the fortune of having The Prophet take one's wife for himself. "God truly holds you in his bosom," Beaufort said before the gathering. Many others had come up to Celia and her father as Beaufort had done to say how blessed their family was to have a member chosen as The Prophet's companion. How they wished they too could be chosen in some way. Some other way, of course. It would be vanity to hope for a blessing as great as Celia's and her father's.

Celia and her father had quickly fallen into a living arrangement that was closer to roommates than parent and child. Celia both pitied and hated him. It was impossible not to feel bad for him. In his typical way, though, he managed to lose even the sympathy garnered from being a man deserted by being a man of inaction. Celia had trouble concentrating on the events that had transpired. When she tried to think about her mother leaving, about her becoming the companion of The Prophet, about her father alone in his bedroom at night and at the breakfast table in the morning, her brain simply wouldn't follow. It would suddenly take interest in a squirrel glimpsed at the edge of the woods or it would circle endlessly around some snatch of song lyric she remembered. She didn't want to think about it. She didn't want to deal with it, and she believed, firmly, that she shouldn't even be expected to. They shouldn't have brought this into her life. It wasn't right to ask your child to comprehend the meanings and feelings that went into something like this. So for now she drifted. Her parents' division manifested itself as a dull ache in her chest whenever she came too close to dealing with it.

"Oh, brethren," The Prophet said. "Be assured, society as we know it will crumble. The streets will run with the blood of sinners."

Celia was assured. She had never been so assured of anything. The Prophet was always right. Like with her mother. The Prophet said God wanted her to be his companion. Her father believed it, so it came true. The Prophet told them all they were strong enough to turn their backs on the world. Strong and faithful enough to turn over all their finances, whatever they had, to him to run and maintain the farm, to provide fuel and provisions, and they believed it, so it came true. The Prophet said. They believed. Prophecies turned true. God's word came to pass.

God spoke to The Prophet and commanded that Celia be allowed to visit her mother in the big house whenever she felt like it. One morning Celia dug her coat out for the first time that fall. She opened her bedroom window, perched on the sill like a bird, then spread her arms for balance and dropped the short distance to the ground. Her father wasn't home, but she came and went through the window almost exclusively now. She liked having her own entrance. It made her room feel more like an apartment.

She walked the path to the big house. It was the narrowest and least traveled of all the footpaths worn into the land. She turned halfway and looked back over the farm. There was the old farmhouse she shared with her father. Gardner's shack and pop-up were just beyond that. Gardner's shack was finally finished, but he was nowhere to be seen. Off somewhere, maybe with her father and some others, hunting or tilling or fixing or building. Whatever work there was to be done. Past Gardner's place was the Town Square, as they called it, where everyone else had arranged their campers, trailers, and shacks in various states of completion. Beyond that was the barn where Trevor lived and the covered amphitheater where they held services. Past that were the fields.

Celia let herself into the big house. The wide living room was neat and unused. She passed through it to the hall that connected the wings of the house and entered the one in the middle. Halfway down the corridor, she found her mother's room on the left. It was one of the rooms Celia had thought looked like guest rooms on her initial exploration. The companion of The Prophet was granted one of these rooms as her own. It was large. Even with the bed there was room for a love seat and a chair, along with a dresser, a wardrobe, and a vanity. It had its own bathroom.

The place was a disaster. Celia's mother had abandoned her love of a clean house along with everything else, tossing it out of her heart somewhere between the cabin and this room when she left. Celia imagined it sprouting into an orderly bed of unpleasant black flowers along that narrow pathway. Her mother sat in front of the vanity on a stool, picking through makeup at random, scattered sticks and tubes and compacts, and applying it in the giant mirror that stretched the width of the faux-marble top that was really plastic. She rubbed rouge into her cheeks, filling them with air as she did it, like a squirrel storing beauty away for the winter. She sat up straight when she was done and turned her head back and forth, checking each side. The jerkiness of the motion made it look like she was listening for predators. Then, with no indication of approval or contempt, she tossed the compact back onto the dresser and removed the makeup with a cotton ball and pitched it into a corner with a dozen others. A pile of white commas separating the list of ways her face had looked that day.

"Hey, Cee-bear," her mother said after Celia stood in the doorway for a moment. Her mother's eyes watched her through the mirror. Her childhood nickname felt cold and dead in her ear, like the wet willies Sloane used to wake her up the morning after a sleepover. "Well, don't just stand there. Come take a load off." She gestured to the couch. "Have a seat." The love seat was covered with dresses as usual. At first, Celia hadn't wanted to visit. She was embarrassed in front of her parents. Embarrassed for them. They were too old to become new people with new habits. The only habits that looked right on them were the ones she had grown accustomed to, the ones they had worn into each other over the years, polished smooth by the flow of their lives together, like a rock in a stream. Separately, their attempts at personhood were too clear, and the effort was an embarrassment. Celia hated to see them trying.

The first time Celia visited, there were three dresses. Her mother was wearing jeans and a long-sleeve top, her usual clothes. "Barrett gave me these," she had said, holding up a dress made of red material that caught and held light in its ripples and folds. She pressed the dress against her body and thrust one leg out, the top of the hanger making a question mark over her nose and mouth. She gave herself a once-over in the mirror. "I don't know if he expects me to wear them around the house or what." She tossed the dress back over the arm of the love seat. "But I'd feel like a prize ass walking around in the middle of the afternoon in one of them, so if that's what he's expecting, he's about to discover the first disappointment of this union." The dresses multiplied along with Celia's visits. The rest of her mother's clothing dwindled. Now Celia most often found her in just her robe, the television playing in the background.

The TV played a daytime talk show now as Celia took a seat amid the pile of unloved dresses. In it, women with ridiculous names found out that their men with equally ridiculous names had been unfaithful to them. The host asked questions in a disapproving tone that tried but failed to elevate her above the situation she had created for entertainment. The audience assailed the show's guests from the safety of their seats. Small print at the bottom of the screen kept television viewers just tuning in updated on the events. "Joebelle caught Zipper cheating on her with her best friend in a Dress Barn parking lot," it read as Celia sat down and watched her mother curl her eyelashes.

"Do you want something to eat?" her mother asked her. "You can make yourself whatever you want in the kitchen, you know."

"I'm fine," Celia said.

"Is your father eating?"

"I guess."

"I suppose you wouldn't let him starve."

"You got more dresses."

"The hits keep coming. He's ever seen me wear one, but he keeps buying them for me." She sighed and turned her head back and forth, examining her latest application. "Must be a pretty special gift."

Celia turned the word *buying* over in her head a few times. It had been a while since she'd heard anyone use it. She knew Barrett left the farm once a week for supplies. He left in the morning and returned late in the day. He brought back sugar, multivitamins, and other things they couldn't produce themselves. He also brought clothes for the citizenry. The clothes were secondhand, picked up from the Salvation Army or Goodwill. Celia's mother's dresses were actually new. They were made of nice material and were well-sewn. Being in their presence made Celia feel grimy. Barrett must buy them for her when he makes the supply run, Celia thought.

"You keeping up with your studies?" her mother asked.

"Yeah. Every day," Celia said automatically. She didn't know what her mother thought she was studying, but she had learned to just answer in the affirmative.

"That's good. You keep on that. What's that you got?" Her mother squinted at the item Celia was clutching in her hand.

"It's your tape player," Celia said. She had carried it over in the pocket of her coat and had been holding it since she sat down, waiting for her mother to notice. Before, when they were all living in the farmhouse, her mother had kept the player, along with her tape collection, in the bottom of a box of clothes under the bed. It would happen like this: Her mother would wake from her spot on the couch with a trace of her old energy. She would smile at Celia and dart her eyes around the cabin with a cartoonish exaggeration, checking to see if they were being watched. Her mother would stand and scurry to the door, flipping the bolt. She would peek through the curtains for a moment then snap them shut, looking around the room like they were about to discuss state secrets and had to secure the premises. Celia's heart would pump blood-hot excitement over this giddy childishness. It was stupid, but it was her mother as she used to be, and

Celia was instantly sucked in. Her mother would tiptoe absurdly into her bedroom and snatch the tape player out of the box, pressing play and running back into the living room, where she'd make an abrupt stop and slide across the floor in her socked feet. The song would kick on, always the same one from the *Dirty Dancing* soundtrack, the singer's voice dropping into the gloomy farmhouse all at once. "Baaaaaaaaby. Oh-oh, baaaaaaaby. Ooooooooh, baaaaaaaby. You're the one." Her mother would grab her hands. Celia always feigned exasperation, but only for a second, and they'd dance, hopping around in circles, twisting their hips, total shrieking abandon, flailing and uninhibited. They would dance nonstop through the song, then her mother would shut it off, toss it in the box, and kick the thing back under the bed.

They never talked about it. Everything at the farm was talked about. It was all discussed. They named behaviors and actions and talked about whether they were righteous. Everything was judged. Caffeine, smoking, wanting to write a letter to family out in the secular world, missing TV, wanting new pants—everything had to be spoken, admitted, so they could decide if it was acceptable or a sin. How else would they know? It was why they were there. Celia and her mother's secret wasn't the music or the dancing; it was their refusal to let it be judged.

"I brought it for you," Celia said now, holding the tape player out to her mother. She had made sure the *Dirty Dancing* soundtrack was in it before she left the cabin. She felt stupid digging the thing out, caring about it, checking the tape. She hadn't known how to bring it up to her mother. "I thought you might want to play it. Or whatever. I thought you just forgot it. Dad would just toss it out if he found it, so…"

"Geez Louise and peas," her mother said, taking the small device from her. She turned it over in her hands, opened the tape slot, closed it again. "Remember when we used to have to hide this?" She shook her head and rolled her eyes. "So silly. All that." She tossed the tape player onto the bed and swiveled back around to her mirror. "Go ahead and play it if you want."

Celia didn't want to play it anymore. She was embarrassed. Angry. Her mother shook a small white pill from an orange bottle and popped it into her mouth. "They're for my nerves," her mother said when Celia asked. "I have a lot of anxiety, being companion to The Prophet and all that." Celia knew her mother would need a nap in about twenty minutes. She stood up and snatched the tape player off the bed. She stuffed it back into her coat pocket. "Where are you going?" her mother asked.

"The kitchen. I'm hungry."

"Bring me a bottled water when you come back, would you?" her mother called after her.

Celia didn't go to the kitchen. She wandered down the third hall. She stopped at the door to Barrett's room and looked inside. The bed was rumpled and clothes littered the floor. Again, the TV was on with the sound off, playing a twenty-four-hour news station. Several parts of the farm had electricity, like their own house, and Celia's father and the other workers were always in the middle of running power to the other parts for heat, hot water, and light, but no one else was allowed to have television. "Doesn't matter if it's allowed or not," her father said. "Why would we want it? It's immoral. It's trash. It turns our minds to filth. No one should even want it, and if someone did, I would question his devotion to God, to his soul, and to this community." He had been holding court on the porch of their cabin. Celia listened to him from her room. Barrett was exempt from this rule, of course, because he was The Prophet and God had decreed that he needed a television to keep track of the horrors of the outside world. He didn't mention if God had given the OK for his companion to also have TV to watch daytime talk shows, but no one really knew what Celia's mother was up to in the house, and since she was out of sight most of the time, it didn't occur to them to wonder.

Celia stuck her head into Barrett's grotto, as she had come to think of it, checking the corner where he had first surprised her to make sure that didn't happen twice. It was empty. The hot tub sat quietly covered in the winter sun. She went to the last door in the hall and looked inside. Barrett's office. The Prophet sat at his desk at his computer. Internet was also an evil the rest of them happily went without, the better to avoid the temptation of the outside, but God had given his prophet the thumbs-up on this, too. There were fast-food wrappers overflowing from a trash can in one corner. The Prophet had grown rotund, putting on weight as though for the winter ahead. Great stores of flesh swelled under the long caftans he wore over sweatpants. His hair went uncut, tangling up and back, growing into itself and knotting. More little orange pill bottles dotted his desk like the towers of a nuclear-power plant.

Barrett stopping his web surfing suddenly, sensing someone watching him. He turned in his chair and saw Celia. She pressed against the doorframe and thrust one leg out. She said, "Hey."

Celia sprawled across the love seat in her mother's room, topping the pile of dresses, and listened as her mother rattled on about her husband. She was the companion of The Prophet now, but her husband was still her husband.

"Still running himself ragged around the farm, I'm sure. Smoking two packs a day like he thinks they'll get him to heaven faster."

"He quit smoking," Celia said.

Her mother stopped sawing at her fingernails with the file and stared at Celia with an expression Celia had never seen before. For a moment Celia thought she had dug the file into her skin and gotten it stuck. "He quit when?" her mother said.

"I don't know when, but I haven't seen him with a cigarette in a few weeks. If he's still smoking, it isn't in the house. The ashtrays are gone, too."

Her mother opened an orange bottle, took out two white pills, and dry-swallowed them. "So, what? He thinks he's Mr. Clean Living now? Well, we'll see how long that lasts. I've never seen the man go more than a day without a cigarette."

"You could if you left your room. He's out there. You could see the man without a cigarette for more than a day."

"No." Her mother crawled up the foot of the bed and made her way under the covers. "No, I'm done with that horrible farm. Barrett wants me to come when he preaches, fine, but that's it. There's nothing out there I need to see again." She lay back and was quiet. Celia stayed where she was on the love seat until the steady breathing from the bed told her her mother was firmly under.

Celia took her mother's usual spot at the dresser. She sorted through the jumbled makeup until she found the things she wanted and arranged them in a neat row. She did her eyes, then her eyelashes, then her lips. She tried on a few of the unworn dresses before finally settling on one that required a minimum of stuffing in the chest to look normal. Then Celia went to find Barrett. She was apprehensive. A knot was thumping in her throat, and it reminded her of the time she'd explored this house on the sly while her mother sat in the circle of followers believing she had gone to the bathroom.

The day before, when she had left her mother and gone wandering the halls, Barrett had welcomed her into his office. He'd given her a soda from a small refrigerator under his desk. Its sweetness provided an explanation as to why bumblebees were always bumping drunkenly through the air. She was instantly giddy from the sugar. He asked her questions about her day, if she liked visiting the house, what things were like on the rest of the farm during the day. His questions weren't accusations in disguise, like her father's ("You think it makes God happy to look down and see you filling your head with the garbage ideas of the secular world?" he'd said the first and last time she asked if maybe she could get some books.) They weren't questions about her father, like her mother's. The Prophet's questions were about her.

Celia found Barrett in his sanctuary. He was in an armchair near the large bookshelf that took up the whole right wall of the room. He looked up as soon as she appeared in the doorway this time.

"Hello, Celia," Barrett said. She crossed the room and sat in the chair across from his. "Your mother put herself down for her afternoon nap, I take it?"

"Yeah, she must have been exhausted from her morning nap," Celia said.

Barrett smiled. "She's been through quite a bit recently, your mom. It's worn on her some. You have to expect that."

"I do?"

"Coming to Christ is difficult. I can ask a lot of my people. Your father had a rough transition, too. I'm sure you remember."

"I remember everything that's happened from the moment you entered our lives," Celia said, studying Barrett's face. He opened his mouth as if to respond but hesitated. His eyebrows dipped slightly. For a second, she saw he was unsure, almost diffident. Celia added, "Christ drawing us in like that, it rescued us. I mean, you drawing us in like that. I don't—" Celia smiled and lowered her eyes. "It's hard to know how to talk to you now." She sat up very straight so her slouching wouldn't shift the stuffing at her chest.

Barrett's eyebrows went back to their regular place, and his mouth closed into a small smile. If he recognized the dress she was wearing as one he had bought for her mother, he didn't mention it. "You just talk to me the way you normally would. I've been sent to make your communion with God easier, not to leave you tongue-tied." He leaned toward her. "You are spiritually wise for such a young age."

Celia leaned forward as well. "I'm not that young."

"How has your homeschooling been going?"

"I just read the Bible. It's the only book we have."

"It's the only one you need."

"That's what my dad says. He says God shouldn't have to compete with the empty-headed bullshit of science." Barrett blinked a little at the profanity. "That's how he says it," Celia added.

Barrett laughed. "That's an aggressive way of putting it, I suppose, but he's right. My father is a jealous God, as I'm sure you've read." Celia nodded. "He wants no other gods before him. That includes science and its perverse desire to explain God away."

"But that doesn't make sense."

"What doesn't make sense?"

"That God is a jealous god."

"It says in the Bible that—"

"Envy is one of the seven deadly sins. How could God commit one of the seven deadly sins? Not only how could he commit one, how could one be a part of his personality?"

"You have questions," Barrett said. Celia didn't think it was much of a question. That this, among other things, didn't make any sense was a fact as she saw it. But she wanted this man's attention. She wanted his focus, the way he was focusing on her now, taking her seriously, giving her the full measure of his thoughts. If "questions" were the way to get it, then so it would be. Barrett went on. "You've been reading the Word but with no guidance. Your father is busy, and your mother is…also busy, in her way." Celia's mother was about as busy as a sack of rocks, but she let it go. "And I see you're filled with desire. To learn."

Celia was filled with many desires, not all of which she recognized. But being in this wing of the house with Barrett, having someone to talk to, something to think about, all this tickled her sense of longing with the feather of relief, of satiation. Something, anything, different. Celia nodded that she was, indeed, filled with a desire to learn.

"Then I guess I'll see you tomorrow," Barrett said, and nodded toward the door with a smile, indicating that for now she should see herself out. Celia got up and headed for the door. "Oh," Barrett said as she went. Celia stopped and turned. "You look very pretty today," he said. He looked back down at his papers, and Celia went back to her mother's room.

Gardner was sitting on a log in the woods. Celia was walking with her thoughts, taking them for a stroll. She thought of Barrett and imagined what their meeting tomorrow would be like. Today her walk in the woods was devoid of anxiety…until she came across Gardner Creech squatting on a log with a rifle across his lap, chewing at a fingernail he seemed to hate. Celia stopped walking, and Gardner kept chewing.

"Heard you coming a mile away," Gardner said around the tip of the finger clenched in his teeth. "You ain't never gonna be able to track nothing clomping around like that."

"I don't track things," Celia said.

"You don't do much of anything," Gardner said. He bit off the piece of himself he'd been working loose and spat it into the leaves. "But eventually you're gonna have to contribute. Your daddy sure likes to lend a hand. Can't turn around without near stepping on him. You and your momma didn't get none of that off him, it seems." He thought for a moment. "Y'all two are more like Beaufort."

What a turd, Celia thought. No wonder his wife gave him the heave-ho.

"My mom is the companion of The Prophet," she told him. "And I'm just a kid. And Beaufort…" She tried to think of some excuse for Beaufort but couldn't come up with anything. "Well, Beaufort's got shingles. They're really painful."

"Pshhht. You ain't no kid. You're just lazy. You want me to teach you to hunt? I'll do it."

Her and Gardner alone in the woods, him whispering in her ear to keep from spooking some poor creature they were about to destroy. No thanks. "I don't think I'd like that," she said.

Gardner snorted and shook his head. "Your daddy's doubled down in his efforts since your momma went to live with The Prophet. Man's up at dawn, working and praying all day, talking up the beauty and grace of The Prophet's vision, how blessed we are."

"We are blessed," Celia said, defensively slipping on her Celia the Chosen One persona. She didn't know what Gardner was after. Or why he was even talking to her. "God has found us worthy. Through us he will enact the revelations in the Bible."

"No doubt, little sister, no doubt. The prophecies of the Bible will come to pass. Sure I know it. But there ain't really any Bible stories where a woman gets thrown in the mix and it makes everything work out, are there? Eve, Delilah, Bathsheba, Mary Magdalene." He spat again. "And now your momma."

"What are you even doing out here?" Celia didn't care much for her parents these days, but she didn't want to hear anyone else voice the same opinion.

"I was here first," Gardner said. "You're the one came traipsing through my peaceful moment." He reached behind the log he was sitting on and hoisted up five dead rabbits strung together on a line. "I was checking my snares. These ones here," he pointed out the four at the top of the line, "came through the rabbit run hustling. You can tell 'cause their back or neck is broke. The trap caught them farther back 'cause they were running. But this one here," he said, jabbing at the fifth one, hanging pathetically at the end of the line, "he walked right up to the thing. Investigated it, sniffed at it, whatever. Got his head bashed in." Gardner looked away from his kills to Celia. "I'll show you how to gut and skin them. Their fur'll make nice mittens."

Celia shook her head. "I got to go." She turned to go back the way she came, put this jerk behind her.

"Not like that," Gardner called. Celia stopped and turned. "You got to sort of edge away while keeping an eye on me. And you want to walk that way first, so I ain't facing you." He stood and gathered up his dead rabbits. "You don't want to learn much, but I can at least teach you this: Don't ever put your back to someone holding a gun." He went past her, putting her to his own back.

"It's the kind of thing you really oughtn't have to tell people," Celia heard him mutter as he moved off into the woods, heading back to the farm.

"So what have you learned so far?" Barrett said. "From the Bible."

Celia had learned that the Bible was dense and boring and that was probably why most people were content to let someone else read it and tell them what it meant. But this was Celia the Chosen One talking to Barrett The Prophet, so that was no kind of acceptable answer. She lobbed out a generality. "I learned the word of the Lord is a deep current that flows through every aspect of our lives. That his love is…" Barrett raised his hands for her to stop.

"Celia, you can talk to me like a friend. Christ wasn't always serious, and neither am I. He was a friend to his disciples. He laughed and joked with them all the time. He was really funny."

"I don't remember him being funny in the Bible."

"Well, the Bible doesn't say that exactly."

"Then how do you know?"

Barrett raised his eyebrows at the question. "I'm his return. The second. Therefore I know, intimately, about the first: Jesus."

"Oh. Right."

"So let's loosen up a little." He took her by the shoulders and gave her a gentle shake. "C'mon, there we go. Get loose." He kept shaking her, and Celia began to giggle. "That's right, shake all that seriousness out." The top of her mother's dress shifted against her skin. The socks she had rolled and stuffed in the chest to fill it out rubbed back and forth, tickling. She couldn't stop giggling. "Yes, yes," Barrett crowed above her. "Get it all out and relax." The shaking stopped, but he kept his hands resting on Celia's shoulders, standing above her in her chair. Celia's giggles subsided, and she caught her breath. She looked up into Barrett's crooked face, the autonomous eye, the twisted smoke of his hair. He was still gaining weight and appeared heavy and powerful. He smiled down at her. "I have an idea," he said. "Something to relax us both."

Ten minutes later, Celia found herself in a large black T-shirt easing into Barrett's hot tub. Her mother's dress was on the floor in a corner of Barrett's bathroom where she had changed out of it. Barrett was already neck-deep in the water wearing a bathing suit. He had lent her the shirt. The tub steamed in the cold air, and the contrast between it and the water made Celia feel as if she were stepping down into a fire that licked its way up her legs as she lowered herself, inch by inch, onto the seat. She tucked the shirt down around her legs, though Barrett wouldn't have been able to see her underwear through the bubbles even if it drifted up a little.

"That's better, isn't it?" Barrett said. "Makes things a little more informal." He stretched out and his foot brushed Celia's leg. He settled back into his seat. "My predecessor would have loved this," he said. "Though he probably would have turned it all into wine." He threw Celia a wink. "So yesterday you mentioned that it didn't make sense for my father to be a jealous god. Is that right?"

Celia nodded. "Jealousy—envy—is one of the seven deadly sins."

"And God shouldn't be able to commit a sin."

"Right."

"And what is sin, exactly?"

"What do you mean?"

"Just that. What. Is. Sin. What is it? How would you describe it?"

Celia felt the T-shirt she was wearing rise along her sides, carried by the bubbles. It caught and pooled under her arms. She didn't pull it back down, instead relishing the thrill of her legs, underwear, and stomach being uncovered in front of this man while staying hidden beneath the screen of water, broken white and churned by the jets, ceaselessly breaching the surface. "A sin is any act against the Lord."

"Right. Any act against something my father commands. And that's where it ends." Celia didn't follow, and her expression must have said so, because Barrett went on. "To act against the Lord is to commit a sin, but who is the Lord going to act against? There's no one above him. He's the top of the food chain. He makes the rules and for you not to follow is a sin. But he doesn't have to abide by the same laws that govern you."

"God doesn't have to be moral?" Celia said.

"God created the world and imposes the rules of morality that are in it. There's no morality as we know it that acts upon him. The moral aspects of our faith, Celia, they're just a reflection of what's best for the group as a whole, for society. Their core value never changes, but their application and interpretation can vary. God lays down laws, and his leaders, his agents on earth, we put them to the people in the way that best serves them, and him. You decide what's best for the group, explain how that fits with the laws my father laid out, and that's morality. Thou shall not kill, for example. Well, of course not. Unless we are threatened by another group of people, like in a war. Then we may kill, and God will be on our side while we do. This is what your question is really about, I think. How can God say not to kill, then lead the Israelites to glory in battle? How can he say not to be envious and then be jealous? But my father is not held to his own decrees, and we appeal to him through our spiritual master here on earth to find out the situations in which we, too, are not held to them. Does that make sense?"

"But how do you know what those times are? How do you know which rules to obey and which to ignore? And when to do it?"

"He is my father," Barrett said, closing his eyes in rapture with either the Lord's grace or the warmth of the hot tub. "I know his will, and my exercise of it is pure and right. He takes care of my needs." The bubbles and jets abruptly quit. The water ceased rumbling and became calm and clear. Celia could see her own legs, white like fragile new roots, extending from the light blue triangle of her underwear. Barrett opened his eyes and also saw. She pictured herself from his side of the hot tub—the pale lines of her legs, the small blue border of fabric that divided them from her stomach with its inward curve from hardly ever eating, and the inescapable fact of her breasts, small but a reality, wrapped in wet black fabric, their bottom halves hidden in the bunched shirt and their top halves rising from the water like two dark moons. Barrett lolled on his side like a boiled ham. He sat up and lunged across the tub. Size and power came straight at her. Celia's breath caught, and she took a rush of pure adrenaline to the head, which pulsed slightly. But Barrett veered to her left and reached outside the tub for the timer. He cranked it once, the bubbling resumed, and he retook his seat.

"My father will take care of your needs, too, Celia," Barrett said. Celia herself couldn't claim to know what, exactly, she needed, but she thought it would be nice if that were true. If someone—God, her parents, Barrett, anyone—could figure out what she needed and arrange it for her. The idea was wonderful, really, the more she thought about it. "You're special, Celia," Barrett went on. "You and me, we aren't like them." He nodded in the direction of the farm, the people working and toiling outside the walls of Barrett's haven. "Our faith isn't like theirs. You know it. You can feel it. I know you can. They believe in God's power and cower before it. It explains away their pain and fears. His power makes their lives livable. They are humbled before it. You and I, on the other hand," he leaned forward and put a hand against her cheek. "We can wield it." He reached down and took her hand. "Think about that some." Barrett lifted their joined hands out of the water and turned Celia's palm toward him. He rubbed her index finger. "You're getting pruney. Better go check on your mother. Make sure she isn't wandering around the kitchen again." Celia stood up out of the water and hustled through the cold back to the house, grabbing a towel off one of the chairs as she went.

"Celia," Barrett called after her. She turned, shivering in the chill winter air. "Come back and see me tomorrow."

Celia changed back into her clothes in Barrett's bathroom. When she came out, he was not in his bedroom, nor his office. The door to the sunroom was closed as she'd left it. She guessed he was still out there in the hot tub. Her mother was facedown in bed, but Barrett was right about her wandering the kitchen. She was clutching a half-eaten slice of white bread.

Back at the cabin, Celia climbed through her bedroom window and listened. Silence from the other room. Her father was not home yet. Her day with Barrett hovered around her like a mist. The memory of his body across from hers in the hot tub, its proximity, agitated and excited her. Celia liked him, she realized. Coveted him, really. Wanted him to love her. She didn't want to hide in this crummy room anymore while her father skulked out in the living room.

Celia went to the kitchen and rummaged through the cabinets. She found the big pot, filled it with water, lit the stove, and brought it to a boil. She added pasta. When her father came in later, she was putting the finishing blob of ranch dressing on a salad, a carefully measured amount to make the bottle last as long as possible. "Hey," she said when he came in. She carried the bowl over the table and put it at his seat. "Wash up. The rest of this will be ready in a minute." Her father remained in the doorway, watching her. "You want to close that? Or are you hoping this pasta'll be as cold as it is outside?" He shut the door.

"What's all this?" he said.

"Dinner. You've been working all day. Aren't you hungry?"

"You just never made dinner before is all."

Celia shrugged. "Guess I never had to, but..." she said, gesturing around the room to suggest *but now all this*. Her father nodded. He went to the bathroom and washed his hands and came back to the table. Celia sat next to him. "Hurry up and bless it so you can start on that and I can finish the rest."

"You can't hurry through thanking the Lord," he said, intent on being his usual self.

"You can if you've already been working for the Lord all day and the pasta needs its sauce," Celia said calmly. She took his hand. "Go ahead."

Her father bowed his head and said a grace that was blessedly short. Celia went back to the counter and sauced the spaghetti. Behind her she heard her father crunching through his salad. It was gone in ten bites. Why did men do this? Why didn't they savor? Every bite was set at total capacity, every day crammed with as much work as could get done. Maybe it wasn't men. Maybe it was just *this* man. Perhaps Beaufort took small, dainty bites like a child.

Celia took away the salad bowl and replaced it with the spaghetti. She broke off a hunk of the bread they baked daily down in the Town Square inside the large outdoor oven Nancy-Lynn's husband, Biscuit, had constructed, and brought it over. She took her seat next to her father.

"You ain't eating?" he asked, forking the pasta over on itself a few times to let off some of its heat. The bowl steamed impressively. The cold cabin never quite warmed up all the way. There was a potbellied stove in one corner they kept burning through the night, but the heat it generated only traveled so far before it lost faith and converted to cold air.

"No, I ate a late lunch. Not that hungry. You eat, though. I'll just sit."

He went back to the pasta, dipping the bread into the sauce occasionally. He looked up halfway through his bowl and said, "This is good. Thanks for cooking," with the air of an actor who has just remembered his lines, forgotten way back, but now coming to him all at once as he finds the means to return to character.

"A man can't work a whole day and come home to no dinner." She'd heard her mother say that. Her mother also told her, "A man's never more content than when you make a meal only for him. If I make something just for your dad and don't have any myself, he looks at me with such relief you'd think he'd just been pardoned. Like it's the first thing he's gotten all day that wasn't a struggle." There were other gems on the subject of men and women: "Men run away from a problem they've created. Women run away from a situation they've got themselves into. And yes, there's a difference." After seeing her parents' behavior over the last year, that one was starting to make sense.

"You see your mom today?" her father said, not looking up from his bowl and appearing all the more pathetic for it.

"Yeah. I'm looking after her for us." Her father put his fork down abruptly and put his hand over his eyes. He sat that way a moment, then took his hand away. His face was dry. No tears. That was her father as she knew him. He sighed.

"I don't...It doesn't always make sense to me, you know? I try...I try to follow the Lord's plan, but I...I feel like..." He sat baffled before his meal.

"The Lord's plan doesn't have to make sense to us. It doesn't make sense why some flowers are yellow and some are red, does it? But you don't go around questioning it. You deal with what's in front of you, let him worry about the logic of it all."

"I feel like Job."

"Job had everything taken away from him. You still have a bowl of pasta." Her father looked up, scanning her face for sarcasm, pondering this statement. "You're not Job. The Lord wants us to appreciate the things we still have. That's what we have to do."

He nodded, cleared his throat, nodded again, and went back to eating. Celia sat with him until he was finished, scraping up every available remnant of sauce with his bread. He stood and said, "I'll wash up. Probably hit the hay after. It's been a long day."

Celia's mother stopped coming to the Service Gatherings. People talked the first time, the way they will when anything they experience as a collective changes.

"I hope your mother's feeling all right," May Altman said to Celia after the second no-show. The Prophet was more or less inaccessible, so questions and concerns went through Celia and her father.

"She certainly keeps Barrett shut up in that house all to herself," Geraldine said. "Of course, who can blame her? What a blessing to have access to that kind of spiritual energy all the time."

"The Prophet decides how he spends his time," Celia said. "And who with." She fixed Geraldine with a smile. "And does it with his father's blessing, obviously."

"Oh, yes, obviously," Geraldine said, quickly covering. "How could it be otherwise?"

"I hope you'll say a prayer for my mother sometime. You're right, May. She's been feeling a bit under the weather lately."

Geraldine and May both promised they would, and Celia and her father walked home. The next day Celia couldn't find Barrett anywhere in his wing. She checked his room, his office, and his sanctuary. Her mother had been loopy when Celia arrived, glassy-eyed and hard to speak to, off in the fog brought on by her orange bottles. Celia was sick of orange bottles, and she was sick of her parents eating what was in them. Her mother's room was becoming a second Crypt, with dresses piled on the love seat, clothes on the floor, and plates and glasses all over the nightstands. At least she didn't smoke, so there were no overflowing ashtrays to add to the funk.

Celia left her mother groggily brushing her hair and went off to find Barrett and hopefully take a soak. When he wasn't in his wing, she wandered the rest of the house. He occasionally ventured out onto the compound, visiting people's homes and checking out the work in progress. Not as often as he used to, certainly; Geraldine had been right about that, though she had been wrong about with whom he was spending his time. It was Celia, not her mother, who commanded his afternoons. Celia's mother hardly interacted with Barrett at all, a fact Barrett had lamented to Celia.

"The Lord has decreed that she be here, that she be my companion, but your mother, like all of us, still has her free will. It's up to her, ultimately, whether she follows the Lord's path or not," Barrett said one afternoon as he and Celia lay stretched on his bed watching TV. They were taking a break from Celia's lessons, a reward for her hard work, Barrett had said. His bed was soft and large. Celia slept on a cot, and the contrast in comfort was almost enough to put her to sleep on the spot.

"I don't think I've ever seen you two in the same room," Celia said.

"We used to have a stronger connection. She knew my father wanted her to be here, with me. But then, somewhere along the way…"

"Maybe she knew my father didn't want her to go," Celia said quietly.

Barrett rolled his bulk toward her. "Do you think that's true? That your father doesn't want her here?" Celia studied his face. There was an air of suspicion.

"My father serves the Lord, so he wants to do whatever the Lord asks. It's still a big change." Barrett's right eye studied the ceiling while the left stayed locked on Celia. "If the Lord wants her here, my father wants her here," she added.

This satisfied him. He turned to the TV with his good eye, the rogue going back to whatever it did, like a family member who always disappeared down into the basement. "Your mother, though, she's here now, that's the important part. She'll come around."

"Was there ever anyone else?" Celia said.

"Anyone else what?"

"Any other…companion. Before all this. Like a girlfriend or anything?"

Barrett didn't say anything for a long moment. Finally, he said, "I wasn't real popular in school. When I stopped going, I didn't have any plans or anything. Just odd jobs. Not the kind that impress anyone, especially women. When I finally received my calling, I focused on that, on my ministry, and I never met anyone. I worried about it some. So when God, my father, told me I was to take your mother as a companion, I don't mind saying it was a welcome order. It was nice to not have to think about that on top of everything else anymore." He rolled back toward her and took one of her hands in both of his. She rolled toward him as well so they lay like girls at a sleepover exchanging whispers. "Celia, I've never told anyone so much about my life, my past life before I was the Second Coming. Before I became all this. I'd appreciate it if you didn't tell anyone."

Celia nodded. "I never had a boyfriend or anything either," she said. "I wasn't popular in school either. Back when I used to go. I only had one friend, really. Sloane." Saying her name conjured Celia's longing for her friend. She wished she could visit her.

"We're very similar, you and me," Barrett said. "I knew you were special the first time I met you, I told you so. You remember?" Celia did. "I don't think other people understand us. People like you and me. They don't get us. We're different."

Celia agreed. The feeling was mutual as far as she was concerned. She didn't understand other people any more than she felt like they understood her. How could Barrett feel the same way though? He was the most popular person she knew.

"Everyone gets you though. They love you," she said.

Barrett smiled. "No, they love my father. They love my message. And that's beautiful, but they don't get the real me. The person inside who's conflicted, who has doubts. They only see what I present to them."

Celia understood. Her outward persona was generated based on the expectations of others, based on the situation, based on the mood in any given room. Suppression ruled her life. Every feeling tamped down and hidden, otherwise she'd be in constant conflict with every aspect of the world that existed around her.

Now, with Barrett nowhere to be found in his wing, Celia was about to leave. She stopped in the front foyer. She heard something. It sounded like voices coming from the unused part of the house, where they used to have Bible study before the amphitheater was built. Celia stood at the top of the hallway, keeping still so her clothes wouldn't rustle. It was definitely voices. Barrett must be having some sort of meeting. She could just come back later, or even tomorrow. Right now she could go see Trevor, or find Rebekah, or, and there wasn't a chance she was actually going to do this but the option did exist, have Gardner teach her how to hunt. She did none of those things, however. Celia hung at the lip of the hall for another few seconds then moved down it, slowly and quietly.

The voices grew from murmurs to actual words. They were coming from a room at the end of the hall. There was nowhere appropriate to hide, so Celia stood in the hall outside the closed door, heart hammering and face flushed. One voice was Barrett's, but she couldn't quite place the other one.

"Of course, you've always been incredibly devoted to Christ, devoted to what we're building here, a wonderful Christian." That was Barrett.

"Then speak with your father, please. I feel a stirring in my heart that says this is the right thing. I can't just ignore it, Barrett. It's too strong." It was a female voice, familiar.

Then it went quiet. Celia started to panic. If she couldn't hear them, they might pop out of the room at any second and catch her eavesdropping. Then she realized Barrett was actually, silently, talking with God. Asking about whatever it was this woman wanted. Barrett spoke up again. "My father wants to know what you see as the benefit to this. He wants to make sure you understand your own intentions."

"She isn't fulfilling the duties of a wife. She isn't being a good companion, you told me as much yourself. She's honoring God's command in a literal sense, but spiritually she's not." Geraldine, that's who owned the voice. And the *she* Geraldine was referring to was unmistakably Celia's mother. "I know you believe she'll get there on her own, that she'll come around, but this will push her there faster. It'll force her to step up and fulfill the role for which she was chosen or prove that she rejects God's orders."

"You think she would do that? Reject God's direct commandment?" Barrett sounded nervous.

"Oh, I have no doubt she'll respond appropriately. I think the Lord is pushing this on me, and believe me, it came as a total shock when I began to get this…this, well I don't want to say message, because those are what you get and this is nothing like the direct connection you have, being the Son of Man reborn, but a push. Yes, it's a push. Like God maybe reached down and gave my heart a little nudge with his finger. And I think he's pushing me this way to fulfill his original command. If she sees someone else upholding her side of the relationship, being devout and following God's will with joy and devotion, then she'll follow suit. I believe the Lord wants me to do this to complete his plan, to bring you companionship, to make you happy, and if that's the case I accept. I'm his and your willing disciple, because I love him and you."

There was a long pause, and Celia pictured Geraldine's face, expectant and pleading, watching Barrett as he closed his eyes and talked all this over with God, his face pitched upward. Finally he said, "Yes, Geraldine, my father put this stirring in your heart. He and I were waiting to see if you understood and you do. You understand completely."

The chicken squawked and flapped aimlessly. It couldn't fly, and no other chickens rushed to its aid as Stacy Harmon batted it gently out of the way and scooped up its eggs four at a time in her strong fist. Her knuckles wore the white char of a dry winter across them, like snow capping a mountain range. Her fingernails almost didn't exist, just tiny semicircles embedded at the cuticle like baby teeth. Celia followed behind her holding a basket to her chest, both arms wrapped around it. Everyone on the compound was a forgiver, or at least declared themselves such as Christians, but you didn't want to be on the receiving end of all that forgiveness if you dropped the egg basket. The community was entirely interconnected. A mistake affected everyone. Drop the egg basket and everyone knew when they didn't have any eggs. Forgiveness was an accusation, an assault, when thirty-odd people smacked you with it all together. Better to not drop the basket with all their eggs.

"I ain't seen not hide or hair of Ger'dine in almost five days," Stacy said. "She gen'ly comes 'round e'ery other day or so. Helps me with the eggs, feedin', regular chores. She ain't sick, is she?" Stacy put a handful of eggs in the basket and gave Celia a look of genuine concern. Just in the head, Celia thought. But she said, "No. Or anyway, I don't know. I just haven't seen her."

Celia hadn't told her mother, or anyone else, what she'd heard transpire the day before between The Prophet and Geraldine. She was launching an investigation. Celia the Chosen One, Girl Detective. She was pitifully confused. Did she like her parents being split up? No. But did she like them at all? No, but she wanted to. She didn't like her parents much anymore, but they were still her parents. She felt the need to protect and defend her family, despite it being a crappy one. She didn't like Geraldine maneuvering against her mother. She also didn't want Geraldine gaining entry to the big house. The current situation there was to Celia's liking. Her mother, though sad, broken, drugged, self-centered, and distant, was still not really with Barrett. She kept to her room. This gave Celia unfettered access to Barrett and his hot tub, to the dangerous flirtation that sparked between them, to the comfortable bed and the television. Sure, she had to listen to a lot of God-talk, but she got to ask questions, and Barrett seemed to be trying to explain something to her, something he didn't talk about in his sermons. Her mother was physically present and mentally absent. Geraldine wouldn't be so easy.

Celia left Stacy with all their eggs in one basket and walked through the Town Square. Rebekah and her mother were hanging laundry behind their place. The Eubankses had arrived with a small camper. Since their arrival they had cut out the back wall and added on, creating a small bedroom for Rebekah, a pantry, and a workroom. Celia grabbed the other end of a freshly laundered sheet and helped Rebekah pin it to one of the clotheslines.

"Celia, greetings in Christ," Mrs. Eubanks said.

"God's blessings," Celia responded.

"How are your studies coming along?"

"They're fine. I have the day off today." Mrs. Eubanks moved off to hang her husband's work shirts.

"Have you seen Aunt Geraldine lately?" Celia asked Rebekah in a whisper.

"No," Rebekah whispered back, not knowing why but taking the lead from her idol. "She hasn't been here in a few days."

"How many?"

Rebekah shrugged. "I don't know." She made a thoughtful face. "I don't know how many days anything is anymore. We used to do the calendar in school, but we don't have one in the camper."

"When are you done with your chores?"

"When the sun gets to there," Rebekah pointed west. "At the top of that tree. Mom says I can go play then." There were other children at the farm now. Celia had seen Rebekah playing with them in the evenings, either from the front porch of the cabin or on her solo trips along the forest's edge.

"You want to go on a mission with me when you get done?"

"Sure, what is it?"

"I'll tell you when I come back. Meet me over by where that cat lives," Celia said, referring to the farm cat no one owned but everyone tolerated because it pulled its weight killing and eating mice. Since it was a cat, it more or less lived everywhere, but it, too, had routines and liked to bed down in a small hollow under the floor of the amphitheater.

"Bye, Mrs. Eubanks," Celia called trotting off.

"Oh. OK, bye, Celia. Say hello to your mother for me."

"OK."

Celia crossed Town Square, waving to everyone she saw. She stopped at the Laundry Shack, which, despite its name, was a sturdy and newly built structure. Inside, eight washing machines churned through the compound's dirty clothes while their owners waited and chatted. Someone with a knowledge of electricity had "tapped the grid," as Celia had heard it described, and wired up most of the homes at this point, as well as the Laundry Shack. Gardner and Celia's father had found the machines somewhere, either salvaged and repaired or bought secondhand. She helped load and unload machines for a while, politely promising to take hellos and how are yous to her mother and casually asking after Geraldine. No one had seen her in a week outside of The Prophet's services. And how was her mother doing, exactly, they wanted to know. Well, they said, certainly hope she's doing well. It must be such a blessing, to be chosen by The Prophet to leave your husband like that and take on such a responsibility as...well, as being The Prophet's companion. Whatever that responsibility is, it must surely be great, but also, maybe a little overwhelming. Was she overwhelmed? Her mother? And her father, how strong his faith was! They never thought they'd live to see a man of such conviction. How was he handling it all? Strong as a rock, wasn't he? It's on rocks like him that God builds his churches. Says so right there in the Bible. But was he lonely at all? Did he want a little company? Oh not to imply anything, he and Celia had each other after all, but all the same, did Celia think he'd like a little company sometimes? Just good neighborly company.

Celia assured everyone that everyone else was doing great. That God's plan was good, that his work was a balm for the soul, that her father didn't need any company, thanks, and that each of them fully understood, believed in, and accepted God's part for them to play and that surely all of them, all of them here on the farm, were pleasing the Lord because look, washing machines! Right here on the farm, saving them toil. Now if that wasn't a sign from God, what was?

Celia waved good-bye to that henhouse and swung back by the henhouse where Stacy still hadn't seen Geraldine but gave Celia four eggs for her and her father. Celia took the eggs back home, where she turned them into a tin of fresh corn bread. She wrapped the corn bread in a clean cloth and marched down the path, through Town Square, and out to the amphitheater, where she found Rebekah already waiting, twirling a piece of pine straw for the cat, whom they had named Fred. Fred batted at the pine straw with bored half interest that said this was no kind of challenge for a tried-and-true mouser such as himself.

"C'mon, let's go," Celia said to Rebekah.

Rebekah laid the pine straw across Fred's head, sending him into a mad scramble to knock it off. Any mouse watching knows his weak spot now, Celia thought. Rebekah fell into step beside her. "What's our mission?" she asked.

"Our mission, should we choose to accept it, is to cheer Beaufort up," Celia said.

"Is Beaufort sad?" Rebekah said.

"I think he's probably feeling a little lonely."

"Sure nice of you girls to come over and visit me," Beaufort said. He was sitting on the RV's small couch on an inflatable doughnut, battling his hemorrhoids.

"How's the war against your ailments going?" Celia asked.

"It's tough. I suffer. I wish more than anything I could get out there and help. I'm envious of your fathers. But," he shrugged, "the Lord gave me hemorrhoids. And the gout. So here I sit. Tell me about your day, though. I bet you two have all kinds of fun out there. And you must be learning so much. Celia, how are your studies coming along?"

"I'm learning so much I can't even keep track of it all."

"Uncle Beaufort," Rebekah said. "My mom says hemorrhoids means your fanny hurts." Celia shot her a look. "What? She did," Rebekah said.

"It's OK," Beaufort said. "That's pretty much it, yes. It means my rear end hurts. I have to sit on this cushion."

Rebekah's hands moved to cover her own behind. "Are hamroids contagious?"

"Ha! No. You'll be OK. You can't catch them. It just happens sometimes when you get older."

"We brought you some corn bread," Celia said, placing her parcel on the small kitchen counter and unwrapping it.

Beaufort bounded up off the sofa, almost forgot his cane for his gout, snatched it, and moved quickly to the kitchenette. "Well, look at that. I'm going to have a piece right now. Can I cut some for you two as well?"

"No, thank you," Celia said. Rebekah shook her head. "We figured you might be hungry, what with Geraldine being out so much and you not being able to get up," Celia said. She watched Beaufort standing easily at the counter, shoving a piece of corn bread into his mouth. "Get up easily, I mean," she added.

"It's tough with my lack of mobility. But Gerry, she just goes and goes. It's in her nature. She's out pretty much all day doing chores, helping out at the laundry, all sorts of things. I think she spends most of the day with Stacy."

"Is that right?" Celia said.

"Oh yeah, I've hardly seen her at all the last few weeks."

Celia thought back to the end of all her "lessons" with Barrett. The sudden dismissals. The prompting to go check on her mother. She worried that Rebekah might blurt out something about Celia asking after Geraldine, but Rebekah was preoccupied with the safety of her backside. She'd covered it with her hands and was eyeing Beaufort's inflatable doughnut with distress.

"In the henhouse," Celia said. "With Stacy."

"That's what she tells me," Beaufort said, cheerily putting more corn bread in his face. "I hope y'all don't mind, but I'm going to finish this. I'm about hopeless in the kitchen and with Gerry not being around too much and all, it's been kinda bare bones." He swallowed the last slice of corn bread.

"I'm gonna wait outside," Rebekah said, jetting for the door. "In case my mom calls me. Bye, Uncle Beaufort." The narrow door to the RV opened, and there was a patch of daylight, then a flimsy slam.

"I don't think she believed me when I said they weren't contagious," Beaufort said, winking at Celia.

"I think you're right." Celia took the cloth she had wrapped the corn bread in and shook it out over the sink.

"Well, there's nothing you can do but let people believe what they believe until experience teaches them different," Beaufort said.

Celia wasn't too sure about that. Experience, in her experience, didn't convince anyone that what they believed wasn't true. Her father had let her mother go, let their family crack into pieces, like the corn bread Beaufort had just crumbled and eaten, and it only strengthened his belief. He needed his beliefs to be true now more than ever, to make all he had lost worth it. On the other hand, right now Beaufort believed his wife was down in the henhouse with Stacy. At the next service, in two days, if what Celia thought was going to happen actually happened, experience would teach him otherwise. Celia tossed the kitchen cloth over her shoulder. What did she know, anyway? Not much, she thought. Except, of course, where Geraldine had really been spending her time.

Celia said good-bye to Beaufort and left through the skinny RV door.

That night Celia made dinner for her and her father and led them in grace. They sat at the simple wooden table that had come with the house. The night sky through the windows was heavy with stars, the air clear and cold and still. The compound below them was quiet, its residents bundled into their homes.

"Heard you were out and about in the village today," her father said. His voice was flat, dinner chatter—almost like the old days, except that everything in the world separated them from those times, the way a war might divide a country into *before* and *after*, leaving what was left of its inhabitants passing one another the breadbasket with one wall and the roof of the house missing.

"I helped Stacy in the henhouse for a while. And I was at the laundry. Visited Beaufort with Rebekah."

"He's got hemorrhoids now, I guess."

"And gout."

"He's got the gout? Out of nowhere? Just developed the gout? Here on the farm? Dang if that man don't hate work."

Celia shrugged. "I guess so. And now he just can't help *gout* around the compound."

Her father exploded so hard with laugher a little food sprayed out of his mouth. It was a sound Celia hadn't heard in a while, one that belonged to their old house. It was almost sacrilegious here in the cabin. They were caught off guard by the moment, stunned by their ease in each other's company.

Celia suddenly hated how this moment reminded her of the way it was. The tension she had felt in her father's presence for so long was gone. It was something she could look at now as though from outside herself. A chunk of time in a glass box that she could look at and study, shaking it a little to make it roll over so she could see it from all angles. She had dealt with a situation, changed it. That time was a dog she had trained to no longer scoot its butt across the carpet of their interactions, but she felt betrayed by how far they had journeyed from normal. The moment lacked her mother, their cornerstone, who had left her corner, leaving them like a two-legged stool. The way her father laughed at her gout joke, it was the laugh that used to belong to no one but her mother.

The joking must have summoned the ghost of their matriarch for her father, too, because when he stopped chuckling, he said, "Did you go up and visit your mom today?"

Celia shook her head. "No, not today." It had been several days, in fact, though she wasn't really not visiting her mother, because her mother wasn't the reason she went up there in the first place. She was not visiting Barrett.

"How is she doing? When you do see her, I mean."

Celia usually just said "fine" when her father asked after her mother. She pretended their actions and decisions made sense to her, didn't affect her. The nearly normal moment that had just occurred, though, gave her pause now. She didn't want to pretend right that second. So she said, "I don't know."

"What do you mean, you don't know?"

"I don't know how she's doing. I don't know how I even would know. She lives up there with Barrett. You and I live here. And we all just pretend it's fine and that it's OK and—" Celia felt the knot in her throat, the irrefutable signal she was going to cry. If she kept talking, she would end up blubbering. She wouldn't be able to swallow, and her words would come out through thin threads of spit connecting her top and bottom lips. She stopped and stared at her plate, unsure of where to throw her emotions or how to put a cap on them.

"All right now, that's enough of that," her father said. Celia tried to choke it all back down, but it was too late, like vomit at the back of her throat she couldn't swallow. "Stop it now, I said." Her father gave her his stern voice, the self-righteous one. "You got no business talking like that or crying over the Lord's—" But her first sob broke and then so did he, his face falling back to its old shape, from when he knew how to love them without God's interference.

"Hey, hey, it's all right, take it easy, take a breath," she heard her father saying. She felt his hands on her shoulders. Her vision was blurry, so she was aware she was moving, but the motions were muscle memory, something her body knew so well from long ago that her brain felt confident forgetting it; she had crawled onto her father's lap, bawling. She gave up trying to control it. Her shoulders shook, and she couldn't close her mouth for the crying pouring out of it and the air she desperately sucked back in as replacement. She drooled. Celia was curled, near-fetal, under her father's chin and against his chest. She felt his heart beating steadily, evenly, against her neck, as though it were trying to communicate calm and ease to her racing pulse—trying to show her own internal machinery how it was done. Her father's body was softer than it used to be. The scalloped background of muscle and bone she had known from this same haven as a girl was still there, but a new softness surrounded it. He could thank his compromised spine for that.

Celia's sobbing slowed. Her breath came in stuttered rags, but the worst had passed. Her father's arms tightened around her, and the same muscle memory that had carried her onto his lap now stiffened her limbs so she'd be easier to carry. He had already hoisted her and taken a step before she remembered and said, "Your back. You can't."

"Hush now," he said. "If my back can't carry you, then I might as well have it ripped out entirely. I'll be fine." He carried her into his own room, the one he once shared with his wife. The air was cold where the warmth from the stove didn't carry. He laid her in his bed and pulled the blankets up around her. He used part of the sheet to wipe her face. "I know it's scary, baby. It ain't easy on me neither. But you gotta believe me when I say it's God's will. That's real. It's not like we got divorced. Or your mom or me ran off with someone else. She's with The Prophet, the Second Coming of Christ. That right there shows you God's hand in this. His approval." He pushed her hair back off her forehead. "Otherwise I wouldn't be able to take it."

Celia watched him above her. His shirt was wrinkled, a pack of Vantages outlined in the breast pocket (so much for quitting), and a streak of dust under his chin that she hadn't seen before, now visible in the lower light of the bedroom. He had stubble on his cheeks and neck because hot water was too long coming to shave every day, and flecks of gray visible in his sideburns just below his ball cap, the one he'd bought at that NASCAR race where he'd had a cooler full of food and beer and the blessing of his two ladies to go off and enjoy it while they watched on TV in case they got a glimpse of him, their man, who they'd only just seen that morning, somewhere in the throngs of thousands so they could say to each other, *There he is, that's him right there, that's our guy.*

"Get some sleep, baby," he said. "It'll all be OK. You'll see." He kissed her forehead and stood, left the room. She heard him clearing the table, dishes being washed in the sink, then the groan of the old couch as he sank into it and the faint smell of a cigarette, freshly lit, seeping through the walls.

Celia was embarrassed, but she felt better. Losing control had a certain reassuring quality as long as someone was there to pick up the reins and say it was all going to be all right, even if they were terribly wrong in that assertion. God's will: Celia was young enough, still close enough to being a subject in the kingdom of her parents, to see this phrase for what it was, the mustachioed twin brother of "Because I said so." It was a cover to keep from having to face what was really going on. Her poor father. He told himself that his wife leaving him was God's will because that let him out of his responsibility to the situation. If it was God's will, then that meant it wasn't his religious militancy, his change in mood and attitude, or his absence that was to blame. Not his physical absence. He had always been around, but first there had been the painkillers. Then God. Then Barrett. He kept finding new things to be devoted to that sapped devotion away from her mother. Desire created value, and he had stopped desiring her mother and replaced her with drugs, then salvation, then his Prophet. Celia's mother lost her value to her husband, and she knew it and couldn't stand it, so she ran to the place where his new value lay. Rather than face any of that, her father wrapped it up in a bundle called God's will.

Her mother left for another man because she felt scorned, plain and simple. Hadn't she, too, labeled that God's will? Celia had heard her mother attribute this chain of events to God, though she snarled a bit when she did it. "We followed God's path, and this is where it led, so now here we are. It's not my fault God wanted me to live up here. Your father will just have to learn to deal with it," she had said, implying her father was somehow not dealing with it, as though he had any choice. She had fixed Celia with her serious gaze then, much like her father had done just fifteen minutes ago. "It'll all be OK, sweetie, you'll see. You just have to have faith." Faith, the refuge of people who were too scared to think things through realistically.

Barrett had faith, though—he was the creator of their faith—and he did not suffer from God's will, he only gained. He told Celia's mother it was God's will she be his companion, and she went to be with him. That simple. He told Celia's father it was God's will his wife left him, and now her father was twice as devoted to him. That simple. After all, he told them he was God, The Prophet, returned. It was Barrett's will (or his father's, however he chose to phrase it) that laid a path for all these people to follow, her parents among them, but he was never ultimately responsible because they came to this, to him, of their own free will. It was their choice. What a racket. That was the side Celia wanted to be on, the side where you benefited from God's will by people deciding for themselves to follow it the way you explained it to them. That was where she was going to stand.

Celia wiped her hand across her cheeks again for good measure, though her tears had dried by now. She felt their salt trails across her face. Lines of barren havoc. Good. That was how her face was staying from now on, no more tears. This was her life, so be it, but she wasn't getting left on the losers' side feeding chickens, living in a shack, and taking the oddly shaped and impossibly heavy burden of God's will on her shoulders. She was going to be on the other side, dictating God's will, wielding it, and sitting in a hot tub. That was where the smart money was, and that's where she was going to be. Let others waste their free will on suffering. *Will*, that was a keyword, as Celia's teachers would have said. Her parents had come to all this on their own. All the misery and unhappiness their free-will decisions had created, this gift God bestowed on them because he cared for them above all. What a cruel trick it was to call this love.

Celia did not go up to the big house the next day. She woke in her father's bed with the early morning sun spreading buttery light across the floor but doing nothing to take the chill out of the room. The sounds of the day intoned and overlapped from outside like the notes of a wind chime. Birds squeaked and blathered, voices called to one another from down in the Town Square, and the cabin creaked with the spinning of the earth. Celia got up and ran across the freezing house back to her own room. She grabbed clean clothes and her coat and jumped into her bed where she changed under the covers, putting the coat on as well. She stayed there until she was hot from the blankets, then she got up and went into the kitchen.

She ate breakfast and drank a cup of coffee. She had slept deeply and late. When her toes began to burn with cold even through her socks, Celia pulled on her boots and went outside and into the Town Square. She started to head to the real henhouse, then changed her mind and started with the laundry. May Altman was there with Nancy-Lynn and the mother of Rebekah's sometimes playmates, the twins. Jill, Celia had heard her called.

"Good morning and God bless you, Miss Celia," May Altman said, smiling.

"Good morning," Celia said, nodding to them all but keeping a neutral expression. She screwed this neutral expression into one of concern and worry and then dropped it back to neutral, like her father shifting gears in his old truck. "Can I help someone separate something?" she asked.

"Got a pile here waiting to go in," Nancy-Lynn said. Celia went to the table where Nancy-Lynn's pile of clothes was heaped and began tugging articles out of the mound. "You feelin' OK, honey?" Nancy Lynn said. "You look a little worn out."

"Are you backed up some? You need to go sit on the toilet?" the twin's mother asked.

Celia shifted the neutral expression up a dozen gears into horror.

"Cheese and rice, Jill," May said. "She's old enough to know when to clear her bowels." To Celia she said, "Her two are still young'uns, never mind her. It's a habit of mothering. You do look a little off, though. Is everything all right?"

Celia stared at the floor for a long moment. "You promise you won't laugh?" she said to the three women.

"You should probably put Biscuit's underpants down before you tell us, if you want that promise held," Jill said.

Celia looked down and saw she had pulled out a large pair of men's briefs. She dropped them like they were an insect. She sighed and went ahead, saying, "I dreamed God spoke to me last night."

Jill and Nancy-Lynn exchanged a look, but May Altman, who had known Celia longer and seen more of her earlier interactions with The Prophet, put a hand to her chest and studied the girl's face. "Has this ever happened before, honey?"

Celia nodded. "Yeah, but never like this."

"What do you mean?" May said.

"Before, I dreamed of this place—"

"The laundry shack?" Jill interrupted.

"No, the farm. Here. Where we all live. I dreamed God came to talk to me and he showed me this place. When we came here for the first Bible study, I recognized it and knew we would live here one day. But this time—"

"Go on. This time: What?" May said.

"This time it was more"—her face went vacant as she searched for a word—"direct. The other time I just sort of knew it was God speaking to me when I woke up. This time he said who he was. He said there was a change coming to the house of The Prophet. There would be two where there was one. Our faith must be strong and open to his will. And that he would make two where there had been one."

May relaxed. Nancy-Lynn picked up the underpants that Celia had dropped and tossed them in the white pile, a classification Celia thought was generous. "Honey," May said. "Dreams are just bits of our day playing back nonsense in our heads while we sleep. I wouldn't worry yourself over it. It's beautiful that you dream of God, but it's just a dream."

Celia put on a grave face and fixed her eyes firmly on May's. "He was very clear, Mrs. Altman. There will be two where there had previously been one." Her tone took May Altman aback. Nancy-Lynn and Jill both raised eyebrows. Celia shut her eyes, as though against a pain in her head, and sighed loudly. "I'm sorry. You're right. I'm not feeling that well. I think I'll go lie down." With that she left the laundry shed.

She marched straight back to the cabin and got back under the covers for a nap. She resisted the urge to put on the same act for others around the farm.

She didn't want to oversell it. May, Jill, and Nancy-Lynn would be enough. Ironically, Geraldine herself would have been the perfect soil to bury Celia's seeds, but Celia needed an audience, not a main character, and Geraldine had wrangled a spot for herself center stage. Everyone in the compound would gather tonight for service. Celia closed her eyes and began to drift off, wanting to be rested for the evening. She was content to let Geraldine have her moment in the spotlight, but only a moment. Celia the Chosen One was coming, and she wanted to be a star.

Celia and her father walked to the amphitheater. Attending the weekly service was easier for him since his wife didn't show up anymore. Celia knew he wondered why she wasn't there. Everyone did. But The Prophet didn't mention it, and no one asked except rhetorically to one another. Most people let Celia's mother off the hook, saying The Prophet must have asked her not to come for reasons beyond their humble understanding of the Lord. Or maybe they spent their time in such deep prayer and reflection that attending the weekly service was redundant. Celia overheard them when they thought she was out of earshot. Only Gardner spoke aloud what most of them only let themselves think: "She's just lazy and don't feel like coming, simple as that. And she thinks she's too good for all this now that she's The Prophet's companion." Unlike the others, Gardner also seemed to make a point of saying this loud enough for Celia to hear, just in case she was out of earshot.

Celia and her father sat in the front row, their unofficial permanent seats, which were always waiting for them, even if they arrived a little late. They'd sat there the first service after The Prophet took Celia's mother as his companion. Celia's father wanted to show his devotion, his certainty that this was God's will. He didn't want there to be any doubts about his faith among their neighbors. They took note and continued to leave the seats for them. Perhaps they needed to see him there. Maybe his faith set an example for them, something they could look at if they ever had a moment of doubt about following The Prophet, living this way. Seeing him they could say, "This guy is still confidently on board, and he's certainly putting up with an awful lot."

May and Kent Altman took two seats behind them. That was an unexpected stroke of luck. May put a kind hand on Celia's shoulder. "You feeling better?" she asked.

Celia kept an impassive face and said, "Yes, much," with no enthusiasm at all.

Her father, who had been praying, she supposed, or maybe just sitting with his eyes closed, opened them and turned to face this interaction. "When were you sick?" he said. Celia saw in his face that he was thinking of her meltdown the previous night.

"Oh, earlier today," May said before Celia could answer. "Just a funny tummy." She gave Celia a quick wink that her father couldn't see. As far as May was concerned, she was saving Celia from the embarrassment of taking a dream too seriously. Did anyone ever tell men anything? Celia was beginning to think not. They were always the last to know. She thought of poor Beaufort—though really, Geraldine had been throwing herself at Barrett since they met him, and Beaufort acted like a total boob. He had no excuse for not knowing what was coming. Maybe that was why so many women didn't bother to explain anything to men; there was no point.

Celia's father was studying her now. "I'm fine," she told him. "I just felt a little…off, earlier." He watched her for another moment, his eyes tracking up, down, left, and right, exploring her face as though a good survey from ear to forehead with a concentration on her chin would provide some clear idea of what was going on in her head. He nodded finally, pacified, and returned to his meditation or whatever he had been doing.

The crowd began to hush and hustle into their seats. Celia knew without looking that this meant The Prophet had been spotted coming through Town Square, his white robe vaguely spectral in the dark, shapeless, like the lingering smear of a light that hovers in your vision for a moment after things go dark. Celia scanned the congregants. Geraldine wasn't among them. Neither was Beaufort, but he was having butt and foot pain simultaneously, and most anyone Celia knew would agree that was a sufficient combo for skipping church. Or work. Or laundry. Or Community Efforts on Tuesday and Friday. Or any of the other things Beaufort's ailments got him out of doing. Celia didn't know what to make of Geraldine's absence, though. Maybe Barrett had shot her down after all and Celia's "dream" of one becoming two would remain just that, an odd moment between a young girl and the three older women who would forget all about it, or only think of it years later, the memory triggered by some stressed-out pair of men's underpants they were folding or throwing away or cramming into a crack in the wall for insulation to keep winter out of one of these homemade huts they all lived in.

Barrett reached the amphitheater and mounted his dais at the front. Rebekah's father and some other men rolled the thick plastic sheeting down on the four sides of the structure and snapped shut the fasteners that joined them at the corners and the ground. The heaters and their own breath and bodies warmed the enclosure, and soon the first line defenses against the cold would begin to peel away: gloves and hats. Scarves would be unwound. For now, though, their mouths still poured steam from their body's factory efforts and there was nothing out of the ordinary except for missing Geraldine, which no one but Celia bothered to notice.

"My family," The Prophet began. "For that is truly what you are: my family in Christ. And you are one another's family in Christ as well. We have been drawn together by no less than the hand of God so that I may bring you to an understanding of the intricate mysteries of the Lord. The great secrets that will be revealed to you in time. And out there"—Barrett raised his hand and pointed as he always did to indicate the religious wilderness beyond the compound—"they would condemn our way of life. They would condemn you. Take your children away from you if they could, in favor of having them corrupted and influenced by secular society, so they might become sexually active, diseased in both mind and body. So they might fall away from God's loving embrace and serve a society that knows no moral compass, which will never understand the exquisite mystery of salvation I can show you. And that society out there, those people, they would not just have your children, but you! Laid low as well, taken away from Christ's bosom. Away from me! They would drive a wedge the size of the world between you and me, leaving you shelterless and damned." The Prophet ambled back and forth across his dais, letting this last bit sink in. Letting them remember their home foreclosures, their desperation in that time. "But would God allow that to happen?" A few murmured noes came from the seats. "I said, would God allow that to happen?" A bark now— "No!"—the crowd finding one voice, like a school of fish all turning as a unit. "Would I allow that to happen?"

"No!"

"I have brought my people in, I have sheltered them, I have cared for them and led them to a new land. People say, 'Where is God in my life? Where is the proof of God's love and existence in my life?' and we say back to them, 'Right here! Look around.' We live in my Father's heart, in Eden, right here in Brock, South Carolina. As free men and women living according to their own proper and right values. Living as God intended, on this beautiful land, in this beautiful country, fulfilling a covenant made with America long ago that this would be a nation of Christian men and women living in sync with God's law and reaping the bounty of that way of life. They say, 'What proof, Barrett, that you are the Son of God, the Christ returned?' and we say that we live in the heart of that proof, that he has led us to a new land and we are not going back and only the faithful may enter. We are no longer beholden to your laws and ways out there. We have seen that our own way is the way of the light and the living Christ. We have proved your way of life wrong and you may no longer tell us what to do. We live only according to God's law now."

The residents were excited. People called out, "Amen," and, "Praise God." Barrett circled his area again, letting them revel for a moment.

"And now, my brothers and sisters, I tell you that my Father, God Himself, has given me a command, a command in keeping with his law from the beginning of time, from the Old Testament. One lived out by his prophets and followers for centuries before their..." he said, pointing again to the heathens beyond their borders, "secular society began imposing their own devilish ways on us. My Father has commanded me to take a second companion, in accordance with his laws as read in the Bible."

The crowd was silent now, tensed. Husbands gave their wives nervous looks. Celia could have told them not to fret. The only husband who needed to worry was sitting in his RV on a round inflatable pillow. There was movement behind The Prophet. The plastic sheeting all around them was fogged with the heat of the congregants' bodies and breath. The throbbing energy of their lives, their constantly running motors, poured into the air of the amphitheater, producing an atmosphere that hung wet on the walls and shone filthy white under the lights. A portion of this whiteness pulled back now, and Geraldine stepped onto the dais behind The Prophet. She wore a simple white robe like Barrett's. The crowd muttered in tongues as their individual comments blended to nonsense and mixed with the shifting of bodies as they all strained and turned trying to locate Beaufort, who wasn't there. Geraldine was followed by Celia's mother, dressed in the same white robe as the new companion.

The two women crossed behind Barrett and sat in the two empty chairs at the back of the dais. Their cheeks were red from the cold; they must have been standing outside the amphitheater shivering, waiting for The Prophet's cue to make their entrance. Geraldine's exhortations on Barrett had worked, it seemed, for here was Celia's mother, attending service again and now in uniform. She sat stiff and still in her chair, dead-eyed as a bored teenager. Geraldine smiled like a queen who had just found out her chief rival had died in a toilet drowning.

The crowd, having decided Beaufort was definitely not in attendance, turned their attention back to their master. "My followers," he said. "The Lord's family will grow. Our numbers will swell. This is only the beginning."

Celia swiveled in her seat to see May Altman staring at her. Celia locked on May's eyes with a serious stare and held up her index finger. One. She slowly raised her second finger to join the first in a V.

Two.

Chapter 6

Sheep bleat; they don't blah—Young ladies falling out of trees—Understanding what her
parents merely believed—Working in some revenge

Celia and her father walked home in silence after the night's service.
Everyone did. People said their good-byes and good nights, straining to sound
normal. Smiles came and went too quickly from their faces as they parted ways
while throwing out pleasantries. Celia had just put water on for tea to warm
them up when they heard the first groan and creak of the porch, followed by a
knock.

Nancy-Lynn and Biscuit came in, followed a few minutes later by Kent
and May Altman. Celia put on more water. The five adults sat around the table
with their mugs of tea, not drinking them.

"You think Beaufort knows yet?" Biscuit said.

"He knows," Celia's father said. "Whether he knew before service or
found out after"—he shrugged—"but by now he knows." Celia imagined he was
thinking of The Prophet's visit to their own house. She doubted Barrett had
bothered to tell Beaufort in person, though. It was more likely he'd left the task
to Geraldine. Beaufort wasn't the kind of man who commanded a face-to-face.

"It's not that my faith in The Prophet is anything less than absolute,"
Kent said. "But, I mean, do you think we should, I don't know, prepare, I guess,
for this to be a, you know like a—"

"A trend," his wife finished for him.

"Yeah, thanks. A trend," Kent said. "Not that it isn't an honor." He
glanced at Celia's father. "But we were sort of wondering, and we thought it
might be a little raw to discuss it with Beaufort just yet, I mean, we were curious
how much choice you had in the matter. And I don't mean to say we'd choose
to, you know, disagree with the Province of the Lord's Second Coming, or leave
or anything like that—"

"Not that we could leave," Nancy-Lynn said quietly.

"Right," Kent said. "And we get that. We made our commitment when
we came here. We understood it, and we turned over all our finances and
accounts, everything, everything we had, to The Prophet, just like everyone else.
And I feel good about it, I mean, who wouldn't trust the Lord to take care of all

that?"

"Look at the birds in the sky," Celia said, and she heard them all turn toward her. She stood at the counter looking out the small crooked window over the sink into the backyard of the cabin. "They do not sow or reap, they gather nothing into barns, yet your heavenly Father feeds them. Are not you more important than they?"

"Right," Kent said. "Like it says in the Bible."

"In Matthew," Celia said. She kept her back to them. Out the window the tree where she and Rebekah had found the baby bird—What was it now? Almost a year ago?—stood skeletal and grim against the moonlight, shorn of leaves and birds alike.

"But something like this comes along," Kent continued, "and you just, I mean, call it a test of faith or just wanting to know what's what, I guess. So we were just wondering, you know, what the level of, you know, choice was in the matter. Not that we wouldn't choose the Lord's path, but, you know."

Celia didn't turn to look at her father. She knew his manner well enough. He was staring down into his tea, hat pushed back on his head, cigarette burning a long untapped ash. He said, "No woman so far has become a companion of The Prophet who didn't want to."

"He's had to set visiting hours already," Celia's mother said. They were sitting in her room, Celia propped up on the bed, watching her mother twist and pose in front of the mirror in a black cocktail dress, her hair washed and blow-dried. "She was over there every two seconds, 'Oh, Barrett you're so great,' 'Oh, Prophet, what do you think about this,' and blah blah blah." Celia's mother did Geraldine's voice in a whining pitch accompanied by a horrible facial expression. "Like a damn sheep."

"Sheep bleat. They don't blah," Celia said.

"What? I don't even know what that's supposed to mean. And where have you been? Don't go so long without visiting me again. I can't believe you didn't think to come see your mother for a whole week."

"I can't believe you noticed I wasn't here. You didn't notice before when I was, even when you were conscious."

Her mother stopped posing in front of the mirror and fixed Celia with a look she knew well, one balanced perfectly atop a mountain peak of hurt feelings or contemptuous and cutting fury. The look was an idling car perched at the apex of those two slopes, and if she released the handbrake, it could careen down either side. Her mother added no comment or threat to this look; none was needed. She turned back to the mirror. "Anyway, it was only two days before she was banned from his wing."

Celia's mother did not like Geraldine Hamilton moving in across the hall (though, to be fair, neither did Geraldine, who had assumed she would share Barrett's room). She did not like her sharing a bed with Barrett two nights a week (though, to be fair, this was because it meant she herself now felt obliged to share her bed two other nights of the week). In short, as The Prophet's companion, she did not like having a companion of her own (again, to be fair, neither did Geraldine who had assumed her presence would force the other woman out entirely). To Geraldine's face, though, she had said, "You should look through some of those dresses. See if you want some. I never wear them."

"Oh, I'm sure they're too big for me, but thank you," Geraldine had said. "Barrett is getting me my own, anyway."

They both smiled.

Celia's mother cleaned her room. All the orange prescription bottles Barrett kept her supplied with were tidied into a single drawer at the bottom of her vanity. She showered each morning now, putting on one of the many dresses Barrett had given her and doing her hair. She no longer nodded out for half the day. She ate her sundry muscle relaxers and antianxiety pills more judiciously. Geraldine wore her new dresses. They sat around in each other's rooms resenting each other to the point of outright dislike but having nowhere else to go. They reminded Celia of the millionaire's wife and the movie star from *Gilligan's Island*.

"She would crawl right up Barrett's ass if he let her. Any time she hears a noise at the front of the house, she runs out there to see if it's him. 'Can I do something? Do you need my help?'" Celia's mother did her impression of Geraldine again. "It's pathetic. He put her on a schedule. She's only allowed in his wing for an hour each evening. It's driving her near insane she's this close to him and can't be right up in his face." Her mother smiled at this. "She's such a twit."

"She'll hear you," Celia said.

"Good. I don't care."

There was a polite knock on the door, and it opened a crack. "Guess who!" Geraldine's voice swirled into the room.

"Oh, hey," Celia's mother said, sweetly.

"Celia! Hello!" Geraldine cried, letting herself in and taking a spot on the love seat. "It's so good of you to come visit us."

"She's visiting me," Celia's mother said into the mirror.

"Oh, I'm visiting everybody," Celia said lightly. She gave Geraldine's hand a gentle pat. "How are you holding up, Mrs. Hamilton? Becoming a companion of the prophet is a big change. It can be a real spiritual challenge." She made eye contact with her mother in the mirror.

"Spiritually, I was more than ready. And, please, it's just Geraldine now among us girls"

"But not out there with the others, right, Gerry?" Celia's mother said. Without turning from the mirror, her eyes flicked back to Celia. "Gerry came up with a new name for us to be called by the regular, nonspecial folk. A title."

"I thought it would be a little more formal and befitting the importance of the Lord's plan for us," Geraldine said.

"Go on, tell her," Celia's mother said.

"I thought Missus Companion would be nice. Or Lady Companion."

"Lady Companion sounds like a polite name for a massage toy," Celia's mother said. She winked at Celia.

Geraldine's eyes stretched open to their limit. "You shouldn't say— Lady Companions don't talk like—"

"Or a leg razor," Celia's mother added thoughtfully.

"Not in front of Celia," Geraldine shout-whispered. "What if The Prophet heard you talking like that?" She turned to Celia. "That's not how a Lady Companion talks."

"Gerry, she's been coming here visiting a companion longer than you've been one. Besides, she doesn't even know what that is."

This was true. Celia had never heard of a massage toy. She could tell by Geraldine's reaction it was something sexual. Nothing induced panic in the farm's citizenry like the thought of unwholesome sex. They fled any mention of it like a crowd scattering at the appearance of a gunman. Celia flared with embarrassment and indignation at her mother announcing her ignorance of massage toys, though. How did *she* know Celia didn't know what it was? Maybe Celia made massage toys in her spare time, between her studies.

"I do too know what it is," Celia said. As soon as the words were out, she understood the embarrassment of not being able to back this statement up was going to be worse than the initial embarrassment that drove her to make it.

"What then?" her mother said.

"Celia, no," Geraldine said. "You don't know what that is. You don't want to know. It's dirty. None of us should be talking about this."

"Well?" her mother said.

"Fine. What is it?" Celia said, ashamed. Her mother's face flashed the pleasure of her victory, but she saw the dismayed look Geraldine was volleying back and forth between the two of them. Celia looked at Geraldine, who quickly looked back to her mother. Celia looked to her mother, who jerked her gaze back to Geraldine. "Well?" Celia said, angry.

"Geraldine's right," her mother said. "It's not appropriate. I shouldn't have said it. Just forget about it."

"Yes, let's all forget about it," Geraldine said. She smiled and resumed her looking back and forth between them, waiting for the slackening of tension and grimaces.

Oh, what a bunch of bullshit, Celia thought, but she said, "I have to go anyway. Studying, you know."

"Honey," her mother said as she stood, but didn't follow it up with anything.

"Celia, wait," Geraldine said as Celia shut the door behind her.

"Let her go," she heard her mother say. "She's a teenager. She's just like this sometimes."

Celia marched to the end of the hall and made a left toward Barrett's wing. She heard her mother's bedroom door open and close behind her and the hustle of feet coming after her. She turned and saw Geraldine.

"Oh," Celia said. Celia realized Geraldine had expected her to be on her way out the front door by now. Geraldine was rushing to Barrett, hoping her news about the inappropriate conversation from her rival would warrant a disregard for the set hours she was allowed to bother him.

"What's up?" Celia said. Seeing through Geraldine's ridiculously obvious plan raised her confidence, smushing a little of her anger and shame.

"Were you looking for—" She glanced at the verboten hallway that led to Barrett. "He really, really doesn't like to be disturbed during the day," Geraldine said.

"I was gonna grab something to drink before I went home." Celia thumbed behind her in the direction of the kitchen. "Where were you heading?"

"The same," Geraldine said, smiling. "Just getting a drink."

In the kitchen, Celia opened the refrigerator and took out a bottle of water. She saw Geraldine watching her and waited for whatever it was she felt compelled to say.

"I don't know if you should take that," Geraldine said, getting a glass out of the cabinet. "The others don't get bottled water. It's something a little special, just for The Prophet. If people see you walking around with it, that might make them feel a little left out." She filled the glass with water from the sink and held it out for Celia. "Why don't you drink this instead?" She held out her other hand for the bottle of water. "Taking those out of here just isn't allowed."

What an irritating busybody this woman was. Her husband had indeed been blessed by the Lord for taking her off his hands and making her Barrett's problem—a problem he was solving by hiding out in a separate part of the house. What did she expect when she went around behaving like this? Celia accepted she wasn't getting down Barrett's hallway while Geraldine was in the house, but she wasn't giving up her lousy bottle of water. She gave Geraldine a sweet smile and put the bottle in her jacket pocket. She said, "I'm allowed."

Celia went out the front door and around to the back of the house. She crouched under the low branches of the fir tree that was mashed against the wood-slat privacy fence at the back of Barrett's courtyard and duck-walked to the trunk. She pulled herself up through the branches until she was even with the top of the fence. A healthy-looking branch jutted over the fence into the courtyard. With Celia's weight, it rested against the fence top, providing stable support. She inched along it until she was almost over the fence, then launched herself out of the tree and into the yard. She landed on her feet, but momentum pitched her forward onto the ground, where she rolled full around and found herself back on her feet once more. She looked and saw Barrett halfway out of the chair where he had been reading. His stance was on its way to a full sprint for cover.

"What—"

"There's someone guarding the end of your hall now or I would have knocked," Celia said. Barrett sat back in his chair and smiled.

"A man can't get any peace in his own home, and now I've got young ladies falling out of trees. I'm living the dream, it seems."

"I'm sorry. I can go. I just—" Barrett put his hand up. She stopped talking.

"It's fine," he said. "I didn't mean you were keeping me from peace. My new companion is quite devoted. I had to be rather firm with her the other day. Come, sit." Celia took a chair next to his. "She's driving me nuts, to be honest. God, my father, is confident in my patience, more so than I would be. She means well, but..."

"But having to say that about people all the time is annoying," Celia said.

"My human inclination is to agree," Barrett said. "But enough uncharitable indulgence. I heard something about you."

"From who?"

"Not what?"

"Huh?"

"You don't want to know what I heard, just who I heard it from?"

"If I know who, I can probably guess what."

"Could you?"

"People are predictable."

"Yes, they are. They're readable, and by being readable, they're predictable. They'll surprise you every now and then, that's undeniable, but you don't train a dog for the day it might learn to fly. Plan for the predictable, and adapt to the surprise."

"Plan for the predictable, and adapt to the surprise," Celia repeated.

"And making predictions based on the predictable is also wise," Barrett went on. "But I don't normally consider myself predictable."

"You're talking about my dream. That's the thing you heard about me." Celia noticed he had not mentioned who told him. May was the obvious candidate, with Nancy-Lynn and Jill the runners-up. Celia doubted it was any of them, though. Unlike Geraldine, they were less inclined to need to speak to The Prophet directly, even during the small amounts of time he made himself available to his followers. He was their leader, their minister, their Prophet. They heard what they needed to hear from the pulpit. No, it was more likely one of their husbands who had brought Barrett the news, sucking up.

"Was it real?" Barrett said. "Your dream?"

"It came true."

"Did it?" Barrett said. His voice became stern, and his face fell into hostility.

Celia didn't answer. She had slipped up somehow. She wasn't playing the game right. Celia the Chosen One had miscalculated something, but she wasn't sure what. What she was sure of, though, was that Barrett knew she had invented the dream, that it had been planned and plotted. How could he know that? What had she messed up? She had planted the seed quietly, allowed it to grow on its own, and now, as she had mentioned, it had come true.

Oh, wait. That was it.

"I mean. It was just a dream," she said, hoping to cover her previous certainty. "It could be interpreted as—"

"No. The people who heard about your dream, the people you shared it with, they think it could be interpreted only to mean you foresaw The Prophet, me," he leaned forward into her space as he said *me*, "taking a second companion." He had never used this tone with her. It was clipped and severe. Not angry. Anger was an emotion. This was emotionless. It was scarier. "They see that as the likely meaning. You, on the other hand, said your dream came true. That this was, in fact, its meaning. Almost as though you knew this was what it would mean the whole time, like you dreamed it specifically so it would mean this."

Celia stared at her feet, angry at herself for messing up, angry at Barrett for catching her. She felt the lump, the swelling gag in her throat that was crying's portent. She fought it, taking smooth regular breaths, trying not to move, like if she froze long enough the impulse wouldn't carry to its culminate point. Barrett continued leaning into her space, staring her down. When she felt the urge to cry receding, when she had held it back long enough to assert her dominance over it and it had shrunk and begun to slink off, she looked up and met his gaze. "You said I was special. That I could wield faith."

Barrett leaned in even more. "And?"

Celia panicked. And what? "That's it," she said. "I just wanted to be like you. And show you I was special, like you thought."

Barrett's expression resumed to its usual shape and he sat back out of Celia's face. "You came up with this all on your own?" Celia nodded. "No one suggested it to you or told you to do it?" Celia shook her head. "You weren't coerced into doing this by anyone else? No one set this up and asked you to go along?"

"No," Celia said. Why would anyone else care about making her special besides her? Barrett sighed and shook his head. He looked like a man who just found out his missing wallet had been returned with all the money still in it. Celia wasn't sure what had upset him so much, though she imagined he took exception to her lying about the Word of God. That was probably a big deal.

"Celia," Barrett said. "I don't think you're special." Of course you don't, Celia thought, because I'm not; you just caught me proving it. "I *know* you're special," he went on.

Celia looked up. "You do?"

"I don't think things, child." He made finger quote around the word *think*. "I know them. I know them from God's brain straight to my lips."

"God has a brain?"

"It's a figure of speech. What I'm telling you is that all my information is fact, because it comes straight from God. And one of those facts is that you, Celia Waters, are a very special girl."

"But I made it up. It wasn't a real dream."

"Yes, but as you pointed out, it came true. My knowledge, my words, they come directly from God. From him straight to me. Other kinds of seers, other people who are special, their information might come from other sources. If it's true...well, God is truth, is he not? It was bad form on your part, sloppy really, to openly know what people would believe about your dream before they themselves had a chance to decide they believed it, though you must have played it better out there than you did here, because people are intrigued by what you told them. And intrigue is better than if they just believed you. If they just believed you outright, right away, then, sadly, they're idiots. They'll believe anything. But if they're curious, if you got their attention and they didn't dismiss you, that means they want you to make believers out of them. They want it to be real, but their pride, their intellectual pride, regardless of the fact that there is nothing intellectual about ninety-five percent of people, demands that they hold back belief a little longer. They're on the peak, Celia, and they just need you to tip them over the edge. To give them the tiny bit of proof that will allow them to stomp their intellect into the dust and open their hearts to belief." He grew excited as he talked, leaning into Celia's space again, this time without menace, though with a tinge of something else. What was it? Madness maybe. He reminded Celia of mad scientists in the old movies they played on Saturday afternoons on the poor channels, before her parents got cable. Perhaps that was what it took, the secret ingredient. She was horribly confused.

"I don't really—I don't understand," she said.

Barrett took a deep breath and smiled. "No, of course not. It's a lot to take in, and I got a little carried away." He took his hands from the tops of her thighs, near her knees, where they had come to rest during his monologue. "But you will. You will understand in time. I want you to come back here tomorrow, like you used to do, but come your new way." He gestured toward the fence. "At least until I find a nicer way for you to come around Geraldine. And Celia?" He leaned forward again, and his hands went back to her knees. "We're going to be talking about some very important things that you can't share with anybody, do you understand?" Celia nodded that she did. "I want to make this really clear," Barrett went on. "You've been very good so far, very discreet, so I believe you'll continue to do so. That you won't let me down. But, if you do." He pressed more firmly on the tops of her legs. It didn't hurt, but she registered the increasing pressure. His good eye stared at her intently while the other circled around her face, like a drone that could swoop in and strike from any angle. "If you let me down, then you will truly understand what it is to experience wrath. And you will come to know why it is considered such a grave sin. Do you understand?"

"I understand," Celia said.

"Good girl." He raised one hand and gently stroked the side of her face. "You truly are special. Not many people in the world would understand how important this is." Celia leaned into his touch. It was a sweet relief after the tension and fear she'd gone through during this conversation, fearing she had already let him down, fearing she might do it again. She wanted to keep coming here; she wanted to keep being around him. She would be a good girl, special, not like Geraldine, who had to wait in the hall. Not like her mother, who couldn't appreciate how good she had it before or how good she had it now. Not like her father, who acted like his faith was the punishment he long deserved, not just for his painkiller problem but his entire life before that. No, she wouldn't be like her parents.

Celia understood what her parents merely believed: that people wanted, craved, something absolute and eternal to apply to them, to their time on earth alive and riddled with consciousness, but they hated the single absolute they were given: death. So they started with death and set about unraveling it, denying its nature straight off with the concept of eternal life. Once they destroyed the only existing absolute with one they preferred, they set about inventing other absolutes, making the rules for God and signing his name on the contract.

Did Celia believe in God? God was the person in charge who enforced the rules, who determined who was good and bad. The person you subjected yourself to. God was Barrett.

Celia leaned into Barrett's palm as it cupped her cheek, and she felt relief. A barrier had been crossed. She was inside a kind of zone of understanding now, past the lingering requirements of pretense. She could shed Celia the Chosen One in front of Barrett now, because it wasn't a game anymore. She had been chosen for real.

"How are my people doing out there?" Barrett said. "Are they at peace with everything?"

Celia opened her eyes. "They're nervous. Some of them. They think their wives might be called upon by God, too. They say they're OK with it, but they're not. My dad told them no one has to be a Lady Companion who doesn't want to, but—"

"A Lady Companion?"

"Geraldine thought a title would be nice."

"That's not a title. That's an abomination."

"Or a massage toy," Celia said, risking having to admit she didn't actually know what that was. Barrett laughed.

"Cheeky, but true." He laughed again, and Celia felt the satisfaction her mother must have felt knowing she could get that kind of laugh out of Celia's father. At the same time she experienced a pang of jealousy. It was the kind of laugh her mother could get out of Barrett, too, she realized. It was her mother's joke, after all. Celia didn't even get it. "That's too mature for you to say," he said mock-sternly. "I'll have to make sure that name doesn't stick." He sat back in his chair. "As for the fear that Satan is sowing among my followers…"

"Satan?"

"When good people begin to question what they know is the will of God, Satan is always to blame. He tempted my first incarnation in the desert. If he is so bold as to tempt the Son of God, he won't have any trouble whispering words of discontent in the ears of these simple people.." He was quiet awhile. He stared off into space. Celia stayed still in her seat. She wanted to suggest they take a soak in the hot tub to help him think but sensed this wasn't the time. Finally he said, "They've been alone too long, I guess. I don't want another Eden on my hands. It's in the nature of humans to grow restless, even in paradise. It all becomes too easy, and they start to feel entitled. What they need is a dose of fresh blood. A little competition to make them work for that spot at the top of the food chain. You can't value and appreciate something you don't fight for." Celia was lost again. "Yes," Barrett said. "Some new meat. It's time I suppose, and I've kept the others waiting long enough."

"Who are the others?" Celia said.

"You'll see. Come back tomorrow. Same place and time. You're going to have another dream." He stood and led Celia back toward the fence, his arm around her shoulders. He turned her toward the fence and stood behind her, placing his hands on her hips and saying, "OK. On three. One. Two."

"What was I?" Celia asked.

"What were you what?" Barrett said, still crouched behind her, waiting to give her a boost.

"Predictable or a surprise?"

"You, my lovely, were a wonderful surprise. One. Two. Three!"

Celia went up and over the fence.

"Go on, baby. When you're ready," Celia's father said. She was standing at the railing of the cabin's small front porch. Spread before her was the entirety of the farm's population. Even Gardner was there, standing off to one side, arms folded across his chest, but looking less hostile than usual. Rebekah was out there with her parents. She waved to Celia. A few people were up on the porch itself, both of the Altmans and Beaufort. Beaufort was in a chair in the corner, holding tightly to the porch rail lest his newly developed vertigo send him spilling to the ground. Celia's father had placed Beaufort there himself, saying, "C'mon, Bubba. Got a spot for you right here." Several things about this were out of place, beginning with her father calling another man by a nickname. More out of place was the fact her father had coined the nickname himself. Her father and Beaufort spent time together now. Previously, Celia's father had thought of Beaufort as a man without a work ethic, without a job, without motivation, and without "any damn sense." Beaufort was, however, newly without something else that Celia's father was also without: a wife. Their common ground. Perhaps it was sympathy for Beaufort over all the things he was without that drove her father to saddle him with something, even if it was a nickname. What else did her father have to give, anyway? Unfortunately, Celia thought, it was catching on, and shouts of, "Hey, Bubba," could be heard all around the farm as Beaufort teetered and staggered from tree to fence to truck looking for balance as he made his way to collect food or laundry. If Celia's father was the high-school quarterback who dug deep and made the big play and advanced the game, the one who sacrificed and showed the drive to carry the team, then Beaufort was the official mascot.

"Has your father asked you about the dreams yet?" Barrett wanted to know when she returned the day after their confrontation in his grotto. There was a ladder at the base of the fence this time. It was tucked discreetly under the fir tree, behind the trunk. As out of sight as possible without looking like it had been hidden. Just forgotten, or left out by some soul too lazy to put it away, probably that crazy Bubba. Celia propped it against the fence and ascended. Barrett must have heard the sounds from the other side, because he was waiting to take her hands and help her down. This time they used the hot tub. Barrett didn't press her for details about his followers right away or tell her why he wanted to see her. He led her into the sunroom, saying, "I thought we might take a soak while we talk. He took her across the hall to his bedroom and pointed to a package on the bed, a small box wrapped in white paper and tied with a small gold bow.

"What's this?" Celia said.

"It's a gift," Barrett said. "A special gift for a special girl. For all your efforts and your dedication to the Lord." Celia ran her fingers over the wrapping. The corners were folded evenly and the ends tucked expertly together, taped from the inside so as not to mar the appearance. "Don't you want to open it?" Barrett said.

Celia nodded. "I do, I just…it's wrapped so nice." She hadn't received a gift in a long time or seen anything wrapped so delicately. The sight of it here, the surprise at seeing something pristine and the improbability that it could be for her were better than anything that might be inside the box. She wanted to savor it but knew if she stood staring at it for much longer she would appear rude. She lifted the box, wishing she could wash her hands first so as not to dirty the paper. It was light, almost as though it was empty. She unwrapped it from the ends, sliding the folds apart with her dirty fingers, being careful not to tear the paper. Underneath was a white box, and when she lifted the lid, she saw a small pile of red fabric. She took it out slowly. It was a bathing suit. A bikini. Bright red.

"I thought you should have a proper bathing suit," Barrett said. "No more old T-shirts."

Celia turned to face him. "Thank you," she said. She moved toward him, then hesitated, unsure.

"It's all right," he said, and she put her arms around his generous middle in a hug, her face settling comfortably into the center of what she couldn't help but notice were his discouragingly ample breasts. A bathing suit. There was only one place such a gift could be used. It meant she was welcome. She was in. Barrett ran a finger around the inside of her collar. "Why don't you change and I'll meet you outside?" Barrett said. Celia nodded and he left, pulling the bedroom door shut behind him.

Celia laid the bikini on the bed and took off her clothes. The bottom of the suit was easy enough—that was essentially underwear—but the top proved difficult. She had never put on a bra. She couldn't fold her arms around at the back to fasten the clasp. Finally she turned the top around so the clasp was in the front, fastened it, then rotated the whole thing back to its proper place and hooked the straps up over her shoulders. She opened Barrett's bathroom door and took a look at herself in the mirror. It was immediately apparent that she was not supposed to have a bathing suit like this. Her mother and father both would have demanded she take it off, and both would have used her full name as they said it. It was that kind of bathing suit, and that was how good she looked in it: Celia-Ann-Waters-take-that-thing-off-this-instant good. She checked herself out from different angles, turning left, right, and craning her neck to see herself from the back. Thrilled, she left the room and skipped across the hall, through the sunroom, and out to where Barrett waited in the hot tub. He turned and leaned over the edge when he heard her.

"Let's see you," he said. Celia stopped and gave him a pose, one arm up the other down, one knee bent: ta-da! "Now give me a twirl." Celia performed a loose pirouette, smiling. "You look amazing, my lovely," Barrett said. "Stunning. C'mon, get in here before you catch a chill."

Celia stood on the seat of the hot tub, submerged up to her knees, and felt the hard, hot bite of the contrast between the water and the late winter air. She eased the rest of her body in slowly until she was settled up to her shoulders. They sat in silence at first, heads propped against the edge, feeling the heat work its way into their bodies, the cold air a harsh necessity of the world from which they were taking a break.

Barrett spoke first. "Has your father asked about your dreams yet?"

He had, the night before. Celia had taken a walk in the woods after she left Barrett. She had come across Gardner again with his rifle. She'd spotted him ahead of her through the trees and thought she had gotten the drop on him. She turned to go back the way she came, taking care to walk quietly. She had only gone a few steps when she heard Gardner call out, "Heard you clomping this way five minutes ago, Miss Lazy Bones." She sighed, gave up being quiet, and clomped back home. When she came in the door, her father was already there, along with Kent and May Altman. They weren't talking, just sitting. Whatever they had to say to one another had been said before she arrived. Celia stared at them and they stared back until her father said, "Come sit down, honey. I want to talk to you about something." Celia stayed where she was and looked from her father to Kent and May and back again. "We want to talk to you about something," he corrected himself. Celia knew what this was about but remembered Barrett's admonishment not to reveal when she already knew what people wanted, believed, or were thinking when she was the one who had orchestrated those thoughts, beliefs, and wants.

"What happened?" Celia said, letting her voice waver a bit for effect.

"Oh, Celia," May said. "Nothing bad. Don't worry."

"Just come sit," her father said. "It's OK." He pulled out the chair next to him. Celia crossed the room and sat. "May told me about a conversation she had with you a few days ago about your dreams."

"Can you tell your dad what you told me?" May said.

"You told me it was nothing, just a dream," Celia said.

"You used their resistance. That's good." Barrett said in the hot tub. "Make them drag it out of you. See why it's better they didn't believe you right away? How it makes their belief stronger in the end? People who just jump in with both feet..." He flapped his hand in the air dismissively and pinched up his face, saying, "...you can't do anything with them. They'll believe in anything. Which is the same as believing in nothing, if you follow me." Celia shook her head that she didn't. "Some people, they don't decide against anything. They love everyone and everything. But love is something you reserve for certain things, otherwise it's meaningless. Love is reserved for the things you value above everything else and more than anything else. If you just say it about anyone, it's not special. It's the same with faith and belief. Faith is meaningless if it's not held despite something. Or despite everything. So it's good they had reservations about your dream. And it's good you reminded May about it. Keep doing that. Sprinkle it in. They're all Doubting Thomases, every one of them. They all have to jam their fingers in the wounds. They don't want to see themselves that way, but of course they're like that. It would be more insane of them not to be. It's better for their faith in the long run to doubt and be refuted. You have to always remember to bring it up. It reminds them that they're sane and logical people, and yet here they are, believers. They like that as a story about themselves. It makes anything seem all the more true because they had to be convinced, and their vanity allows them to think that only a powerful truth could convince someone like them."

"And it is a real truth, right?" Celia said. She was arching her back so she could see the twin red triangles of her new bathing-suit top break the surface of the water. She was a Doubting Thomas herself when it came to good fortune, and she needed to see the bright red fabric over and over to know it was real.

"Of course it is, but the most important truths are never obvious, so people have to be convinced."

The most important truths, Celia thought, were actually the ones that were the most obvious. Don't put your hand in boiling water or you'll get burned. Get out of the speeding car's way or you'll be killed. All any of them really needed to know was spelled out clear as breathing. The veracity of Celia's dreams was, in reality, completely useless to everyone. What they had done was they had all decided that these other, nonobvious, truths, or whatever they were, should be important because they had all mastered the really important truths and now took them for granted. They were interested in something more complicated now. Celia kept this to herself, though. She was here to learn from Barrett, not to point out the things he missed.

"What did you say next?" Barrett said.

May had actually spoken next, not Celia. "I know," May said. "I did say that. I'm sorry, but you seemed so upset and it sounded like it was just a dream, but then..." She made a gesture that said *you know*.

"Geraldine," Kent finished for her.

"Yes, Geraldine," May said.

"One became two," Celia added to throw in a dash of the mysterious. She kept her eyes down as she spoke.

"That's right," May said. "One became two."

"This is what we need to talk about," Celia's father said. "I need you to tell us exactly what you dreamed."

"And what did you say to that?" Barrett asked her as they sat in the hot tub, Celia's red-wrapped breasts surfacing every few minutes like scarlet seals peeking up from below.

"No," Celia had said, keeping her gaze firmly on the table, partly for effect and partly because she was scared. She had never outright defied either of her parents, and their situation—their lives, family structure, all of it—had changed so much she could not sense how her father might react.

"Excuse me?" he said, indignation in his voice.

"I don't understand," May said. "You told us all at the laundry not three days ago. God came to you in a dream and then what?"

"Celia Ann Waters!" her father said, still smarting from being told no, and at this, at the end of the three words that named her, the ones only ever used together in anger, like blasphemy, Celia flinched away from her father as though expecting to be hit.

The effect this had on the room was immediate. Her father, who had never struck her in his life save for the mild spanking he'd administered (at her mother's insistence, she remembered) when Celia was five and she used a rock to scratch a heart into her mother's driver's side door for Mother's Day, stopped saying whatever he had been about to say and looked puzzled. He would have had no previous memory of his child reacting to him in such a way. Perhaps he recognized the motion as one from his own childhood now seen, confusingly, from outside himself. The Altmans both looked to Celia's father, their eyes wide, which was when her father realized the implication buried in all this and his puzzlement turned to defense.

"Honey, hey, c'mon now, what's all this? What's the matter?"

"You just always get so mad at me," Celia said, still not looking up for fear she wouldn't be able to go through with this if she did.

"That's not true. Why would I get mad?"

"I have dreams. I see things in them I don't understand. I wake up scared and can't go back to sleep. In the mornings I'm tired and you get angry. You tell me I'm lazy, a bad Christian. You said it all the time in front of The Prophet and Mom. You're always so mad." Celia let this hang in the following silence. Her father sat staring at her with his mouth open. The Altmans stared at them both.

"I'm sorry," her father finally said. "I didn't—how could I know? I just—" he turned to the Altmans. "Parenting. Rise and shine and all that, I didn't—" He broke off and turned back to Celia. "Baby, I'm so sorry. I didn't know. How could I have known?"

Celia wasn't finished. "Everyone in the laundry practically laughed in my face."

"Oh, Celia, we didn't laugh. We just didn't know either. Like your dad said, how could we have?" May said.

"When I told you Barrett was the Second Coming," Celia continued as though none of them had responded. "You all kicked me out. Snapped at me. Made me go outside. After I brought you the news."

"Celia we just—you told us such a big thing, we needed to discuss it and, well, sometimes adults need to talk among themselves," Kent said, fielding this one since neither his wife nor his friend seemed willing to step out there again and try to justify themselves to this bitter child.

"No, always," Celia said.

"Always what?"

"Adults always need to talk. Talk and talk and talk. So go ahead and talk. I don't want to be here."

"But you're what we need to talk about," Kent said. "I mean, not about *you*, but about your dreams. What they might mean. We need to talk about—"

"With," May interrupted and shot her husband an incredulous look. "Talk with you about your dreams." She lowered her voice and said to Kent, "Did you not grasp what she was just tellin' us?"

"That's inconvenient for you then," Celia said. "Because I don't want to be talked about or with. May I be excused?"

"Celia—" Kent began.

"Or do you want to force me somehow?" Celia said before he could manage anything else.

"You're excused, honey. Of course," her father said. Kent raised his eyebrows in alarm but kept quiet. Celia stood and went to her room and gently shut the door.

"Sounds like you had quite a bone to pick," Barrett said from his side of the hot tub when Celia finished her retelling. "See you worked some revenge in there."

"He always thinks he knows everything and he has to be, like, the center of everything. Like the dreams don't count or can't be serious until he's heard about them and given his opinion. Like he wants to take them from me. And he always has to be telling me what to do just because I'm the only person in his entire life he's ever been the boss of. It makes him feel like a big shot to boss me around and criticize everything I do, even though he's the one always doing something wrong, getting hurt, or getting on drugs, or losing his job. He just," Celia tried out a word she had never used before, "sucks. He sucks."

"He's your father. God commands that we honor our father and mother," Barrett said. "But I see what you mean. Your father is a frustrated man, and he's come to his faith through the fire. He's been tested mightily and has endured, but it hasn't been easy for him. That difficulty can get passed onto the child." Celia decided this meant Barrett took her side in the matter. "Besides your personal grudge though, you did a good job. You left them all slightly shamed. That's so important. Shame reminds them they aren't worthy. It makes them try harder. Tell me what happened after you went to your room."

As soon as Celia had shut the door to her room, she'd been slammed with anxiety and excitement. She paced back and forth. She had gone through with something she couldn't take back. She had committed to something. Her personal dedication made an idea she had conceived of real. It had been dragged through the hearts and minds of others and accepted. If they had called her on it or if she had panicked and admitted it was a trick, their whole world would be different, but now it was going to be this way because of her will. She made something true.

And it *was* true, wasn't it? Barrett said it was. He said it wasn't really a lie. If she said something was going to happen and it did, she hadn't lied. Whether she really dreamed these things or knew about them some other way was a meaningless detail. "Saying you dreamed these things is the framework to get them to hear the truth. And truth is what's important. God is truth." This feeling of being the edge, the point at which two possible worlds diverge, this must be how Barrett felt all the time.

Celia didn't explain all this as they sat in the hot tub. When Barrett asked what she had done afterward, she simply said, "I went to sleep. I was exhausted."

"Good. That's good. And then you had another dream of things to come in the near future."

"I did?"

"Yes, you did. And even though you got upset before, you know that God's words need to be shared with the people. You had a very specific dream. Let me tell you what it was."

This was how Celia came to be standing on the porch of the cabin facing almost everyone she knew. She was nervous. Even putting on the mental cloak of Celia the Chosen One couldn't relieve the jitters. Her father introduced her, so to speak.

"Glad y'all could come," he said loud and clear over the small crowd pressed in at the rail. "Most of y'all have heard at least a little bit about my girl, Celia's, dreams. Now, I'm not here to tell you they're prophecies, and neither is she. Do I believe there is a divine element at work here? Yes, I do. But you're going to have to make your own decision when it comes to that. But I will tell you that I have discussed this with The Prophet." Celia went dopey with confusion when she heard this. Then part of her brain, the same part that always thought of the perfect comeback five minutes too late, put everything together. Of course. It had been her father who first told Barrett about her dream of the one becoming two. May told Kent, and Kent told her father. He had no doubt been to see his prophet every day since then, too, just like Celia. Barrett wasn't letting all this run on chance. He was the Son of God after all. Chance is what the actions of God look like to humans who can't see the complexity of the operations at work.

"I have discussed this with The Prophet," Celia's father continued. "And he counseled me to listen to my daughter. To not ask questions. To not make rash or quick decisions, but to listen and open my heart to the possibility that God might have more than one way of talking to us. Just because he talks to us through Barrett doesn't mean he can't talk to us other ways, too. In the Bible

God sent people dreams all the time, even when he himself was talking to those people and telling them stuff when they were awake, too. It was his way of helping them understand his actions. Now I guess you all know Celia had another dream, and that's why you're here. I'll get out of the way now and let her tell you about it." Her father stepped back and gestured for Celia to take his place at the porch rail. Barrett told her father what to do in order to draw Celia out concerning her dreams, which legitimized them for him, and Barrett told Celia what to do in order to make her newfound power the most appealing and believable.

"When your father comes home this evening be waiting for him," Barrett had told her in the hot tub. "It makes an impression on people when they find you waiting for them. Throws them off slightly. Tell him you had another dream. That you have to tell someone. You want that someone to be him."

"Won't he wonder why I want to tell him now after I refused to tell him last night?"

"Tell him that in the dream you were told to tell him. Then tell him the dream. And the dream is this…"

"I was standing in the field down below Town Square," Celia told her father. "There was no one else around. It was like everyone else was still asleep or something and I was the only one up. Animals started wandering out of the woods into the field. Just one at first. A moose. I was watching the moose when a deer came out. Then a cat. A dog. Then it was just, like, animal after animal. They poured out of the forest like a stampede. Then suddenly the rush stopped and they were all standing in the field looking at me, and Christ was by my side. The animals stopped looking at me, and I could tell they were all looking at him. He turned to me and said, 'They have come in from the wilderness and must receive shelter.' Then he pointed out at the woods, and there was smoke coming through the tops of the trees like out there all around us the world was burning. Then I woke up."

Celia's father looked at her a long time after she finished. Finally he lit a cigarette. "What do you think it means?" he said.

"When he asks what it means," Barrett had said to Celia, "tell him, 'When we came here, we left the world behind, but we aren't the only ones who need a place to go.'"

Her father considered this after Celia repeated it. "You think something or someone is coming? Here? To the farm?"

"You don't know any particulars," Barrett had said to Celia in the hot tub. "This is why you have to share it with him. You don't know what these things mean exactly. You're too new at having these dreams to be good at interpreting them with any kind of clarity yet. But what you do know," Barrett said, as he leaned forward. "What you do know…"

"…is this," Celia told her father in the serene quiet of their cabin as evening dimmed around them outside and the room became pregnant with importance the longer they spoke. "We didn't come to this place with Barrett, with The Prophet, to hide. We came to set an example. And now that we've settled and we've set an example for ourselves and one another, who's next?"

"Tell him if anyone else wants to hear about your dream they can come tomorrow evening. You'll tell anyone who wants to hear about it," Barrett had said. He took her face in his hands. She floated across the tub toward him, her legs mixing and brushing against his below the water. He pulled her face close to his. "And remember. It's very important that you do not discuss anything we've talked about, or even that we talk at all, with anyone." Celia nodded, their faces so close her nose almost rubbed his as her head went up and down. He put his mouth by her ear and said, "Good girl." Then he had released her to float back to her own side.

Now, on the cabin's front porch, Celia's father stepped away to relinquish the space and the crowd to her. Celia stepped up to the rail. She had habitually thought of faith as it affected others—her parents and their friends—and had never given her own faith much thought. It was hard to think of something that wasn't there. Looking out at these people, though, seeing what Barrett had so easily wrought, being a part of it, at once a participant and a pawn in his design, Celia felt the spark. Deep in her being the match was struck, and the sulfur flashed and burned hot. Celia believed. She believed in Barrett.

Celia glanced behind her, where her father stood.

"Go on, baby. When you're ready," he said. "Don't be nervous."

But she wasn't nervous. She didn't have to think of what to say. Barrett had already told her. She faced the crowd and delivered to them God's message.

Chapter 7

New blood—Wake up, faker—How can you have God in your heart and hate me so much?—A real bombshell—A couple of drunk beavers—Maybe fear is the beginning of wisdom—Matthew is upset—Science is way too hard—Another seed of doubt being sown—God needs soldiers—The first shipment—The rabbit can't be caught—This girl can cook—An outcome both horrific and hilarious—Better to be married than be on fire—A hand with nothing to hold, a heart with nothing to pump—A pure woman in the eyes of God

Celia watched the butterflies toss themselves between tree branches. They moved faster and more gaily than she ever realized. The ones she had known in Garden Estates flew low, flower hopping. She had never seen them like this back then, in the woods. Hadn't realized how high they flew into the trees, flapping through the branches and leaves like brightly colored paper caught in an updraft. Celia lay in a small clearing in the woods, watching dawn take over and the butterflies rise and fall like sparks from a fire. She had awakened around five that morning and let herself out the window. Gardner wouldn't be out here this early. He went fishing at dawn, but he cut through a different part of the woods to get to the river. It wasn't just Gardner, though, that drove her to take sanctuary this early. Their community had had a population boom. The farm was now a bustling compound. Barrett had been busy, locked away in his wing of the house shaped like an E. His online ministry was as powerful as his face-to-face work. He had dozens of new believers waiting to leave their broken secular lives to come live in his paradise on earth. They began arriving a week after Celia's second dream, while there was still a chill in the air, before the mosquitos.

The new arrivals came as families, couples, and singles. Celia used to share the woods with Gardener, but now the two of them shared with everyone. There were more children now, and when their chores were done, they roamed in packs. "I'd be scared I'd shoot one by accident, but they're louder than you even," Gardner grumbled to Celia one evening when they met crossing the Town Square.

"Maybe you should train them to hunt," Celia said. "You'd have a little army."

"Don't think I'm not working on it," he said. "Offer still stands for you, too. Teach you something useful, other than sleepin' and dreamin', Miss Lazy Bones."

"No thanks."

"Problem is there ain't nothin' out there to shoot when them kids are clomping around and hollerin'. Keep having to go farther out. Sooner or later I'm gonna run out of woods."

Gardner was pressed deeper into the forest, and Celia was left getting up before dawn to come out for a quiet walk.

Barrett's website and Facebook page referred to their home as the New Zoar Temple of the Blessed Tabernacle, named, the About page went on to explain, for the land where Lot and his daughters went to live after the fall of Sodom and Gomorrah. Some residents still occasionally referred to it as the farm, but with all the new people going around calling it Zoar, the old name mostly fell out of use.

The old citizens heralded the arrival of the new with a showcase of enthusiasm and warmth achievable only by people drowning in apprehension. Grumbling about Lady Companions dried up as the spring rains poured.

Barrett had been right about the place needing some fresh blood. The recruits came with unlimited energy for their new lives, and the original citizens shook off whatever complacency had crept into them and perked up as well. They had no intention of appearing to love God, their Prophet, or Zoar if that's what they were calling it now, any less than these Johnny-come-latelies. The Gatherings became wild, devotional affairs. And there was so much to do now! A few of the new followers came with campers, but most of them needed homes. Among the newbies was a young woman named Beth, who was staying in a tent until she could get a better--quality shelter. Celia and her father met Beth one night after a Gathering. She came up and introduced herself.

"You're the first," Beth said after they exchanged names. She was a slightly plump young lady with hair so dirty blond it was almost the color of dust. She wore jeans and a fleece pullover.

"The first?" Celia's father said, confused.

"The first follower. The first to come and live here. You were the first to heed The Prophet's call. You led the way. Without you," she said, shaking her head, baffled by the awful possibilities, "none of this would be possible."

Celia's father chuckled and fiddled with the brim of his hat. He took a cigarette out of his shirt pocket and stuck it in his blushing face. "Ha. Well, that's a nice thought, but it's really Christ and The Prophet made this possible. I can't take any credit other than being a sinner who needed saving."

"The Prophet is the mountain, that's truth from God. But you're the first drop of melted snow that starts the river," Beth said.

"Well, thanks," Celia's father said.

"It was nice meeting you both," Beth said. She waved good-bye and walked off into the night, back to her tent.

Celia looked at her father who was chewing on his cigarette filter and watching Beth recede into the dark. "What a strange thing to say," he said. The next morning he walked down to her tent and began making her plans for a small house.

Dawn yielded to morning. Celia had enough of the butterflies and the peace and quiet. She gathered herself up and left the woods, coming out near the barn. She went inside and found Trevor flopped over on his side looking entirely dead. She crouched by his head. He kept his eyes closed. His breath had blown a clean patch on the dirty floor. "You're not really asleep," Celia said. She poked gently at his nose. "Wake up, faker." Trevor opened one eye and regarded her. He snorted and stretched his head toward her, accepting a bit of petting along his snout, then shut his open eye and went back to sleep. She let him be.

Celia left the barn and walked toward the big house. People were emerging from tents, RVs, campers, and the slowly multiplying "Gardner Model" of home. This was what everyone called the style of house that Kent Altman and Harmon Landross had first built for its namesake. The style was a mash-up of the two men who invented it, combining a suburban and pioneering mentality. The homes were a long rectangle, with the back wall six feet higher than the front and the roof sloping down from back to front. One end of the long rectangle was walled off inside to make a bedroom, and a loft was built above this if someone needed room for kids. A small porch came off the front and back doors. There were three windows in the front, three in the back, and one on each end.

"They'll keep you warm in the winter," Harmon liked to say, which was sort of true. "And dry in the rain." This was a little truer. "But they'll burn like a matchbook, so be careful." This was very true.

Celia reached the big house and went in through the front door. She didn't have to go over the fence anymore. Having dreams that foretold future events qualified her as someone who had business with The Prophet. Geraldine's winning hand continued to pay lousy dividends. She was a trooper, though, Geraldine. Celia had barely shut the front door before she appeared at the end of the hall wearing her nightgown and no makeup. Early morning was the only time the companions looked like anyone else at Zoar.

"Celia, it's so early. I don't think—"

"It's OK. You can go back to bed," Celia said. "Get some rest." She walked past Geraldine toward Barrett's wing.

"I didn't mean for us. I meant for The Prophet." Geraldine trailed Celia through the door at the end of Barrett's hall.

Celia turned and faced her. "What are you doing?" she said.

"I think it's too early for you to be here. It's an inappropriate hour for a young lady to wake a grown man who—"

"Geraldine, The Prophet called me here in a dream. He has come to me in my sleep and beckoned me. Now, please, trust in the Lord."

"I do trust in the Lord," Geraldine said. Her tone was unamused.

"Then why do you insist on disobeying him and standing in the way of his commands?" Celia asked, matching Geraldine's intonation with some of her own. "You've been asked to be a companion, you have special time set aside to see The Prophet, which isn't now, and yet you feel the need to interfere where you have no business. I have the actual work of Christ to do, not just keeping someone company."

"That is out of line and—"

"If you want to disobey The Prophet, then do it. Tell him you don't care for his decisions, but don't keep me from my task. So if you're coming, come on. Otherwise, excuse me." Celia turned and went down the hall. She didn't look behind her until she got to the door of the sunroom. Geraldine had gone back out and was closing the door at the end of the hall. Celia waited a moment or two at the sunroom door to make sure Geraldine didn't surprise her, then turned and went into Barrett's bedroom. It was better if Geraldine thought she was meeting him somewhere less personal. Not that she was really meeting him at all. When she opened the bedroom door, he was asleep. He breathing was a hideous sucking that sounded like the hollow bones of a rib cage being dragged up and over the last of a set of stairs. Her father breathed a racket in his sleep as well. Some men couldn't do anything peacefully, she supposed. Everything had to have a knock-down-drag-out quality to it.

Celia crawled onto the bed next to the wheezing Barrett. He didn't move, just continued to wheeze.

"Faker," she said. "You're not really sleeping." Barrett's breath caught, and he hoarked, snorted, and sighed, like his mouth had caught a fly, accidentally swallowed it, and found that he enjoyed it. Celia reached over and gently poked his cheek. "You're a faker. You're not really asleep. Wake up, faker."

Barrett groaned and opened his eyes. "It's not a prophecy if it's self-fulfilling."

"If it's what?"

He rolled onto his back and rubbed his face with his palms. "Self-fulfilling," he said. "What time is it?"

Celia shrugged. What difference did it make? There was day, then the night, then another day. There was light or there wasn't. Barrett pointed to a bottle of water and a bottle of pills on his nightstand. Celia handed them to him. "What does that mean?" she said. "Self-fulfilling."

"It means you say I'm awake and the sound of you saying it wakes me up, thus proving you right. The statement renders itself true. Or maybe it's a tautology, or a bit of both. I just woke up, so it's hard to sort out." He tossed two pills from the bottle into his mouth and chased them with a swallow of water.

"Isn't that the way it works, though? You say something and make it so?" He handed the pill and water bottle back to her and gestured at the nightstand. "What are these?" Celia said, shaking the pill bottle.

"They make me wake up. Those on the other side make me go to sleep. And others," he said, waving his hand, his way of dismissing details he deemed unimportant or didn't like, "do other things."

"What about the self-fulfilling prophecies? Aren't those all prophecies? Doesn't a prophecy only rely on itself no matter what? I mean, it can't come true at all unless you make it, right?"

"Honey, it's…" He palmed his face again. "It's early. I just woke up. Even the Son of God needs a little time to collect his thoughts. OK? Just…just go across the hall and wait for me. All right?" Celia slid down off the bed. "Celia," Barrett said as she started to leave.

"Yeah."

"Tea. Put on the tea"

Celia filled the electric kettle in the kitchen and carried it back to the sunroom. She heard the shower running across the hall and wished Barrett would hurry up; adults were so slow. She needed to ask him things. Everything. She needed to ask him everything. Since her conversion to the faith of Barrett Higgins, she had simultaneously felt on the verge of understanding everything and nothing. Barrett told her how people's minds worked, the way to reach them, and the way to manipulate them. Only he didn't put it that way. That was the part where she came up feeling like it was all a big muddle. Barrett would never say it was manipulation. He would say he was steering people toward salvation. It was like her game of playing Celia the Chosen One, but he refused to acknowledge it was a game. Celia's "dreams" were obviously inventions, they both knew it, yet he insisted that because they came from him it was the same as if she'd really had them.

"God comes to you in a dream or God's human form on earth tells you a dream, it's the same difference," he said.

She loved him, though, despite this quirk, and she went along with the belief under which they all lived. That was all anybody really wanted, if you thought about it, whether it was Rebekah, her parents, her teachers, or Barrett.

Just play along. She couldn't help having questions, but Barrett thought her the inquisitive student thanks to this habit, and that made him happy. And Barrett happy made her happy.

The door opened and Barrett entered the sunroom. He was wearing a blue silk robe tied with a white sash in a strained knot around his ample belly. His hair was still wet from the shower, slicked back, all the fight taken out of it.

"Were you out in the hall tormenting poor Geraldine earlier, or did I dream that?" he said, taking a seat on the couch.

"I wasn't tormenting her," Celia said, rolling her eyes. She put his cup of tea on a saucer and put the saucer on a tray, the way he liked. "I was keeping her from tormenting you."

"She doesn't torment me," Barrett said. "Sugar, my lovely, you're forgetting the sugar again." Celia set the tray down and added the bowl of sugar. "You're a bright girl, but Lord knows you aren't a natural for tea service. Lord knows. Ha." He chuckled at his joke. "She doesn't torment me, she's just a bit overenthusiastic. She has a devout heart and a fierce passion for the Lord." He nodded approvingly. "Fierce passion. Thank you, my dear," he said as Celia placed the tray on the coffee table.

"She's a busybody," Celia said. "She can't mind her own business."

"Just be nice to her. I mean it. Now, what was it you were asking me?"

"Aren't all prophecies self-fulfilling, since if you don't make a prophecy, then whatever the event is just becomes this thing that happened, like everything else?"

"No. Self-fulfilling prophecy is a term used to indicate when someone *makes* something happen. When a real prophecy is fulfilled, that's it. It was fulfilled."

"But—"

"You're focusing on the wrong thing here. Prophecies aren't about the relationship between the prophecy and the event that happens. They're about the relationship between the person who makes the prophecy and the people who hear it. Power must be proven, it demands to be proven, it wants to show itself, and people want to see it. They want to see the monster truck crush the car, or one wrestler jump on the other one's head. Making a prophecy isn't about the thing you predict, because whatever the event is it was going to happen anyway. Making a prophecy is about showing other people that you know. It showcases knowledge, shows that you have access to information they don't have, and that having it places you apart from them. That's what power does: It sets you apart and above by your show of strength. Because it takes guts, moxie, intestinal fortitude, whatever you want to name it, to stand up and put it all on the line like that. Making a prediction and standing by it shows your strength and sets you apart, and these are the two points from which one derives power. Might, and separation from the herd."

"Did I show strength when I made my dream prophecies?" Celia said. She enjoyed having him tell her about herself, being the hero of her own story.

"You certainly did, my dear. That's why people responded. The strength to say what you knew to be true in the face of potential disbelief, or even ridicule, shows people your might. And they instinctively know God will not have his will made manifest by cowards." Barrett paused and took a long sip of his tea. "Ralph Waldo Emerson said that about God's will in an essay called 'Self-Reliance.' I should have you read that."

"Doesn't quoting from something called 'Self-Reliance' go against the spirit of, you know, self-reliance?" Celia said.

Barrett ignored this. "And bringing about God's will, knowing what it is and bringing it to fruition, that, young Celia, is true power. That's what faith is, what religion is. Religion is power for the weak. When they have no money, no options, nowhere to turn, they can find power and strength in their beliefs. Those people out there, farming, building, hunting, making lives for themselves to be lived in pure, clean service to the Lord, they derive their power from me. One day, maybe from you. Everything they have, the lives they lead, I made that possible. The Lord made that possible. I bestowed it on them. So don't worry so much about the actual prophecy itself. The important thing for you concerning prophecies is that you can make them, not what they foretell. In fact, it's best to make them a little vague. That way there's room for a little interpretation. You say a guy in a red shirt is going to show up and the guy turns out to be wearing a blue shirt, that's all people will talk about—how you were wrong about the shirt. Doesn't matter that the guy showed up. All they'll focus on is that the shirt color was wrong, so maybe you're wrong about other stuff as well. Maybe this isn't even the right guy." He drained off the last of his tea and Celia filled his cup. "Just causes a headache. Keep it vague and avoid specifics. People will fill in the blanks themselves. It makes them feel better, like they figured something out. 'A great upheaval is coming' or 'Expect a messenger to bring important news.' Stuff like that is better. That way when a guy shows up, it doesn't matter what color the shirt is, or even if it's actually a guy. Could be a woman. She could tell them a pig in the next town over got sick, and they'll go, 'Well, hey. That's a message, ain't it? This must be the messenger. This is what was foretold.' They'd rather be the ones who put it together. They get all proud of themselves like they just solved the Word Jumble or something, and they'll go around convincing doubters for you. It's almost cruel of them, when you think about it, making us jump through these ridiculous hoops to save their souls. To bring them salvation. Making us orchestrate these elaborate details so they can accept their own happiness and joy. Like children who need their father to dress up like a clown at their birthday party to entertain them. You really have to present your vision in such a way that it can let itself become true for them."

"In a way that lets it fulfill itself?" Celia said, innocently.

"Yeah, something like that," Barrett replied. He sat back and stared out the glass at his grotto. Celia's red bathing suit was laid across one of the lounge chairs, left to dry the previous day. Celia rolled her eyes and gathered up the tea tray to leave outside the door. Geraldine always collected it after her visiting hours with The Prophet. Barrett was quiet now, lost in thought, and Celia didn't bother him. She left the tray in the hall, pouring the last of Barrett's tea around to make more of a mess for Geraldine. When she came back inside and shut the door, Barrett said, "I guess that's why we get what we get."

"Get what?" Celia said. Sometimes Barrett kept on talking in his head and would start vocalizing again four or five thoughts further down the line from where he had stopped.

Barrett gestured absently all around them. Celia figured he meant the house, the grotto, the comfortable bed, and air conditioning—all the relative luxuries he operated within while his followers built their homes by hand. Barrett gazed out the windows a moment longer, then shook his head, slapped his thighs with both hands, and stood. "I have to get to work," he said. "You should go visit your mother," he told Celia. Out in the hall, though, he opened the door to his bedroom rather than going into his office. "Do me a favor," he said, placing a hand on Celia's shoulder. "Send Geraldine to see me, please."

"Why? It's not her time."

"I need to speak with her."

"Is she in trouble?"

Barrett turned in the doorway. "Celia, love, please, no more questions. Send Geraldine."

"Should I tell her you'll be in your office?"

"No, tell her I'm in my room." Celia stood staring at Barrett, wanting to prolong their time and shorten Geraldine's. Then she remembered something. Her face must have changed. "What's the matter?" Barrett said.

"I told Geraldine that you called me here this morning. I said you came to me in a dream and told me to come see you."

Barrett's eyes narrowed. "Why would you say that?"

"I didn't think—"

"Did you and I discuss that?"

"She was—"

"Did. We. Discuss. That?"

"No."

Barrett placed a hand on the side of her neck. His thumb brushed the length of her throat. His tone was even and serious. Too calm by half. Something happened in Celia's stomach whenever Barrett spoke to her this way. It was terror, terror from the not-so-veiled anger she had provoked, the potential wrath that may ensue, possible expulsion from the inner sanctum and benevolence of Barrett.

"Have you said this to anyone else?" Barrett said.

"No." The pressure of his grip on her neck increased slightly. "I promise," Celia said. "Just this morning, to Geraldine. She didn't want to let me in."

Barrett's hand moved up to the side of her face, against her cheek, the sign the anger was not permanent. At this Celia was flooded with warmth and relief. She suddenly felt the need to breathe through her mouth.

"Don't tell anyone else things like that," Barrett said. "Do you understand me? Don't go off script." He pulled her in close, her small frame pressed against his larger one. Her breasts, which, in addition to being practically nonexistent, were now letting her down by being sore and painful to the touch, fit between Barrett's own full chest and his belly. "We'll speak about this more tonight. Come in the other way. Don't use the front door." He let her go with a slight push, separating them. "Now go visit your mother and send me Geraldine." He turned and shut the door to his room, leaving Celia alone in the hall.

Celia found her mother in her room, the windows thrown open to the cool morning, a cup of tea steaming on her bedside table. She looked up from folding laundry when Celia walked into the room. "Geraldine's mad at you," she said.

"I bet I can make her happy again," Celia said. "Watch this." Celia stepped across the hall and knocked on the door Geraldine had closed when she heard Celia coming. There was a noise from the immediate other side of the door after Celia knocked: Geraldine listening, Celia realized, probably hoping to hear her mother chew her out for being rude this morning. Celia smiled at the thought of knocking right into Geraldine's ear as it was pressed to the other side of the door. She stifled the smile when the door opened. "The Prophet requests your presence in his chambers," Celia said.

This confused Geraldine. "Now?" was all she managed.

"It's not her time," Celia's mother said behind her.

"Any time is her time if he asks for her," Celia said. Geraldine said nothing. She turned and snatched a small sweater from the back of one of her chairs and hurried down the hall. Celia watched her retreating back. "You're welcome," she said, mainly to herself, and went back into her mother's room.

"Next time she wakes me up at six in the morning because you've upset her, I'm not going to be real pleased with you," her mother said.

"Sorry," Celia said in a singsong voice, flopping down on the bed.

"So he wanted to see Geraldine first thing this morning in his bedroom, huh?"

"How did you know he wanted to see her in his room?" Celia said.

Her mother eyed her for a moment but only shrugged. "Lucky guess," she said. There was something implied here, Celia realized, a layer that wasn't being hidden from her exactly, but one she couldn't see and that no one was going to point out to her. Before she could give it much thought, her mother said, "That'll make her day. She gets so depressed about only being allowed to see him at certain times. Sometimes he forgets or he's too busy and whew." She shook her head. "That poor creature is beside herself."

"I thought you didn't like her."

"I get frustrated with her, but you have to remember, Gerry and I have known each other for years, since around the time you were born. She's the one who gave you Daniel, that stuffed bear you carried around everywhere when you were younger."

"I remember Daniel. His eyes fell out."

"Something was bound to happen to him. You hardly ever put him down."

"So you like Geraldine now?"

Her mother let out an exaggerated sigh, the one she used when she wanted Celia to feel like her questions were bordering the absurd. "I always liked her. I was just...frustrated, honey. Your father was doing his thing and—"

"What's his thing?" Celia sat up straight and watched her mother, who sat back on the love seat and stared at the ceiling for a while, thinking.

"Your father couldn't let himself be forgiven, and that left me out. It was like mere forgiveness wasn't enough. He felt like he had to go and become a whole different person, and that different person wasn't my husband. And all that, it was hard, and it hurt, but it was part of God's plan and it was for the best. God wants me with The Prophet, and that was the way it had to be for me to be able to do that. You understand?" Celia absolutely did not. She shook her head. "Maybe when you're older," her mother said.

"No," Celia said. "I don't want to understand when I'm older. I want to understand now. I have to understand math. I have to understand history and science and the power of Christ. I don't see why I don't get to understand this until I'm older."

"Honey, it's hard to explain."

"If you can't explain it, then you don't understand it either."
Her mother stared at her but didn't say anything. This was borderline back talk,
which her mother preferred to practice on others rather than experience herself.
She just nodded though, and after thinking for another moment, spoke. "Your
father thought he'd failed us. Let us down, with the painkillers and everything."

"He did," Celia said, coldly.

"He did," her mother agreed. "But he made it right. Cleaned himself
up. We lost the house and all, but it wasn't his fault. The economy and those
son-of-a-bitchin' bankers, all that was God's way of bringing us here. But once
we were here he just couldn't—He gained faith in the Lord, but he lost all his
faith in hisself. And that shut me out. He wasn't the same man, and it was sad
and it hurt, but that was what had to happen so I could end up here. That time,
the troubles, the anger: that was the path I had to follow to get to The Prophet.
This is where God wants me, and that's how he got me here."

"It must be nice being able to just change your mind like that," Celia
said.

Her mother stopped with her tea partway to her mouth. Celia met her
gaze. "How can you have God in your heart and hate me so much?" her mother
said. She got up, slamming down the mug of tea so hard it broke. Tea escaped
the shattered vessel quickly, instantly, as if it had been waiting for its chance.
Liquid always wants out of whatever it's in; it'll take advantage of any hole or
crack, and the tea spread across the table, then fled over the edge and down into
the carpet. Celia's mother went to the vanity and sat down. She kept her eyes off
the mirror.

Celia had never hurt her mother like this before, never wounded her so
with her own words. She felt bad about it. Then, after feeling bad, she felt angry
that she felt bad. But still. She looked at her mother opening a bottle of pills
taken from a drawer, popping one in her mouth, looking around, remembering
the broken mug, the lost tea, and dry-swallowing the capsule.

"I'm sorry," Celia said. "I don't hate you."

Her mother shrugged and nodded. "So what were you visiting Barrett
about this morning, anyway?" she said, back to her smooth regular tone, as
though the previous conversation hadn't happened.

"My dreams," Celia said. "What they mean. Why I have them. Stuff
like that."

"And what does The Prophet say? Why do you get them?"

Celia shrugged. "God chose me to be his messenger. He chose dreams
as the message." She thought for a moment if there was any more to it. "That's

about it," she said.

"That's about it?" her mother said with a chuckle.

"The gist of it," Celia said, smiling.

"Oh, you know," her mother said, riffing on the theme now. "God comes into your dreams, gives you a little message for the faithful because he feels like it. That's all."

"The tall and skinny of it."

"The general idea."

"So easy I could do it in my sleep," Celia said.

Her mother burst out laughing. "It really is a wonderful gift, honey," she said when she had gotten it together. "Not as good as dreaming of tomorrow's lottery numbers, but pretty special all the same."

"What are those?" Celia said before she realized she was going to. "Those pills you always take?"

Her mother turned to face her. "They're for my nerves," she said, casually.

"Are they what Dad used to take?"

"Your dad didn't take anything. He abused them."

"Are they what Dad used to abuse?"

Celia's mother was quiet for the extra second people take when they're deciding how best to lie. "No, they're different. Not the same at all. Your father was on heavy-duty stuff for severe pain. These just relax me, make me less tense. The Prophet gives them to me. They come with his blessing."

"What are you tense about?"

"Just 'cause you commit to going over the waterfall doesn't mean the ride down isn't still scary."

Celia flopped onto her back on the bed. They were quiet for a moment. "Hey," her mother said. "Sit up."

Celia lifted her head. "Why?"

"Sit up. C'mon," her mother said, rising and standing at the foot of the bed.

Celia sat up. Her mother narrowed her eyes and studied her, leaning over with her palms down on the bed. "You're being weird," Celia said. "What are you looking at?"

"You're getting your boobs," her mother said. Celia instinctively covered her chest with her arms. "What are you doing?" her mother said. "Stand over here and take your arms down."

Celia stood next to the bed facing her mother. "They hurt," she said.

"God, I remember that. That's normal. Don't worry about it." She pressed the upper and lower parts of Celia's breasts. "That sore? When I do that?" she said.

Celia nodded. "You really think they're coming in?"

"Don't *think*. I know." She gave Celia's breasts a gentle squeeze, one in each hand. Her mother gave her a hug, and Celia felt her chest pressing against her, the pain coming from her mother's breasts to her own in a dull throb, like a bass note.

"Do you think they'll get as big as yours?" Celia said when her mother let go.

Her mother pushed out her own chest. "Probably. Or pretty close to the same size, at least. Maybe bigger. It's hard to know exactly, but your mamma's working with a pretty sturdy rack, so they should come in pretty full." She held Celia by the shoulders and looked her up and down like a picture she was about to hang on the wall. "You're going to be a stunner, honey. A real bombshell."

Nothing anyone ever said to her had made Celia as happy as this. She looked at herself in the full-length mirror on her mother's closet door: her legs that were still too skinny, her hips that were largely theoretical—now they seemed primed with potential. "Will I get my period soon?" she said.

"I expect so. You shouldn't be in a rush to cross that bridge, though." Her mother stood next to her and looked in the mirror, too. Side by side, they looked like a before-and-after photo. But before and after what? Dad, Celia thought. I'm still with him, in the before, and Mom is gone, in the after. The aching in Celia's breasts took on a new tone. The soreness became a reminder, a bell tolling in her chest, ringing in the future, a future of being a bombshell, a real stunner. Celia and her mother turned back and forth in the mirror, giggling and striking poses. "Your mamma was pretty hot stuff back in the day," her mother said.

"Still is, it looks like," Celia said. She remembered something she hadn't thought about in a long time. A memory of a memory that wasn't even hers. Her mother, younger, walking across a parking lot in the hot sun of a southern summer. Her father chasing after her, a happy fool, not caring who saw him, needing to talk to this girl striding toward her car. The smell of grass clippings and gasoline and sweat and a storm off in the distance that wouldn't be there for hours. Just like that the tip of her happiness, the peak, was worn away, eroded. The apex of her high passed and all the rest of reality was still there, waiting for her descent. Next to her, her mother's face was growing slack; the dreamy look was beginning to emerge.

They heard Geraldine coming down the hall a few seconds before she appeared in the doorway, the white noise of clothes lightly rustling and footsteps on carpet.

"That didn't take very long," Celia's mother said.

"The best things never do, do they?" Geraldine said.

Celia's mother turned back to the mirror, her stare growing to a thousand yards. She turned side to side. "No," she said. "They certainly don't."

Geraldine's time with The Prophet seemed to have purged her memory of being mad at Celia. Eventually Celia's mother drifted off to sleep. Celia said so long to Geraldine and went out to walk the compound. From the minor height of the big house, Celia observed the bustle of activity. The cold morning had thawed now that the sun was up and doing its job. All over, work was being done with the vigor and enthusiasm of people who know winter is at their back.

Celia looked out over Zoar. She could tell who was new and who was an original. It was in the gestures and posture of people building, farming, and at the laundry. The originals were demonstrating, giving directions, while the newcomers listened in groups of three or four, occasionally performing some task, then looking over their shoulders to receive nods of approval, a bit of advice, a pointer or two.

Down the slope from Celia and her father's own cabin, there was work being done on a new Gardner Special. Celia saw her father among the workers and walked down to the site.

"Hey, Cee-bear," her father said as she approached. "Where you been all morning?" Celia pointed up at Barrett's house, not specifying whether she had seen The Prophet or her mother. She felt guilty every time she had to tell him she had seen her mom.

"What are you doing?" Celia said. Her father normally worked on what machinery they had, drove things and people around, and oversaw and organized others. Physical labor was kept to a minimum on account of his back. He definitely didn't haul lumber, which is what he was doing currently.

"Building a house. What's it look like?" He was chipper, grinning. "I even got Bubba to lend a hand, look there." He pointed out Beaufort, a dozen feet away, lurching around the work site with what looked like a wooden crate. Occasionally he stopped to pick up something off the ground and drop it into a cup taped to the crate.

"What's that thing he's clomping around with?" Celia said.

"I made him a walker out of some scrap wood. For his vertigo. Helps him balance."

"I thought the point of him having vertigo was so he didn't have to work."

"Yeah, well, I had about enough of that. So I built him that box."

"What's he doing?"

"Picking up stray nails, wood screws, and whatever else gets dropped that can still be used."

Beaufort spotted Celia and waved. He staggered and dropped his hand back to his wooden support.

"For all the nails he's going to bother picking up, you probably could have just saved the ones you used making him that hobble horse," Celia said.

"Hey, c'mon. Why you want to give Bubba a hard time?" her father said.

Celia felt slighted. A very short time ago that line would have had her father cracking up. Beaufort shuffled past like a man dragging a broken chicken coop. Her father bent down and picked up an armload of two by fours.

"What are you doing?" Celia said. "Your back. Put those down."

"I'll be fine. Your dad's a strong guy. A few boards won't hurt me."

"Daddy, no. Are you crazy? Why are you even doing this?"

"Celia! Hi!" a voice behind her said. Celia turned and saw Beth, the new woman they had met after the Service Gathering, walking their way. It looked like she was coming from Celia and her father's house. "Peace of Christ be with you on this beautiful morning," Beth said.

"Were you just in our house?" Celia said.

"I'm letting her use the facilities while we get her place in shape here," Celia's father said.

"This is going to be your house?" Celia said to Beth.

"We're going to be neighbors. Can you believe it?"

"We believe Barrett is Christ reborn. Yeah, I think I can swing the concept of neighbors."

"You smart-ass," her father said, playfully. He put a hand on the back of her neck and gave her a gentle shake.

"Stop," Celia said, ducking away from his grip. "And put those down." She turned to Beth. "He's got a bad back. He's not supposed to lift things like that."

"I know," Beth said, her voice filling quickly with concern, like a shallow sink. "I've been telling him that, but he doesn't listen."

"But you're letting him build your house."

"Would both of you stop?" her father said. "I'm fine. It's not a big deal."

"You're just supposed to be supervising," Beth said. "Give me those." She started taking the lengths of wood from him. She gripped them awkwardly, with no sense of order, struggling under their weight.

"Beth, you can't carry all those," Celia's father protested.

"Yes, I can. Look," she said, staggering absurdly toward the base of her future house. She and Beaufort passed each other like a couple of drunk beavers with their supplies.

"Look. See?" Beth called out.

"She's a real ball of energy, that one," Celia's father said.

"See? Look, I'm fine," Beth's voice sailed back to them.

"Smart, too, let me tell you."

"Look. See? I got it."

"And devout. She loves God so much. A real disciple. I mean, you can't stop her. She just gives and gives and gives. Here she is with no home yet, and the other day she was holding reading classes for the kids down in the Town Square. I mean, can you believe how selfless she is?"

Celia stared at her father staring at Beth, who said, "Look."

That night after dinner, Celia saw her father wince as he got up from the table. "You hurt your back," she said.

"It's just a little sore."

"Go lie down. I'll bring you something."

"It's fine."

"No!" Celia said. "We don't have a tub for you to soak in, and there aren't any doctors here. If we don't take care of this, you'll be as useful as Beaufort, except he can't make you a walker, so the two of you will be sharing the one you made him like two idiots clinging to a stack of popsicle sticks."

"All right, all right, take it easy," her father said.

"Go lie down in there." Celia pointed to his bedroom. He walked slowly to his room like she ordered. Celia followed him a few minutes later. "Roll over," she said. "Onto your belly."

"What is that?" her father said as he rolled. He was looking at the light blue blob Celia was carrying. It had the bladder-style look of a hot-water bottle, but the shape was wrong.

"It's for your back," Celia said. "I borrowed it today. I knew this was going to happen. I filled it with hot water."

"Yeah, but what is it?" her father said, again. "Ah. That feels better already."

Celia adjusted the warm blob on his lower back. "It's Beaufort's hemorrhoid cushion," she said.

"Aw, hell," her father said, trying to roll back over and swat away the offending blob.

"No!" Celia said, pressing on his shoulders, trying to pin him down.

"I ain't lying here in Bubba's butt sweat," he said. "I'd rather be crippled."

"Oh, lie still. I washed it," Celia said.

He stopped squirming and looked up at her. "How well did you wash it?"

"It's been thoroughly disinfected, I promise," she said. He settled down. "You're lucky he had it to lend."

"Him having it means no work from him, more work for everyone else, and that this," he jerked a thumb toward his back, "was more likely to happen than not. *Lucky* don't seem like the right word."

"Well, now, there's a thought," Celia said. "You've been pretty friendly with 'Bubba' lately, though."

"I'm feeling less charitably toward him lying under his butt cushion."

Celia sat next to him on the bed and felt the warmth of the cushion. "This should be good for another half hour or so, then I'll refill it."

"Hey, that Beth is something else, ain't she?" her father said.

"Something else to half kill your back. You can't go back down there and keep building that house." Her father sighed. "Daddy, I'm serious. You're being crazy. What are you going to do if you can't walk anymore? Just sit here in this cabin?"

He buried his face in a pillow. Celia heard a muffled roar of anger and frustration come out of him. He said, "I hate this. I feel old. Do you know how awful it is to not be able to do the things you used to be able to do?"

Yes, Celia thought, I do—things like see Sloane, or go to school, or visit a grocery store. She said, "Older is wiser. At least there's that." She felt the butt cushion again, as they were apparently calling it now. It returned steady warmth to her hand. She imagined the heat was emanating from her father, that somewhere inside him was a glowing rock pulsating a healing heat.

"That's a lie," he said. "Older ain't wiser. Older's just slower, so it looks like you're taking your time and thinking things through, but really you're just hoping you can make it there at all before you completely give out."

"Make it where?"

"Anywhere."

"Maybe that's wisdom. Just focusing on getting there."

"It's scary more than anything."

"Maybe fear is the beginning of wisdom."

"Hell, I don't know."

"No, you don't. And not knowing isn't very wise. So see there? Not wise, therefore not old."

"What a depressing compliment."
"You're welcome."

Celia woke in her father's bed, curled against him in the chilly room. His breath was slow and even. Celia was returning to sleep when she remembered the butt cushion. It was on his back, which was why he was on his stomach, which was why he wasn't breathing a holy racket. She sat up and felt the plastic. The heat was gone. She must have drifted off only briefly. Then she remembered Barrett. He'd told her to come back that night.

Celia went to the kitchen and heated more water in the kettle. She emptied and refilled the cushion and returned it to her father's back, lifting his shirt this time to place it directly against his skin. He didn't wake as she inched his shirt up, the flannel soft from a thousand wearings and washings. She placed her hands on his lower back for a moment, on the place where he was spoiled. Then she put the hot cushion back and pulled his shirt down over it as best she could. She crossed the cabin to her own room and dropped easily out the window.

Around back of the big house, she set up the ladder and went over the fence. Barrett's grotto was deserted, lit only by the underwater lights of the hot tub. It looked like a cauldron awaiting eye of newt and hair of wolf and all the other impractical ingredients that represented the origins of organic cooking. The quiet, and the witching-hour nature of the glowing hot tub, put Celia on edge. She slid open the door to the sunroom and went through to the hallway, where the bright ceiling lights nearly blinded her. Barrett's room was empty, the door open, TV on but silent, and the bed a mess as always. That left only one place.

Celia pushed open the door to Barrett's office at the end of the hall. He was at his desk with his back to her. The computer in front of him showed a bank website. There was a long column of numbers she couldn't read from whatever account he was logged into. Music played softly from speakers on either side of the monitor.

"Good evening, my dear Celia," Barrett said without turning around. His voice was thick and slow, familiar somehow.

"Hey."

"Have a seat." Barrett pointed over his shoulder at the couch along the wall behind him. He didn't turn from his screen. "I'll be with you in a moment."

Celia sat on the half of the couch that wasn't heaped with papers, but papers from the nearest pile slid onto her lap when she sat anyway. She stacked the sheets neatly, absently reading the one on top. It was from another bank, but it was addressed to someone named Barbara Josener. There was a red stamp that said COPY across the text. Over at the computer, a small box with a man in it appeared in the upper-right corner of the screen. The man looked tired, like he had been awakened. Then he moved and his voice came through the computer speakers over the music. "Barrett, you still there? Let's get this done so I can get back to sleep, if you don't mind."

"I'm here," Barrett said. "I'm thinking. Just be patient."

Celia went back to the paper on top of the pile she was neatening. She scanned the text under the COPY stamp but couldn't draw any sense from what it said. Who was Barbara Josener? What was a lien? Whatever it was, Barrett had one against "the property located at 7606 Route 52." Route 52 was the road you turned off to get to Zoar. Barbara Josener must be the lady who gave Barrett all this land. A lien must be some legal thing for giving someone your property.

"OK," Barrett said to the man on his screen. "This all looks fine. Set up the transfer, but don't execute it until delivery. I'll call you when everything arrives. Then we can all call whoever we need to call to verify the things we need to verify and part ways happy."

"Great," the computer man said with zero enthusiasm. "Now can I—" He stopped talking and squinted, leaning into the screen on his end. "Barrett, who is that?" the man said, his finger jabbing out of the screen and obscuring his face momentarily. Celia realized he must be able to see her on his own screen in a small box in the corner, sitting behind Barrett. She waved. The man looked surprised, finally fully awake. "Barrett, what the fuck?"

"Watch your language. She's an instrument of the Lord," Barrett said.

"What?"

"She's fine. Don't worry about her."

The man rubbed his bald head. "Barrett, do you grasp what we're doing here? And how inappropriate it is for you to have a guest during this discussion?"

"I said, she's fine. Don't worry about her," Barrett said, and Celia recognized the danger in his tone. "Do we have a problem?"

The man on the screen stared into the room. Celia pretended to be reading more spilled documents. "No," the man finally said. "We're good to go." His box in the corner of the screen went dark. The music coming from the computer speakers got louder. Barrett pushed himself back from his desk and swiveled around to face Celia.

"Matthew is upset," Barrett said.

"Sorry," Celia said.

Barrett closed his eyes and shrugged. "What can be done?" he said. His voice came out in a slow pour, and Celia realized why it was familiar. It was the voice of her father on his painkillers and her mother on her nerve pills. Did being an adult hurt so much? What was it that was so painful for these creatures who, as far as Celia could tell, went around doing whatever they wanted?

Celia said, "I don't know."

"It was rhetorical," he replied. "Now then. Celia, instrument of the Lord." Barrett clapped his hands together and held them in front of his chest. He blinked hard and opened his eyes wide, perking himself up some. "The crime you stand charged with is…" He looked thoughtful. "What was it you did again?" he said. This time Celia opted to believe he was being rhetorical. "Oh, yes," he said. "The crime of taking liberties with the talking of—of speaking of things you do not—uh. Of saying things of a divine nature without, you know, checking with me first. How do you plead?"

Celia didn't understand what Barrett was going on about, but he was in high spirits about the whole thing, which was a relief. She had been waiting for this all day without being able to decide what she felt. Fear or excitement?

"I'm sorry," Celia said. "I shouldn't have told Geraldine that—"

"Guilty!" Barrett exclaimed. "Celia Ann Waters pleads guilty with apology. Come over here, Celia, and throw yourself down and have a seat on the mercy of the court." He patted his lap. Celia stood and caught some more papers that wanted to fall off their pile. She went and sat on Barrett's lap. He snaked his arms around her waist and pulled her in tight. Celia's heart beat harder and higher than usual. "Put your arms around my neck," Barrett said. Celia did. It felt natural. Comfortable. The feel of another body against hers opened a pressure valve, relieving an agitation she hadn't realized was there. With her arms around his neck and her body pressed along the soft cushion of his own, Celia's face and Barrett's were inches apart. She saw that his pupils were practically his whole eye. Barrett put his one good eye on Celia. The rogue was beyond insouciance; it was in outright rebellion, like a kid on a sugar high, unable to stop himself running in circles. "You know what you did wrong?" Barrett said.

"I told Geraldine you had—"

Barrett put a finger to her lips. "Do you understand why it was wrong?"

"Because it wasn't part of your—" Celia said, just to see if Barrett would put his finger back on her mouth, which he did. His hands were soft and cold.

"We don't have to rehash it as long as you understand and don't ever do it again," Barrett said. "And I'm sure you won't do it again. You know why?"

"Because I'm a special girl," Celia answered.

"A very special girl," Barrett said, leaning so close to her face that Celia felt his breath on her mouth. He stood up from the chair, still holding her, and began to sway. "Dance with me, special girl. Do you know how to dance?"

Celia had made up lots of dances with Sloane and Rebekah, but she had only danced with a partner, like grown-ups did, once before at a wedding with her father when his boss, Dwayne, got married for the third time. Her mother had bowed out of attending, saying, "I went to the first two weddings and they didn't last. I'm beginning to think I'm bad luck. Take Cee-bear."

"What do you think, darlin'?" her father had said, scooping her up and tossing her gently into the air before catching and holding her. "You want to be your daddy's date to Dwayne's nuptials? I'll have the best-looking girl of the whole wedding on my arm. Just you and me, baby." Celia couldn't think of anything more exciting.

Dwayne was marrying a big fat woman this time, having decided that, "them skinny bitches is trouble," as he put it when Celia and her father congratulated him after the ceremony.

"'Cause a woman who don't eat has too much time to think of how to make you crazy," Dwayne's new bride added helpfully, then laughed so loud that now the laugh was the only thing Celia could remember about her. A laugh as big and strong as the woman who made it.

Celia's father had hoisted her into his arms when they were invited to join the new couple during their first dance, and afterward he kept her in his arms for song after song. Celia could see all the adults on the dance floor at face level rather than staring up at them. "Them skinny britches make trouble," Celia repeated, and her father laughed almost as loud as Dwayne's new wife. Later he told Dwayne what she said, and Dwayne called her Skinny Britches forever after that night.

Now, in answer to Barrett's question, Celia shook her head. She didn't properly know how to dance. Barrett lowered her feet to the floor. "All right, face me. Like that. Your hand goes here on my shoulder." His own hand took its place on her waist. "Now take my other hand here, like this. And we're just kind of stepping around in circles. You follow me. I'll guide you."

"You're in a good mood tonight," Celia said.

"I'm always in a good mood."

"An especially good mood tonight."

"Do you know why I'm so good at what I do?"

"Because you're the embodiment of God on Earth and it wouldn't make sense for God to be bad at being God."

"What? No. I mean, yes, but outside of all that." Celia didn't know they were allowed to think anything outside of that. "It's because I understand religion. I understand what it is, what people want from it, and how to use it. Do you know what people want from their faith? From a religion?"

"Redemption."

"They want to be right. That's it. They want to be right where others are wrong, and if you do it properly, you can give people a way to be right about any and everything. The murderer sees himself carrying out God's vengeance. The thief convinces himself he's stealing from the wicked. The bigot thinks he's opposing things that are abominations in the eyes of the Lord. Religion should be vague enough to include anything and also vague enough to exclude anything. And if you give it to people in the proper way and with the proper mind-set, they're grateful, so grateful they'll give you anything you ask for: money, women, power. The Catholics understood this best back when they were selling indulgences to the highest bidders, but they were so crass about it that sooner or later people were bound to revolt and jump ship for the first better offer that came along. Luther knew an opportunity when he saw one. And nailing his thesis to the church door like that. What a showman! It's right out of a movie."

Celia was lost in the monologue. She didn't know who Luther was and she had never met a Catholic as far as she knew. Barrett held her tighter, really pressing himself against her now. He planted a leg between hers and pushed her backward. "This is called a dip," he said. He brought her upright again. "Good girl. You're a natural. What I understand, and what I do, is give people that amazing ability to be right about anything. Religion is the most wonderful way to make any desire you have seem logical. Even when it's not. Especially when it's not. Oh, you cheated on your wife and now your wife wants to leave you? But you don't want your wife to leave? Well, first, pray to God for his forgiveness, which, if you're truly sorry—and you are, of course, your wife is about to leave you, who wouldn't be sorry about that?—he will grant you. Then check the Bible and find where it says 'wives, obey your husbands.' That's another point for you along with the forgiveness. She's a Christian, too, isn't she? She's not allowed to disagree with God. If God can forgive you, who is she to withhold forgiveness? Here you are, feeling terrible about all this, praying for forgiveness, suffering, and she can't find it in her heart to forgive you? That's not fair. And right there, dear Celia, that's the best part. That's when you know you've got them."

Barrett pushed Celia's hair gently out of her face. Cradling her head and neck, he dipped her again and leaned close to her ear. "When they feel like they're the victim. That's the real money shot." He straightened them up again and resumed leading the dance around the messy office. "Oh, Celia," Barrett said. "That's when they're yours." Barrett's hand slid down her back and came to rest at the foot of her spine, setting up base camp where the curve of her bottom began, in its lowest elevation. Celia was flushed and dizzy from the dancing and Barrett's diatribe, which she was only partly following. "That's the feeling they're really looking for," he went on. "That's what being right feels like: being a victim and your victimhood being important. And what could be more important than standing up for God? You can spit right in the face of science in the name of God. Be the victim. Science with all its proofs and facts and evidence and its theory of evolution—it's attacking you with all these things."

"A lot of my father's faith comes from science being too hard," Celia said.

"Science is way too hard!" Barrett said, laughing and spinning them in a renewed frenzy. "But you can act like you don't need it and claim it's wrong with no experience or knowledge as long as you have your religion. It's an illogical patch that allows you to connect any two thoughts you otherwise can't reconcile. There's evidence that dinosaurs existed, you say? But there's no mention of dinosaurs in the Bible. Well, that must mean the devil put the bones in the ground to trick modern man into not believing in God. It's a shortcut in rational thinking. And it means, my dear child, my special girl—" Barrett stopped the dance and stroked her cheek. His other hand wandered from her back down to her bottom and gave it a gentle squeeze. Celia felt a rush. "It means anything can be right. Anything can be justified and defended. It means I can do anything I want. And they, them out there"—he made a sweeping gesture around them—"they can do anything they want as well." He brought his hand back to her cheek. "As long as I allow it."

The song faded. There was a moment of quiet before the next one. Barrett's bad eye sought out whatever it could find on the periphery of his face, and his good eye looked down at Celia, its gaping pupil like a black hole she was approaching at the edge of space. Whatever energy had been fueling Barrett leaked out of him. The resolve left his posture. Celia felt it go, felt the slackening pressure of his grip on her body. Barrett took a deep breath and let Celia go, making his way to the couch. He lowered his bulk, and the pile of papers next to him tipped and spilled across his lap. Celia sat on the arm of the couch and leaned over him. "Are you all right?" she said.

"Just need to rest my eyes for a few minutes," he mumbled. He swatted at the pile of papers but failed to move them in any meaningful way. Celia gathered the loose pages together and put them back in their pile, then moved the pile to the floor. When she looked back up, Barrett was asleep. She tried to heave his legs onto the couch so he would be more comfortable, but it was like trying to lift a car tire with the car still attached. She sat in the space where the paper had been and leaned against Barrett. His body was soft. Celia stretched her own legs down the length of the couch and, using Barrett as a headboard, began reading through the stack of papers on the floor.

Celia woke in a panic. It was just before dawn. She was on a couch in a strange room where she had apparently fallen asleep while doing someone's taxes. There were bank statements and letters from finance companies all over her. The pillow she was using shifted positions and snorted, and she sat up in shock. Barrett. The office. Right, the dancing and the man on the computer and all that.

Celia put the documents back in their disorganized heap and left Barrett sleeping. She went out back to the fence, dragging a chair over for a boost. She didn't feel like bumping into Geraldine again, or worse, her mother, and explaining what she was doing in the house at that hour a second day in a row.

Sunlight from some hidden place below the tree line and the curve of the earth leached into the sky, mixing with the tail end of night and turning the world gray. Neither day nor night, just the dingy, gray, purgatorial wash of predawn. Through this haze, Celia saw Gardner leaving his Gardner Special in hunting gear. She went past her own cabin and broke into a jog to catch up with him. He heard her when she was still thirty feet behind him and turned. "Well, it's about time," he said. He looked her up and down and added, "You ain't dressed right."

"I'm not coming with you. I wanted to ask you something."

"What exactly do you do all day?"

"Please?" Celia said, in a tone she hoped suggested she wasn't in the mood for this right now.

"All right, what?"

"Help build that house over there. Please." Celia pointed to the barely begun shack that made the third point of a triangle with her cabin and Gardner's own home.

Gardner looked from Beth's future place up to their cabin and then back to Celia. "Your dad was over helping on that one yesterday."

Celia nodded. "And Beaufort," she said.

"What Beaufort does ain't called help where I come from."

"Fair enough."

"Your daddy's got a disk all chewed up somewhere in his spine." Celia nodded. "And you don't want him making it worse building that place, so you want me to help instead?"

"That's right."

"Why's he working on it, anyway? He knows his back's for crap."

Celia shrugged. "Because he's nice?"

"Yeah, that's what everyone says about him. I think that Beth woman asked him to help her."

"You know who she is?"

"I've seen her around. She came in with the new recruits. Wears that pullover. Brown kinda hair. 'Bout yay tall." He held his hand to his chest. "Big eyes."

"Yeah, I guess."

Now it was Gardner nodding. "I've seen her around," he said again.

I guess so, since you know everything but her shoe size, Celia wanted to say, but refrained. She was asking for a favor, after all.

"All right," Gardner said. "When I get back. Figure I got an hour or two before anyone's up and eaten and started in on the place. See you then." He turned and marched off into the woods the way he had been going before Celia stopped him. She turned, too, in the opposite direction to check her father's butt cushion and maybe nap a bit. She was pleased but confused. Gardner had agreed more easily than she expected. Celia figured he would have least made her learn how to fish.

Two nights later at the Service Gathering Celia sat with her father, who still had a bit of a mood on about Celia scheming to have Gardner take over his work site. People stopped by her and her father's seats on the way to their own. This was new. It had started when Zoar's freshman class arrived. A middle-aged couple headed their way. The wife was short, and her breasts and stomach seemed to be all the same piece, a large curve of flesh that drew her along as she walked. Her husband was inverted the other way. He was thin and wiry, but slouching had become his default stance somewhere over the years. They walked over like a question mark following a comma.

"I'm Rosemarie," the woman said.

"Clyde," said her husband.

Celia and her father introduced themselves.

"We just had to come over and say hello," Rosemarie said. "It's such an honor to meet you both. We heard you talk at your place the other day." She was referring to Celia, who had revealed another dream the day before. In this one, Christ had appeared to her at Zoar, Barrett told her. He took her to a treetop, where they'd looked out across the land and viewed all the citizens going about their day. Then the sky darkened with storm clouds. From the tree-top where she stood with Christ, Celia saw the first lightning bolt strike and kill someone. Then the second. The third. Lightning poured from the black heavens, obliterating bodies. But some people were not struck, and behind those people Celia saw "creatures so beautiful, so pure, that I knew right away they were angels. But no matter how beautiful, how awesome, these angels were, I could see that they were fierce, strong beings. Protectors of heaven. They carried swords of fire. Their wings were a white so bright it hurt my eyes to look at them, but I couldn't turn my gaze away. When lightning tried to strike a person the angels watched over, their wings covered that person and protected them like a shield. I asked the Lord, 'Why are some under the protection of angels and some are not?' And Jesus responded, 'My child, because there are some who claim to believe in my Second Coming but who do not believe it in their hearts. They do not have the strength to accept the truth, and when they are called to action, they will not be able to act. Better they be struck down now than fail me when I call.'" Then Jesus turned into a lamb and jumped down from the treetop and started grazing on the bodies of the dead, who turned to grass before Celia's eyes. Or mind's eye—whichever one was correct when you were talking about a dream.

"Could you tell who exactly was being struck down by God's lightning?" Rosemarie wanted to know. "Do you know who the nonbelievers are?" She and Clyde waited. They were concerned it might be them, Celia supposed. It's harder than it seems, measuring your own level of belief. They had followed The Prophet here, given over the reins to what money and property they had, but what if that wasn't enough? They hadn't been here as long as the others. Would that be held against them? They could never truly be sure they were good enough; there was always another seed of doubt being sown.

"They weren't specific people," Celia told them. "I didn't look down and recognize people I knew. It wasn't like that. The people in my dream were kind of stand-ins for all of us here. They represented us as a people."

"So you just couldn't make out the faces of who was being struck down and who was being saved?" Clyde said.

"It wasn't actual people who live here," Celia said.

"But you said you looked down and couldn't recognize anyone," Rosemarie said. "Maybe we were just all killed already and those people in your dream were new people you just haven't got familiar with yet."

Celia was losing control of the impression the dream was meant to have. Wait. Or was she? Let them fill it in; don't be specific—that's what Barrett had told her. The dream was supposed to scare them. That was the point. Fine, let them be scared. "It's possible," Celia told Rosemarie and Clyde. "The

Lord doesn't give us direct orders or tell us exactly what's coming our way, because it would violate our free will. But he favors us, so we're allowed a glimpse. One thing is for certain. A dark time is coming. And we can either be ready for it or suffer through it." That ought to do it, Celia thought.

"Amen," Clyde said.

"Would you pray for us?" Rosemarie said.

Celia told her she would. "I pray for us all. I hope you will, too."

Clyde and Rosemarie went to find seats. Celia's father said, "There's been a lot of that since your dream. The people know. They know something's coming." He seemed about to elaborate, but the voices of the congregants drained away to nothing, which meant his wife, along with The Prophet and Geraldine, were about to appear.

The two companions took their seats, and The Prophet mounted his dais and surveyed his people. He didn't speak. The people shifted and fidgeted. After a full minute of silence from The Prophet, a palpable fear was coming off the crowd. Then, finally, "I know you all love one another here," The Prophet began. "And you love the Lord. And you trust in him. In me. You all work together. We produce almost all our own food. Those of you who helped found this community have opened your doors and your hearts to our new residents. And those of you who are new have opened your hearts in return, learning our ways and pitching in. And it seems like a nice place to live."

The Prophet strolled around his stage, letting that last line stand naked a moment. "It seems like a good place." Another terrible stretch of silence. "But," he went on, "I worry you all think that's enough. I worry," his voice rose, "that you'll all become complacent here, tucked away from the challenges of so-called civilization. Because let me tell you something about civilization," he said, pointing blindly, out beyond the borders of Zoar. "The alleged civilization that you all left behind? It isn't civilized," he bellowed. "Here, you come out of your home in the morning and greet your neighbor saying, 'Good morning, beautiful day God's made for us,' and your neighbor will say, 'God's peace be with you, friend. It is indeed a beautiful day.' You say something like that out there in the civilized world and someone's likely to take a swing at you. Or tell you to go screw off or some worse profanity. Or maybe they'll tell you that your talking about God violates their rights—the rights they only have because of this one nation under God. These are the same people who don't want your kids to pray at school. They hate for children to pray, because it makes them harder to corrupt. Harder to turn them into consumers. They don't want God's name in the Pledge of Allegiance. They want God's name off their money. And let me tell you, God agrees with them on that one. He doesn't want his name on their vile and filthy dollars anymore. And it wouldn't hurt his feelings much to have it taken out of the Pledge, either. This country has turned its back on God. And the time is coming, friends…" The Prophet let this trail off, his eyes closed, his head back, as if speaking with the Lord right then. "Out there," he began again. "They would just as soon spit on you as greet you. But that challenge, the challenge of living your faith, living the way God intended everyone to live, makes you stronger. It's that assault from the so-called civilized and secular world that weeds out the fair-weather faithful from the true believers. It's easy to be a good Christian when you're immersed in a Christian environment. It's a luxury. But God doesn't need merely good Christians for what lies ahead. No, God needs soldiers. Christian soldiers willing to fight for their faith, who are strong in the face of oppression from the secular world. They are the ones who truly keep the Lord's favor. They will be the ones the Lord raises up, the ones he will make a place for in heaven. The ones who are truly his children and who he will save. And I worry, friends…I worry there are those of you here who don't have the fight in you."

The Prophet had come right out and said it. The crowd had long sensed the direction he was going but hoped they were mistaken. Now here it was. Their leader, their Prophet, had doubts about them, just as Celia's dream had provided doubt within themselves. "I worry that bringing you here was a mistake. That it's made you soft. That I've taken you away from the hostile world of modern America with its consumerism, its abortions, its Muslim terrorists, its liberal atheists, its illegal immigrants, its stolen jobs from hardworking folks, its pornography posing as sitcoms, its Victoria's Secret catalogs that just show up at your house, its blasphemous music, its science that tries to disprove the Bible, its homosexuals prancing around trying to recruit you, or worse, your children, its war on Christmas, its unions and affirmative action, its assault on family values, and its absolute and total disrespect for our Lord and Savior Jesus Christ. I worry that without the world out there right in your face, reminding you of the evil that exists all around us, you might have forgotten the fear. The fear that the world might take you and your family, and that when judgment day comes the Lord won't take you. It's that fear that spurs a person to fight. To become a soldier for Christ, and I worry, no, I fear, you all may have become complacent." The Prophet stopped and circled his dais. "Have you become complacent?" he said quietly.

There was silence until a voice next to Celia hollered out, "No!" It was her father, startling her out of her reverie. She had been examining her nails.

"Brother Waters, you've always been a strong man," The Prophet said. "You couldn't be complacent if you tried."

There was another shout of "No!" that Celia recognized as Gardner, probably mortified he hadn't been the first.

"Are you complacent?" The Prophet asked again.

"No!" came the unified response, solid and vigorous. No one wanted to be left out.

"Have you forgotten the evil that is out there waiting to take your soul?"

"No!"

"Have you lost your drive to fight that evil no matter the cost?"

"No!"

"Are you ready and willing to be a soldier for Christ?"

"N'yes!" They hadn't quite been ready for the switch to the affirmative, but they recovered in time.

"I said, are you ready and willing to fight for your faith, to be a defender of God's kingdom, a protector of heaven, and a soldier for Christ?"

"Yes!"

The first shipment of guns arrived a few days later.

Shots cracked like tree branches in a storm. Every morning and afternoon it sounded like the surrounding forest was being blown to destruction by an unfelt wind. The days after the guns arrived grew beautiful and mild. Spring scents of growth and warmth mixed with gunpowder. It was a tang in the taste of the air. The citizen's enthusiasm for target practice was matched only by their zeal for the Lord.

"Guns and God," Celia's mother said. "They should have called this place Texas instead of Zoar."

Gardner, of course, became insufferable. "'Bout time we started teaching these people some practical skills," he said to Celia one day when she found it impossible to avoid him on one of the paths without being obvious. "Ain't seen you at gun class yet," he said. "Do you just hate fun or what? Come fire off some rounds. Learn how to clean a gun. They don't bite."

"I thought that was exactly what they did," Celia said.

"Not if you know how to handle them properly, they don't."

What was it like, Celia thought, to be one of those people always trying to convince others that dangerous things weren't dangerous. Someone who always wanted others to believe skydiving, or guns, or rugby were perfectly harmless. She said to Gardner, "Thanks, but—"

"No, thanks. Yeah, yeah, I know. Your pops has sure taken to it, though."

He certainly had, Celia was happy to notice. Since the night The

Prophet had stated, in front of the compound's whole population, that Brother Waters couldn't be complacent if he tried, her father had been a new man. Well, not exactly new, but he was back to being satisfied with his own righteousness. All his dedication, sacrifice, and effort finally acknowledged with a short public platitude and he was content. It made Celia remember one of Barrett's diatribes. Not a late-night painkiller-fueled diatribe, but a lucid midday explanation he'd delivered over tea.

"It doesn't work if they completely get it. They can't ever have the ultimate prize, because then you'd have nothing left to sell them," Barrett had said.

"Sell them?"

"Figure of speech. Listen. Once the dog gets the rabbit, it stops chasing it, right?" Celia figured that was probably true and nodded. "So things always have to be just out of reach. Slightly hazy, off in the distance. The people always have to remain sinners. You have to remind them of their flaws, keep them down. The rewards come later."

"When they're dead."

"No, when they are reborn into eternal life. Death is what we're defeating here. It's what they're all scared of. Getting around death, ducking that inevitability, that's what we're promising them. But you have to keep them working at it. Got to keep them chasing that rabbit."

"Don't they get, like, defeated after a while?"

"You have to throw them a bone now and then. Tell them they're special."

Celia was hurt. "You told me I was special."

"You are special, child. So special. That's why I'm explaining all this to you. That's why you're here and they're out there: because you weren't chasing the rabbit in the first place. You already seemed to get it. You know the rabbit can't be caught."

Celia accepted this and felt better.

"The best way to do it," Barrett had said, slipping back into his lesson, "is to lay a heavy emphasis on mystery. That there are deep and complicated things most people can't understand or even fathom."

"But there are mysteries, aren't there? Things people can't understand?"

"Of course. People don't understand how their TVs work. Or lightbulbs. God, the universe—suggesting there's more than they can know about these things meets with little resistance. You never directly explain any of the mystery. You talk about how there are people who know and people who don't know. People who understand and people who don't understand. And whomever you're talking to and paying attention to will assume they're in the group that knows. Or that will know, as long as they keep listening to you and following you."

"Know what?"

"It doesn't matter. It's a mystery. But it keeps them going. Chasing the rabbit. Feeling like they're one step closer than some unseen group of others."

That's what Barrett had done for her father—thrown him a bone to give him a little more energy to keep chasing the rabbit, made him feel special. Celia was happy her father was happy again, but the whole thing was a bit sad when you stripped away the context and saw it for what it was.

Celia was happy about her father's passion for the soldiering side of his faith for another reason, too. It kept him from trying to build Beth's stupid house. Or anyone else's house. Or from helping with the farming. Barrett had given them both that. Something her father could throw himself into—which was the only way he could do anything, throw himself at it—that wouldn't lead to him dragging himself around with a trashed spine. Gardner had taken over completely on Beth's place. Beaufort was immediately fired.

"I ain't watching a nonretarded man hobble around like a drunk picking up dropped nails," Gardner had said. "Ain't dignified."

Instead, Gardner assembled a crew of kids. They kept the work site clean, and Gardner taught them what all the different tools were and how to use them. He led a gun-safety course for them as well. He was building up to a hunting trip when enough of them showed firearm proficiency and learned "to keep quiet longer than it takes to fart." He was a self-styled scoutmaster.

"Mr. Creech is funny," Rebekah told Celia.

"Are you sure?" Celia said. "He mainly seems grumpy."

"He's super grumpy. That's why he's so funny."

Celia thought Rebekah might be a bad judge of what was humorous, but she didn't say so.

Beth was still around even though Celia's father was no longer building her house. Celia came home one evening and found her father at the kitchen table, cleaning an assault rifle, and Beth at the stove boiling all the flavor out of some poor vegetable.

"Hey there, Cee-bear," her father said. "Beth is making us dinner. Ain't that nice of her?"

"It was the least I could do. Your father has been so welcoming. He started my house and all, and now he's teaching me how to use a gun."

"You got to know. With all The Prophet is talking about coming down the pike, it'd be insane not to know how to safely and effectively use a gun." Celia excused herself from dinner, saying thanks but she wanted to lie down; it had been a long day, and she'd eaten with The Prophet after their lesson and prayer session. "All right, baby," her father said. "Get some rest. But you don't know what you're missing. This girl can cook." He smiled at Beth. "I mean, check out this spread."

Celia looked at the boiled food plopped sadly onto their two plates and resisted the urge to throw one of the heavy glass ashtrays at her father. Fool man, going on like no one had ever cooked him a meal. She went to her room and slept.

Celia woke before dawn. She peeked out her door. Her father was asleep on the couch, which meant Beth must have taken his room. She stayed with them sometimes while her house was being finished. Celia's father had encouraged Beth to stay with them permanently until her place was ready. He did this in front of Celia without any warning or discussion.

"You should just stay here. We have plenty of space," he had said, gesturing around their tiny cabin. "Celia and I would love the company, wouldn't we, Cee-bear?"

"We don't have that much room," Celia had said. "Beth might feel a little cramped."

"Your dad is so generous," Beth said to Celia. "But I couldn't impose like that. I stay with friends. The Lord provides for me. And there's so many wonderful people here who've opened their doors." She patted Celia's father on the arm. "Besides, you know me. I can take care of myself."

Letting other people open their doors to you isn't taking care of yourself, Celia thought, especially when those other wonderful people mainly meant Gardner. She kept these thoughts to herself. If her father didn't see fit to ask her before inviting Beth to live in their cabin, then she didn't see fit to keep him informed of the goings-on around the compound. Celia had found Beth staying at Gardner's on a nighttime walk a few weeks earlier, a little after Gardner started working on Beth's house. From a distance, Celia had seen Gardner exit his pop-up camper and relieve himself next to the truck. Why wasn't he in his house? Celia wondered. She waited until Gardner was back inside the pop-up, and hopefully asleep, then crept up to his home. She pressed her face against the bedroom window, and there was Beth, asleep in Gardner's bed. Now she paid attention to the nights when the light in the pop-up glowed dimly through its small windows. How many times in Gardner's life, Celia wondered, had a woman relegated him to sleeping in that thing?

Now, Celia gently closed her bedroom door and left her father asleep on the couch. She didn't have to wonder how many times a woman had relegated him to that spot. She had seen him live on a couch for the better part of a year in his painkiller days. She packed a clean change of clothes into a small bag, slid her window open, and hopped outside. A few other early risers were moving around by the barn. Celia saw them in the morning's pale light. There was some activity around Town Square, too. People getting an early jump on the day's chores. At her end of the compound, though, Celia was alone. Gardner was either sleeping in or was already out hunting or fishing or whittling or whatever.

Celia headed for the big house with an aim to using Barrett's shower, or better yet, taking an early morning soak in the hot tub, then a hot shower. The weather was turning, but the water in the cabin still barely crossed over from freezing to tepid.

Celia walked around back to the fence. Her ladder was gone. She checked under the fir tree just to be sure. Nothing. The last time she used it she had laid it on its side and leaned it against the fence, like always. Had someone else been here? None of Zoar's other inhabitants ever came up to the big house, with the exception of Gardner, who was occasionally called up and dispatched to do some errand or other. He would never have any reason to be around back. Who had moved her ladder?

Celia felt paranoia creeping in and an unsettling feeling, like she was being watched. She went back around to the front of the house, too uncomfortable to keep speculating while standing at the scene of the mystery. Barrett must have just needed the ladder for some normal ladder-related purpose—changing a high lightbulb or something. She would just have to take her chances with the front door.

Celia let herself in and closed the door quietly behind her. She crossed the den like a thief. She was almost to Barrett's wing when Geraldine rushed out of her own hallway. "Celia, no," Geraldine said.

"Geraldine, I'm not in the mood right now," Celia said. "The Prophet is expecting me."

"No, he's not," Geraldine said, and the surety of her tone made Celia pause. What was going on here?

"What do you know about my ladder?" Celia said, puffing herself up as much as she could and stepping close to Geraldine.

"What ladder? What are you talking about?" Geraldine said. She moved around Celia and blocked the entrance to Barrett's hallway. "The Prophet is busy right now, and you're not to bother him."

"I never bother him. He asks me to come here."

"Well, he didn't ask you this morning. You need to go."

Celia wasn't going to continue pretending she had been summoned, either by divine communication or regular old talking. Geraldine was too sure of being right not to know Celia was lying. Celia didn't know how she knew, but she did. Nothing to do about that, but she wasn't getting kicked out by Geraldine, a wannabe who had wheedled her way into Barrett's inner sanctum, whereas Celia had been invited.

"Get out of my way," Celia said, and she tried to break through Geraldine's human barricade.

Geraldine braced herself with her arms out, her hands against the walls. "Celia, are you crazy? Stop it. What's the matter with you?"

Celia kept pushing through, grabbing one of Geraldine's arms and prying it off the wall. "Move it, old woman," Celia said. The two of them struggled, shoving against each other.

"Celia, you're being insane. Stop it. Get off me."

"I'll get off you when you get out of the way."

"Celia—" They grappled in the hall's entrance. "Celia, this is for your own—" Geraldine's sentence cut off with a grunt as she got Celia around the waist like a football player and tried to drive her back. Celia pressed a hand against either wall and tried to propel herself forward. "It's your mother," Geraldine finally hissed from down by Celia's rib cage. Celia let go of the walls, and the two of them fell. They sat up on the floor, both panting from the exertion. "It's your mother," Geraldine repeated. "She's with The Prophet doing her Lady Companionly duty. You understand?" Celia sensed her mouth was hanging open, but she couldn't seem to make it close or say anything. "That's why you can't go see him right now. He's with your mother."

Celia sat on Geraldine's bed finally understanding the appeal of all these painkillers adults took. She knew this was part of it, of course—being a Lady Companion or whatever these two called themselves, but she had never been confronted with it outright. It existed in the ether, like using the toilet. Everyone knows everyone else has to do it, too, so there's no reason to go talking about it and being impolite. Now, here it was. Down that hall she knew so well, behind a closed bedroom door, in a bed she had sat on just as she was sitting on Geraldine's now, her mother was having sex with Barrett.

Barrett, who was supposed to think that she, Celia, was the most special. Who taught her the secrets of being The Prophet and leading these people.

Her mother, who was supposed to be with her father. Who had ditched him for a better life and left Celia with the scraps.

Geraldine was talking. "...why you need to listen to me. To adults in general, honey. We know what's best. Your mother and The Prophet, they're expressing a beautiful covenant blessed by God, but they need privacy. That's why it's no good for you to just go barging around. You're always welcome here, but you have to remember you don't actually live here. You wouldn't like it if someone just showed up at your house, right? Just barged right into your life?"

"I don't like it."

"Right, no, you wouldn't."

"I'm sorry I tried to run you over."

"Thank you," Geraldine said. Some of the starch went out of her. She patted Celia gently on the leg.

"It's just that I had a dream I wanted to discuss with The Prophet. It scares me, this dream. Not like the others," Celia said. "This dream made me think, like, that everything was over."

"That does sound scary."

"That wasn't the scary part. The scary part was that everything had been over for a long time. I just hadn't really believed it."

"Do you want to tell me about it?" Geraldine said. "As a Lady Companion to The Prophet, I have a spiritual knowledge that can help guide—"

"That's OK," Celia said. "It was probably just a regular nightmare. I'm going to use my mom's shower and change." She stood to leave.

"Oh, I don't know if that's a good idea, since everyone can't…" Geraldine trailed off as Celia's gaze found hers. Perhaps it was empathy, or maybe she felt that one victory was enough for the morning. Or maybe she didn't want Celia trying to go through her again. She nodded and said, "I'm sure it'll be fine this once."

Celia went across the hall to her mother's room and shut the door and locked it. She stripped down and ran the shower as hot as she could stand. She shivered under the steaming water when she got in, as though a chill deep within was wreaking what havoc it could as it was warmed out of her.

Then she cried. Not much and not hard, but she stood and poured her water along with the shower. She felt nothing but rejection. How could Barrett want her mother over her? How could he tell Celia she was special, share so much with her, then take her mother into his room? Her mother who left Celia and her father behind and didn't even have the decency to act like she was happy with her choice. Because they think you're a child, a voice in Celia's head answered her. Even while they hang the enormity of the adult world on you, they look at you and see a child.

Out of the shower, Celia took a seat at her mother's vanity and brushed her hair. She opened a drawer. Her mother's little orange bottles of pills looked up at her, their white tops like blank eyes. She closed that drawer and opened another. Her mother's makeup. Celia chose a lipstick, foundation, blush, eye shadow—the tools of the trade for covering up what was human and presenting what was desired. She dropped these into her bag along with her dirty clothes, dressed, and left, blowing by Geraldine's open door without saying good-bye.

Outside, she paused on the front porch and looked down to her cabin. Beth and her father were out front with a pair of handguns. Her father was demonstrating arm and shoulder alignment in the firing position. He gestured at his own arm, then got behind Beth as she took position, wrapping his arms around hers, pressing against her, adjusting and tweaking. After a few minutes, they holstered their weapons and went down the path, presumably to the firing range. They stopped at Beth's nearly completed house, where Gardner stopped what he was doing and began demonstrating something with his own gun for Beth's benefit. Celia's father's gun came back out and he began counterdemonstrating. The two men waved their guns around for Beth to see, keeping their arms straight and swinging their weapons in dramatic arcs to keep from pointing them directly at each other or her, sticking to safety protocol. From a distance it looked like they were doing yoga or some other pagan practice. What a couple of assholes, Celia thought. Finally her father holstered his gun and Gardner his, and Beth and her father continued on their way.

Celia went down to the cabin and made herself breakfast. She lay down and napped for a few hours. When she woke, she took out the makeup and tried on a few faces before settling on one she liked. She put on her smallest shorts and a tank top that was so worn it was nearly see-through. It was almost noon by the time she was ready. Her mother would be back in her own room by now, in her own bed. Celia pulled on a sweater to fight the chill and went back to the big house. Her ladder had been returned to its regular place. Celia hopped the fence and let herself into the sunroom. She pulled the sweater off and threw it into a corner, then went down the hall to Barrett's office. The door was open. He was at the computer, his back to her. The room was strewn, as usual, with stacks of paper and fast-food wrappers, but now there was the addition of three crates of assault rifles stacked against one wall.

Celia pressed herself against the doorway until Barrett sensed her and swiveled around. "Miss Celia," he said.

"Hey."

"I believe, if I'm not terribly mistaken, that I heard you fighting with Geraldine again this morning."

"Yeah."

"I was very clear how I felt about that after the last crack-of-dawn fight you got in with her."

"Yeah," Celia said, looking down at her feet. "I was bad." She left the doorway and went and sat in Barrett's lap. He looked confused but drew her in. She put her arms around his neck. "I'll be good from now on," she said. "I promise. It won't happen again."

"You'll be good?" Celia saw his eyes drop to her chest.

She nodded. "I'll be good."

"Well, who could deny such a sincere apology," Barrett said.

Celia felt his arms encircle her a bit more firmly, and she hopped up out of his lap, breaking his grip, leaving him wanting. "Show me how to shoot," Celia said. She went to the stack of crates and looked in the topmost. The long gun lay nestled in squiggly scraps of paper that looked like curly hair. She raised the gun, barrel first, and admired it for a moment stood upright, its full length on display. Men were so proud of these things. She lifted it out of the crate and turned back to Barrett. The gun was heavier than it looked. She held it awkwardly across her stomach. "Show me? Please?" she said.

"You can't shoot it inside, obviously," Barrett said. "But I can give you some tips." He heaved himself from his chair and slid around behind her. He put his arms along hers and positioned the gun. His body along the length of hers was plush and yielding. Celia pressed her backside gently against his crotch. Barrett cleared his throat. "OK," he said. "Now, whatever you're aiming at, you're going to sight it right along here. That's how you set up your target."

But of course, Celia already knew that.

"Will you take me over there one day?" Rebekah asked Celia.

They were in the barn with Trevor.

"To the big house?" Celia said. She was braiding Rebekah's hair. They were taking a break from playing a game where Celia was the queen and Rebekah was her most loyal subject. It was fitting, since when Celia had found Rebekah playing with some of the compound's other children and asked her to leave them and come hang out with her, Rebekah didn't have to give it any thought. She left the others without even saying good-bye.

"Yeah, to The Prophet's house," Rebekah said. "I bet it's rapturous. Like being as close to what heaven's like here on earth."

Celia thought back to her morning. She woke up in Barrett's bed after sneaking over in the night. (Beth was in Gardner's house, she noted on the way over; Gardner was in his lousy pop-up.) She woke because Barrett had scooted up behind her and was rhythmically pressing something hard against her bottom. His hand snaked around to her chest, and she came awake more fully. She was drowsy. She wanted to keep sleeping in his magnificent bed, so much better than the depressing cot in her own room, but this was the price of admission: to the bed, to the house, to Barrett's magnetic presence. She let him go on for a bit longer, and when his hand went under her shirt, she counted to ten, then gently removed his hand and rolled over to face him. "Someone is energetic this morning," she said.

"My body is still human, though my soul is divine," Barrett said, not for the first time since the afternoon Celia had come over for a gun lesson.

"I know my Prophet," she said. He liked being called this. "But my body is still divinely pure, though my soul may be human." This second part he didn't like so much, though he couldn't come right out and say so. "A young lady must keep her body pure for the Lord. You taught me that."

The day Barrett showed her how to hold a gun she had wriggled and squirmed against his body until he tossed the gun back in the crate and turned her around to face him. There was something base and animal in his expression. His wild eye suddenly made sense on his face. She pressed even tighter against him, and he lowered his head and put his mouth against hers. His lips parted, and hers followed instinctively. His tongue flicked shallowly across her mouth, and she pushed her own out to meet it. Relief. Relief that he liked her. Relief that he wanted her. Relief as her body stirred and whirled inside, taking over and responding with a surge to the touch of another body, another mouth, this ancient and embedded practice recognized. It was her first kiss. In the instant before their mouths met, Celia felt cataclysm. Fear and power combined. She was impressed with what she had brought into being: this moment. She was scared of where it was all leading.

She kissed him again, lying in his bed that morning. Kissing was becoming commonplace in a pleasant way. The kissing riled him up again, and he pulled her to his body with its singular want. Celia made out with him for a while before pushing him away. "I can't defile my temple," she told him. "But," she said, slipping her hand inside his underwear, "my left hand need not know what my right hand is doing."

Barrett groaned. "Say it again," he said.

Celia found the source of all this trouble and wrapped it in her hand. "My left hand," she said, using that hand to stroke his cheek, "need not know what my right hand"—Barrett groaned again—"is doing."

It was only a short time before Barrett made his mess, then sighed, kissed her, and fell back asleep. This was an outcome Celia was coming to find both horrific and hilarious, like burping a baby till it spit up, then went down for a nap. Celia got up and washed her hands, then went back to sleep herself.

"Like being as close to what heaven's like here on earth," Rebekah was saying now in the barn.

"Yeah, it's pretty rapturous, I guess," Celia said.

"So will you take me some time?"

Celia thought of all the competition she already had for Barrett's attention. She looked at Rebekah, who had turned to face her with this request, with her bright eyes and sincere devotion, her long white legs. She imagined Barrett telling Rebekah she was special. "I don't think I'm allowed to bring visitors," Celia said. Rebekah deflated. "You wouldn't like it anyway. It's just a bunch of adults doing boring adult things."

"I thought The Prophet was in rapture all day."

"He is, I guess, but he's, like, alone in his room in rapture, so the rest of the place is quiet and boring, and you can't go look at him or anything. Here, Trevor looks hungry." Celia ran her fingers through Rebekah's hair, unraveling the loose braid. She stood and took the younger girl's hands and pulled her to her feet. The barn was still and cool, but outside the warm sun pushed through the cracks in harmless dusty blades, like a magician's sword trick. The compound had a tractor, rendering Trevor obsolete as anything other than a factory for a minimal amount of fertilizer. It would have been hard to imagine anything enjoying its obsolescence as much as Trevor, though he maybe wouldn't have felt that way if he knew how much Harmon wanted to eat him.

"A beast of burden that don't work's just a burden," Harmon said. "Lotta good meat on him."

Fortunately for Trevor, life on the compound was never so hard up that any of the others felt hungry enough to eat donkey. Celia and Rebekah fed Trevor and stroked his head.

"This is where The Prophet revealed himself to you, right? That he was the Second Coming?" Rebekah said.

"Right in this very spot," Celia said.

"I bet it was amazing."

"Oh, yes," Celia said, looking around the dusty barn while Trevor twitched away a fly with his ear. "It was wondrous indeed."

Celia floated her legs to the surface of the hot tub and rested her feet against Barrett's chest. Barrett's head was tilted back against the tub's edge, his eyes closed, half a bottle of beer sweating nearby. He'd only taken a single sip to chase down a couple of pills. The other half he had poured into a glass for Celia.

"Are you trying to get me drunk?" she had teasingly asked him.

He had scowled. "I didn't enjoy being around drunk teenagers when I was one. You can handle half a beer."

Barrett absently rubbed Celia's feet without opening his eyes. "What do you think of this Beth woman?" Celia said.

"Who's Beth?"

"She came with the new people a while back." Celia took a sip of her beer, which she liked being allowed to have more than she actually liked its taste.

"What about her?" Barrett said.

"Do you think she's pretty?"

Barrett grudgingly opened one eye. "Is she the one that goes around with Gardner?"

"And my dad."

"Right, that whole thing," Barrett said, closing his eye and rolling them both beneath the lids.

"What whole thing?"

Barrett waved his hand. "Forget it. Nothing. No, I don't think she's pretty."

"Me either," Celia said.

"Well, I'm glad we cleared that up."

"Can I stay here tonight?"

"I think you should stay at your own house tonight."

"Why?"

"Because sooner or later someone will notice you're not sleeping in your own bed, and it would look bad if you got caught sneaking in here."

Celia came across the hot tub and straddled Barrett. "Please," she whispered in his ear.

"Celia, darling, I don't—" but he stopped as she ground herself against him. Celia felt him stiffen under her, and she rubbed herself back and forth along his length, a tingle and desire rising inside her. That had to be ignored, though. Barrett was the focus here; for her the goal was being wanted, not being attained. She was driving this car and needed to keep her attention on the road.

Celia put her mouth against Barrett's as she felt his hands creep up to her breasts and slip under the fabric of her bathing suit. She let him, whispering, "Please, please, please, please."

The next day Barrett announced that the Lord commanded him to take a third wife.

Once again, The Prophet sat at the kitchen table in the small farmhouse.

Celia's father sat slumped across from him. Beth stood back from the table, behind Celia's father, her hands folded at her chest in prayer or pleading, it was hard to know. The Prophet greeted her when he came in and referred to her by name. She hadn't moved since. She appeared frozen by his presence. Celia resisted the urge to roll her eyes.

"Brother Waters, it is good to be in your home again," The Prophet said.

"Mighty good to have you," Celia's father said uneasily. "Though technically it's your home, I guess. We just live in it."

"I gave it to one of my most faithful followers," The Prophet said, reaching across the table and placing his hand atop Celia's father's. "You and I, we've been through a lot together, haven't we?"

"That's certainly true."

"Since the beginning," The Prophet said. He looked over to awestruck Beth. "You know," he said. "Brother Waters here was one of the first to understand, the first to really get it. To see what was going on in the world and comprehend the magnitude of what was coming. He is one of the rocks upon which all of this has been built."

Beth nodded. "I hope I can be one of the new rocks," she said.

Inwardly, Celia made a face. Barrett beamed, though, and opened his hands. "I love to hear that. And the Lord loves to hear that, Beth. It's that faith and heavenly spirit that makes our mission possible." He turned to Celia's father. "The Lord, my father, has been speaking to me, Brother. He has a plan as you know, having participated so closely in its being put into action."

"I've been incredibly blessed."

"God has commanded me to take another wife in keeping with his true law, which is the Bible. You are familiar with the Bible's teachings."

"I am."

"And you're aware that God says the legal age of marriage is at puberty."

Celia's father had been keeping a dignified face despite almost curling into a ball in his chair as The Prophet spoke. Now he straightened up and looked confused. "Puberty?"

"Yes, puberty. It is better for a woman to be married than for Satan to tempt her through loss of self-control. Better to be married than be on fire."

"Corinthians," Celia said, always pleased to cite sources.

Celia's father looked over to where she was sitting beside Barrett, then looked to his prophet, then to Beth. "You mean *Celia*?" he said.

"God calls Celia," The Prophet said. Beth dropped her folded hands and also looked perplexed.

"But you can't take Celia," her father said.

The Prophet's voice dropped to frozen steel. "The Lord, your master, does not take anything. For all that he views is already his domain."

"I didn't mean…of course he doesn't take. I just…what with her being so young."

"God has a special plan for Celia."

"I truly believe that he does. I mean, I always believed that. Being smart as she is and all. Even when she was just a little thing, she was super smart. I knew she was bound for something important. But it just seems"—he swallowed and went for delicacy—"to my human understanding, which is, you know, limited before God, like it would make more sense to wait until she was older."

"God's plan does not have to make sense to us," The Prophet said.

"Pardon me, Prophet," Beth said, taking a seat now beside Celia's father. "But don't we find peace and comfort in God because he brings sense to a senseless world?"

"Stay out of this, Beth," Celia snapped.

"Hey!" her father said.

"Now, Celia," The Prophet said, shooting her a look. "Questions of a theological nature are always welcome. Beth, the sense that God brings to the world is the comfort of knowing that he is in charge. That he is there to guide us through our lives and bring us into an eternal peace when we die as his servants. This is what makes sense of the world. We do not have to understand his plan, just that it is his." Beth nodded. "Celia," Barrett said.

"I'm sorry," Celia said. She reached across the table and took Beth's hand. "Christ be unto you," she said with a smile.

"Brother Waters," The Prophet said. "Clearly you have a very special daughter with a very special purpose. She is spiritually mature beyond her years and touched by a gift from God: her dreams. They show the early stages of direct communication with our father. He has told me that she is to be my third wife. I am already her teacher and her guide, as well as her prophet."

Celia turned to her father. "Daddy, don't worry. I know this is right. The Lord has reached into me and filled my heart with peace on this matter. He has been leading me to this: when The Prophet revealed himself to me, then with my dreams. This is God's special plan, just for me. And almost as much as I want this, I want you to be happy for me and to let everyone see how happy you are for me."

Celia's father sighed and smiled weakly. "My," he said. "But I am blessed."

Celia jumped up with a squeal and went around the table and put her arms around his neck. "Thank you, Daddy."

"Oh my, but I am blessed."

Outside, as they walked back to the big house, Celia said, "How did I do?"

"Perfect, my love," Barrett said. He put an arm around her. Celia slowed her own quick steps to keep pace with his ambling. "The Lord prefers his will be done smoothly and with as little fussing and talking as possible. So if your father can tell people how happy he is for you then, well, that greases the hole a little before we slip the news in, right?" He gave the side of Celia's breast a playful pinch that actually hurt, but she kept quiet. "Not that God needs his followers' approval, but why do things the hard way?" They walked in silence until Barrett said, "You know who I don't care for? Though she is one of my followers and, of course, one of God's children."

"That Beth woman."

"You got it." Barrett took a bottle of pills out and dry-swallowed one. "Now let's go give your mother the happy news."

Celia, her mother, Geraldine, and The Prophet sat around a table in one of the unused rooms in the unused part of the house shaped like an E. It was the room where Celia had eavesdropped on Geraldine and Barrett discussing her becoming his second companion. Celia's mother looked a little spacey but lucid. Geraldine looked thrilled to be there. Celia figured she thought this meeting was to discuss Celia's behavior.

"I'd like to begin with a prayer," The Prophet said. "Join hands." Celia got her mother's hand and Barrett's. "My Heavenly father, hello. It is your son, your humble servant and earthly avatar. This is a beautiful day, Father, for we are about to bring your decree to fruition. We are all so close, Father. A family. Your family that you have hand-selected to be the head of the larger family that is the rest of the community here." The Prophet stopped and tilted his head back, eyes closed, mouth ajar. "Yes, Father," he shouted after a moment. "Yes, we accept your command with glad hearts and joyous praise, Father. Our family welcomes our newest member. In accordance with your wishes as put forth in the Bible, we have become a family of one man and multiple wives. It has made us strong. And now we welcome our third wife." Geraldine's and Celia's mother's eyes shot open. Celia had been watching them, waiting for their reaction. She stared back at them. The Prophet continued. "We go humbly, Father, down your path. We go graciously, Father, down your path. And we go blessedly, Father, down your path. In your name we pray, amen."

The Prophet opened his eyes and they all dropped hands. "Barrett, what the hell is this?" Celia's mother said.

The Prophet slammed both hands down on the table and stood, roaring, "You will not use that language in the presence of my father."

The shock of the outburst left the room silent and still. Celia hadn't been expecting it. She had never heard anyone talk to her mother that way. To judge from the stunned look on her mother's face, she wasn't used to being spoken to this way either. She looked scared and confused. For a moment Celia felt great pity and affection for her. She wanted to come to her aid and defend her, take her someplace safe, away from Barrett and Zoar and Geraldine and farmhouses. She wanted to protect her family, her blood. But the moment passed and turned to loathing. Where was this woman's fire, her heat and passion? If there had once been a woman like that, she was gone a long time now. Only something from a childhood memory, like Daniel, the stuffed bear she had loved till his eyes fell out and his ears wore away. And now? She wouldn't even begin to know where to look for him.

"Barrett, what is this?" her mother whispered.

"This is the will of the Lord," he said, still hulking above them. "This is what is happening next."

"This is my daughter. This is sick," her mother said.

"If you blaspheme like that one more time," Barrett said. "I will exile you without a second thought. You have not contributed nearly so much that I can't afford to throw you away."

"Prophet, please," Geraldine said now, stepping in. "You must understand. She doesn't know what she's saying. It's just so...sudden. And it's her daughter. Of course she's going to be concerned. I mean, she's so young it's—"

"The Bible decrees puberty as the age limit for marriage. And God decrees that this young woman is to be his Second Coming's third companion."

"But surely she can't be spiritually mature enough to take on the mantle of being a Lady Companion."

"Geraldine, what did I tell you about that ridiculous name?" The Prophet said, pinching the bridge of his nose between his thumb and forefinger.

"Celia, honey," her mother said, turning to face her now. "You don't want this. You don't understand what you're doing."

"I'm not doing this. This is a calling from God," Celia said.

"No, it's not. This is not God's will."

"Why not?" Celia demanded, raising her own voice. "Why was it God's will when it was you but not me?"

"Celia, please—" Geraldine began.

"No!" Celia shouted. "Answer me. Why was it God's will for you two but not me? Geraldine, tell me about your message from God. It was pure, wasn't it? There wasn't any cunning or ulterior motive, was there? You certainly didn't sit in some room with The Prophet, bargaining, did you?"

Geraldine looked like she had been punched in the gut. It took a long moment before she managed to say, "Of course not."

"Then why would you suggest something less than God was at work for me?" Geraldine only stared at her and didn't answer.

"You don't want this," Celia's mother said again.

"When was the last time you knew what I wanted?" Celia said.

"OK," Barrett said.

"Or where I was?"

"All right," Barrett said.

"Or what I do?"

"Celia, that's enough."

She stopped. They were all quiet.

"Ladies, this is God's plan. I have not led you astray before, and I do not lead you astray now," Barrett said. "Look at me," he said to Celia's mother. "I have taken care of you." Her mother's eyes dropped to the table. "Look," Barrett said, commanding them back to his face. "I have taken care of things as I promised. Nothing has changed. Do you understand?" Celia's mother tried to break his gaze again and he reached out and grabbed her by the chin. "I said, do you understand that I have taken care of everything?" Her mother nodded. "Good, good. Then there's no problem here, is there?" Her mother shook her head. Barrett let go of her face and turned to Geraldine. "And you trust your prophet, don't you?"

"I do."

"Then continue to trust." Geraldine looked hurt she didn't get as intense an admonishment as her counterpart. "Celia will be announced tonight at the Gathering."

Celia's mother turned to her again. "What about your father?"

"What about him?"

"You're just going to leave him?"

"You did."

"But you were there. He had someone."

"Well, now he's got Beth."

Barrett winced. Geraldine looked as though she was about to ask a question, but before she could, Celia's mother beat her to it. This time it was *her* voice that was raised, triumphing over the slight slur in her speech and coming through loud and clear.

"Who the fuck is Beth?"

Celia stood behind a pine tree in a gauzy white gown that dragged its last few inches along the ground when she walked. Barrett had given it to her to wear for her debut at the night's Service Gathering. She was behind the tree in an attempt to maintain an element of surprise as to who the new companion to The Prophet would be. Fred the cat circled around her in the dark, rubbing against her shins. On the other side of the tree she could hear The Prophet preaching to his people.

"You get the feeling something's wrong," he was saying. "That your values aren't being represented in your own country. That queers and immigrants and minorities are taking over what is rightfully yours. That heads of corporations are only interested in votes. Your values and rights as hardworking Christians, the backbone of this country, are being thrown away. But the thing they forget is that this country was founded as a Christian nation. America can only be a God-fearing land where we know that the Lord Jesus Christ, my forebear, died for our sins and three days later was raised from the dead to open the kingdom of our salvation. If you don't recognize that—recognize and believe it—you're not an American. It's as simple as that."

Barrett had not exiled Celia's mother for her profanity upon learning of Beth's existence. He had kicked Celia and Geraldine out of the room and attempted to calm her down. Out in the hall, listening to the barely muffled fury of her mother, Celia turned to Geraldine. "Guess I'll be coming in whenever I feel like it now, huh?" she said. Geraldine turned and marched out of the hall in angry silence. Through the door, Celia could hear her mother steamrolling through her list of grievances and disgusts with the Beth situation. She didn't stay to listen. What was left for her to learn from her mother's anger? Everything was just indignation that the world was not the way she wanted it to be. Celia didn't know who her parents were anymore, because they themselves didn't know.

"I am an American," The Prophet was saying to his congregants. "But the law out there, the law heathens and politicians have forced on the citizens of this great country, that law would have me arrested and jailed. Why? Because I have the strength of faith to live my life according to the Bible, which makes clear the blessed practice of multiple wives."

Celia knew her father would be in the front row as usual, probably with Beth, his sole consolation prize in the parade of losses that made up his lifeline. Her mother would be behind Barrett as usual, staring fire at the other two. Her father would know her mother was angry and he would be defiant in the face of this, hoping she would respect his defiance as strength. Her mother would know his defiance and grant it no quarter within her feelings. He would know her stubbornness like a familiar touch and set it as the rock against which he refused to be broken. Was this not love still, Celia thought. Was this not biblical? These two had been her religion since she was born. Now she sought to leave their church. There had been a corruption of the dogma.

"The Bible clearly states the age for marriage is puberty," The Prophet went on. "There's a reason it's puberty: to prevent the corruption of the woman in the eyes of the Lord. Out there in your old lives among the wicked you saw what it was like. Pregnant teenagers, openly defying their parents and the Lord, getting their own TV shows. Defiling their bodies, ruining themselves for marriage, turning into whores. Pop starlets making sex tapes. High-school girls texting naked pictures of themselves to boys. Oral sex, anal sex, pornography. American law is turning America's teenage women into whores and sluts, because pharmaceutical companies want to sell them birth control and condoms and abortion pills. To teenagers!"

Maybe it had always been this way, Celia thought. Was her father nothing more than an unskilled laborer with the absolute minimum amount of education America would legally allow? Was her mother a vitriolic bully with no greater capacity than pushing around someone like her father and doing clerical work? Could Celia's memory of them as something more, something not just wholesome but also whole, complete, be attributed to the veil of childhood?

Certainly childhood colored her perception, but it was more than that. They had been a family, and that title elevated them above what they were as individuals. Then they were cleaved apart and lay strewn and useless as severed limbs. Here was a hand with nothing to hold. Here, a foot with no weight to carry. And here a heart with nothing to pump. It was all gone now, but they had possessed it, like their real house, for a little while at least.

"The real law, God's law, exists to protect young women from that corruption," The Prophet was saying. "It exists to put them into a loving, blessed relationship that is pure in the eyes of the Lord and that salvages their purity. God has instructed me, his tool, his instrument, and his son, to take a third wife, so I may continue to be an example to you all and continue to shepherd you, my flock, to the promised land when the day of atonement comes. And rest assured, it is at hand. The wicked ways of the world anger the Lord. He will tear asunder the society that flaunts his laws, that refuses his grace and lives in the bosom of the serpent. But you will not be among those harmed. No, we are a family of Christ. We are a family dedicated to knowing God's way. We worship him. We praise him. We know his way is righteous. We live only for him, only because of him. He wants to see us kneel? We kneel. He wants to see us beg? We beg. He wants us to be clean. He wants us to be pure. He wants us to be saved and so, by God, we shall be saved."

The crowd was excited now. They were calling out, affirming their devotion. Celia felt tears running down her face. Dogs lick your face when they know you're sad. Bobo, the stupid, stinking, always-loose, mutt from the Blue Wave had consoled her in such a way once when she fell in their gravel driveway and skinned her knee. His slobbery tongue bathed her face, head, and knee, and the shock of that empathetic wetness had soothed her there in front of their trailer, where everything had always been too close in the best way. The smell of cigarettes, cooking food, nail polish, glow of the TV, sound of the air conditioner, brush of someone passing, the heat of the oven, scent of laundry, slam of a door, flush of the toilet, springs of the bed, slap of the alarm clock, click of a lighter, crack of a beer, clink of a toast, clack of dinner plates, whoosh of the sink, steam from the shower, brush of wiped shoes—the sounds, scents, and sights that said we're all home.

"Follow me," Barrett said. "Follow me and find salvation. Follow me and be clean and pure before God. This is it, brethren. You are witnessing your own salvation and that of the world for we are the ones who will rebuild a kingdom worthy of heaven. Welcome the third wife and companion of Christ's Second Coming."

Celia wiped her face and took a breath. She smoothed the front of her dress. She stepped out from behind the tree and began the walk toward The Prophet and all the shouting believers. She pushed the Blue Wave and all that had been there from her mind.

Good-bye to all of that.

Could this rightly be called her wedding night, Celia wondered. Barrett stood before her in his room. He pulled one strap of her dress off her shoulder and, with his free hand, stroked her cheek. "This is ordained now," he said. "Put forth and accepted by God." God was doing little to nothing to assuage Celia's fear. The hand that had relieved her shoulder of its strap moved between her legs. It grasped her thigh through the dress, then slid up to her privates. "Let me make you pure," Barrett breathed into her ear.

Her breath caught at his touch, but what pleasure there was to be taken from it was overwhelmed by horror, guilt, shock, and most of all embarrassment. "Stop," she said.

Barrett pulled back. The hand went away. "Why? What's the matter?"

"Just…turn around," she said.

"Celia, honey, this is ridiculous. I've seen you in that bathing suit and—"

"Please?"

He raised his hands in surrender and turned. She took relief at the sight of his back. Now what? She pulled down the other shoulder strap and the dress fell to the floor. She slid her underpants down and kicked them under the bed. Her hands were shaking, and she was breathing too fast. She got into the bed and pulled the covers to her chin. "OK," she said.

Barrett turned back. "You're nervous," he said. "That's fine. It's going to be all right. You'll see. This is going to be wonderful. I'll take care of you every step of the way. You know I love you and would never hurt you, right?"

She nodded.

"So just relax." Barrett began unwrapping the yards of fabric that swaddled him. He got down to his waist, and Celia saw his penis, dangling from beneath the ring of flesh that drooped from his midsection, like the clapper inside the dome of a giant church bell. She had seen his penis before, from a distance, spying on him from the tree by the back fence. She had touched it with her hand, felt it press against her through his robes, but this was too direct. Her view was too clear, all of it too embarrassing. She shut her eyes and didn't open them again until she felt his weight depress the bed next to her, like a cliff ledge suddenly giving away. Then he was above her. "Just relax," Barrett said again. "We'll go slow."

The hand came back. She closed her eyes again and tried to appear relaxed as the hand fumbled between her legs, opened her, explored her topography. A finger slid inside her. The base of Barrett's palm pressed against her most sensitive area, and a rhythm began. She slowly became more present but less aware, her concentration turning inward. She felt as though she were gathering weight, pressure, internal mass and when she got enough she would fall through some invisible membrane that was the barrier to pleasure. Right before she got there, though, it all stopped. The finger was too quickly removed, startling her.

"You're ready," Barrett said. He rolled on top of her and entered her.

The pain was searing, sharp and unfamiliar. It was internal, like a broken heart in her guts. Something tore. She cried out for him to stop. Her nails dug into Barrett's back. He hissed a little at the scratching and caught her arms and pinned them above her head by the wrists. "It's OK," he said between thrusts. "It hurts a little the first time. It's natural. You just have to get through it." She had no choice *but* to get through it; he wouldn't stop.

The severity of the pain was matched by brevity. The Prophet found salvation quickly, calling out to God as he spasmed above Celia. He collapsed on top of her. He was huge. She couldn't breathe. She had a vision of dying like this. Surely she must be dying. Barrett groaned contentedly and rolled off her. She sucked air and found herself alive.

With the heat of Barrett's body and breath gone, she felt cool air on her face and realized it was wet with tears. She hadn't known she was crying. The bed was wet underneath her bottom and her legs. She didn't dare look. She wiped her face quickly so Barrett wouldn't see, but he had his eyes shut and it didn't matter. "That was amazing," he said. He sounded drowsy and already half-asleep. "There'll be some blood. Don't worry. It's natural. Your hymen broke." The tears started again. They fell silently, unaccompanied by sobs. Celia lay still. "You're a woman now. Unsullied. A pure woman in the eyes of God," Barrett said.

Celia lay quietly crying. She heard Barrett's breathing become even and regular, and she knew he was asleep. Her birthday had been two weeks earlier. No one had said anything and she hadn't brought it up. It was the first year no one remembered. She was fifteen.

Chapter 8

Everything about the next life and nothing about this one—Shifting sands at best—Celia basks—God doesn't like barbecues—Skinning and boiling the head—Better talent in the last bunch—Celia's own crime scene—South Caro-f—ing-lina—Enough paper to clog a toilet—A planet of burgers—Celia in the driver's seat—Champagne

Celia woke to the maraca sound of a shaken pill bottle. Barrett was on the hunt, snatching up bottles and shaking them. They were scattered all over his wing. Celia woke up on the couch in the office when he finally found one that held what he wanted. The mess of pill bottles was better, Celia supposed, than his habit of leaving fast-food hamburgers out in their paper sacks. He ordered twenty at a time when he made runs into town, sometimes more, and ate them over the course of several days. He left them by the bed, next to the computer, in the bathroom—anywhere.

"Just get a mini fridge," Celia told him. "Or a regular fridge for that matter. You have the space. You're going to get sick leaving them out like that."

"No such thing will happen," Barrett had declared. "The Lord won't let me get sick as long as I'm doing his will."

Barrett was always shirking some minor responsibility or another and dumping it on God's plate. Celia learned there was no point in arguing. Celia had learned a lot of things in her first month of being Barrett's partner (she refused to go by Lady Companion). She learned that sex eventually stopped hurting so much, and she learned to always be on top to avoid being crushed. She learned there were many things she still had to learn. The day after Barrett deflowered her, Celia went down the second hallway in the house shaped like an E to her new bedroom. It was prestocked with clothes, same as her mother and Geraldine's. Celia's closet wasn't filled with cocktail dresses like the other two, though. Hers had childish sundresses, pink crop tops, a cheerleading uniform, the kind of skirt and button-up white shirts that private school girls wore, and some sort of nightie. She had shut the closet door unsure what to make of the ensembles. Postvirginity she felt a tickle in the back of her mind, reminding her a milestone had been unchangeably reached. Her thoughts all tasted of the thrill of accomplishment but with the bitter aftertaste of a lost purpose—a trip ended. With this, too, came the repulsive violence of the act itself, which had shocked her more than it pleased her and scared her more than it freed her. But still, she had wanted Barrett and she got him. She wanted Barrett to want her and she made it happen. Now they had each other. Things would improve. Right now, though, Celia was sore in a very delicate place, and there was blood crusted on the inside of her thighs and a little on her bottom. She had been too embarrassed to use Barrett's bathroom to clean herself, so she threw on the white gown from the night before while he was still asleep and came to her new room.

Celia pulled off the gown and ran a hot shower. She cleaned herself gently. She was tender, and her insides felt wrecked. She toweled off and brushed her hair, then sat gingerly on the closed toilet seat to survey her surroundings. Her own bathroom, clean and tidy with hot water and proper pressure. The memory of the night before popped into her head—the sex, violent and uncontrollable—but she blotted it out and focused on the bathroom. She didn't want to think about the night before right then. The memory wasn't going anywhere (unless she was lucky); it could wait. She returned to studying the bathroom. It was just the right size, at that moment, to give her a sense of safety and security. After a while she wrapped the towel around her chest and went out into her bedroom. Her mother stood in the doorway.

"What?" Celia said, startled and guilty and immediately angry.

"So you've officially joined the ranks of the unfulfilled," her mother said.

"No," Celia said. "I was fulfilled with a connection to our prophet and to God. I was totally fulfilled."

Her mother smiled in a way Celia hated. She had meant something else, something Celia's answer just proved she didn't know. Something, no doubt, having to do with sex and the adult world and something she wasn't going to share with Celia. Celia felt sick thinking about it, thinking about the night before. Here she was across the line—a woman who has had sex—and she was still unschooled, unknowing, and it was obvious. One more thing she had yet to learn. She felt like she had gone behind enemy lines without a map simply because no one thought to give her one. She was surrounded, Celia realized, by people who were always telling her any and everything about the next life and nothing about this one.

"I'll let you get dressed," her mother said, still smiling that obnoxious smile. She shut the door, and Celia heard her go down the hall to her own room. Celia rummaged through the bag she had packed the day before and found the old tape recorder with the *Dirty Dancing* soundtrack still in the deck. She locked her bedroom door and went back into the bathroom. She sat in the tub and balanced the tape player on the tub's edge. Celia turned the volume low and pushed play, letting the tape's secret existence fill the small room.

Despite the neighbors, Celia grew to love her new room and enjoyed sleeping there, but Barrett always wanted her in his wing. In the plus column, this drove Geraldine and Celia's mother nuts because it reduced their time with The Prophet. It also highlighted the fact that the privilege of staying the night in Barrett's wing was never extended to them. Celia relished their agitation. In the minus column, however, registered the fact that Barrett always wanted sex, snored like a baboon, and took up too much space in the bed. In the end, Celia had to stake her personal happiness on the misery of the other two. Shifting sands at best.

Waking up now, on the couch in Barrett's office, Celia cursed herself for not taking advantage of a perfect time to slip back to her room. It was late. She had fallen asleep while Barrett droned on to Matthew—always an irritated little box on the computer screen glaring at Celia in the background—about shipments and payments and locations for meeting someone that night.

"They're annoyed they keep having to meet you in these obscure locations," Matthew had said.

"Where do they want to pick up six crates of automatic weapons? A KFC parking lot?" Barrett had replied.

"I'm just the messenger here," Matthew said.

"They have GPS and they all have those enormous four-wheel drive SUVs. What do they think the four-wheel drive is for? What do they need with that in Atlanta? I'm finally giving them a reason to own those stupid trucks."

Matthew sighed. He was always sighing, always exasperated, always wound tight. Celia wished he would either loosen up or get a new job. He was a black cloud hovering over Barrett's keyboard. "I'll take the coordinates when you're ready," he said. Barrett read a long string of numbers to him, and Matthew wrote them down and read them back.

"That's it," Barrett said.

"How about the other customers?" Matthew said.

"The Aryans don't care about meeting in the woods. That's right up their alley," Barrett said.

"I didn't mean that, I meant in general. Are they happy with the money, the situation?"

"Yes, they're thrilled the blacks want their guns to murder one another with. They find the arrangement quite satisfactory."

The two of them moved on to discussing finances and Celia had drifted off to sleep on the couch. While she was asleep, Barrett had gone off to sell his guns and Celia had missed a golden opportunity. Now he was back, clattering pill bottles and weaving around the room.

Celia kept her eyes closed and pretended to be asleep as Barrett banged around the room. Hopefully he would just stumble around for a while, then pass out in bed. She sensed him next to the couch and tried to keep her breathing regular. He poked at her gently. Celia pretended to stir a little but remain asleep. Barrett ran his hand down her side, stopping at her hip for a moment before ending the journey at her backside. If he kept it up, she would have to feign waking and have sex with him; it all depended on how long he kept at it and how many painkillers he had eaten. This time the painkillers won, and he let it go. He gave her bottom an appreciative squeeze, then stepped away from the sofa and, as it sounded to Celia, collapsed on the floor.

Celia's eyes shot open, but she didn't move. Barrett was sitting with his back to her, between the sofa and the desk. The sound must have been him sitting down. She had never seen him on the floor. He was picking at the carpet and mumbling something. Celia worried he might be having some sort of episode, taken too many of his little pills, but just as she was about to break her pantomime and get up to check on him, a perfectly square piece of carpet came free in his hand. Next Barrett lifted out a piece of floorboard the same size. He Frisbeed these off to one side. He fiddled with something inside this hole, and after a few seconds, he opened a lid. It was a hiding place.

Celia watched, unmoving on the sofa, as Barrett pulled stacks of bills out of a duffel bag he must have been carrying when he entered. He dropped the first few stacks in by hand then grabbed the bag impatiently and tipped it open over the hole in the floor. As he shook it, stacks of bills banded around the middle with white strips of paper tumbled out and disappeared into the hole. Barrett flung the empty duffel bag into a corner and closed the lid of the hiding hole. He fumbled with the piece of floorboard and carpet, then struggled to his feet, using the edge of the desk to help hoist his girth back into the air. He gave the carpet over the hole a few good stomps, then weaved his way out the door, tired and drugged, with the air of a man who has just completed the day's last task. He clicked off the light as he left, leaving Celia alone in the dark.

Celia spent the mornings either sleeping in or serving Barrett tea and breakfast and basking in his attention. She wore the outfits from the closet in her room—school-girl uniforms, skirts and crop tops, short dresses with odd, ruffled petticoats she had to put on underneath. The Prophet started his mornings slow, in a fog, until his wake-up pills kicked in and the tea and the food and then Celia's outfit all conspired to get his blood up. He would pull her onto his lap, lifting the skirts or yanking them off roughly and then mirroring that action with his own robes, hiking them up over his white legs, doughy like the contents of a ready-to-heat biscuits tube, flopped over the edge of the couch. The Prophet would jab himself inside of her, an abrupt and awkward unpleasantry that Celia endured before sending him off to tackle the rest of his day. She spent afternoons in the hot tub and alternately lying in a chair next to it, basking in the sun. Sometimes she walked through Zoar, visiting the residents and basking in their curiosity. The weather had turned a corner, and spring was now official. So Celia basked. It was a fine season for it.

Celia met Gardner late one afternoon as he was coming along a path carrying the head of a wild boar. His arms were coated in blood up to his elbows. He held the severed head out to one side by a tusk.

"Hello there, Gardner," Celia said. "Peace of Christ."

"Peace of Christ yourself there, Queen Bee," Gardner said.

"You look…" Celia looked down at the boar's head dangling at Gardner's side, "…well, I guess." Drops of blood fell from the neck onto the pathway.

"Caught this beauty coming through one of his runs." Gardner hoisted the head so it was facing Celia. "Everyone's gonna be eating good tomorrow night. Harmon and me's gonna get the pit going early tomorrow and slow roast this sucker about twelve hours. Get everybody down in the Town Square tomorrow night, have a big time. You gonna come?"

"Absolutely," Celia said. "What should I bring?"

Gardner smiled. Celia realized it might be the first time she had ever seen him do that. "Shoot, Queen Bee, I knew even you couldn't say no to a barbecue."

This would be the third barbecue they'd had at Zoar. The first two had been fun. Everyone had made food and brought it to Town Square, potluck style. The barbecues reminded Celia of the ones Dwayne used to have every summer for his crew and their families. The whole compound turned out for these things and for a night it was a joyous and raucous atmosphere, almost like they were regular people out in the regular world enjoying a party, instead of Christian soldiers waiting for the end of civilization—which was why Barrett hated them.

"They're a distraction," he had told Celia before the last one—before they were joined by Christ and he had taken her into his bed—when she asked him if he was going, childishly hoping he might be her date. "It's best to keep people working toward the common goal with serious hearts and determination. Things like these cookouts, they take people out of the moment and make them a little too much themselves."

"Too much themselves?" Celia had said, deflated by his reaction.

"Yes. It's fine for them to relax a little, appreciate a hard day's work, but you don't want them to have fun. Fun is a problem."

"But you and I have fun, don't we?" Celia had said, thinking of the hot tub and their long talks.

"Yes, but we're special. We're different," Barrett had said, retrieving Celia's heart from where it had fallen and sending it galloping. "With the kind of work we're doing here, with the residents—I mean, God's work that we're doing through the followers, those people need to be unified as a group. Fully realized individuals with their own thoughts and ideas about God, about what's right and wrong—that's no good. Individuality makes it too hard to get people on the same page, thinking the same thing and doing the same thing. People start thinking as individuals and the whole thing falls apart. They have to be pieces of a whole, united as a group. If you've got no group, you've got no congregation. No congregation, no followers, and if you've got no followers, well, then what? Who are you saving? Who are you bringing to Christ. Who's listening to you? That's why, when you first bring them into the fold, you start with faith. Start with their souls. Start with what they're afraid of: death. Get them on the side of the angels, back under God. Then you use their faith to set the rules and laws for them. What they can and can't do, according to their faith. Next you tell them what their work should be, again, according to their faith. God wants them to work the land here at Zoar, keep the place running. When the rules and their daily lives are joined together like that under the umbrella of their faith, you stamp out that independent streak. They're part of the flock then, never quite full individuals. That's what you want." Barrett paused, nodding to himself, agreeing with his own pronouncements. "So you can save them, of course," he added. "But when you take them out of that zone and they start having fun, you risk the spark of individuality coming back. They start thinking about feeling good. About enjoyment and pleasure. About going off and getting a place of their own and making it comfortable, having a party every weekend. About living to feel good instead of living to serve." Celia must have been wearing a conflicted look by that point, because Barrett saw her face and said, "Go and enjoy yourself. Don't worry about it. Fortunately Gardner doesn't shoot a wild pig all that often. I just don't encourage these things."

"But why even let it go on, then?" Celia said. "Why not tell them the Lord doesn't approve? They'll do anything you say. Tell them God doesn't like barbecues."

Barrett sighed. "I've spent my whole life in the South. If there's one thing I know for sure, it's that no southerner is going to believe you're a prophet if you tell them God doesn't like a barbecue."

"Brownies, maybe," Celia said now to Gardner. "For dessert."

"May's putting a list up in the laundry so people know what everyone's making. Just check that first," Gardner said.

"And what about that?" Celia said, gesturing to Gardner's parcel. "Your head. Please don't bring that tomorrow night."

"This? Nah, I'm gonna skin it and boil it. Me and Harmon'll eat that tonight. And Stacy. I imagine we're the only three interested in that particular delicacy. Then I'll keep the skull. Hang it on my wall probably."

"That's nice," Celia lied, in an effort to be pleasant. "All this time hunting that thing, it's no wonder you haven't finished Beth's house." Celia had noticed recently that the work had stalled. She suspected Gardner enjoyed having Beth stay at his place and was dragging his feet on the project. Maybe he wanted her in his house long enough to impress her with his nasty severed boar's head. Celia had only brought it up to tease him a little, but now she saw all his prior happiness dribble out the downturned corners of his frown.

"Shoot, ain't no point finishing it. She ain't never gonna live in it."

Celia felt her own good mood evaporating in the hot glare of what she suddenly knew was coming next. "Why not?" she said.

"She's with your daddy all the time now," Gardner said, scowling. He caught himself and tried to seem casual. "Stays at his place. Seems someone moved out and left an empty room."

"Beth lives in my old room?"

"People talked a little at first, but…"

"But what?"

"Your daddy's always been an honorable man, they said, and I guess you can't argue 'em there. If he says the arrangement is chaste, then it's chaste. Still, can't be long before he asks the Prophet to make it legit. The man ain't got a wife anymore and not through any fault of his own. Guess there's no reason he can't remarry."

"No, I guess not."

They were both quiet.

"Well," Gardner said finally, with a false note of his previous good humor. "Guess I better go and get started skinning and boiling this head."

"Right, just another normal evening," Celia said.

Gardner winked at her. "See you tomorrow night. You best show up now. Don't you disappoint me."

"Wouldn't dream of it."

"Certainly hope not. Your dreams tend to come true." Gardner stepped around her and continued on his way, carting his bloody head in his bloody arms. Celia watched him. Farther along, Rebekah and some of the compound's other children ran over to greet him. She watched Gardner squat down and hold out the head, explaining something and pointing to the tusks. Then he jumped to his feet with a roar and chased after the children with the head. They scattered and screamed in horrified delight.

Back at the big house that evening, Celia said to Barrett, "There's a cookout tomorrow night."

"Yes, I heard. Gardner went and shot another wild pig." Barrett shook his head. "I preferred it when he was afraid of those things."

"Gardner was afraid of wild boars? Why?" Celia said. She had a hard time imaging Gardner being afraid of anything. On the other hand, one didn't become the gun enthusiast Gardner was without being afraid of quite a lot of things now that she considered it.

"Oh, yeah. A boar gouged him a few years ago when he was out hunting. Tore his leg up pretty bad. He almost bled to death. He got lucky, he had a radio with him, like a walkie-talkie or something, and some other hunters happened to be near enough to pick up his calls. A father and son, which was just salt in the wound that pig had ripped into him. They got him out of the woods and to an ambulance. Saved his life."

"Why was that salt in a wound?"

"Gardner always wanted kids. Surely you know that. It's why he's so fond of you. Asks about you all the time. It's why he likes all the kids around here, why he runs the Junior Christian Soldiers."

"The what?"

"The thing with the kids. Hunting lessons, gun safety, what tree bark you can eat, how to tie weird knots—all that nonsense. He calls them the Junior Christian Soldiers. Everybody has to name these little groups."

Celia had never considered that Gardner liked her. The opposite, actually—she thought he resented her and her family. "Why didn't he have any kids? He was married, wasn't he?"

"His wife didn't want them. Real evil bitch, that one." Celia was startled. She had never heard Barrett use profanity. He said it so casually. "Just mean and nasty. Sneaky. I gather that Gardner got her to try and get pregnant at one point and it didn't take. She made it seem like that was Gardner's failing, though I'm sure it wasn't. She was deceiving him, never seriously trying to get pregnant in the first place."

"How do you know that?"

"Because I spoke with God on the subject. Some women's only aim is to trick their men, especially men like Gardner."

"Who are men like Gardner?"

"Simple men. Uncomplicated men. These women pretend to be no-nonsense, hardworking, salt-of-the-earth types, then once they get their claws into a guy like Gardner, they turn into mean and twisted cunts." The word was thrown into the sentence with such ease that Celia felt it like a sucker punch.

"Just want to run a man down, belittle him, pick him apart. Make him feel stupid about every aspect of his life. Gardner got one of those." Celia didn't know what to make of Barrett's language. The c-word was bad, she knew that. Almost as bad as the n-word. She had heard both being screamed inside various homes around the Blue Wave. Her parents impressed upon her the importance of never using either.

"She was a mean and vicious little shrew of a woman, constantly letting Gardner know what a disappointment he was to her." Barrett stared off out the sliding doors into the night. "Never worked herself." He got quiet again, like he was picturing her. "Reminded me of my mother."

"Did you meet her?"

Barrett came back to the present. "Yes, I had the misfortune."

"Are they divorced now?"

"No, she'd never divorce him and risk him being happy."

"So they're still married."

"No, I had Gardner declared legally dead."

"What?"

"I had him declared dead."

"You can do that?"

"I did it."

"Can you get in trouble for that?"

"I did it with God's blessing, so no."

"So his wife didn't throw him out?"

"How's that?"

"I always thought he came here because his wife threw him out."

"Oh yeah, she threw him out all the time. Not the time he came here, but pretty regularly. He would sleep in that pop-up camper thing."

"I knew it!"

"When he came here, that was when I had Gardner leave her. He deserved to get to walk out on her at least once after all the times she tossed him. A few days later I reported the truck stolen. A few days after that a body turned up—"

"How'd a body turn up?"

"Bodies are always turning up. The indigent and homeless die all the time. Arrange a little paperwork and now the body is Gardner. You might not realize this, but ninety percent of modern life is just paperwork. Only we don't do it on actual paper so much anymore; we use computers, but it's basically the same. Birth certificate, high-school transcripts, college transcripts, mortgages, insurance policies, cell-phone contracts, Internet contracts, cable contracts, zoning permits, bank statements, marriage license, parking ticket, police report, divorce, foreclosure, death certificate. It's all just paper, or electronic paper, that moves around the desks of various peons who never actually set eyes on you. Most of your life is just a pile of paperwork."

"How'd you arrange the paperwork?"

"Know the right people and pay the right price. And I know lots of people. It would have been worth any price to see the look on that twat wife of his's face when she found out his million-dollar life-insurance policy went to charity."

"Gardner had a million-dollar life-insurance policy? Why?"

"Because I took it out for him."

"What was the charity?"

"Zoar. Here, though the paperwork makes it look like the charity is an organization that provides clean water for African kids."

"You kept it?"

"It was mine. I took out the policy. This place needs money to function. My mission needs money. I need money."

"So the African kids don't get any water?"

"Africa needs to learn to stand on its own two feet. The rest of the world can't keep stepping in to explain simple things like needing clean water to live." Barrett washed down a giant bite from his second burger with a mouthful of soda.

"Isn't that illegal?"

"According to man's laws, not God's. We're in a battle for the soul of mankind. And we must win at any cost. To fight the evil of the secular world, it's best to use a weapon the secular world understands. Paperwork. It's an incredibly powerful weapon because it's the basis for everything. How much money someone has, what they own, even their name—it all exists as data, paperwork, numbers in a computer. Legal decisions, medical records, deeds. All of it's just paper. You slip in the right piece of paper that says Gardner's dead. Presto, he's dead. Slip in another that says he's worth a million, presto, he's worth a million. Then you get another piece of paper. This one's a check. Never underestimate paperwork. It's the true weapon of our age."

"Then why are we giving everyone guns? Shouldn't they be learning how to, like, type and file?"

"Simpletons need guns. It's the only way they understand the ideas of war and power. Plus it gives them something to do. Hunting, target practice. Keeps them focused."

"So Gardner's not married anymore? You can't be married if you're dead, right?"

"No, I would say Gardner is definitely not married anymore. Why?"

"That Beth woman is living in my room."

Barrett looked up from his third hamburger. "Who? Someone's in your room?"

"Beth, that woman who goes around with my dad and Gardner. She's moved into my room back at the cabin."

"Oh," Barrett said, and went back to his food.

"I think my dad is going to ask you to marry them. Or join them. Whatever it is we do here. Gardner liked her. He was building her a house."

Barrett shook his head. "I don't get it. Am I just not recruiting lookers anymore? There had to be some better talent in that last bunch."

"What are you talking about?"

"Nothing, never mind."

"I want her gone."

"Excuse me?"

"Give her to Gardner."

"Give her to Gardner?"

"Yes."

Barrett put his burger down on the coffee table. "I can't *give* her to Gardner."

"Why not?"

"What's wrong with your father having someone in his life who makes him happy?"

"Not her."

"Why not?"

"Because I don't like her."

"That's not—it's not your decision. It's your father's. He's an adult. She's an adult."

"Give her to Gardner."

"I can't do that."

"You mean you won't."

"Same thing."

"Why not?" Celia had found such a perfect solution to the problem that had been living in her gut like a bacteria—the unstoppable creep of Beth into her father's life. Beth with her gray vegetables and desperate need for her father's attention. Now Barrett was simply refusing to help when he could fix all this with a simple decree. Celia was getting angry.

"Because it doesn't benefit me in any way to get involved in these people's private lives."

"Since when? And since when is anything their decision? I thought you made their decisions for them. Are you afraid you can't do it?"

Barrett's expression hardened. "Calm down."

Celia did not calm down. "There's no paperwork you can forge while you're hidden away some place, so you're afraid you can't do it? Are you afraid they won't believe you if you say God says it has to be this way? Afraid they won't listen to you?" She watched him sitting there with an old burger in his hand. "There are limits to the power you pretend to have, and you know it."

Barrett stood. "That's enough, Celia."

"You're scared of them finding you out. You don't think you're strong enough to make it happen, so you're hiding behind excuses about it suddenly being their lives and their decisions. You're chicken."

"Celia."

"You're no prophet. You're a bullshitter."

"Enough!" Barrett roared. He grabbed the edge of the coffee table and overturned it, sending burgers, soda, french fries, and pill bottles sailing into the air. He grabbed Celia by the throat with one hand and squeezed. She felt the instant panic of choking and swatted at Barrett's meaty arm. His face was red and grim, the loose eye finally focused, she saw, on her and her pain. She felt herself going under, but before she managed to die, Barrett relaxed his grip and, with his free hand, slapped her so hard across the face she actually came up off her feet as she fell. She couldn't see anything, lying on the floor in a pile of spilled soda and burgers, the layers blown apart and scattered. She struggled to regain her breath, her airway crushed and incapable of taking in what it needed. Her vision straightened out just in time for her to see Barrett coming at her. She tried to back away, but she was coughing, still trying to breathe normally. Her hand came down on ice cubes from Barrett's drink. He grabbed her by the front of her shirt and yanked her to her feet, pressed her back against the sliding glass door. Celia felt something cold pressed between the back of her arm and the glass. A tomato slice, she knew, though she didn't know how she knew or why, at that moment, her brain was wasting time on such things. Barrett grabbed her face by the jaw and cranked her head so that she was staring at him.

"I'm weak, am I?" Barrett said. "Does anything about this feel to you like I might be weak? Not the physical strength, of course. I'm naturally stronger than you. Most people probably are. I'm not referring to anything so banal as that, as just our physical difference. I'm talking about my willingness. Willingness is a good measure of strength of character. I am willing to break your neck, or smother you, or bash your head through the glass of the door here, then hold you under the water in the hot tub outside until your thrashing peters out and your body goes limp in the blood stained water. And nothing"—he leaned in closer to her face—"nothing would stop me. And nothing would happen to me. I could throw your corpse out in front of the house and leave it there as a warning. A sacrifice. An offering. However I want to feel about it. Do you understand? This is the power of God. The power to smite." With his free hand, Barrett reached up and brushed some of Celia's hair out of her face. "I created you. I allowed you to become the minor little celebrity you are around here. And I can smite you, your father, your mother, Beth, whomever I so choose. Now, I don't want to do that. I don't want to smite you, honey. I love you. I really do, with God as my witness. I don't want to destroy you. But make no mistake about it. If you ever speak to me like that again, I will pull your pretty head off this neck and use it to beat the rest of your family to death." Barrett tightened his grip on her face and pressed her harder against the glass. "Do you understand?" he said. Celia tried to nod but couldn't move her head. He felt the effort, though, and let her go. She dropped to the floor. "Good. Now clean this up," he said, striding out the door and slamming it, leaving the room and the girl in it a wreck behind him.

Celia picked up the scattered food. She righted the coffee table and used a dish towel to soak up the spilled soda. She used glass cleaner on the sliding door, wiping away the smears and smudges the tomato slice stuck to her arm had made. Celia did all this without thinking, her mind blank with incomprehension. Her attention was a free-floating thing, deliberately unmoored and unwilling to land on any particular thing, for fear it would have to address the situation at hand. Barrett had gone into his office and shut the door. Celia finished cleaning up her own crime scene and stood staring at it for a long time. She wanted to run away, to go to her mother or her father and cry and sob and tell them all the things that had happened to her, but they already knew, in a way, and they didn't care. And this, living here with Barrett, Celia had wanted this. She had fought her mother on the point, dismissed her father outright; there was no comfort or sympathy waiting for her in either of those two corners. She was overwhelmed to the point of exhaustion. Barrett's door was closed, and she imagined he was halfway loaded with pills and on his way to unconsciousness. Celia trudged down the hall back to her own room and fell facedown on her bed, clothes still on, and slipped under almost immediately.

Something woke Celia from a deep sleep. She was in her own bed in her own room. A pair of hands was making out her shape through the covers. She thought it must be Barrett, which was confusing because he refused to visit this part of the house. "I can't go to that wing," he had said once, when it was still only inhabited by Geraldine and Celia's mother. "It's too feminine. Small boxes sitting out, pieces of makeup…" He had looked baffled and thrown his hands up. His own wing was a sour mess except for the sunroom, which Celia kept clean. Celia couldn't tell if Barrett thought his wives' wing was distasteful because of the women's influence on their surroundings or if he called it feminine because he associated femininity with cleanliness and found cleanliness itself restricting.

Either way, someone was shaking her awake now. Celia remembered the beating she had taken earlier that evening and panicked. Was Barrett not finished with her? Had he woken with his blood up and found her missing and come to claim his nightly piece? He must want sex pretty desperately if he was willing to cross into the woman-zone. When she clicked on the small lamp by her bed, though, she saw her mother flinch in the light and shield her eyes.

"What are you doing?" Celia said.

"Celia, honey, are you awake?" her mother said.

"Obviously. I just asked you a question."

"What?"

"A question."

"What?"

"What do you mean, what? I asked—oh. You're high." Celia flopped back on her pillow. She had gotten a clear look at her mother's face and recognized the bleary expression, the swollen pupils.

"Celia, there's an accounting—"

"I know, I know, there's an accounting coming. A reckoning. A great upheaval. How could I not know? I dream of one day causing it myself so you'll all shut up about it."

"No, there's an account." Her mother struggled for a second with the words. "A bank account."

Celia pushed back the covers and got out of bed. She helped her mother up to a standing position from where she knelt by the bed, like a child saying her prayers. "Come on," Celia said. "Let's go back to bed."

"Listen," her mother slurred. "I'm not supposed to say. Barrett's got…and me. We're names until you're eighteen, but it's trust so he can't have it or me, but you should know. You got to know why it was for, and I was unhappy too, but you—"

"OK, OK, shush. Take it easy," Celia said, leading her mother down the hall to her own room.

"Listen," her mother said, in the habit of inebriated people the world over who mistake a lack of comprehension as a fault of the listener's ears rather than their own mouth. "It was part of the deal. When I came here. To the house. To Barrett."

"A bank account?"

"Trust. A trust."

"OK, Mom. Lie down, huh? There you go. It's late. We don't want to wake Geraldine up, do we?"

"It's for you. I made him open it for you so you could leave here. One day."

"Sh," said Celia gently.

"Don't have to spend your life."

"Sh. Be quiet."

"In South Caro—"

"Sh."

"Fucking -lina."

Her mother quieted down and Celia sat on the bed beside her. She brushed the hair out of her mother's face and pulled the covers up around her. She took the pill bottle from the nightstand and slipped it back into its drawer in the vanity. She closed the door behind her and stood in the hall. The house was still. Celia padded down the hall into Barrett's wing. She pushed open Barrett's bedroom door. He was a mountain range running north to south along the horizon of the bed. She stepped near him and gave him a few gentle shakes. His breathing rumbled on undisturbed. She stroked his shoulders and arms a bit, but he remained still. Finally she ran her hand down his belly and stopped at his crotch. Nothing. She gave him a few gentle pats in that area, and when he showed no signs of waking, she was convinced his pills had made him sufficiently comatose. She left the bedroom.

Celia let herself into Barrett's office and pushed the door most of the way closed, leaving it open a crack so she could hear anyone coming down the hall. Barrett had left a small desk lamp burning. It cast enough light. Celia ignored the papers on the couch. She had looked through most of them already and besides, Barrett wouldn't leave anything out with her name on it where she would see. She opened various desk drawers. She found a couple of handguns and bullets. There were bank statements crammed in haphazardly with the names of Zoar's citizens on them.

She closed the final drawer and stared at the floor. Celia had been hoping it wouldn't come to this. It was one thing to be caught with an open drawer. She could claim to be looking for nearly anything; she was in this room all the time. It was another thing entirely to be caught with part of the floor removed rifling through piles of cash.

She approximated where Barrett had slumped to the floor that night and dropped down there herself. The carpet didn't show any obvious seams. Celia pinched two fingerfuls of nap in the spot she remembered and pulled. At first there was just the expected resistance, but she kept up the pressure and a corner pulled free. She grabbed it and peeled away the square of carpet. Beneath it was the wooden floor, and she saw a finger-hole drilled through this. She lifted out the wooden square. There was the hidden space. It was deeper than Celia was expecting, at least three feet, and was filled with little bricks of bundled cash stacked in a tower and pressed into the corner. Three rows of stacked bills, followed by three more, followed by a final three. Nine small towers of bills pressed together to form a rectangle. The sides and bottom of the hidey-hole were thin plywood. Celia could make something out in the dark space next to the stack of money. She got the desk lamp and brought it over to the hole in the floor. She shined the light into the darkness and pulled out a thick plastic folder with a press-seal at the top. She opened it under the lamp light. There was a deed for the property at 7606 Route 52 in the name of Barbara Josener, the woman from the lien statements. There were several thick packets of documents about the lien. There was a death certificate with "Gardner Creech" printed on the important line and a copy of a life-insurance policy for Gardner. There was a cell phone, turned off, the kind you could buy at a gas station. And at the back of the folder, clipped together, were statements and a small bank book for a trust account in Celia's name with Barrett and her mother listed as something called custodians. It was real. Celia scanned the documents and found a number: $250,000.00. She went back to the first page and double-checked that it was, in fact, her name on the documents. It was. Those were the two indisputables: her name and the figure. Celia Ann Waters, $250,000. Then she heard the toilet flush in Barrett's room.

Celia closed the plastic folder and threw it back down into the hole. She put the wooden cover back as quietly as she could. It felt painfully slow. She was fitting the carpet back into place when she heard the doorknob of Barrett's bedroom door turn and open. She mashed the edges of the carpet with her palm and lifted the lamp back onto the desk. She grabbed the bank book and statements for the trust fund from the floor and flattened herself against the wall behind the door just as it swung open and Barrett came into the room.

Celia caught the door lightly with her fingertips before it smacked her in the face. She held her breath. She heard Barrett at the desk opening and closing drawers, shuffling papers, moving things. Had she disturbed something he would notice? Had he heard her when he was in the bathroom? Barrett crashed around the room some more, and Celia's heart sank lower and lower into her stomach. She was positive that at any moment he'd yank the door away and find her. Her breath burned in her lungs, but she didn't dare breathe. Then she heard the familiar sound of a paper bag being opened, recovered from some corner of the office. She heard the sound of thinner paper being torn away and the smack and grunt of Barrett taking a bite from an old hamburger.

There was a swish of movement, the creak of the floor, and the shadow passing the gap at the door hinge as Barrett left the office and went back down the hall. The door to his room pulled shut and Celia heard the sound of him climbing back into bed with his hamburger. She let out her breath and huffed air back into her lungs in huge draws. Finally, when she had her wind back she tiptoed into the sunroom, slid the door open, and hopped the back fence out into the night.

Celia sat in a circle of lantern light in the barn with the papers she had taken from Barrett's hidey-hole spread out in front of her. There was the paperwork that had opened the account, statements, the bank book, and her social-security card. This last item was tucked into a small plastic sleeve. She didn't know much about banking, but she understood that in some way these flimsy pieces of paper meant she was rich. It wasn't even that much paper. Not enough to make a book or a magazine. Enough, perhaps, to clog a toilet. The words on the pages were vague and nongrammatical, mixed with numbers and codes and strange abbreviations. Yet somehow this small pile of paper, barely enough to start a fire, amounted to $250,000. It was more elegant, Celia supposed, than Barrett's tower of money, but less reassuring. You could put your hands on Barrett's money; these documents Celia had required faith in a system she couldn't see and didn't comprehend. A vision, that of her mother, had come to her in the night, like Gabriel to Mary except high on pharmaceutical-grade narcotics. That vision had also spoken to her like Gabriel to the Virgin Mary, except her mother was slurry and Celia wasn't a virgin anymore. That vision, though, the one of her high-as-a-kite mother, told Celia that unto her a trust fund was created. High-yield, according to this statement. Yet another thing Celia was supposed to accept and believe because someone else said so. Because her name was on a piece of paper hidden in a hole in the floor. Her mother and Barrett had taken care of this for her. It was all for her. One more thing to believe on faith.

Celia had had it up to here with faith. Barrett's, her mother's, her father's, and all the nimrods of Zoar who believed the idiotic dreams that Barrett made up for her. Barrett, who made up these dreams and didn't have the courage to admit he was doing it. Barrett, who, it now seemed, had essentially bought her mother out from under her father with this trust fund for Celia. Barrett, who told everyone what to do and think and say. Barrett, who didn't really talk to God, only to himself, and was vain enough to think that was the same thing.

Celia had wanted Barrett, to possess or be possessed by him, so badly because he was the only thing there was to want. That was his greatest trick. He had pulled it on all of them. He found people with practically nothing, then he took even that away so there was truly nothing for them to desire except him: his attention, approval, words, blessings. Now Celia had him and saw clearly what an illusion it all was. She had worked so hard to get him: an addict with a hot tub and a god complex, who sold guns from dubiously acquired property while he ate himself to death and got cranky if he went too long without a hand job.

Was there really a God? A place called heaven and a place called hell? In the Gospel of Matthew, Jesus tells a crowd to observe the lilies and plants, to observe the birds and how they didn't worry because God provided for them. It was an analogy. If God took such good care of the birds, he would certainly take care of people—but it was nonsense. Birds worried all the time. Celia had seen a bird worry hysterically, up close, that day she and Rebekah found its hatchling fallen from the nest. That mama bird had swooped and shrieked with worry. She had seen other birds fight over seed scattered on the ground, over mates, over territory. They scrambled to get twigs and branches for nests they had to guard, worried that something would eat their eggs or kill their babies. In fact, if a person watched a handful of birds for even just a few hours, they would see enough to know that passage from Matthew was complete and utter rubbish. Jesus may have been a swell guy who showed kindness to the poor, but he was a lousy naturalist. If there was a God, who cared? He was off minding his own business, not even looking after the birds. And if there was a heaven, who wanted to go there and hang out for eternity with jerks like the ones she was surrounded by here at Zoar? And if there was a hell and God sent people there for not figuring it all out before they died, then she didn't want anything to do with him. Because she wouldn't send anyone to hell for eternity; she had more mercy in her heart than that.

Her life was awful and having access to a real house and a hot tub was lousy recompense for Barrett stuffing his horrid thing up inside her all the time. And now? She reached up and brushed her fingers along the impact line of Barrett's hand against her face and felt the tenderness of a developing bruise.

Celia didn't share the beliefs of the people around her, but she had to live her life under the umbrella of their faith. Fine, she thought, folding the trust papers neatly around her social security card and sliding it all into the back pocket of her shorts. She could operate under their faith. Their petty, self-serving, vainglorious faith. But one thing was certain. She wasn't hanging around this dump any longer than she had to. Whether she found a way to access the trust money or not, she was done. She was leaving her parents, leaving Barrett, leaving Zoar, and maybe, as her mother sloppily suggested, even clearing the hell out of South Caro-fucking-lina.

Celia went back over the fence and into the house with a few hours left until dawn. She let herself into Barrett's room and got into bed next to him. She felt a little sick as she did it, but she reached under the covers for his manhood and began coaxing some life into it. She needed to be back in his good graces, however repulsive that may be and however inappropriate it was to call his attentions "graces." Down below Barrett began to stiffen, and up above he began to stir. He opened his eyes and saw Celia.

"What's this?" he said, but he didn't try to stop her.

"I'm sorry," Celia said.

"'I'm sorry, *what?*" he said, a hand reaching gently up to her throat.

"I'm sorry, Prophet." His touch at her throat remained gentle. Celia kept going. "I beg your forgiveness."

"'You beg my forgiveness *what?*"

"I beg your forgiveness, Prophet."

Barrett rolled onto his side and roughly yanked down her shorts. Celia thought of the papers, folded in her back pocket, but with her steady rhythm on his penis, he didn't notice them—or if he did, he paid them no mind. He tossed her shorts away, then kissed her. Celia was prepared to climb aboard him and do what she needed to do, but instead he pushed her, facedown, onto the bed and rolled on top of her. Barrett opened her legs with his knees and she felt him fumbling down below, but he seemed to be confused. He was trying to put it in the wrong place. "Forgiveness comes at a cost, my dear," he said. "Do you truly seek the forgiveness of your Prophet? The absolution of the new Savior?"

"Yes," she said, scared. She blocked out what was happening to her as best she could. A habit she was beginning to excel at.

"Then I need something from you. Something I haven't had before. Are you truly sorry?"

"Yes."

"Say you want my forgiveness."

"Please forgive me. I want to be forgiven."

"Do you want to be saved?"

"I want to be saved."

"Then you shall be saved."

And then it began.

And then it was over. How quickly didn't matter; Celia couldn't register anything like time through the pain. She did not stay in The Prophet's room that night but got up in something bordering a fugue state, closed off in a corner of her mind as far away from real life as possible. She dressed, and as she was about to leave, Barrett grabbed her wrist. "You are forgiven now, my child," he said. Celia managed to nod. "What do you say?" Barrett said.

"Thank you," Celia said. Then, before he could prompt her, she quickly added, "Thank you, Prophet."

"I'll see you in the morning." He let go, and Celia left, walking gingerly back to her room.

The morning came only a couple of short hours in which there had been no sleep later, only a daze where she couldn't tell dreams from her mind's wandering. She crossed paths in the kitchen with her mother, who gave Celia a puzzled look. "Were you in my room last night?" she said.

Celia was tired and sore, and it took a minute for her to understand the question. "I stuck my head in to say good night. You were already 'asleep,'" she said, making finger quotes.

"I remember," her mother snapped. "I just asked you about it, didn't I?"

"Oh, fuck off," Celia said, throwing the refrigerator door closed and leaving with her tray of tea.

"What did you just—"

"I said, fuck off," Celia squawked over her shoulder without looking back. "I just said it, didn't I?" she added in a mocking voice. She went down the hall to the sunroom and composed herself before entering. Barrett was on the couch studying some papers. He looked up when she came in and tossed the papers on the coffee table. Celia smiled. "Good morning, Prophet," she said, relieved to hear her voice come out normal.

"Good morning," he said, watching her as she placed the tea tray down on the coffee table and began preparing his drink. He watched in silence until she was done. "Come here," he said, making no move to drink his tea. Celia came around the table and stood in front of him. "I have a surprise for you," he said.

"A surprise?"

"Over there." He pointed to two grocery bags in a corner of the room. Celia made to go investigate, but Barrett caught her arm. "Take these off," he said, tugging at her shorts. Celia slid her shorts down and stepped out of them. "And these, too," Barrett said gripping her underpants and yanking them down himself. The swiftness of the movement startled Celia, but she stayed put and said nothing, only began peeling her shirt off as well. "No," Barrett said. "Leave that." He nodded toward the grocery bags. "Go on," he said. So, naked from the waist down, Celia crossed the room to the three grocery bags in the corner. She stood over them, feeling exposed. "Squat down," Barrett said. "And look at what's inside." Celia squatted, feeling humiliated and feral. The bags contained several boxes of brownie mix, as well as eggs, milk, sugar, and other ingredients. "Get on your hands and knees," Barrett said, now. "And look through them." Celia did as she was told. "Wider," Barrett said. Celia looked back at him, not understanding. "Make your legs wider apart," he said. She readjusted and checked back to see if he was satisfied. He must have been, because his robes had been pulled up to expose his already-hard member, reaching up and back against the curve of his belly, like Atlas, holding up a planet of burgers. Barrett's hands were by his side, and he looked pained. "Do you like your present?"

"Thank you, Prophet," she said over her shoulder, not understanding.

"I went this morning. Early. You wanted to make brownies. For the barbecue. There's enough there to make a hundred."

Celia was taken aback. She hadn't been expecting this. "Thank you, Prophet," she said again, feeling more sincere this time. She was stunned and confused. There was no dignified way to thank someone for brownie mix when you were naked from the waist down like Porky Pig, on your hands and knees. And saying thanks in this particular predicament felt traitorous to herself in any case…yet she was so relieved by the brownies that she did, in her heart, feel genuine gratitude.

"Come back," Barrett said. Celia started to get up. "Crawl," he ordered. Celia turned and crawled, hands and knees, across the room to Barrett, who was still splayed back on the couch, fully erect, with his robes bunched up over his belly and under his armpits. Celia stopped in front of him. Barrett's penis twitched slightly every second or so, as though with his heartbeat. "I can't touch it," Barrett said. "The Lord, my father, prohibits Onanism."

"Like if there was a demon inside you?"

"That's exorcism. But it's like a demon. It's the remaining human piece of my divinity. My human urge. And it wants out." Celia realized he meant the white stuff, the mess, that came out of him when he climaxed. She reached out and took him in her hand, but he stopped her. "No, I need more than that." Celia began to stand, hoping he wanted to put it in the right place this time. Again he stopped her, pushing her back onto her knees. He cupped one hand around the back of her neck. "Open your mouth."

"Prophet, I—"

"Open it," he yelled.

Celia did, and Barrett shoved her head toward his crotch, the length of his penis filling her mouth and gagging her. She choked and tried to cough. Barrett began a violent, regular thrusting. He moaned loudly. Celia's eyes watered, and she huffed air through her nose. Her hands instinctively fought to push herself away, to gain the ability to breathe properly again, but she wasn't strong enough. Barrett gripped her head more firmly and pressed harder. "Don't fight," he snarled. "Don't you fight the vessel of the Lord." He was quickened by her struggling, though, and he finished with a yell, his fingernails digging into the skin on Celia's neck. He held her another shuddering moment more, then released her with a toss, collapsing back into the couch. Celia fell back against the coffee table. Her spine slammed against the wooden edge, and she bounced onto the floor, spitting and coughing and crying. The room was still. Barrett gave a grunt of satisfaction, then stood and extended a hand down to Celia on the floor. "Get up." Celia raised a hand, and Barrett hauled her onto her feet. "Come," he said. He led her out of the sunroom and across the hall to his bathroom. "Sit," he instructed, gesturing to the toilet. He kneeled, with some effort, by the bathtub and ran the water. Celia hoped he was going to drown her and end all this.

When the bath was drawn, Barrett told her to get in. Celia lowered herself into the water, tentatively, against its heat. "Easy," Barrett said. "Easy. There you go." He took a washcloth and began to gently wash her face. Celia would have been less surprised if he had thrown a handful of burgers in and made her into a soup. "Here, lift your leg," Barrett said, running the wet cloth over her foot and the length of her leg. He scrubbed her chest and stomach, occasionally pausing to add more hot water to the bath. "C'mere," he said, easing her head onto his shoulder and beginning on her back. Celia relaxed, despite herself. It was such a gentle touch, such a soothing sensation, the warm cloth trailing long lines down her back. This was how she had always thought it would be. "I love you so much," Barrett said, as he bathed her. "You know that, right?" Celia nodded against his neck. She wanted to press her face as deeply into him as possible and sleep right then. "The depth of my love is infinite," he went on. "Divine beings have needs that regular humans can't comprehend. Earthquakes, floods, hurricanes, diseases, violence, and war—God my father has a need for these things, otherwise they would not exist. And if my father created them, they are good, they are noble, and they are just. Even if they are painful for the people who experience them, they are good." Barrett squirted shampoo into his hand and massaged it into Celia's scalp. "It's the same with me. But nothing I do changes the love I have for you or makes my actions any less good, any less just. Lean back." Barrett rinsed her hair. He drained the tub and wrapped Celia in a towel, planting a kiss on her forehead. "Come see me after the barbecue. Now go make your brownies."

Celia stood in the kitchen with her first batch of brownies cooling on the counter and the second in the oven. She was mixing a third. She regretted wanting to make brownies for everyone, but she was so relieved Barrett had showed her some kindness, both in buying the ingredients and in the bath, that she felt bad complaining. She felt lucky to have this chore, and after all, it had been her idea. She wanted everyone, especially the kids, to have a treat. The residents of Zoar were fed, but they never had so much as to be able to waste milk and eggs on something like brownies. She wanted to do something nice.

Something nice turned out to take almost eight hours. Celia had to double- and triple-up batches in the oven. Geraldine came in at one point to fuss.

"You should let people know if they're not going to be able to use the kitchen all day," she said.

"Why can't you use the kitchen?" Celia said, impatiently. "Do you need the stove?" Celia pointed to the clean and clear range atop the oven. "Or the microwave or the counter? Everything works. Why do you think you can't use it?"

"You've been monopolizing the oven all day. If I needed to—"

"Do you need the oven?"

"That's not the point."

"I'm sorry, Geraldine. What *is* your point then?" Celia said, removing one pan of cooked brownies, moving two other pans up a level each, and sliding a new pan in at the bottom.

"That if I needed the oven I couldn't use it."

Celia turned and faced Geraldine. "So if everything were different than it actually is, you'd be having a problem that you aren't actually having. And you see that problem as being so unfixable that you couldn't solve it by simply asking me if you could use the oven." Celia took the dish towel from her shoulder and tossed it by the sink. "You know, Gerry, I hear you call yourself a spiritual leader, but that attitude doesn't sound very spiritual. Or like leadership."

Geraldine had turned and marched out of the kitchen she didn't need. Celia went back to her brownies. When they were done and cut into squares, Celia stacked them on all the serving dishes the kitchen held, plus a good number of the regular dinner plates. There was no way she could carry them all down to Town Square herself, and this was not the house in which to seek help. Everyone in it was boycotting either the barbecue or her. Celia got the keys to the truck from Barrett's office and pulled it around to the front of the house. She loaded the brownies onto the front seat and floor, then changed clothes and drove down to the gathering crowd in Town Square.

Celia drove slow so as not to kick up dust. She braked to a stop at the edge of the festivities and waved to May Altman, who came to the passenger-side window.

"My goodness, girl. It's not so far a walk you had to drive down here, is it?" May said. Celia pointed at the passenger seat and floor, stacked with brownies. May's eyes got wide. "Celia Ann Waters, you are too sweet," she said. "I can't believe y'all made all these."

"No y'all, just me," Celia said, loath to let anyone think for a moment that Geraldine or her mother had contributed.

"I figured as much," May said. "I was just being polite. So I guess those two aren't coming, then?"

"No," Celia said.

"Will The Prophet be coming?" May said. "I heard he might come."

"He's sorry he can't make it tonight," Celia said. "But you know how it is with him. Work, work, work." She didn't like defending Barrett much, but he was happy at the moment, and she was scared of doing anything to upset that. Even out of his sight, she didn't want to risk it.

"Well, much as I'd like to see him come down and have a good time, we all benefit from his efforts, so God bless and keep him."

"Amen," said Celia.

"Whooee, look at this," Gardner said, emerging from the crowd and joining May at the passenger window. "Queen Bee, you made it. And it looks like you outdid yourself with all these brownies."

Gardner sounded different to her now, Celia noticed, after hearing Barrett's story about him. The tone she always heard before, the irritation it caused her, was gone. She recognized the playfulness behind his words. Before she had only noticed his gruffness, his grumpiness, and his grim expression. Now she saw that he was trying to be nice, friendly even. The poor man just didn't have the natural face, demeanor, or voice for it.

"Hey, Gardner," Celia said. "How about giving us a hand with these so I can take the truck back up and get it out of everyone's way?"

"You know it, Queen Bee."

Gardner, May, and Celia each stacked an armload of brownies and headed into the thick of things. People were setting up chairs and spreading open blankets. Celia caught bits of conversation as they walked.

"—weather's cleaning up so nice I think we're gonna get a good output from that final field we planted. I wasn't too sure how it'd go when we started—"

"—to convince our neighbors to repent and be saved for years, but it was like The Prophet said. They'd just as soon spit on us. I fear for what's gonna happen to them at the end-times, but all you can do it try."

"The wind comes through this chink in the wall so bad I thought we were liable to freeze one night. Got to fix it before next winter."

"I prayed about it, but the Lord just couldn't save that bean dip."

"—more ammunition. There's gonna be desperate sinners roaming around. Funny thing is a lawless world is probably what they think heaven's like anyway. When they come trying to take what's ours though, all they're gonna find is hell."

"The Lord'll cut 'em down."

"Never enough sugar in her tea. I swear she's half a Yankee."

There were people playing guitars and singing hymns. Children raced between the adults, chasing one another, chasing balls, boys chasing girls, girls chasing boys, all of them yelling out new rules whenever it pleased them, changing teams and sides and allegiances on a whim as it suited their chances of being victorious in whatever made-up game they were playing. A few of the stalwart cried foul when this happened, but most of them took it as a cue to do the same when the tide turned against them.

Celia, Gardner, and May came to a long row of tables. They were stacked with casserole dishes and bowls holding beans, corn bread, coleslaw, collard greens, potato salad, corn on the cob, yams, sweet potatoes, fried okra, macaroni salad, fried chicken, rice and gravy, and mashed potatoes. They made room for the brownies on a table. Out beyond the party line, Celia saw a small cluster of people around a smoking pit. Celia recognized Stacy Landross and waved. Stacy came loping over, her crooked smile matching her lilting gait. She surveyed the brownies being unloaded. "You make all these, sugar plum?" she said. Celia nodded. "Too sweet. 'Tween you and this dessert, the whole compound'll have a cavity or a fit, won't they?" Stacy wrapped Celia in a muscled hug that smelled of smoke and earth and wind. Celia gripped her back with a desperation she hadn't intended. Stacy. Why couldn't Stacy have been her mother? "Whoa, I missed you too, child," Stacy said playfully.

"How was the hog head?" Celia said, letting go and regaining her composure.

"Haven't had a treat that special in a while."

"I can't believe y'all ate that," May said.

"Harmon, Stace, and me prefer you don't approve," Gardner said. "Means we ain't gotta share."

Stacy cackled, and May held up her hands in a do-whatever-and-keep-me-out-of-it gesture. A voice behind Celia called out, "Hey there, Cee-bear." Celia turned and found a special treat of her own: her father minus Beth. They exchanged a hug. Gardner said, "Waters," and nodded.

"Celia made dessert," May said, gesturing.

Celia's father took in the mountain of brownies. "How'd you get all these down here?"

"Drove down in the truck."

Her father made a face both impressed and surprised. "You drove?"

"Barr—The Prophet has been teaching me." Her father made an even more cartoonish face and Celia smiled. "It's only fifty yards, Daddy."

"Last time I saw you behind the wheel, you drove straight into a wall."

"That was a go-cart and I was eight."

"You have the truck down here now?"

"Yeah, it's over there. C'mon, I'll show you. I'm really good. Ride back up with me."

"All right, give your old man a lift." He put his hands together in prayer and looked up at the sky. "The Lord will protect me, I reckon."

"Oh, stop. C'mon, you'll see."

They said see-you-soons to May, Stacy, and Gardner and went back to the truck. Gardner and Celia's father were polite but formal with each other, two men now on the finished side of a competition.

They were almost to the truck when Celia heard the lyrics to a song she herself had invented. She scanned the crowd and saw, in the space between two shacks, a group of young girls practicing a dance routine, singing, "My Savior's back and you're gonna be in trouble..." There was Rebekah, leading three other little girls through the choreography. "No, it's turn, then right-foot step, then the arm, like this," Rebekah was saying. The four of them took it from the top, finishing with the arm raised on the "Hey la, hey la, you'll roast in hell."

"Good," Rebekah said. "Now in the next part, we end on 'prepare for hell.'"

Celia and her father reached the truck and got inside with the lingering smell of brownies. Celia started the engine. Her father was staring at her. "What?" she said.

"It's just funny to see you in the driver's seat. I always figured I'd teach you how to drive, and here we are and you already know how."

"Barrett only showed me a little bit. I'm still figuring it out. You can still give me lessons." Celia put the truck in reverse and checked behind her. She did a one-point turn and started them back up the way to the big house.

"I don't imagine there's much left for me to teach you about anything," her father said.

This struck Celia as so sad she considered driving them into another wall and putting them out of their misery—or, preferably, driving them away from Zoar forever, bearing to the right past the house and following the rutted dirt road out to Route 52 and just keeping the pedal down. To where? Didn't matter. Back to the house with rooms they could paint any color they wanted. Back to the Blue Wave. Or just keep driving until they were in another state. Or all the way to Canada. You could make a fresh start in Canada, right? If not there, then where?

But no. Her father didn't want to leave his Prophet, and Celia didn't have anywhere to go as a fifteen-year-old. She could turn herself over to the state, she supposed, but if this, Zoar, was how the world was run by the adults that cared about her, she didn't want to fathom being looked after by the ones who didn't. This place was all they had left. So she said, "How's Beth?" instead and kept on toward the house.

"Great, she's great," her father said. "In fact," he said, turning toward her, getting all animated like he always did whenever he was excited, "I wanted to tell you something. Beth and me—"

"I wanted to tell you something about Beth, too," Celia said over top of him, in lieu of holding down the horn to keep him from saying what he was about to say. "I had a dream about the two of you." She wasn't supposed to make up dreams on her own. Barrett was supposed to dictate them to her. Barrett who hurt her. Barrett who could be so sweet when he wanted to be. But if Celia wanted to leave Zoar, maybe she could make her father want to leave, too. This might make him want to leave and take Celia with him, right? This might work, right? Too late to wait for an answer—she was already talking.

"You had a dream about me and Beth?" her father said, his voice going flat.

"I dreamed The Prophet came and knocked on the door to the cabin. You answered it, and The Prophet asked for Beth. He walked with her to Gardner's house where he knocked again. Gardner answered and Beth went into his house. Then Jesus came down from heaven and blessed both homes. Yours, and Beth and Gardner's," Celia said quickly.

Her father was quiet as Celia came to a stop in front of the big house and put the truck in park. "What's The Prophet say about your dream?" he finally asked. "You tell him?"

Celia shook her head. "Not yet."

Her father nodded thoughtfully. "Don't even need him to interpret that one, do we? Pretty obvious what's gonna happen."

"It's just a dream, Daddy."

"Your dreams aren't just dreams. You've been blessed. It's been proven over and over. Just wish I understood it. Understood any of it. Seems like...seems like whenever I find a little peace—"

"There's more," Celia interrupted. Bring them down and raise them up, that's what Barrett had taught her. "That's the wave you make them ride," she could hear him saying in her head. "Give them all the bad, all the fear, all the ways they are sinners without a drop of good inside them. Then, when they're about as low as they can get, you throw them a lifeline. You give them a little hope. Tell them how you can redeem them. How you, along with the power of the Lord can raise them up. After they're dead of course. You can't do much about them being lowly sinners in their day-to-day." Bring them down, then raise them up. Celia said it to herself like a mantra.

"Daddy, you said no. In the dream you rejected the Prophet."

"What does that mean? Why did I do that?" her father said, looking alarmed.

"Then Jesus, He faded away and the devil was standing there. Satan had been posing as Jesus. The whole thing had been a trick of the devil's." Should she add some more? Tell him that in the dream he had come to get her, Celia, and they had left together? Gone out to start a new life. Did she even want that? Christ, she didn't know. She just knew she didn't want whatever it was she had. She didn't want this anymore. So she said nothing else.

"What are you telling me?" her father said.

"Just my dream, Daddy. That's all."

"Is there more?"

"No, then I wake up. Every time I have the dream, that's when I wake up."

"How many times you had it?"

"A bunch."

He got out of the truck. Celia got out, too, and walked around to his side. He stood with his hands on his hips, looking intently at the big house. "You know," he said. "I haven't been inside there since she moved out. I never got invited again."

"Do you want to go inside now?" Celia said. Her father shook his head. "What were you going to tell me?" Celia said. "A minute ago. In the truck."

"Nothing," he said. "Nothing important." He turned and started back down to Town Square. Celia followed, walking a little behind him.

Celia returned to the house after the barbecue and reported to Barrett's room, as requested. As she came through the door, he slid off the bed and came at her. He grabbed her by her hair and steered her toward the bed, where he bent her over. With one hand he held her head down on the bed and with the other undid her shorts and yanked them down to the carpet, along with her underwear. Celia felt his robes pull aside and the heat of his skin against hers, then he entered her. His other hand came up to her head now, too. Barrett turned her face into the mattress and pressed. For a few seconds Celia was fine, relatively speaking, but she soon ran out of air and couldn't breathe. Still Barrett held her there. Her body took over again and began fighting to get away, to get up, to take a breath. Barrett moaned and pressed her down harder. She struggled, trying to press up with her arms and kick away with her legs. Somewhere in the distance, beyond her fight to live, she heard Barrett cry out as he pressed himself into her so deeply she would have gasped and cried out if she could have gotten any air. He shuddered as he finished and then suddenly let her go.

Celia came up heaving, hair stuck down her face and getting sucked into her mouth. She didn't care to brush it away; she only wanted air and could tolerate whatever was dragged in along with each wonderful breath. Behind her, Barrett was also panting. He withdrew from her and turned her toward him, taking one finger and hooking the hair away from her face. He led her to the closet, where he took out a robe and put it around her. Then Barrett picked her up and carried her to the bed, where he laid her gently against the pillows. He went around the other side and pulled out a large glass bottle. "This is champagne," he said, popping the cork, which ricocheted off the ceiling and shot into some unseen corner of the room. He poured some into a tall, thin glass and handed it to her before climbing into the bed next to her. Celia rested her head against his shoulder and took a swallow of the liquid. It was like tiny, sweet firecrackers in her mouth.

Barrett sighed with contentment and turned up the volume on the silent TV. A man and a woman were arguing on a news show. Celia drained her glass and held it out for a refill. She was back with the sweet Barrett now, the one who loved her. He filled her glass. The man and woman on the television were both yelling at the same time. "Idiots," Barrett said.

"Why are they idiots?" Celia said.

"Because they're liberals. Liberals are idiots. They don't get it."

"What don't they get?" Celia presented her empty glass again.

"You should really pay more attention to national politics. Nothing is more educational in terms of people's willingness to be convinced of things that stand to benefit others."

"I like it better when you explain it to me. What don't they get?"

"Liberals constitute a party, the Democrats, that prides itself—defines itself—on ideals and beliefs that center around tolerance, fairness, open-mindedness, generosity. Things like not being racist and helping the poor."

"Oh, no," Celia said, taking a drink. She felt a warmth enveloping her, numbing the pain and soreness she felt.

"The thing is, that's how everybody already sees themselves. Everyone thinks they're fair and open-minded and that they care about the right things. People have high opinions of their own decency. The conservatives, on the other hand, pride themselves on a tough-truths stance. They say out loud the things the average shmuck might feel pressure not to say, things closer to the fear-center, closer to the bone of self-interest. They give people a group to belong to where they can say all the things that come after the *but*. 'I'm not racist, *but* look at the crime statistics in black neighborhoods.' 'I'm a giving person, *but* most of these poor people aren't even trying to get jobs and they have all these kids even though they can't support them.' Liberals don't offer people anything more than what they already believe themselves to be. Conservatives at least give them something."

"What's that?"

"The right to be angry and victimized. As far as converting people, they've got a better plan of action. Of course they're all selling a false god, getting people to worship at the altar of government, regardless of which one it is. All government is godless, especially the ones that try to include God. That's the thing about…"

Celia drained the rest of her glass and held it out for another refill. She half listened to Barrett explaining the world, boiling it down and compacting it into theories and categories that he could throw here or there, shift this way and that. She wanted him to ramble on just like this. She'd missed it. His voice and that of the TV melded, the champagne pooled around her fears and worries and they melted, and with the warmth she felt inside and out Celia drifted, feeling, for the moment, safe and at peace.

Chapter 9

Three teams, three answers—You don't like it? Start a riot—Beaufort is happening—The falling of the scales—The people seized them all—A poor excuse for a eulogy—Field surgery—Umbrellas make lousy parachutes

Gardner went missing.

No one knew how to react at first, so they didn't react at all. When he didn't show up to meet the maintenance crew that first morning, they all assumed he was with the home-building brigade. Gardner was a work-leader and original settler, so he wore a lot of hats. The home-building brigade assumed he was helping the farm team. The farm team figured he was with maintenance or, heck, doing something for The Prophet. The Prophet slept in that morning, so he didn't think much of anything. It was the Junior Christian soldiers who raised the alarm. Eight of them milled about near the firing range waiting for Mr. Gardner to arrive and teach them how to make a bow and arrows from things they could find in the woods, because when the Armageddon came the ammunition wouldn't last forever. Mr. Gardner didn't arrive. Mr. Gardner was never late, and he did not tolerate lateness in others. It was a lesson they had all learned, a point of human decency, as their leader liked to call topics that were dear to him, that Mr. Gardner held in high esteem. "There's no such thing as 'on time.' There's early and there's late," he was fond of saying. When it became clear to the Junior Christian Soldiers that Mr. Gardner wasn't coming, they kept their wits about them, as they had been taught. They formed three teams, split the compound into zones, and dispersed to ask if anyone had seen or spoken to Mr. Gardner that day.

Three teams, three answers. Gardner was missing.

Search parties assembled slowly. People didn't want to overreact. This was partially due to a natural tendency in people to avoid the embarrassment of making a fuss. In this case it was exacerbated by the natural tendency in the citizens of Zoar to avoid being on the receiving end of Gardner's derision if he came strolling out of the woods or popped up out of some well he'd dug himself and began demanding to know what they were all doing thinking he was lost. As more people compared notes on the last time they had seen or spoken to the man, though, it became apparent that he was, indeed, missing and there was cause for concern.

There was also the issue of going into Gardner's private quarters. "Ain't right," Biscuit said. "The man might just be off in the woods or gone to town for something. He's got a sovereign right to privacy as an American." But none of the compound's vehicles were missing, and it was unlikely Gardner had decided to walk to town, which was more than twenty miles away. They were standing in a group between the pop-up and Gardner's house in the last good evening light before dusk. Celia stood with Rebekah and her parents. Kent and May Altman were there, Nancy-Lynn was by her husband, and Harmon and Stacy and Celia's father and Beth and ten or so others debated what to do.

"Look, I agree," Harmon said. "But we're talking about my friend's safety. No one's seen him all day, and it ain't like him to vanish and not come back. We need to check inside."

"Beth could do it," Celia said. "You've been a guest of Gardner's before, haven't you?" Celia and the others looked over to Beth, who kept her eyes locked on the ground in front of her. She shook her head. "Can't go in there," she said.

"'Cause it's not her right," Celia's father added quickly, shooting Celia a frown. "Biscuit's right. Gardner's entitled to his privacy. His home is sovereign, like all the rest of ours as free Christian Americans. He's probably just camping out in the woods for a few days. You know how he is." He rested his hand on his sidearm at his waist.

"We're all camping in the woods. That's what this place is," Celia muttered under her breath.

"You know that for a fact?" Harmon said to Celia's father. "You talk to him today?"

"No. I ain't Gardner's keeper. Just don't think there's any reason to get worked up about a guy going missing who disappears off into the woods all the time like he's Davy Crockett."

"I agree," Rebekah's father spoke up. "I say we give this a few days. Gardner could be anywhere, and he wouldn't want us making all this fuss about it. 'Specially wouldn't want us going through his house."

"Huntin' rifle's gone," a voice called out. They all turned to see that Stacy had let herself in while they were arguing and done an inspection. "But his tent and sleepin' bag's still here, and he ain't take enough shells to be out there more'n a day at most." She reappeared in the doorway. They all stared at her. She looked to the house and back, reading their expressions. "Sovereignty nothin'. Gardner's my friend. I go in his house all the time whenever I want. You don't like it? Start a riot."

Harmon and some others rustled up flashlights and paired off to search the woods in the dying light. "Just gonna end up with more of y'all lost is all," Celia's father said. Beth kept quiet and stared at the ground some more. Celia watched the two of them and tried to decide what had happened—something to do with Gardner, obviously. Celia thought her comment about Beth being his guest would get a different reaction than it had. She turned to Rebekah. "Do you want to be my search-team partner to help look for Mr. Gardner?"

"Rebekah's coming home for the evening," Mrs. Eubanks said.

"What about Gardner?" Celia said, surprised Rebekah's mother wouldn't let her help search for someone she so clearly admired. Whatever Gardner's other faults, mainly his personality, he was beloved by the Junior Christian Soldiers who seemed to find in him, through his leadership, the one adult at Zoar who was telling them something practical.

"Gardner's fine where he is," Mrs. Eubanks said. She paused. "I mean, I'm sure he's fine. Everyone is making a commotion over nothing." She took Rebekah by the hand and started back toward their house. Rebekah looked back at Celia, resigned, stoic, and calm. She hadn't once said she wanted to look for Gardner. She hadn't once wondered where he could be.

That night Celia stood staring out the glass doors of the sunroom at the brightly lit hot tub, holding her third glass of champagne and thinking. Barrett was on the couch behind her, tapping at his laptop. He had already defiled her, but she was learning things. He now invariably cut off her air while humping her. For reasons she didn't understand, he climaxed almost immediately upon feeling her struggle and fight to escape. She fought early now. Barrett hardly had to palm her mouth and nose closed or press her facedown into a pillow before she was flailing and kicking. Then it would end and she would have champagne. More and more frequently she would have champagne before, too. There were bottles everywhere. Barrett kept a healthy supply, never one to skimp on recreational substances.

Celia stood naked at the window with her champagne, staring at the hot tub while Barrett's typing slowed in correspondence to his pills taking effect. The hot tub. Did anyone else know it was here? Did her mother know?

Geraldine? They had to, though it had never come up among them. They were all three keeping a secret the others knew. No one outside the house knew about the hot tub, and the three of them were keeping the secret so well they didn't even slip in front of one another. So one world, the big house, kept the other world ignorant of its goings-on. So what did that other world keep from the big house? Celia was really thinking about Gardner. The evening search party had been fruitless. It got dark too soon after it began. No Gardner anywhere. Behind her, the typing stopped. Rebekah had been so unconcerned. Celia drained the last of her champagne and turned away from the glass doors. Barrett was slumped over on his side on the couch, laptop tipped over to the side with him. His mouth was open, and the wheezing was just beginning, the quick catches and splats in his throat, sounds like blobs of mayonnaise hitting a clean kitchen floor.

"Darling, I think I might go out for a bit," Celia said, filling her glass from the half-empty bottle on the coffee table. "The night is so warm I can't see how clothes are even necessary. Do you think I should bother getting dressed? No, of course not. You never see the point in me being dressed." Barrett continued his early-unconsciousness breathing, it was gaining an edge now, like a heavy stick being dragged down a dirt road. "But if I never got dressed, what would you take off?" Celia said, turning back to the window and taking a drink. "What would be the fun for you if there was nothing to unveil? Nothing to tear away?" She took another swallow. "Oh, just a stroll, that's all. Get some air. And maybe stop in to visit an old friend. Ha-ha. A young friend, actually. You'd like her." Celia finished off her drink. "Yes, you would like her quite a lot. Well, I'm off." She put her glass on the coffee table and slid into her shorts and shirt. "So long, my darling. Don't wait up," she said, and she left the sunroom.

Celia went out the window in Barrett's bedroom, crossed the compound, and let herself in the window of Rebekah's room, clamping a hand tight over the younger girl's mouth as a way of waking her up. Rebekah's eyes went wide, and she began to struggle. "Sh," Celia said in a voice so light it was barely more than breath. It was lost in the sound of cicadas and crickets. "It's me." Rebekah lay still. Celia put a finger to her lips and pointed at the window. Rebekah nodded, and Celia removed her hand and went back out the window into the night. Rebekah followed.

They walked to the barn in silence. Celia lit the kerosene lantern that was kept there. They sat with Trevor, who didn't bother to get up to greet them. "What's going on?" Celia said. Rebekah looked at her thoughtfully but didn't answer. "I'm not stupid, you know. I can tell something is up. What is it?" Rebekah stared at the donkey, her face scrunched as she considered. "Something is happening," Celia said. "Tell me what it is."

"Beaufort," Rebekah said. "Beaufort is happening." Then she told Celia a story.

The Unexpected Rise of the Prophet Beaufort

Beaufort wanted his wife back. When Barrett, their prophet, took his first wife, Celia's mother, Beaufort smelled a rat. "Just seems like the Second Coming of Christ could get his own woman rather than taking someone else's— or that, if she was destined to be with the Second Coming of Christ, she would be single, rather than having married some guy years ago," he reportedly said to Geraldine the night after the announcement had been made. Geraldine had snapped at him. "That's blasphemy. It's not our place to question why the Lord does what he does. Especially not yours. Christ's own mother was engaged to another man when God called her." She had been in a real mood since finding out The Prophet was taking a wife, Beaufort said. That wasn't that strange. Geraldine was almost always in a mood, he never knew why. So he had just stretched out on the sofa to take a nap before bedtime while Geraldine finished cleaning up the kitchenette. He put the whole thing out of his mind.

Then, of course, things changed for Beaufort. The Prophet took Geraldine and Geraldine took nothing from their RV, a fact that upset Beaufort as much as losing his wife. "How could she not want any of her stuff?" he said. "Her stuff meant so much to her." And he should know. He was the one who sat with it in the RV all day under strict orders not to touch anything while she was out running all over Zoar. Now he was alone in the RV. Could he touch her stuff now or not? He didn't know and couldn't find out. Geraldine wouldn't talk to him. No one talked to him really, except Celia's father, Brother Waters, who was really the only person who could understand what Beaufort was going through. And it was Celia's father who told the others about Beaufort's plight; he was the one who really put it in perspective for them.

Celia's father described to the rest of them what it was like for Beaufort. Here was a man, Beaufort, who went to Living Faith Church only because his wife wanted to go, who moved out here to the compound on the good faith that this was a holy and truly Christian community. Now his wife was gone, living with another man who, Beaufort confided in Celia's father, he suspected might not actually be the Second Coming—a shock, Brother Waters knew, to those listening. A shock for certain and blasphemy, too, but only if Beaufort was wrong, and Beaufort had put a pretty strong case before Celia's father. And, it just so happened, Celia's father was privy to a dream The Prophet didn't know about. From his own daughter. Had anyone else noticed how fat their prophet had become? Was that not gluttony? A true Christ wouldn't be capable of getting fat. It was one of the seven deadly sins. Just pure logic said it couldn't be done. If it was a sin, the Second Coming wouldn't be able to do it. Also, shouldn't the Second Coming be leading them to a paradise on Earth? Barrett mainly just sat around his nice house. It was them, the citizens, who did the backbreaking work. Even Beaufort. Sure, he didn't contribute as much actual work as the rest of them, but at least he tried. That was how he kept getting hurt, by getting out there and making the effort, shoddy and pathetic though that effort was.

And the taking of the wives. Not just that Barrett took multiple wives, but the fact that he literally took them from other men, from his followers.

Now, Beaufort wasn't concerned merely because his own wife was taken from him, though that did give him pause. It was the fact that she left everything behind; that was the thing that really struck Beaufort. That and the fact that she never came back to check on him, to see if he was eating, if he was feeling OK. It nagged and nagged at him. See, here was the thing, if Geraldine had packed up, moved out, made a transition that involved the closure and tying up of loose ends that the ending of a marriage might entail then Beaufort would have been able to say, "OK, this is being done for God. It's just the way it has to be and eventually the righteousness will become apparent to me though I am sad to see this woman go." But to just one day never come home, to never check on him or come back to the RV—she left dishes in the sink! She didn't even leave him a single dinner in the fridge. No, this wasn't God telling his Prophet, his Second Coming, what to do. For a woman to leave her husband in that manner, there was only one logical explanation: demons. Only demons could explain this behavior. An evil force must be working over Geraldine's mind and controlling her, sucking her into the abyss. Certainly with all the Christly work the compound had accomplished the devil was lurking right in their midst and hoping to spoil it all. It seemed he'd finally found a way. When it had happened—how it had happened—Beaufort couldn't say, but poison had seeped into the veins of Zoar and it was going to kill them all.

Beaufort had been scared when he came to this realization, and he was even more frightened about telling it to anyone else. Who could he talk to about something like this? Then the answer came to him: the only other man who could honestly confirm or disconfirm his feelings. That was how Celia's father came to be talking to select people about what was really going on around Zoar. Most of them probably knew him, he would say, as a guy always near the front line around here. He was the first to move to the compound, a close confidant of the Prophet, and a guy who sometimes found himself out testifying to others, a leader in their community, though he'd never asked for that. He wasn't that kind of guy; he didn't want the limelight or the attention. It had all just happened to him, and he always pulled back, tried to get away from it. "No, not me," he'd say to God. "You don't want me for this, to speak to people, to lead them in your name. That's Barrett's job. I got enough jobs around here." It was always there, though, this invisible push to get out in front. It wasn't until Beaufort came to him that he understood why. This was what God had been prepping him for, what he had been pushing him into, because someone had to say it in a way that people would get. He'd had to go through all he had been through so he could deliver this message and deliver this place back to God. He went through all this so people would believe him when he stood before them and spoke to them as he did this very day, to certain people whose judgment he respected because they were true Christians who could tell the light from the dark. Because when Beaufort first came to him he was scandalized, no two ways about it, and horrified. Much like the people he was speaking to—good Christian people he could trust, who could see things for what they were because they had their heads on straight. But even though he was scared, because everything he'd been indoctrinated to believe was being challenged, it was as though the scales had fallen from his eyes and he could see clearly. Beaufort's words had a profound and immediate effect on Celia's father, like a spell had been broken. He came up into clean, free air and suddenly he saw it all: the corruption the demons had wrought, how they had been hard at work soiling the purity of Zoar. The demons had gotten hold of their beloved Prophet and turned him from the true path. It happened to Solomon and it happened to Barrett. There was precedent here; you could find it right there in the Bible. You didn't need to look any further than that. Prophets lost their way. It happened before, and it had happened again, now, to them. Was he not example enough? A wife taken and then, on top of that, his precious daughter. She was only fourteen! [Fifteen, actually, Celia thought, realizing he still didn't realize she'd had a birthday.] The demons had blinded him to what was happening, to the wrongness of it all, or he would have refused, taken the exile and gone off to live back in the world. What father and husband wouldn't do that for his family? They all knew him: he was a man dedicated to his family above all else, yet the demons had tricked him and made it all seem legitimate. That was their greatest power, to come disguised as blessings, but to leave only a curse. Now they were at it again, sending Beth to be with Gardner, breaking another holy union. Did any of them listening, Celia's father would ask, believe that they had a holy union with their wife or husband? Because if their union was truly holy, it was only a matter of time before the demons came to break it, to send their wives off with Barrett or one of his cronies. They didn't have to look any further than him and Beaufort to see this was true.

Kent Altman was on board. When he heard Beaufort's message, spoken by Celia's father, the scales fell from his eyes, too. May Altman also lost her scales, right then and there, as soon as she heard the words. She didn't want to be Barrett's wife. Biscuit and Nancy-Lynn accepted the message and lost their scales before Celia's father even finished talking to them about all this, that's how open they were to living without demons. And then others, all of them couples, were recruited and converted, set free from their constraints, set free from the demons, and set free from their fears by Beaufort, the unexpected prophet of the New Zoar.

Rebekah finished her story. They sat in the white noise of the black night, crickets and cicadas screaming over the rustle of the trees and Trevor's heavy breathing.

Celia, still feeling the champagne, chose her words carefully. "Do you believe it? That The Prophet has fallen."

Rebekah nodded. "My parents said it was true. And it doesn't seem right, does it?"

"What's that?"

"Having three wives. And they're other men's wives on top of that. And one of them is so young."

"You didn't think it was wrong before."

"But that was because of all the demons. We were all blinded to the perversion by the devil. Beaufort opened our eyes."

"I thought you were afraid of catching his hemorrhoids."

"He's been healed. Now that he's exposed the sin all around us, he's done the Lord's work, so God has healed him. He doesn't have vertigo anymore either. All his ailments and injuries, and he had a lot when you think about it, they've all been taken away."

"He can work now?"

"He could, but he doesn't, because he won't do the devil's bidding by helping Zoar while it's under Barrett's corruption."

"So he was injured all the time and couldn't do any work, and now that the Lord has healed him, he won't do any work that will offend the Lord?"

"That's the power of Beaufort." Rebekah peered closely at Celia's face. "So I'll turn your question back on you. Do you believe it?"

"Do I believe what, exactly?"

"Do you believe you should be married to the same man as your mom?"

Celia wasn't ready for such a direct question. She didn't think of her mom as married to Barrett, she thought of her mother as being married to her father. This thing with Barrett was just part of a feud between her parents, a fluke, something that could be fixed if only the right person told them God said it was fixed. Celia had wanted Barrett for herself, of course, but now she regretted that. She had only wanted to be the one who held his attention, this special man they all worshiped. "No," Celia said, in answer to Rebekah's question.

"Do you believe your mom should be married to The Prophet? That he should have taken her from your dad?"

"Of course not."

"Do you believe that this is the way things should be?" Rebekah put her hands on Celia's shoulders. "That any of this is the way it's supposed to be?"

Celia felt a knot in her throat. "Stop," she said, without any conviction.

"Do you believe you should be married and sharing a bed with a grown man?"

"No," Celia said, crying now. "No." Rebekah pulled her in close, and Celia wept against her shoulder, building to a full, wailing sob.

"It's OK," Rebekah said, stroking her hair. "Your eyes have just been opened. You've been saved by the power of Beaufort."

"Your dad is going to rescue you."

"He is?"

"Yeah. He's got a whole plan, and he thinks the time is just right. The Beaufort movement has enough believers now to make it happen. He's going to get you out of there."

"And my mom?"

Rebekah didn't say anything. "What about my mom?"

"It was against the Lord for Barrett to take your mother away from your father, but..."

"But?"

"Just because your father's eyes have been opened to the devil's work doesn't mean hers will be. And he figures they probably won't be opened any time soon, and Beth is part of his redemption away from the corrupt prophet. So he's going to be joined with her by Beaufort. Then he's going to rescue you and deal with Barrett and drive your mom out of Zoar."

"What about Geraldine?"

"Beaufort says her eyes will be opened once Barrett is gone."

"My dad says my mom can't be saved, so he's sticking with Beth.

Beaufort says Geraldine can be saved, so he's getting her back. Then Beaufort is going to marry Beth and my dad and kick my mom off the compound."

"Yeah. The joining of your dad and Beth will be Beaufort's first official act outside of Barrett's corrupt rule. It's meant to be a statement."

"What happened to Gardner?"

"That was your dad's first act outside of the demonic influence."

"Where's Gardner?"

"It had to be done. He was going to take Beth from your father and there's already been enough of that."

"What did my dad do?"

"'So the people seized them all, and Elijah took them down to the Kishon Valley and killed them there.' Kings."

"No."

"'Everyone who would not seek the Lord was to be put to death.' Chronicles."

"What happened?"

"Your dad went hunting with Mr. Gardner."

"And?"

"Mr. Gardner had an accident."

"I thought you liked Mr. Gardner."

"Not as much as I love my mom and dad and don't want my mom taken away."

"Of course."

"I'm glad your eyes were opened. I'm glad you're on our side. I was nervous about testifying to you about Beaufort. Your dad and Beth really didn't want you to know. They know you're helping because you told your dad about your dream, but they didn't think you should know—especially Beth."

"She didn't, huh?"

"But I knew you wanted to be saved. And when you came to my room tonight, I knew it was a sign from God that I was supposed to testify to you. With your gift, your communion with God through your dreams, the Beaufort movement will thrive, and the blessing of Christ will return to Zoar."

"Let's not mention that you opened my eyes to my dad or Beth or your parents or any of Beaufort's followers, if that's OK. If there's a plan in place, it's better if they just follow through with it. Let it run its course. God will guide it."

"Yeah. You're right. And they might be mad at me if they knew I talked to you about it. I wasn't supposed to. And I'm not supposed to sneak out at night, either. But still. I'm glad I got to be the one. It feels special. I'm glad I told you."

"Me too. I'm very glad you told me."

Celia watched Rebekah fade into the darkness as though it were fog. It was offensive to anyone's intelligence to think Beaufort had anything to do with his own rise. Her father was obviously behind this. Her father had obviously been taking some lessons from Barrett as well. Her father who had murdered Gardner. She said it to herself out loud, her voice a blasphemy against the still of the night, "Dad murdered Gardner." She tried it again with a twist: "Dad murdered Gardner because of me."

Celia used the ladder and went over the back fence. Barrett was still comatose on the couch. The Prophet: knocked out on painkillers and sexual assault. She thought of the phrase *sleeping like a baby*, but that wasn't right. Babies fussed and jabbered and cried out in the night. Maybe it was gas that bothered them or they were lonely in their crib, the first cage. Or they woke and stared at their mobile or played with a toy or tested their ability to make sound. To truly sleep like a baby was to be engaged with life. Barrett slept like a patient in a hospital who had been dosed with something to kill the pain. He slept like someone who was sick.

Celia went into the office and stood staring at the floor. She didn't know where to go or what to do. Her father had murdered a man, and she was responsible. She'd told him The Prophet was giving Beth to Gardner, and that had been the final straw. Through her self-disgust she managed a stab of anger at her father. Beth had been the final straw. Not her, Celia. Not his wife. Not the marriages to The Prophet, not the destruction of their family, but Beth. Boring, pointless, nothing Beth. Now, after following Barrett all this way, after hanging on every word he said and believing it unquestioningly, these people were turning on him, on everything they had enabled with their belief, and following a puppet prophet, Beaufort. They couldn't possibly believe Beaufort had some divine inspiration, could they? Of course they could, she realized, they were capable of believing anything. That's how they had ended up here.

Celia sat on the floor and leaned back against the couch. A pile of papers toppled, cresting over her head like a wave and spilling into her lap. She stayed still, papered and defeated, and thought about crying. Instead she kicked at the pages, grabbed handfuls of them and balled them up, tossing them here and there in a burst of rage that was quickly doused by futility. Celia stared at the scattered pages. She wanted to set them all on fire, just burn it all. The idea gave her the first inkling of peace she had experienced in a while. Everything was beyond saving. How nice it would be to just burn it all down. Perhaps, Celia thought, that's exactly what I'll do.

The next morning Celia let herself out of the house and walked through Town Square. Now that Rebekah had told her about the insurrection, she saw signs of it everywhere—in the suspicious looks she received when people thought she wasn't looking. From the corner of her eye, she saw the wariness and hostility on their faces until she made eye contact and they broke into a fake smile. Celia saw men in groups of three and four talking low and conspiratorially. Or was she just imagining it? Celia thought of the picture of a piece of toast her father had shown her once, when they still had the house in Garden Estates. It had been nothing but a piece of toast until her father pointed out the face of Jesus in the heat pattern. After that, Jesus was all she could see. The formerly meaningless pattern of toasting couldn't be found. It was the same now. In Town Square Celia could no longer see the old patterns of the compound, random, regular, and devoid of specific meaning. The same was true for everyone else, too. Now that the idea of Barrett as a charlatan and Beaufort as a spiritual leader had been suggested, that was all they could see. The old pattern had been lost. Not everyone believed in Beaufort, or, more accurately, her father, but it must be a significant portion of the citizens for them to feel confident enough to attempt a coup.

How ugly their humanness was when it masqueraded as the divine. She and her mother living with Barrett, her father on the couch with Beth in his bed, Beaufort alone in his RV, Geraldine in her room impatiently waiting her turn, and all the rest of them scattered across Zoar wanting their lives and the choices that brought them here to be sanctioned as the will of God. She'd always known this in the back of her mind, and not even that far back. She had never been slapped so hard in the face with it, though, as she had this morning. The impact of Gardner's murder was finally too much, the last piece that toppled the pile of fear, desperation, and emotional and sexual abuse, like the papers avalanching off Barrett's couch. It was doubt. Barrett railed against it in his sermons: "The doubt that creeps in and threatens your faith." He spoon-fed his people doubt, then chastised them for feeling it. Barrett also told her faith was meaningless if it was not held in spite of something. This was where doubt came in, why it was such a necessary ingredient. Doubt was reality—the world as it actually was and people as they actually were—and it had to be defeated or it would overtake faith. Reality would kick open the doors and break out the windows on faith and all they would be left with was the real. The reality that all this, Zoar in its entirety, from its beginnings in that strip-mall church to right this second, was built only by human hands and human wants: the multiple wives, the money they all turned over to Barrett, the escape from bad jobs or no jobs, taxes, bills, schools, mortgages; all of it had been driven by mere human wants and desires. The only element of the divine here was that they existed at all. God was whatever they named him to be, and they'd named him Barrett. That was why Barrett never pulled back the curtain or dropped the facade, why he didn't acknowledge playing a game the way Celia did. He had faith, too, in himself. He wasn't playing a game; he was setting the rules.

Celia crossed Town Square, traversed a field, and stepped into the woods. She pulled small flowers growing in patches of sunlight as she walked, adding leaves and twigs until she had a wild bouquet. Celia followed Gardner's usual path through the woods when he went hunting. She came to the small clearing where she had found Gardner the time he accused her of crashing through the underbrush and stopped. Holding the bouquet to her chest, she spoke aloud.

"Gardner," she began, "I'm so sorry you were killed by my dad." This was something Celia never thought she would have a reason to say. "And I'm sorry if I had any part in it. I'm sorry you didn't end up with Beth, that my dad took her instead. I'm really sorry this is how it all ended up for you over such a dishrag of a person." This was a mean thing to say in what was, essentially, a prayer, but what good did it do pretend you were someone other than who you were while you prayed? "I think Barrett took advantage of you. He takes advantage of everyone, so it's not your fault. I hope God lets you into heaven and everything you believed about the afterlife, and how to behave to get into it while you were alive, works out for you. And I'm really sorry I thought you were such a creep for most of the time I knew you. You weren't a creep. You were just…weird. I was just starting to like you, and now you're dead."

Celia laid the bouquet on the ground as a memorial, the only one Gardner would ever get. Then, as she stood to leave, she heard a voice behind her say, "Hell, Queen Bee. That's got to be the worst eulogy I've ever heard." Celia spun around in terror, her body moving out of time with her brain, and there, leaning against a tree trunk, was Gardner. "You ain't no quieter than you are a good speaker for the dead," he said. "I heard you coming a mile away."

Celia saw blood soaked through his shirt along his left side. Gardner limped toward her using his hunting rifle as a cane. He was pale. She ran to him and let him lean on her. "Thanks, Queen Bee," he said. They shuffled into the clearing, and Celia helped lower him to the ground and prop him up against the trunk of a fallen tree.

"You're alive," was the only thing Celia could think of to say. She touched his face. "You're alive."

"No thanks to your daddy." Gardner's voice was steady, but low, like his injury had turned down his volume. "Son of a bitch shot me."

"I know."

"I know you know. I heard you prayin', if that's what you call that sorry performance. How can someone who speaks directly with the Lord offer up such a lousy prayer?" Gardner said. Celia met his gaze, looking directly into his bloodshot eyes, silently imploring him to come to his senses. Gardner sighed. "The Lord doesn't really speak to you, does he?"

"Of course not."

"Does The Prophet know?" Celia stared at him again, mildly incredulous. "Right," Gardner said. "He's the one who put you up to it." He sighed again. "Things you didn't see before start to become clear when you're lying shot in the woods."

"Gardner, what happened?"

"Your daddy shot me."

"I know, but—"

"I was gonna shoot you, just now, when I heard you and realized who it was. Thought you might be, I don't know, coming to finish me off. Then I heard you talking. Realized you were being decent. Kind of."

"Gardner, please. I don't understand. What happened exactly?"

"Your daddy asked me to take him hunting. We ain't exactly close, but I figured bygones could be bygones and all that, so I said yeah, why not. We left early. Before sunup. He was being awfully jumpy, nervous and all. I just figured the man ain't never been hunting before. The woods in the dark can be a little intimidating. You know, normal explanations. Whatever I thought, it wasn't that the man was about to shoot me in the back."

"Then he shot you in the back."

"Coward. He must have taken off after he fired. Didn't check I was dead, I guess."

"You don't remember?"

"I remember but, like, in pieces. I didn't know what happened at first. Just heard a shot and felt an impact, and got knocked down like it was all one thing, at the same time. I was lying there, waiting for him to come check I was all right, though I knew I wasn't. He never came. That's when I realize he was the one done it and that I'd been shot. I was in and out for a bit, but I heard him running back the way we came. Louder than you even. Must be genetic."

Celia looked down at Gardner's side and gently lifted his shirt. He hissed a little in pain but let her go ahead. He had bandaged the wound and wrapped his torso in tape, but the angle he had to work with, compounded by the pain he must have felt, made his work sloppy at best. Celia pulled back the ill-fitting bandage and almost vomited. She scooted away from Gardner in a backward scuttle and stopped when she bumped against a tree. She sat taking deep breaths, trying to get her stomach settled.

"So it looks as good as it feels?" Gardner said, unmoving.

"I'm sorry. I didn't mean to freak out. It's just…"

"It's just bad. You can say it. I can sure as hell feel it. Your daddy had a twenty-two on him. Ain't the most stopping power, but it'll rip you up pretty bad. The bullets'll run along a bone once they get in you. They'll ricochet around inside a body, tear it up in there. I got lucky."

Celia pointed to his injury. "Gardner, I don't think that's lucky."

"Still alive, ain't I? Your daddy can't aim anyway. And he was probably half-blind with fear. The bullet came out of me. I think it hit a rib and ran along the bone, then blew out my side." Celia gagged. "Pretty bad exit wound, but it didn't get any organs or I wouldn't be sitting here. Or I would be sitting here, I'd just be dead."

"You bandaged yourself?"

"I got tore up by a boar once, out hunting, some years back. Got lucky and someone found me. It's when I realized someone upstairs was looking out for me. Learned all I could about field medicine after that. Can't expect a second chance more than once, you know. He say why he shot me?"

"What?"

"He must have told you he shot me if you thought I was dead and knew he did it."

Celia stared at him, she was stumped. She wanted to lie, tell Gardner she didn't know why, just bad luck maybe, but her last lie had put him in this situation. She was responsible for that. She was partly responsible for all this: the rise of Beaufort, the compound on the brink of a coup. All of it created by lies and lies and lies, hers among them. Gardner was lying here shot, possibly still near death. Her father willing to commit murder. She didn't just want to get away from Zoar, she wanted out from under its spell and its ways. Celia had wanted to burn it all down. She should start with her own role. "I told my dad I had a dream that Barrett was going to give Beth to you. That he was going to split them up."

"Why would you do that?"

"I thought it would finally be enough. He'd take me and leave. Maybe take my mom and we'd all leave and go back to—"

"There's no back."

"Yes, there is! Why can't there be? It's just down the road."

"We gave The Prophet everything. This is all we have now. This is the way forward."

"We always talk about the bad people, who don't bother to work, who don't make the right lives for themselves. What are they supposed to be doing? And why can't we just do that? Why can't my family just leave and do the things we think everyone else should be doing?"

"The Prophet—"

"There's no prophet! He makes it up. Why don't you see that? You don't know what he does to me. You don't know what—" Celia stopped. She didn't want Gardner to know what had happened to her, the things she had done with Barrett. She didn't want anyone to know. Ever.

"What happened?"

"Nothing."

Gardner nodded.

"There's no prophet," Celia said. "There's no dreams. I'm sorry. I'm really sorry. I just wanted to go home. I thought it would make him want to leave. I thought it would…"

"Break him."

"Yeah. I thought it would break him."

"Well, congratulations."

"I'm so sorry. I'm glad you're OK."

"I'm not OK. I'm shot, but I appreciate the sentiment. And the memorial, such as it was. I need you to run back and fetch Harmon and some of the others. I heard people last night, but I didn't know if they were friendlies or what. Didn't want to risk it. I need a hospital." Celia noticed his voice getting quieter, weaker. "Lucky I found you Queen Bee. Maybe God wants me to have a third chance after all."

"I'll be back," Celia said, standing up. "Sit tight."

"Don't think I could go anywhere even if I wanted to."

Celia started to run back to the compound. She got a few feet and stopped, suddenly remembering everything else that was happening. Even if she got Harmon, who she was sure would never accept Beaufort as anything but a nincompoop, what would the rest of them do when they heard Gardner was alive? They might march out here and shoot him and Harmon both, maybe even Stacy.

"You ain't running, Queen Bee," Gardner said from the ground.

Celia turned back. His eyes were closed. "I didn't tell you everything," she said. She knelt down next to him and gave him an overview of Beaufort's ascendancy and Barrett's impending overthrow.

"Beaufort?" Gardner said when Celia had finished. "You trying to hasten my death, Queen Bee? That bumbling faker? You're telling me he's been gathering a following that's going to overthrow The Prophet?"

"I think my dad's behind it. Beaufort's just a—" she looked for a word. Gardner found one for her.

"Decoy. Beaufort's just a decoy so your daddy don't gotta be out in front of his own insurgency. Your dad's a real shit, you know that?" Celia looked at the ground, and Gardner closed his eyes again. "Sorry," he said. "It ain't your fault."

"I'm afraid to go back and tell anyone you're here. I don't know what they might do. And Harmon'll come running out here, but he won't be able to get you out of the woods without everyone finding out, and I'm scared everyone will freak out and—"

"All right, all right, take it easy. Just—just shut up a minute. I can't—" He winced and for a moment couldn't speak. "Queen Bee, I'm gonna die if I don't get out of here and get to a hospital soon."

"Can you even go to a hospital?"

"'Course I can. I got shot in the damn back."

"No, I mean because you're legally dead."

Gardner stared at her without expression. "You being funny?"

"Barrett had you declared legally dead so you could get away from your wife who wouldn't divorce you." Gardner continued his dead-eyed stare, and Celia realized he hadn't known any of this had happened. "He took out a life-insurance policy on you. For a million bucks."

"This ain't a funny time for you to be telling me this if it ain't something you know for one hundred percent fact," Gardner finally said.

"I saw your death certificate," Celia said, quietly. "I thought it was something the two of you came up with together."

Gardner was silent with closed eyes for long enough that Celia got worried before he said, "No. It ain't something we came up with together." He opened his eyes. "You gotta patch me up if I'm gonna make it."

"Patch you up?"

Gardner pointed at the bulging pockets of his cargo pants and the pack he wore around his waist. "Get out the first-aid gear."

"I don't know how to—"

"You're going to learn, or I'm going to die. That's the two choices here. And seeing how this is partly your fault, I'd say you owe it to me to opt for learning. There's a ground sheet in the pack. Take it out and open it, spread the first-aid kit out on it. Keep everything clean." Celia unpacked Gardner's pockets and pack and did what he said. She found his canteen and gave him some water, then squatted by the spread. "All right," Gardner said. "You have to clean my wound out and close it up. First you're gonna take those antiseptic wipes and clean your hands and put on those rubber gloves. Then you're gonna take that big syringe there, fill it with that solution—it's isopropyl alcohol—and spray it into the wound. Spray it all through the damage. It's called irrigation. You gotta get out any dirt, shrapnel, anything that don't belong in there. You're cleaning a wound, so use your common sense and make sure it's clean, or it'll get infected. Then you gotta close me up with those strips there. Squeeze the opening together and close it up tight. Then cover the whole thing in that antibiotic ointment and put on a new bandage. Everything's gotta be tight and clean."

Celia had started shaking her head at the word *syringe*. "I can't do this," she said.

"But before you start spraying into my wound and all that, you're gonna take that hypodermic needle there, fill it with the anesthetic in that little vial, and inject it around the opening."

"No. No, Gardner, I can't do this."

"Because this whole thing hurts so bad I almost want it to kill me to make it stop."

Celia stared at the hypodermic needle and felt a wave of nausea ripple through her. She thought of pulling off Gardner's bandage and staring into the mess of flesh and blood that was his injury, then stabbing it with a needle. "I can't do that," she said, almost a whisper. She thought of the needle again, the gaping wound, the needle pressing through Gardner's skin. "I can't do it," she repeated.

"You can't let me die is what you can't do," Gardner said. "I'm going to sit here and die in the woods like an animal if you don't do this. Now clean your hands and get that anesthetic ready."

"I can't."

"Listen, yes, you can. It's just a shot. Now look at me. Look up. Actually look at my face." Celia raised her head and met Gardner's gaze. "You don't have to not be scared of doing it," he said. "But you do have to do it. You understand? You can be scared when you do it, but it's gotta be done." Celia kept her eyes locked on his, trying not to look at the sealed plastic package with the needle. She forced her breathing to as regular a pace as possible. "OK?" Gardner said. Celia nodded. "Good girl. You can do this. Now clean your hands and get the needle out."

Celia cleaned her hands and opened the package with the hypodermic needle. There it was, medieval looking. There was a small bottle of clear solution. "That's Novocain," Gardner said. "Unscrew the cap. See how the top is a little rubber stopper with a real tiny hole in it? Take the cap off the needle, carefully." She did. It was so thin it looked like thread. "Put that in the top of the little jar and pull the plunger back on that hypo till the barrel there is filled to the number twenty."

Celia followed his instructions. She focused on the task at hand and tried not to think ahead to the next steps that would require her to actually jab this thing into Gardner's back. "There you go," Gardner said. "That's plenty." He shifted onto his side, wearing considerable pain on his face as he did so. "Come around back here and pull that bandage off." Celia moved behind Gardner and peeled away the bandage, stiff and brown with blood. Gardner growled and sucked air through his teeth. He took a stick from the ground and held it up near his face. "OK, OK," he said, his voice higher than usual, talking to himself more than Celia. The wound looked back at her like an exploded eye. There was a small black hole in Gardner's back where the bullet had entered, and a pulpy wet splatter where it had exited. She gagged again but steadied herself, adrenaline riding hard over sickness and repulsion. "You gotta make the injections around the damage," Gardner said. "Each injection is two CCs, so do two little marks on the barrel. You got ten injections' worth of juice there. You gotta spread them around the wounds, OK?"

"Have you ever done this before?" Celia asked him.

"No, have you?"

"Not funny," Celia said.

"You got it?" Gardner asked. Celia didn't respond. She was trying not to black out. "Hey, you understand or what?" Gardner said.

"I don't think I can do this," Celia said.

"Enough of that. I'm the one's gotta lie here and get stabbed in a place where I already got shot. You should be holding my hand through this, not the other way around."

Celia took a breath. He was right. She reached out and took his hand in hers. "What are you—not literally. Use both your hands back there. Concentrate. Steady yourself. Do it right."

"OK," Celia shouted. "OK, here we go. You ready?"

"Do it," Gardner said, and bit down on the stick he was holding.

"Here it comes." Celia stuck the needle in just to the right of the bullet's entry point. Gardner let out a furious yell around the stick. Birds shot out of the trees above them with a sound like fleeing applause. Celia hit the plunger for two marks' worth of Novocain, pulled the needle out, then did it all again.

Gardner was comfortable now. As comfortable as a shot man could be, anyway, post amateur surgery. The Novocain made the cleaning and closing of the wounds far more bearable for him. Afterward, Celia repacked the first-aid kit and helped Gardner move over to the cover she had spread on the ground. She gave him some more water and found something called a Meal Ready to Eat in his pack. He accepted the little bag of food, but it just sat in his lap.

Gardner sighed and looked up into the green canopy that separated them from the sky. "I didn't think it would be like this," he said. "And I ain't one to generally express surprise at life's red lights. But this?" He shook his head. "I am, in fact, surprised. Shot in the back by one guy. Done greasy by a man I put—" he stopped and took a breath. "By the man I put the full conviction of my faith behind. And now being cared for by the one kid in the whole damned compound I didn't train in any kind of emergency survival." He looked over at Celia. "No offense. You did a real good job."

"Why *did* you follow him?" Celia said. "What made you come here?"

"Same as you, I guess."

"Your parents moved here and you didn't have a choice?"

Gardner flashed a thin smile. "Fair shot. That's how kids end up places, isn't it? No, obviously I came here on my own. I started going to Living Faith, trying to find some way to save my marriage, and I met The Proph—Barrett. And I just...All of a sudden someone was telling me that the way I thought the world ought to be was also the way God thought the world ought to be. Feels awfully good to hear God agrees with you, when it seems like nothing and nobody else can even stand you. That pretty much carried me along for everything else." He thought for a moment, then said, "Your family was already living here. I came in on pretty much the same ship as Geraldine and that idiot husband of hers. By myself, though. Your dad had this great family, and I was envious. I tried not to be. Prayed on it. Problem is, sometimes praying doesn't actually do anything but make you feel like you're off the hook for feeling something because at least you prayed about it. So when your momma went off with the Prophet like she did, I probably wasn't especially sympathetic to your father. Or you. That envy clouded my reaction somewhat, as to whether any of that was right or not. Then Geraldine went off with the Prophet too and, you know, that just seemed...Who cares about Beaufort? He don't help out or nothing, so obviously people aren't gonna get all riled up on his behalf. Then after Geraldine, there was you. By then we'd let the first two happen. And God was behind it, allegedly..."

Celia felt the nausea coming back. She didn't want to talk about being with Barrett or what had happened with Barrett. She didn't want to think about people knowing the things she had done with him.

"...you were too young to be married off like that," Gardner was saying.

"It's fine," Celia said quietly.

"'Specially to a man who was already with your momma."

"I wanted it," Celia said.

"Don't matter. I wanted to jump off my roof with an umbrella when I was a kid. Don't mean my parents should have let me."

"It's not your fault," Celia said.

"Yes, it is."

They didn't say anything for a bit. The birds called out and answered one another above them. Finally Celia said, "Your parents let you jump off the roof when you were a kid?"

"My daddy thought it'd teach me a lesson. Broke both my ankles."

"Geez Louise."

"Umbrellas make lousy parachutes."

"They barely keep off the rain."

"That's the truth."

"You need a hospital," Celia said.

"Also the truth."

"I have a plan. The Gathering starts pretty soon. Just before dusk. I'll come back here with Trevor and—"

"Who's Trevor?" Gardner said, looking alarmed.

"The donkey."

Gardner looked confused. "The donkey," he repeated, like he was tasting a foreign dish for the first time.

"The donkey's name is Trevor. I'll bring Trevor, *the donkey*, out here and you'll ride him to the compound. It'll be dark by then and everyone will be at the Gathering. We'll come out of the woods by the big house. I have the keys to the truck. We'll go to the hospital."

Gardner considered this. He nodded. "Sounds like you have a plan."

"You'll be OK, right? Until I get back?"

"What are you gonna do about it if I ain't?" He flashed a brief smile. "You be careful now, Queen Bee." Celia got up to go. "Wait," Gardner said. "What if someone catches you coming back for me? Insists on coming with you?"

"I'll refuse."

Gardner shook his head. "Don't go doing nothing brave on my account. They'll just find me eventually anyway." He reached over and dragged his hunting rifle across his lap. "It'll be dark, so we need a way so I know it's you."

"How about I call out to you, 'Gardner, it's me'?"

"Smart-ass," he said, but a smile hit the corners of his mouth. "If you ain't alone though…Listen, I ain't asking you to put someone in harm's way. It'll be up to you how you handle the situation. But I've already been near killed, and if someone's forcing you to bring them to me…"

"I'll sing. If you hear me coming through the woods singing, it means someone's along with me, and they're not friendly. I'll tell them it was supposed to be the signal so you knew it was me coming and not someone else."

"So if it's all good, you'll call out that it's you. And if something's rotten in Denmark…"

"I'll sing."

"What'll you sing?"

Celia thought about it. "Um…"

"On second thought, no, don't tell me," Gardner said. "Whatever it is, let's just hope I never have to hear it."

Chapter 10

Idiots never are—The unpredictable option—It comes to pass—Kids and their
music—Three denials—Following the path

Celia ran through the woods. She imagined Gardner shaking his head at
the sound. She went over her plan as she dodged around the trees. She had about
two hours until the Gathering began. She would lay low and skip that. The
Prophet would have to get used to only having two wives there to support him,
because when she got Gardner to a hospital, Celia was never coming back to
Zoar. Once everyone was in the pavilion listening to Barrett drone on about the
end-times and immigrants, she would get Trevor, load Gardner onto his back,
and walk him through the woods to the back of the big house. It would be no
good coming out and trying to cross the compound with a bloody Gardner on a
donkey. Even with everybody in the pavilion, that ran too high a risk of
attracting attention. Better to come out of the woods by the house, creep around
to the front, throw Gardner in the back of the truck and head out to the highway.
Right now, she would go to Gardner's house and wait. That would keep her off
everyone's radar. It was the one place she could count on to be empty;, plus she
could get Gardner a change of clothes. After the doctors at the hospital fixed
him up, he would need something to wear.

Celia went around Town Square and came up on Gardner's place from
the back. She was running around to the front when the first part of her plan fell
apart. She heard voices. Celia came to a stop at the corner of the house. She
peeked out and saw Kent Altman in front leaning against one of the compound's
work trucks. Celia dropped to the ground and rolled under the house. There was
someone inside as well. She heard their steps through the floorboards above her,
then they started speaking again.

"That's everything, he don't got no more," the voice in the house said.
Celia recognized the voice of Nancy-Lynn's husband, Biscuit.

"Is that all the ammo too?" Kent answered from outside.

"I got two more boxes here and whatever I already tossed out."

"Yeah," Celia heard Kent say, his voice low, talking to himself. "I
enjoyed picking up all those shells after you 'tossed' it."

"What?" Biscuit called out.

"Nothing. Doesn't matter." From under the house Celia saw Kent's
legs as he moved to look in the bed of the truck. "He had another rifle," he

called into the house.

"Well, it ain't here," Biscuit called back. "Must be the one he had with him."

"You sure? When this goes down tonight we don't need any extra guns lying around for someone to get a hold of. There's going to be plenty to deal with already."

"I'm telling you it ain't here. Ain't Stacy said his hunting rifle was gone when she went barging in here last night? He had it with him. What we got is all there is to get."

"Fine. Anything else in there we should be worried about?"

"More knives than a chef's kitchen."

"Grab those, just to be safe."

Celia heard Biscuit moving around and the sound of knife blades clanging against one another as they were dropped into a bag.

"You nervous?" Biscuit called through the open door. "About tonight."

"Of course I am. Aren't you?"

"Not overly."

Kent sighed and said, "Idiots never are," in his low voice.

"You got to speak up, man. I can't hear you in here."

"I said, why aren't you nervous?"

"Well, God's on our side, ain't he? I'm confident of that. So we can't lose. It's like a law of nature that God can't lose. And most everyone is on our side and knows this is God's will. Majority anyway, I think. And the ones who ain't, well, they'll see a gun pointed at them backed by the power of Christ, and they'll come to understand that this couldn't be possible without God's blessing. So they'll get right on board. 'Specially once they hear Waters explain Beaufort's position. And the ones who don't get it are obviously agents of Satan who won't never be able to understand God's plan because, you know…Satan."

"We're talking about a heavily armed group of people here, Biscuit," Kent said. "I just think that warrants some concern is all."

"Once they see that false prophet and fake god on his knees with a gun barrel in his mouth and realize that if he really were the Second Coming none of this would be happening, they'll calm right down. Long as we keep everyone rounded up in the pavilion and keep guards all around the compound on high alert, we'll be fine. Keep this place on lockdown until we get the believers sorted from the Satanists. Then it's all smooth sailing after that, with the wind of God blowing at our backs, right?"

"Right."

"I will say, I guess I'm a little worried about Waters's kid."

"Celia? Why? She'll be fine."

"Won't look good if she wants to stay with the false prophet over coming with us and her daddy."

"Nah, she's the one that gave her dad the heads up about Barrett giving Beth to Gardner in the first place. She knows what time it is. In a way she's the real instigator of the Beaufort move—Hell's bells, Biscuit!" Kent suddenly yelled. Celia saw his legs as he jumped to one side and a second later there was a metallic crash as though someone had dropped a silverware drawer. "What's wrong with you?" Kent yelled.

"I thought you could catch, I guess is what's wrong," Biscuit said. Celia heard the door to the house close, and Biscuit came down the front three steps.

"Why would you throw the most violent collection of knives in the compound at someone?"

"They're in a bag."

"Is it one of those magic bags, impenetrable by eight-inch hunting knives?"

"It's canvas."

"Oh, OK. Yeah, that's the fabric I thought I recognized as it came hurtling toward me. Stop throwing weapons, stop throwing ammo, stop throwing giant sacks of razor-sharp knives designed to kill and disembowel." Kent's voice rose from casual sarcasm to a near-scream as he spoke.

"Dang. Sorry," Biscuit said, bending over to pick up the bag of knives. He walked around the far side of the truck and got in, tossing the bag into the bed as he went. Kent sighed and climbed into the driver's side. The truck started and pulled away. Celia gave it a few minutes to clear out so they wouldn't see her, then crawled out from under the house.

So the coup was to take place that very night, and the compound was going on lockdown. It was Celia's turn to sigh, now. She would never get Gardner out of the woods if that happened, and then his death would be on her hands after all. That left her with only one option. Again, she sighed. One rather unpredictable option.

Celia was sprawled across Barrett's bed when he came in from the sunroom, where he had been updating his website. Celia was freshly showered, sipping champagne and watching TV. Barrett pulled his robe over his head and flung it into the corner, making for the bathroom to take a shower himself. He lingered by the edge of the bed, staring at Celia.

"I'm just going to get sweaty during my sermon anyway," he mused, lumbering onto the bed. Celia set her glass of champagne on the nightstand. Barrett grabbed her by the ankle and slowly dragged her toward him, holding her foot up near his face and putting her toes in his mouth. Celia was sprawled before him on her back. Barrett kneeled on the bed, looming over her, clutching one ankle and staring down at her with his one good eye while the other looked off into space as though searching for a new deviancy.

He was just reaching down toward her chest when Celia said, "Shouldn't you be planning your sermon?"

Barrett lazily pushed her shirt up, exposing her stomach. "I don't plan them, as you know. They come to me directly from God, in the moment." He ran a finger around her belly button, then hooked it under the waistband of her shorts, giving them a gentle tug. He began undoing the top button.

"Did God tell you anything special about your sermon this evening?" Celia asked. She pressed her bottom against his stiffening manhood. His eyes closed briefly, enjoying the moment. He pulled his underwear down and let himself out, then yanked Celia's shorts and underwear free and scooted them along her legs, which were pressed along the length of his stomach and chest, her heels resting near his collar bones. He didn't take them all the way off, but left them wrapped around her ankles, tucked under his chin against his throat. He reached down, preparing to enter her.

"What would be special about this particular sermon?" Barrett said. He was at the gate, about to barge in.

"That it's going to be your last."

The citizens filed into the pavilion. Half of them were silent and jumpy, doing a poor job of keeping up the appearance of business-as-usual. The other half tried to chat with their neighbors only to end up confused by the clipped responses they received. Celia took a seat on the dais next to her mother and Geraldine.

"Oh, no. He made you dress up too?" her mother said, taking in Celia's outfit, a dress that wouldn't have looked out of place at a prom. Celia's mother and Geraldine were both in finery as well. Celia saw that Geraldine had been crying. The sight of Celia's dress started her fresh. "Oh, c'mon, Gerry. Get it together," Celia's mother said.

"I just don't think I can take it," Geraldine said.

"What's her problem?" Celia said.

"Why do you think he made us dress up like this?" her mother said. "He's bringing in another wife. Her mother scanned the crowd with narrowed eyes and a grim expression. "I wonder what little twit he's found now." Celia didn't bother to get offended.

"It's just can't believe he's doing this to me," Geraldine whined.

"For Pete's sake, Gerry, you were second yourself. Or don't you remember?"

"But I was one of the first."

"That's not—that doesn't mean the same thing. There's first and the rest."

"I didn't say I was *first*. I said I was *one of* the first."

"So what? If he takes fifteen wives, this new girl will be one of the first, too."

"No. She. Will. Not," Geraldine said, like Celia's mother had suggested they resort to cannibalism.

Celia's mother shook her head and looked over at Celia. "Now you'll see what it's like," she said.

"If there was going to be a new girl, I think she would be the one about to see what something was actually like," Celia said quietly. "And regret everything." Celia's mother stared at her. Celia kept her eyes on the crowd. They were tense and restless. The rebels sat rigid and ready in their seats, and the others sensed the menace in the air but didn't comprehend it, like dogs before a storm.

"She'll have made her choices," Celia's mother replied. Celia said nothing. What did it matter? Her mother said, "Wait, did you say 'if there was actually going to be a new girl'?" Then The Prophet came out of the darkness beyond the amphitheater and took the stage. Her mother would get her answer soon enough. The citizens quieted and The Prophet began.

"You've all come a long, long way," Barrett said. "Spiritually. Physically. You've come a long way. When we started, we were a small group in a storefront church with nothing beyond an inkling that things around us in the world were not right. That this was not how things were meant to be. That God intended for things to be different, better, more in line with the message of Christ. And the inkling, that spark, what did it become?" A portion of the crowd murmured unintelligibly. "Yes, a fire!" The Prophet exclaimed, not slowing down for them. "It became a fire, and that fire consumed. It consumed your old lives in the wicked secular world, and it cleansed each of you and brought you here to live in direct communication with God's word, with his incarnation on earth, bringing forth life from his land, following his path.

"We've talked a lot about the end of days, about the coming upheaval that will loosen the bonds of evil across this once-proud land and set Christian men and women free to live as God intended without constant assault from the demons and evil spirits that want to modernize, secularize, abortionize, consumerize, profitize, and dehumanize your existence. We've prepared for judgment day, gotten ready for it. But…" The Prophet turned his face up, awaiting the rest of this message, channeled directly from God to God-figure. The citizens waited, and Celia thought of her conversation an hour before, with her own face upturned, awaiting a response from a man who claimed he was God.

"Wait, what?" Barrett had said, when Celia told him his next sermon would be his last. She'd explained about Beaufort and felt The Prophet go soft against her leg.

"Beaufort?" he screamed. Barrett had ripped the television from its place on the dresser and smashed it against a wall. He put his fists through another wall twice each and kicked the bathroom door to pieces, which he then stomped. Celia lay on the bed with her champagne and watched, fascinated by the carnage and the huge man producing it in nothing but his underpants.

"Ungrateful, miserable sinners. How dare they?" Barrett panted as the last of his energy drained away during the stomping of the door bits. "How dare they challenge me?" He leaned against the pockmarked wall, breathing heavily.

"So you should probably cancel the Gathering, huh?" Celia said, pouring herself another flute of champagne. If the Gathering was canceled, the insurrection would probably be postponed, Celia figured. Based on what she'd overheard from Kent and Biscuit, they were counting on the citizens all being in a group when they made their move, allowing them the luxury of containment. If the insurrection was delayed, then Celia would be free to move around the compound that night and get Gardner to a hospital.

Barrett stood up from the wall. "Absolutely not. I'm not canceling anything. I will lay that traitor low. I will wreck everything in these people's world. I will flatten this whole land."

The champagne flute stopped halfway to Celia's mouth. "I really think you ought to cancel it," she said. "For your safety," she added.

Barrett shook his head. He straightened up and waved his hands, as though clearing away the whole situation. "You can't get too attached to the places. That's all they are: places. And you must always recognize the signs. Signs show you the way out. Ignore them at your peril." He ran a finger around the inside of one of the holes he had made in the wall with his fist. "I'm going to miss that hot tub, though." He sighed, then shrugged. "Oh, well."

"What are you talking about?" Celia said.

"Pack whatever you want to take with you. A small bag. Something you can carry. We're leaving tonight." He went to his dresser and pulled out a clean robe. He tossed it on the bed and went to the bathroom and turned on the shower, calmly resuming where he had left off when he entered.

"Why don't you just cancel the Gathering? Then you can plan something. Then they can't make us leave," Celia said, rolling over to the edge of the bed and staring into the bathroom.

Barrett leaned out the door. "They could never make me leave," he said. "We're just leaving. Regardless of what happens. And probably tonight, so you should pack." Then he shut the door, and Celia heard the curtain close.

Now, in the yellow glow of the amphitheater in the warm summer evening, Barrett was The Prophet again, striding back and forth in front of his flock as though nothing were wrong. Celia was counting minutes. She needed to get back to Gardner. She wasn't sure how she was going to ditch Barrett, who thought she was leaving with him tonight, or what the end result of this Gathering was going to look like, but whatever was going to happen, she needed it to happen soon. Gardner needed it to happen soon.

The Prophet had his face raised, listening to the message the Lord was allegedly giving him to pass along to his flock. His face darkened. He looked as if whatever he was hearing was painful. "What if I told you—" Barrett shook his head, as though powering through a dizzy spell. He resumed speaking, his voice regaining its weight and pitch. "What if I told you the end-times were not just going to happen? But that they had to be brought about? Made to happen. You've all been preparing, getting ready for them to take place, but the Lord's plan is deeper than that. It always is, isn't it? For all this time, the Lord wasn't preparing you as an army just to survive the coming rapture. He wasn't preparing you just to be defensive. He expects you," Barrett pointed at his followers, his finger sweeping the crowd to encompass them all. "You specifically, to go on the offensive. The Lord, your God, the Almighty, is not just going to sit back and wait for his creation to crumble. He's not just going to sit by while the beautiful world, the beautiful creatures—you!—made in his image, are gradually laid low, sullied and tarnished by sin. No! Do you think God is just going to wait for his world to be broken?" The crowd shouted back in the negative. "Do you think he's just going to let it all be taken away from him? After he worked so hard to build it?" Again, the crowd roared back that, no, they did not think this. Celia found Kent and Biscuit in the crowd. Their faces showed concern. They twisted and turned in their seats, trying to catch the eyes of their cohorts. They all looked like people who wished they had made their move earlier.

"Do you think that after bringing you all here, after the effort and energy that he put into building you into what you are today, he is just going to roll over and let it all be taken without a fight?" The Prophet roared. Celia found her father in the faces and saw comprehension dawn. He, too, was looking wildly around the amphitheater, trying to catch the eyes of his compatriots. To call things off? To give them a reassuring look? Celia didn't know, but the crowd was growing agitated and unruly. "The Lord wants his world back. And he is going to take it back," Barrett bellowed. "You—all of you—you are the instruments, the soldiers, the army, that is going to get it for him. He has brought you here not to wait for the rapture, but to bring it about. You are not going to wait for the sin-sodden world to crumble. You're going to tear it down. The apocalypse will not be a reaction, but an action, and you will—"

Barrett staggered and sank to one knee. The crowd, who had been bordering on a riot a moment before, gasped. Several people in the front rows lunged out of their seats and began to approach their Prophet, but Barrett put a hand up and held them back. He turned his face to the heavens, then looked back down and rose to his feet with what appeared to be (and, due to his weight, actually was) great effort. "The Lord," he began, far more quietly than he had been just moments before, "has been striking at my soul with a message while I've been speaking to you. And the strikes have been getting harder and harder." He took a deep breath. "I would never ignore a message from my father, but this one is so...so painful that I have a hard time—" He stopped and threw his head back, his arms out, as though struck by invisible lightening. "Yes, all right, Father," he yelled. "As you say, Father." The crowd was silent. The Prophet held his pose along with a look of intense internal discomfort. "Father, yes, as you command," he shouted and then went limp, as though invisible strings had been cut. He slumped, swaying before the crowd who waited silently for whatever would come next. The Prophet straightened himself up, breathing heavily, looking like he had just finished an intense workout. "There is a false prophet in our midst," he hissed. "A shepherd for the damned who seeks to lead my flock astray. His followers are out there among you now." Celia had not been able to find Beaufort in the crowd before, but he was easy to spot now. About half the eyes in the amphitheater, his followers, had turned to look at him. Celia's father was looking around wildly, half-out of his seat in what looked like an attempt to prompt the rest of the team to spring into action, to signal them that now was the time. But his signal went unheeded in the face of The Prophet's performance and he was left half-standing like someone with a stomach cramp until Beth yanked him back into his seat, her face angry and scared.

"God has informed me," the Prophet went on, "that an agent of Satan is among us, falsely speaking in God's name. Corrupting the souls of faithful followers and filling their heads with sulfurous thoughts and fallacies!" The Prophet walked to one side of the amphitheater, the side where Beaufort sat. Beaufort was looking around, same as Celia's father, awaiting a rescue that wasn't arriving. "Who among you has followed this false leader, this snake in the garden who would lead you to your death?" Those in the crowd who had been involved in the Beaufort movement seemed to regard this question as rhetorical, no one spoke up. Beaufort looked to Celia's father, across the space, for help. Celia's father kept his eyes on the floor. Beaufort was in a panic, twisting and turning to look for help, gesturing to people who averted their gaze. Those who had no idea any of this had been brewing could now clearly see that Beaufort was the target of both God's and The Prophet's anger. Their shock was tempered slightly with confusion that the man with the homemade walker and hemorrhoids was leading people to Satan.

"What's going on?" Geraldine whispered. Her view was obstructed by the Prophet's enormous body.

"Beaufort is an agent of Satan," Celia's mother whispered back. "Who's been leading people down a path to hell."

"My Beaufort?" Geraldine said, straining to see around the Prophet.

"You sick and sinister charlatan," the Prophet was saying. "Face me!" Beaufort, who had until then still been trying to urge his followers into action, whipped around at this outburst. He had been half-out of his chair, and now he stood, nervous, visibly shaking. "You would dare to lead these people into Satan's maw, to take them away from the light of Christ." The Prophet was roaring.

"Cowards," Celia said to herself, looking through the crowd as people did nothing to help the man they had put in this position.

"Who?" her mother whispered.

"Everyone," Celia said. "All of us."

"You would have them risk their souls," the Prophet went on.

"I just want my wife back," Beaufort said.

But he was drowned out by The Prophet yelling, "God wants this man punished. God wants him brought to justice. If you would accept God's mercy, if you would accept God's love, if you would accept and take God's redemption of this wicked world, would you not prove yourselves worthy of it first?"

Beaufort began to edge his way out of the row where he had been seated. A few people looked away as he went past, fellow rebels who had balked at their opportunity for action. Others, stirred by The Prophet's energy, glared at Beaufort or shoved him.

"Will you not show God that you are ready? That you are deserving of a changed world. That the time for false prophets is over. That the time for a world steeped in sin, steeped in homosexuality, promiscuity, abortion, greed and technology, tolerance of all manner of behavior, and desiccated American values is over!"

The crowd rumbled and stirred. Their voices calling back blended together like the roar of wind and spray and crashing waves. Beaufort cleared the end of the row he had been sitting in and disappeared into the fresh evening darkness.

"God wants this world punished. God wants this man punished. He is giving you the chance to dispense this punishment, to enforce his will. It is through the eradication of this man from our community that God will know you follow his true word and do not kneel at the altar of false prophets. And it is through the eradication of the crimes of the secular world that he will know you truly want his presence on this earth. Then he will truly know you are ready for the end-times, for the return of God's law upon the land. Are you ready? Are you willing? If you would have this world be other than it is, then go! Go forth. Go and make it so!"

The Prophet's voice released them like a broken levee, and Celia watched them fall, fall, fall, over chairs and one another out into the night.

Celia stood at Barrett's office window and watched men and women with rifles and shotguns march past the house. Behind her, Barrett had yanked up the square of carpet and was on the floor throwing money into a duffel bag. He tossed the plastic folder onto the couch with a flourish of apathy toward its contents. Celia's mother was consoling a hysterical Geraldine down their own hallway.

Matthew's head was on the computer screen being frantic. "Why is there never any warning that this is coming?" he was saying. "Why can't we ever just make a quiet plan that we enact and then fade away?"

"That's not how it worked out," Barrett said from the floor.

"It could be how it worked. You could start cutting your losses earlier and then—"

"I'm not debating this right now, Matthew," Barrett said in a warning tone. "Just hurry up and get me some coordinates."

Matthew sighed and held a piece of paper up to the camera on his end with neatly printed numbers written across it. "Here, this is where I'll pick you up."

Barrett grabbed a piece of paper from the stacks around the sofa and a pen that had rolled off the desk. He scrawled the numbers along the paper's edge, then balled it up and threw it across the room to Celia. "Hang on to that. It's where we have to meet Matthew."

"That's not—Can't you write them down better than that? And what?

You're bringing her? Oh, that's just great. Yeah, let's add that to the mix." Celia gave Matthew the finger. "Real cute," he said. "Wonderful. Do you still get carsick? Maybe I'll throw some coloring books in the back of the truck so you don't get fussy. Barrett, this is a terrible idea."

Barrett looked up at Celia. "I thought I told you to pack. Where's your stuff?" Celia waved the tape player she was holding over her head without turning from the window. Somewhere in the distance there was the bright flash of fire breaking the darkness. Barrett went back to emptying his hidey-hole. "You kids and your music," he muttered.

"I think they just set Beaufort and Geraldine's RV on fire," Celia said.

Barrett flopped the last of the bills into the duffel bag. He pulled himself to his feet using the edge of the desk, where he snatched up a paper bag of old hamburgers and tossed that into the duffel as well, along with his laptop. He zipped the bag and slung it over his shoulder. Barrett yanked open a desk drawer and took out a square metal can with a spout on the end. He put a hand on Celia's shoulder and steered her toward the door. "Matthew, we're leaving now," Barrett said.

"Then why can I still hear and see you?" Matthew replied.

"Oh, right." Barrett tossed the duffel bag into the hall and marched back over to the computer.

"Do it right, Barrett. Please. It's important. Get a screwdriver and take the back off the—"

Barrett yanked the computer tower free of its cord, and the screen blinked off and went quiet. "Good-bye, Matthew," Barrett said in a singsong voice. He raised the computer tower over his head and smashed it down against the corner of the desk. The housing broke open. Barrett lifted and smashed it again, and the whole thing came apart. He yanked at the housing some more, exposing wires and circuit boards and threw the mess on the floor next to the plastic folder from the hidey-hole. Barrett pried open the spout on the metal can and sprayed liquid into the guts of the machine, onto the papers piled on the couch, the desk, the carpet, the walls, and then another hard blast into the broken shell of the computer tower. Celia smelled the tang of lighter fluid. Finally Barrett dropped the can itself into the computer's guts and came back to the doorway where Celia was watching. He produced a pack of matches and tossed one on the floor. Fire took the room with a tearing sound as the flames yanked the air apart, eating the oxygen.

"C'mon," Barrett said, shouldering the duffel and tugging Celia away from the spectacle of the fire. The plastic folder melted, turned black, and caught aflame. The piles of paper on the couch went up so fast and bright it was like a camera flash. Barrett paused for a moment at the door to the sunroom. He sighed. "I'm really going to miss that hot tub," he said, shaking his head. He went down the hall and was heading to the front door when Celia stopped him.

"What about my mom and Geraldine?" she said, as smoke began to inch out of the hallway.

Barrett pulled a face as if he'd realized he was about to leave the house without his car keys. He went to the entrance of the women's hallway and pounded his fist against the wall, shouting, "Fire in the hole, ladies. You're going to want to clear out. Fire in the hole."

"What?" Celia's mother called back, stepping into the hallway from Geraldine's room.

"Fire," Barrett yelled, just as the living-room smoke detectors began screaming the announcement in their own way. Barrett turned for the front door again and Celia followed.

"Wait, Celia," her mother yelled after her. "Gerry, get up. We have to get out of here. Get! Up! Now! Celia, wait."

Celia didn't turn or look back. She followed Barrett out into the night. The largest of the fires so far was definitely Beaufort and Geraldine's RV, though the big house would soon take top honors. Other smaller fires flickered around the compound, Gardner Specials that went up easy and burned down fast. "We need to get to the barn," Barrett said.

"This way," Celia pointed them toward the perimeter of the compound, a way she had walked a hundred times before, night and day.

"I'm not sure—" Barrett began, but then they saw one of the compound's work trucks roll by, the bed filled with the faithful, all armed and shouting, and he hustled off in the direction Celia had pointed. They walked down the gradient of what passed for a hill in the flatlands of South Carolina. Behind her, Celia heard a man's voice calling her name. She saw her father, approaching from a different direction than the one she was headed, running toward the burning house calling for her. Celia's mother and Geraldine were coming out the front door, her father running toward them; behind him Beth struggled to keep up, and again Celia turned her back on it all and kept following Barrett.

Celia and Barrett skirted Town Square, where groups of armed believers were piling into cars and trucks and yelling about heading into town and exacting God's wrath. Celia wondered how many of them had been ready to overthrow Barrett only a few hours earlier. The houses of people suspected of being in cahoots with Beaufort were burning steadily, and screams and shouts rose from different directions every few seconds. There was an occasional gunshot. The big house was blazing now, casting a primal glow on the chaos below. Men and women with guns jumped into vehicles, people ran for the woods or out into the fields, and there was wailing and fear and violence. Barrett, The Prophet, had been right. The End had been right around the corner. It had come to pass.

Barrett plunged ahead toward the barn, breathing heavily, jogging. Celia kept the same pace walking behind him, occasionally turning to see the residents disappearing along the road that led out of the compound and back into town. Off to reckon with the evil world. They came up to the barn and Barrett pushed through the doors. Celia screamed and covered her eyes. Beaufort was hanging by his neck from a rope tied to one of the rafters. His mouth gaped open, and his eyes were huge with surprise and pain. There were scratches on his neck where he had struggled. "Judas," Barrett said, and he spat on the dangling corpse. Celia turned her back and edged around the gently swaying Beaufort, not wanting to see.

Trevor the donkey stood in the corner, unimpressed. Barrett stood on a bale of hay and clambered onto Trevor's back. Trevor shrieked and honked.

"Shouldn't you go lead your people in God's name?" Celia said.

"Very funny. Honey, God wants me to get out of here in one piece so I can continue his work. I can't do that if I've been arrested or shot."

"But they'll triumph, right? Isn't God on their side?" Celia knew she was being a brat, but she had to know how deep Barrett's charade ran.

"Of course God is on their side, which is why they don't need me. This is what God wants. He wants us to get out of here and meet Matthew. And he knows I don't like to walk very far or fast, so he wants me to ride the donkey."

"Trevor."

"Right, Trevor. This is his plan. It doesn't have to make sense to us. We just need to follow it." He kicked at Trevor's sides. Trevor brayed in disgust. "I think you're going to have to lead him," Barrett said. He fumbled in his robe and pulled out a glowing GPS and squinted at it. "What were those coordinates?"

"Here," Celia said, holding out her hand. Barrett gave her a doubtful look. "Let me take care of it. I can read it, and I have the coordinates. I know my way around these woods, so I'll lead the donkey—just let me handle it for you." Barrett nodded with relief and handed the device over. Celia found a rope and tied a makeshift lead for Trevor. Being careful to keep her eyes averted, she led The Prophet and the donkey past Beaufort's body and out into the burning night. The big house was gloriously ablaze, an unredeemable tragedy so far out of control that no one could undo it now, save God himself. It burned on, giving Celia a sense of peace. Nothing to do but move forward.

The Prophet was always going on about God's plan making sense, assuring people against the illogical. But that was all wrong: people weren't looking for sense; they already had sense, and it left them cold and scared before a brutal world that clearly did not favor them. No, what people sought was meaning, God up there in his heaven tallying their tiniest sins and most mediocre kindnesses, imbuing them with meaning. And one day God would stop everything he was doing and take them into account, because they were important. No one cared if it made sense.

Celia led Trevor down to the edge of the woods. She thought of the plastic folder melting and burning to ash in the big house. She had made the right call earlier, before the Gathering, when Barrett had gotten in the shower. She had gone into the office and pulled up the carpet and floor over the hidey-hole and retrieved the folder. Celia had taken everything out, the bank books, the legal papers, the death certificates, the insurance forms—all of it—and had replaced it with a wad of random papers from a stack on the couch. Barrett, in his haste, hadn't even noticed. All the documents were neatly folded and stuffed, somewhat uncomfortably, down the back of Celia's dress, an awkward lump Barrett had also failed to register. And now he had handed over both the GPS and the reins, such as they were, to his transportation. If she hadn't been able to get him into the woods, she would have just run for it; it wasn't as though he could keep up with her, or anyone else, for that matter. She thought of Gardner, propped against the log just a short walk away with his gun and his bitter energy. She had told him she would sing if there was anyone with her. She hoped he was ready, because she wasn't just going to sing, she had brought accompaniment. Her tape was all set to exactly her favorite part in the song. *Baaaaaaaby, oh-oh, baaaaaaby.* She hummed a little, getting ready. The GPS glowed faintly in her hand. Afterward she would load Gardner onto Trevor along with his gun, and take him to meet that pansy Matthew and the truck. Then she would drive Gardner to a hospital.

"Are you sure this is right?" Barrett was saying behind her. "This is the way the GPS says to go?"

Celia turned and smiled. "This is the way. We're following the path." Then she led them into the woods.

The End

Epilogue

"I want to be in front of the house, but not *in front* of it. If the smoke looks like it's coming out of my head, I'll be a meme five minutes after this airs. So just, figure it out, no smoke out of my head. Though, like seriously, this whole farm is still smoldering, so maybe it doesn't matter. We should be wearing masks or something, probably. All right, Davis, you ready? They're cutting to us in what? Five, four...OK, OK, nice and easy, but serious.

"Thank you, Carol. We're here live at the site of one of the deadliest citizen uprisings in this nation's history, where the members of a fundamentalist religious sect launched their attack on the town of Brock, South Carolina, and had their final standoff with local and county police. The group called itself the New Zoar Temple of the Blessed Tabernacle. Behind me, smoldering in ruins, is the house of their leader, a man known to them as The Prophet, but known to law enforcement officials as Bartholomew Carrius Higgins, a.k.a. Carry Higgs, a.k.a. Barrett Higgins.

"Higgins served two years in Fulton County Correctional Facility for fraud, impersonating a government official, and illegal weapons sales before being released four years ago. Upon his release, he violated his probation and has been wanted since. The house and property here officially belong to Barbara Josener, a ninety-three-year-old woman in a retirement home in Dillon, South Carolina. Though details are unconfirmed at this time, it is believed by investigators that Higgins acquired the property through a false lien and moved the widowed Ms. Josener to Dillon himself, taking over the property. Down here, to my right, Carol, you can see various dwellings. Some are campers, some are shacks, and some have been burned to the ground—this was where Higgins's followers lived. Now, we aren't allowed to get to close because investigators are still combing the area, but as you can see, there was a full community working here. Officials are estimating that more than one hundred people, including children, were living here before the events of last night.

"Though we're still not clear on the details of what exactly triggered the attack, and I think, after speaking with law enforcement, it is safe to call what happened an attack, it appears that the members of the New Zoar Temple set fire to several of their own homes and buildings here, executed some of their own members—dissenters perhaps—then moved off the compound and headed for Brock proper, essentially stopping at any home or establishment they found along the way and executing any people they found there and setting any buildings, public or private, on fire. A shocking and disturbing number here, Carol—right now police are estimating that fifty-seven people were murdered by the group, including fourteen officers. That number is not official yet, which is all the more upsetting, as it most likely will only grow.

"Many members of this group, which some are already calling a cult, have been arrested and are being questioned, and an estimated thirty-three of them were killed in gun battles with law enforcement. Officials are leaving no stone unturned here. Law enforcement, along with many volunteers, some of whom lost family members in the attack, are forming search parties. They are combing the surrounding woods, putting up posters, and blasting the message on social media to be on the lookout. So far, Bartholomew Carrius Higgins has not been found, meaning his body has not been identified among the dead or as any of the group's members.

"Early investigators have discovered at least one body so far in the surrounding woods, an unidentified man who had been shot several times. He was unresponsive when he was found and is currently in critical care at Brock Memorial Hospital. It is not known at this time whether he will survive. He joins the list of fifteen other individuals in critical condition, a list including four officers and eight civilians, as well as four individuals, including the John Doe found in the woods, who police suspect were members of the compound.

"Sheriff Richard Owens will be holding a press conference in about half an hour, and we're expecting further updates at that time. Back to you, Carol."

Excerpt from an article in the *Brock Independent*

…Brock Memorial and other hospitals in the area have been overrun following the Zoar Massacre, as it is being called. Almost the entire staff at Brock Memorial has been working around the clock since the first victims arrived, including ER nurse Maggie Todd Kane. "There hasn't been a break. You want to stop and go somewhere and cry for all these people, but there isn't time. It's disgusting something like this could happen here. This is a nice town with good people, nice families. One of the first victims we treated was a man who had been shot. His daughter brought him in. She had to drive him here because he was so bad off. Imagine being that girl, having to load your father into his own truck and drive him to the hospital after watching him shot by strangers. She was so brave about it. She said, 'You have to save him. If he dies, I don't know what I'll do. I don't think I'll be able to take it.' She's who I think about while I'm tired and the bodies keep rolling in. When something like this happens, that's what you have to do: Focus on the heroes, the ones trying to help."

Neighboring counties are sending volunteer medical staff to area hospitals in a tremendous outpouring of aid and assistance…

www.ingramcontent.com/pod-product-compliance
Lightning Source LLC
Chambersburg PA
CBHW070849250626

47159CB00003B/1000